MW00928490

Time Jumper

A Novel

Matthew Bayan

Timeline Books ™

Time Jumper
Copyright © 2017 by Matthew Bayan

All rights reserved. No part of this book may be reproduced in any form or by any electronic or mechanical means, including information storage and retrieval systems, without permission in writing from the publisher, except by a reviewer who may quote brief passages in a review.

The Timeline Books name and logo are trademarks of Timeline Books.

The characters and events in this book are fictitious. Any similarity to real persons, living or dead, is coincidental and not intended by the author.

Other books by Matthew Bayan

Fiction
THE FIRECRACKER KING
THE FIRECRACKER KING: PAPER GOLD (Winter 2017)

Non Fiction
EAT FAT, BE HEALTHY: When A Low-Fat Diet Can Kill You
CLICK AND RETIRE
GUN 101: A Writer's Guide to Using Firearms in Fiction (Summer 2017)

CHAPTER 1

The green dragon jumped into a rusty sky.

"Happy Birthday, Beth," Ethan said, shielding his eyes from the searing afternoon sun.

"It's wonderful. The crown jewel of my collection. Where'd you get a Tibetan festival kite?" His wife grinned as she let out more twine. The four-foot dragon kite soared even in the light breeze, its silk shimmering in the light.

"Friends with the Dalai Lama."

She turned and gave him a withering look, then pursed her lips into a kiss. "What a great way to celebrate my senior citizenship."

"Honey, you're only thirty-four."

"Thirty-four is the new sixty." She wiggled her hips at him.

"You're a nut." He grinned at the leggy, tawny-haired woman whom he still couldn't believe had married him. She bounced like a cheerleader as the dragon rose higher into the sky. In her blue T-shirt and cut-off jeans she still looked like a schoolgirl. "Can it do tricks?" he said.

"Not this kind of kite."

"I want tricks."

Beth turned and winked. "Later you'll get tricks."

Ethan sat cross-legged in the tall grass a dozen feet behind Beth, the breeze tossing his dark hair into his eyes. His foxhound, Buzz, leaned against Ethan's thigh and poked his cold nose into his pack leader's right ear, a signal that his own ears needed rubbing.

From the hilltop, Ethan gazed across the valley. A blue haze of humidity rose off the fields and almost obscured his farmhouse in the distance. His family had prospered here in Boonsboro, Maryland for seven generations.

He wiped sweat off his forehead and noticed that Beth's legs and arms sparkled as if covered with tiny gems. "Beth, we should have done this in the morning. We're sweating like pigs."

"Lover, women do not sweat. We glisten. Only men sweat. Filthy beasts."

Suddenly, Ethan's guts felt like he'd swallowed a bag of ice cubes. His sight blurred and thunder boomed in his head.

3

He glanced at Beth. She didn't hear it. Buzz hadn't moved.

No, this is something only I see.

I've always hated lightning.

He bit the insides of his cheeks until he tasted blood, panic ripping through him like a fever. He fought for control as he got to his feet.

"Beth, we need to get off this hill."

She turned and frowned, one hand holding the twine, the other on her hip. "We just got here."

Her gaze shifted to something above and behind Ethan and her brows rose. Ethan turned to see a dark cauldron of clouds bubbling up from the Potomac River valley. The humid breeze turned to cold wind and the kite line almost wrenched out of Bethany's grasp.

"Honey, let's get that kite down." As if to punctuate Ethan's words, a silver ribbon sizzled across the southwestern sky. Thunder boomed nine seconds later. "Less than two miles away. Let's hustle."

Ethan began pulling in the kite line.

Beth grabbed what looked like miniature ladders off the ground and spooled twine onto them, but couldn't keep up with Ethan. In less than a minute, he had the kite in hand. Seeing Beth trying to spool the string, he yelled, "Forget that." He pulled a pocket knife from his jeans and sliced the line. "Let's go," he said as goose bumps rose on his skin.

The kite yanked and twisted like a wild falcon tied to his wrist, but he held on. As they double-timed it to the floor of the valley, fat raindrops slapped the ground, falling so wide apart it seemed possible to avoid them. The race with the storm lasted another minute before the sky darkened as if a hand snuffed out the sun. Charcoal clouds disgorged a frigid deluge.

They broke into a trot, Beth laughing and shrieking as thunder ripped overhead. Delay no longer separated the flashes and the booms. A hundred yards ahead, their red barn loomed out of the downpour. Despite his longer legs, Ethan fell behind as nettles of pain blossomed in his knees, another reminder of the toll college hockey had taken on his body. In contrast, his wife bounded over the corn stubble like a fawn.

Bethany turned and, running backwards, slowed enough to let Ethan catch up. She shouted, "You wanted tricks? Try to find me in the hay loft. I'll be the naked one."

4

"Go. I'll catch up," he shouted.

Bethany pulled ahead, sprinting toward the shelter of the barn. Ethan slowed to a walk. His knees hurt too much to run. The rain pounded down with such volume that the field was rapidly turning to mud.

A hundred feet away, Bethany trotted toward an ancient dead oak that stuck out of the field like a pale withered hand.

A million tiny worms crept into Ethan's scalp and crawled down his neck. Adrenaline squirted through his system. He screamed, "Beth! GET DOWN!" The wind ripped his words away as easily as it snatched the kite from his hand.

Lightning strobed high above, throwing the landscape into a series of snapshots. Beth in mid-stride. Beth nearing the oak.

Ethan ran though his knees felt like fire, each step now requiring the added effort of pulling free of mud that sucked at his shoes. Between thunderclaps, he yelled, "BETH!"

This time she heard him and turned, just under the oak.

He watched in horror as a faint spidery tendril of light wavered from the highest branch of the dead oak and wound its way into the sky.

"BETH, GET DOWN!"

She looked like a bewildered child as she stared at Ethan and cupped her hands behind her ears to hear him better.

Sound Dopplered down the spectrum as time stretched out for Ethan. Everything around him moved, in flux, but he seemed slowed as if in quicksand.

The spider of energy thickened and whipped above the tree, searching, searching.

Ethan pointed above Beth, trying to get her to see the danger. His knees screamed as he closed the distance. He had to reach her, tackle her. Couldn't she feel the charge building?

Bethany finally looked up. Ethan saw fear in a face that seemed so pale against the darkness. She dropped to her knees, then flattened into the mud.

Not even knowing it, Ethan whispered, "Not now, God, no." He drove himself forward, each step a distinct battle. He blinked madly to see through the wind-lashed water that hammered like buckshot against his face.

Thunder crashed at such a low frequency that Ethan's

stomach vibrated. He looked up at the oak.

The bright feeder tendril fattened and reached higher into the sky.

Until it made its connection. "No, no, no..."

A searing rope of light blazed from the top of the bleached oak and whipped upward, coiling and writhing, a coruscant, crackling, living thing of purest silver. Smaller ropes arced across the ground from the tree to the barn. With the tree at its center, a translucent blue ball of energy ballooned outward, sizzling like bacon on a hot skillet. Bigger it stretched, engulfing Beth. When the glowing ball expanded to the barn, it suddenly collapsed and the tree exploded like a grenade, hurling wood shrapnel in every direction. In that last moment, Ethan saw Beth's prone silhouette etched against the flash. Then the splinters hit him and he fell into the mud in a ball.

Momentarily blinded, Ethan peered through the rain until his vision returned enough to see that the old tree had vanished. Flames engulfed the barn.

Time spun back up to normal as Ethan struggled to his feet, his knees feeling like broken glass. Blood oozed from his forehead and scalp and arms. Hundreds of splinters protruded from his bare skin. He ignored the pain and the taste of blood in his mouth. Barely able to make headway against the lashing wind, he limped toward where he had last seen Beth. The earth lay fused into a glassy strip of hot blackness that hissed and spat in the rain. Buzz trotted up to it, sniffed, and then ran for the house as if wolves were chasing him.

Ethan dropped to his knees, then lay flat, his face only inches above the steaming glass. No trace of Bethany remained. Could lightning vaporize someone?

Despite the wind, Ethan smelled a chary, ugly stench. He rolled to his right and vomited in the mud.

A sound in the wind caught Ethan's attention. Moaning? Beth?

He realized the sound came out of his own throat, the sub-vocal plea of a wounded animal.

He had felt it coming.

He should have known.

He collapsed into the cold mud and tried to hate himself into oblivion.

CHAPTER 2

"Barry, where the hell are you getting your information?" Clark Fanning leaned back in his leather chair and spun his Cross pen on his rosewood desk.

At the other end of the call the farmer, Barry Meeks, hesitated, twisting his phone in a gnarled hand. "Well, not sure I can say."

"C'mon, cut the crap. I need to know how you do it before I commit us to something really risky." Fanning looked out his window and frowned. Semi-crappy view. On Wall Street, the more you made, the better the view. He really needed a better view.

"Information's reliable. Leave it at that."

With the skill of two decades of sales, Clark Fanning said, "Barry, do you want to retire or do you want to keep working your farm until you're an old man?"

"Christ, I'm already an old man. Feel like one anyway. Wake up every mornin' with a dozen old aches and half a dozen new ones. Hell, fifty-nine, I've had enough of farmin'. Want to move to Florida and get the dirt out from under my fingernails."

"Then tell me, Barry. Where are you getting this information?"

After a few seconds of silence, Barry Meeks said, "Just between us, Mr. Fanning? Don't want nothin' to kill the golden goose."

"Just us, Barry," Fanning said, consciously using the farmer's name again. He remembered his first boss telling him how people loved the sound of their own names. *"Say their names enough, they'll love you. They love you enough and you'll get rich on commissions."*

"Okay. There's this guy Ethan West lives outside Boonsboro. Twenty years ago, his grandfather dies, both his parents are gone, so he shows up from Boston, takes over the family farm. City slicker, college boy, never grew so much as a house plant. Bunch of us neighbors offer him help, but he says no.

"The guy never has a bad harvest. Sidesteps drought, grasshoppers, mildew, every damn thing nature can throw at a farmer. Thought we needed to help *him*, but it's us needs the help. We're havin' good years, some bad, but he's got good harvests every single year.

"Stopped hittin' my head against the wall some years back and started watchin' this guy. If he planted corn, I bought corn futures. Bad Midwest weather pushed up corn prices and I made a bundle. When he didn't plant corn, I went short on corn futures, figuring it would be a bumper crop for supplies and prices would drop. You know that's exactly what happened. I'm makin' ten times more money tradin' commodities than from farmin' my Goddamn land."

"You've parlayed a respectable portfolio, Barry, but these last five years could just be luck. Before I let you risk everything, I want more information."

"Okay, one time he grew watermelons. Everybody laughed their asses off. Nobody grows watermelons in Frederick County. Season's too short. Well, that year we had the longest summer I ever seen. With five hundred acres in melons he made a killin'. Next year, some farmers tried melons and an early freeze in September wiped 'em out. But that year this guy grew tomatoes. Two days before the frost, he hires pickers. Frost hits and his fields are bare. How you explain that?"

Fanning said, "I can't. But there must have been times he screwed up."

"Never."

"You sure, Barry? Sure enough to take a big risk? You're wrong, you'll lose everything."

"I'm sure."

Clark Fanning pondered. He had taken flyers on less. "Okay, Barry. Here's the play."

If this hick was really onto something, Fanning had big plans. And if the farmer was wrong, well, it was the hick's money, not Fanning's. He'd make commission either way.

CHAPTER 3

The October sun beat unseasonably hot on Ethan's shoulders as he pulled up the yellow tape the police had staked around the remains of the old oak. A crime scene? He felt like strangling one of the stupid bastards who'd kept him away for a week as they poked around the spot where Beth had disappeared. When they finally accepted that Ethan hadn't killed his wife, they lost interest. Now he was free to do the only thing he could think of. He pushed a spade deep into the coffee-colored earth, heaved aside the damp loam. Again and again. It felt like digging a grave, except his purpose was not to bury something. Just the opposite. Soon sweat dropped from the end of his narrow nose in a steady rhythm that matched his movements.

His scalp and forehead itched from hundreds of tiny scabs left by the splinters. He stopped digging and ripped sweat-soaked bandages off his arms and let the sun beat on the swollen skin. A week after the storm, the pain of his wounds had barely diminished. The infected areas throbbed in the heat of the sun. What did pain matter? He deserved this pain and more.

It took an hour to clear surface soil and dig around the dark nightmare. Where the lightning bolt had struck Beth, the ground had fused into black and brown glass with a hollow center that corkscrewed down at an angle into the earth. Uncovered, this last evidence of his wife's existence stretched over five feet long and a foot wide, a twisted mass of silica and carbon, the result of over six thousand degrees of heat.

A piece of the sun.

Ethan ran his fingers along the convoluted curves, some smooth as Steuben glass, others rough and textured like charcoal.

Ethan attacked the glass. With each powerful arc of the twenty-pound sledge, he smashed the glazed artifact into chunks, then fragments. Then, like a prospector, he sifted through the pile of shards and dust for some hint of Bethany.

After an hour of sifting, Ethan sat in the grass and stared at the shattered remnants of an energy beyond his comprehension. Not a bone nor a button had been captured in the thing. No wedding ring had fused inside its translucent mass. It was as if Beth had never existed. Could lightning do such a thing?

His eyes drifted to the bright sky but they saw nothing except his own guilt etched in the clouds. It crushed down on him with a weight that made him lightheaded.

Sitting here on this spot where she had left the earth, Ethan felt some faint energy, some remnant of her thoughts. His mind flashed the image of her pale face, so terrorized in those last instants.

He should have sensed the storm earlier. He should never have taken Beth up that hill. A life of hiding had dulled him to the clear signals of danger.

Deep inside, I knew. Why didn't I understand?

Why did he hide? He was no longer a child. But his training ran deep. His mother had seen to that.

He had thought he would find closure by digging up the glass artifact, but instead he felt only turmoil. His forty years of life seemed wasted, withered. What good were his skills if he didn't use them?

And now using them didn't matter.

When Ethan had started digging, Buzz sniffed at the black glass, but wrinkled his nose and settled in the grass ten feet away. Now, sensing Ethan's turmoil, the dog sidled up to his sitting master and poked his snout into Ethan's ear, delivering a two-lick kiss.

Ethan scratched the top of Buzz's head, then gathered his shovel and sledgehammer and trudged back to the barn. The sun's heat did nothing to warm his soul.

CHAPTER 4

The farmer sounded breathless at the other end of the line.

"Slow down, Barry. Tell me that again."

"Ran into Ethan West in the supermarket. He had a shopping cart full of vacuum-packed coffee beans. Like twenty-five or thirty cans."

"And?"

"When I asked him about it, he got nervous, changed the subject."

"So, Barry, what's your point?"

"Coffee's goin' up."

Fanning didn't want to believe, but he had to believe. This had happened too often. "What do you want to do?"

"Put all my money in."

"You're sure?"

"I'm sure."

"Okay." Clark Fanning pulled up the trading screen on his computer and made the trades for the Barry Meeks account.

Then he did the same for his own account.

* * *

"You're sure about this, Fanning?"

"Mr. Churchill, this is a safe bet."

"There's no such thing as a safe bet or it wouldn't be called betting. How much room do I have on margin?"

"Close to a million."

"Leverage the whole thing."

"Yessir." Clark Fanning smiled as he put down the phone. A fat commission, in a growing list of fat commissions that he'd been able to turn because of the information coming from that Boonsboro farmer, Barry Meeks. Not to mention his own portfolio trades.

Another year like this and he'd retire to a sunny beach and fill his days chasing anything that wore a bikini. And he'd catch them too. Didn't matter he was bald and fat. Have enough money and you can catch anything you want.

* * *

Andrew Churchill frowned as he put down the phone, buyer's remorse rising like bile in his throat. Could that broker

11

be trusted? He was making weird trades, but Churchill had already seen his initial investment increase twentyfold.

If this went wrong, he faced ruin. But if it went right, it would buy his company another six months of life. Maybe long enough to float a public stock offering and get out of the bush leagues. Yeah, maybe. He hit a speed-dial button.

"Egany, get in here. Bring the financials."

"Mr. Churchill, this is the third time this month. We've used up all the accounting tricks."

"Maybe we missed something."

They'd walked a tightrope for the past year. They needed breathing space. Churchill dialed the extension of his research team.

"Dolci."

"Cliff, how soon before we get results on the Memnon clinical trials?"

"Still crunching numbers."

"I need good news and I need it yesterday."

"Well, in that last run of testing, most subjects scored about five percent better than the law of averages."

"That's the group. What about individuals?"

"One guy scored nineteen percent above the group."

"Dolci, drop the test subjects who scored under five percent and print up a preliminary report. I want it on my desk yesterday."

"Mr. Churchill, that would taint the study. When we get it peer reviewed, we'll get crucified."

"Dolci, I need better results from you or this company's in the shitter. Maybe you like the idea of getting government cheese and unemployment checks?"

Dolci didn't answer.

"Just do it," Churchill said.

Andrew Churchill dialed his contact at the Pentagon and took a deep breath, scratching his long fingers across the stubble of a crew cut he'd had since childhood.

"DV Ops. Harrington here." Churchill recognized the voice of colonel Walter Harrington, head of the government's Distance Vision Project.

Andrew Churchill took a breath. "Colonel, I have some good news for you."

He felt no embarrassment about the lies he was about to tell. He knew a lot about lying.

CHAPTER 5

The stock broker's voice sounded like music on the phone. "Mr. Churchill, the Brazilian government announced that an excessive rainy season has severely cut coffee production. I liquidated your options before the market closed. You net about four million."

Andrew Churchill rolled his blue eyes and leaned back in his chair. "You beautiful bastard." No matter what else happened, this would keep those private investors off his back.

"Do you want me to look for another position?" The broker sounded hungry.

"Clark, let me enjoy my spoils for five minutes, okay?"

"Sure, it's just that I could parlay this up. I'm more confident now."

Something in Clark Fanning's voice caught Churchill. "More confident? Why would you be *more* confident about option derivatives? They're risky as hell. I know ten guys who lost their asses with only one trade, but you've been batting a thousand. How?"

"Well, I can't really say."

"Bullshit. We're talking millions now, Fanning. I'm not going to let you parlay a goddamn thing unless I know how you're making these trades."

"Mr. Churchill, most people are just glad to make the money."

"Well, I'm not most people and we're talking serious coin. I started with a lousy fifty grand. How are you doing this?"

* * *

Fanning hesitated. He thought of his ethical obligation to his client, the farmer, Barry Meeks. He thought of the hefty commission he'd made on this four million-dollar trade plus the fat profit he'd made in his own portfolio. Meeks was soon to become a *former* client, selling his farm and retiring to Florida. When that happened, Fanning would lose his link to the information that was making him rich. Realistically, how much would he owe Meeks after the well ran dry?

Andrew Churchill, on the other hand, Fanning's *current* client, planned to take his pharmaceutical company public. Being the underwriter of a hot public offering was every broker's dream score. Clark Fanning would ride the rocket to retirement. No, Clark Fanning decided he wouldn't really need that damn farmer's information anymore.

Fanning said, "There's this guy, a farmer named Ethan West..."

* * *

The black Lincoln Continental lumbered up the driveway so slowly, it barely raised dust. Buzz's barking drew Ethan from the back of his house where he was repairing a downspout.

To the two suits who got out of the Continental, Ethan said, "Mornin'."

Buzz sniffed the air and barked. Ethan thought of how he and Beth had learned to trust Buzz's instincts and had coined the dog's analysis of strangers as the Buzz test. Ethan picked up a small branch and threw it at the dog. "Buzz, no!" Buzz sat on his haunches and shut up, but his eyes never left the strangers.

"Mr. West?" The taller one spoke.

"Who are you?"

"Are you Ethan West?"

Ethan squinted. "Two suits in sunglasses come to a man's house and start asking questions. No hello, no pardon me. Cops or salesmen. Which are you?"

"We've come to offer you a business proposition."

"I'm a farmer, not a businessman. Good day, gentlemen." Ethan started for the rear of his house. The two suits squinted at each other. The shorter one stepped forward.

"Excuse my associate, Mr. West. We didn't mean to offend you. But we would like to talk about something that could be beneficial to you."

Ethan turned.

"We represent Neural Research Laboratory from down in Rockville. We explore aspects of human brain activity, memory, things like that for the Defense Department."

"What's that have to do with me?"

"We understand you have a unique talent. Predict what to plant, that sort of thing. We'd like to pay you to let us conduct some tests to see how you do what you do."

Ethan's senses tingled. He had dipped his toes in forbidden waters to make a living, thinking it harmless. But crocodiles lurked under the surface. What good was hiding if people found you? "How you know anything about me?"

14

"Mr. West, people in this valley have noticed your uncanny ability to pick the right crops to grow, year after year. People talk. The story got to us and we wanted to look more closely at this ability. We'd pay you very well for some of your time."

"I'm just lucky, is all."

"Mr. West, luck is ability that's not understood. Maybe you have such ability and maybe you don't. But we're willing to pay to find out."

"How much?"

"Five thousand dollars a day."

Forbidden waters looked inviting. Bethany's funeral had been expensive, even without a body.

I can deal with crocodiles, Ethan thought. Even if they wear suits.

CHAPTER 6

"Andrew, nobody has scores like this." Clifford Dolci stabbed his finger into the stack of green-bar paper, pushed it across the oak conference table to his boss.

"Good?" said Churchill.

"No, bad. Distance visualization, card guessing, all the usual ESP tests, West gets everything wrong. I couldn't believe it, so we ran the tests again. Same result. Very unusual."

"How so?"

"Take the card guessing. In a fifty-two-card deck on average you should guess the suits of thirteen cards. This guy scores near zero deck after deck. It's impossible. The law of averages says you have to guess some cards right eventually."

"He's unlucky," said Churchill.

"No, I think he's doing it on purpose."

"That would make him quite remarkable."

"Yes."

"What makes you sure he's faking?"

"I think he's aware of his abilities and hides them. He likes the money. Figures we'll get bored, go away, and he can buy a new tractor or some crap like that."

"I've made four million dollars off this guy. Yeah, Dolci, he must be faking." Churchill rolled his eyes.

Dolci rose from the conference table and pulled a video dolly across the room to the edge of the table. Dolci punched a button on his video remote. "These thermal brain scans are interesting. On the left is a test subject. The image on the right is West. See a difference?"

"West's brain looks hotter. What are they doing?"

"This is the control sequence. They're in a dark, quiet room. Watch this."

A moment of static appeared on the screens, then both images resumed.

"Jesus. What are they doing now?" Churchill leaned closer to the screens.

"Card guessing."

"West makes the other guy look like a popsicle brain."

"Yes." Dolci pointed to areas of the screen. "The difference is striking. The control subject goes from cool blue to green with a little yellow. Notice that West's cerebral cortex

16

is uniformly yellow with areas of orange. Much greater activity. And also his medulla oblongata. Interesting juxtaposition. One controls higher thought, the other instinct."

"Is he okay?"

"Yes. No outward signs of agitation. What fascinates me about these images is that his brain does something similar to what Memnon does for our test subjects. More brain activity, more blood flow. It's an interesting parallel."

"What would happen if you goosed him with Memnon?"

"I assume his brain function would increase even further."

Churchill pondered for several seconds. "Do you have any idea how good he is, Cliff? I mean, this is all rather vague, so far."

"He says he can't do anything. It's just luck."

"Well, we know that's a load of manure, from a farmer, no less."

"What do you think we should do? I'm out of my field here."

"I have an idea," Churchill said.

CHAPTER 7

In the testing room Ethan sat at a computer screen divided into quadrants. At random intervals the computer beeped. Three seconds later, the computer generated a blip of light somewhere on the screen. After each tone and before the light blip appeared, Ethan was supposed to touch the screen in the quadrant where he thought the light would occur.

He was into his second run when the ceiling lights in the room blinked out and the monitor went dead. Ethan sat back in his padded chair and waited in the dark. Several minutes went by and nothing happened. In the distance, he heard a siren wailing. He smelled smoke. Then water hissed from the sprinkler system overhead.

The smoke became thicker and Ethan dropped to the floor to avoid the worst of it. He groped to the door and felt around until he found the doorknob. It turned, but the door wouldn't open. Panic seized Ethan. He saw a faint reddish glow higher up the door. Ethan's fingers ran up the jamb to chest level where a ten-key security lock glowed dull red. This door had never been locked before. The red keypad had never been lit before. But why would they want doors locked in an emergency?

A deep rumble vibrated the walls and Ethan's heart rate accelerated. He began coughing. Nobody was coming to release him; he was on his own. The smoke got so thick he had to put his face right up to the door. He stared at the keypad and in his head saw a number. He punched in seven digits. The keypad glowed green and clicked. Ethan yanked at the doorknob and the door opened. He staggered into the hall.

The fluorescent tubes in the hall beamed brightly; the carpet remained dry; no sprinklers had gone off. Except for smoke spilling out of the testing lab, the air was clear. What the hell was going on?

* * *

In the control room, Clifford Dolci tapped a monitor labeled Test Lab Number 2 Infrared View. "Did you see that, Andrew? He got the code on the very first try. A *seven* digit number."

Andrew Churchill sat back in his chair, steepling his fingers, a smile twisting his pale lips.

18

"Uh-oh," said Dolci.

"What?"

"He's bugging out."

Andrew Churchill glared at the screen. They'd stumbled onto something here. He didn't know why, but he needed this farmer. It took Andrew Churchill three seconds to weigh the possibilities and reach a decision. "Call security," he said.

* * *

As Ethan loped down the wide corridor, his skin prickled. With each step his thoughts screamed, "They know, they know, they know..." He cursed himself for what he had done – the witching his mother had tried to beat out of him since childhood. He had always kept his head down, made a modest living to avoid attention, but this easy money had sucked him into something he now regretted.

He felt them ahead, so he veered left into a corridor of the same white walls, same gray carpet, the same progression of endless oak doors. But Ethan had a precise sense of direction. He knew exactly where he'd parked his truck and no matter how many times his route might twist and turn, he could find it.

Hearing a shout, he snatched a quick look behind. A mountain in a blue uniform swept toward him. Now he had to really run. His knees still ached from sprinting through the thunderstorm with Beth, but he had no choice. "Damn." Ethan cut right and broke the line of sight, charging down the first corridor that appeared. Fifty feet ahead he saw a gray metal door, behind which he would find open air, his truck, and an end to this foolishness. But he felt someone ahead about to intersect his line of flight. He accelerated, focused on the gray door that led home.

He arrived a second too late.

A door on his left swung open with such force it banged back against the wall. Two guards spewed from the opening and collided with Ethan. The trio went down in a tangle, Ethan ramming his right knee into the groin of the nearest guard. The man screeched as he swung an elbow at Ethan's face. An instant too slow, the man's elbow never connected, as Ethan's knuckles broke the guard's nose. Blood gushed and the man howled. His attack stopped.

As the second guard grabbed Ethan's neck from behind, Ethan spun left and got a leg under himself. With huge effort, he lifted himself and the second guard long enough to slam backward against the wall, crushing the breath out of the man who clung to him like a limpet. The guard's grip loosened and Ethan drove an elbow backward catching his attacker in the front of the rib cage. A high squeal came out of the man and Ethan almost shook loose. Through the corner of his eye, he saw motion and heard the slamming footsteps of the man-mountain rapidly approaching.

Reaching up with his left hand, Ethan felt behind his head, located his grappler's face and rammed a thumb into an eye socket. The guard let loose with a guttural roar. Ethan shook himself free. Without looking back, he hurled himself at the gray door. He had his hands on the horizontal throw-bar, when a crushing weight hit him from behind. The impact drove him through the doorway, sprawling him across a concrete landing.

For a brief instant, Ethan lay in the sun. But as helpless as a calf in the jaws of a crocodile, he could not fight the enormous strength that yanked him back through the doorway.

CHAPTER 8

His skin increasingly itchy and hot, Ethan watched clear fluid drip out of a transparent IV bag into a plastic tube and down into the needle stuck in his arm.

He lay in a bed in a beige room with white enameled cabinets along three walls. Bundles of wires trailed across the floor, like multi-colored pythons. Ethan's inclined bed faced the fourth wall which held a gigantic sheet of mirrored plate glass from floor to ceiling. He sensed people behind the glass.

A door opened and a short, bespectacled man in a lab coat entered. Ethan quietly pulled at his restraints as he catalogued the thinning gray hair, the watery brown eyes.

"Mr. West, in a room somewhere in this building, a person is looking at a photograph and trying to project to you what is in that photograph. I don't know if it is a man or woman and I don't know what is in the photograph. Your job is to try to tune in those thoughts and tell me what is in the photograph." The man's calm, professional voice complemented his thin, academic face.

"My job? You're out of your mind. Do you know this is kidnapping? I'll have your ass, you little jerk."

The creases in the man's forehead deepened. He said, "You signed a release for extended research in a residential environment. You'd have a hard time proving you were held here involuntarily, especially since we'll be making a large deposit to your bank account every week."

When the man turned, Ethan strained against the nylon straps that secured his wrists until veins popped out on his neck and forehead. Brute force was not the answer. He needed another way. He folded his fingers down as far as they would go, felt along the edges of the cuffs. Velcro. Ethan extended his long fingers. His right hand could barely touch the end of the Velcro strap around his wrist.

Ethan scowled at the mirror wall.

The man in the lab coat wrapped a pressure cuff around Ethan's left arm, then flicked on the automatic blood pressure monitor.

Ethan nodded his head toward the line that dripped fluid into his arm. "What the hell is that?"

"It's a little cocktail called Memnon. It stimulates neural

21

receptors. Kind of a tune-up for your brain."

"Why?"

"To make you more able to do what you do."

"And that would be?"

"Don't be coy, Mr. West. I've seen your test scores."

"Yeah, they're lousy."

"Conveniently so. I've also seen the security camera video of your little adventure."

Ethan's eyes narrowed.

"Ah, I see you understand the significance of that. Let's not play games. You have abilities you're hiding. We want to see what you can do."

No. Ethan clamped down every shred of his control. He tried to blank all thought from his brain, tried to block all information as he felt his mind jump. This damned drug was doing something to him. Thoughts sparked across his cerebral cortex and he saw images of things he didn't want to see.

The man checked his wristwatch, then ran his right hand nervously through his hair. "Try to relax."

"I'm not giving you a goddamn thing. Let me go."

"That's not in my power, Mr. West."

"Why not? You're just a powerless little shit?" Ethan tried to stay in the moment, wanting to argue with this drone to keep his mind away from images that were forming against his will.

The man stood a little taller. "I'm a senior member of the research team."

Ethan had the end of the Velcro strap between his middle and ring finger. Pulling part of it free, he kept talking to camouflage the sound. "You're a veterinarian? You take care of the lab animals?"

"I'm a clinical psychiatrist."

Another inch of the strap came free. "Look like a glorified nurse to me."

With open smugness, the man in the lab coat said, "I assure you, I'm more than that."

Ethan let out an artificial laugh and stared at the one-way mirror. "Good one, you horse's ass."

The man leaned over Ethan and shined a penlight into his eyes.

Ethan said, "See anything?"

"Nothing abnormal."

"No? How about now?" Ethan spat into the man's face.

The man's eyes flashed and his pale skin turned pink. A vein in the center of his forehead stood out like a blue worm.

"What's the matter? Never had a lab rat fight back?" Ethan squinted at the man's name tag. "You're looking a bit vexed, *Doctor* Gunderson. Except you're too much of a gutless prick to do anything even when a man spits in your face. Am I right, *Doctor?*"

Gunderson took off his glasses, wiped his sleeve across his face. In the instant Gunderson's eyes were covered, Ethan's fingers yanked the rest of the Velcro strap free. His right fist crunched into Gunderson's throat; the doctor fell back, gasping for breath. Ethan's free hand released the other.

He sat up and freed his left ankle just as Gunderson rushed him. Unable to get totally free, Ethan rolled to his right side, pivoted his left leg at the hip, and kicked Gunderson in the ribs. As the smaller man hit the floor, Ethan released the last restraint, yanked out the IV needle, and hopped off the bed.

Then the door opened.

The man who stood in the doorway wore a white lab coat, but any other similarity between him and the doctor did not exist. Here stood a tub of muscle behind a grin. Hands like hams reached out and shook Ethan, then slammed him against the bed.

"Be a nice little fellow there, Mr. West, and do like Doc wants." His python fingers wrapped around Ethan's throat and immobilized him while Gunderson re-strapped Ethan to the bed and reconnected leads. Then, just for fun the big man squeezed his fingers and gave Ethan a good shake. Ethan's face turned red from the pressure around his neck. "You try any bullshit like this again and I won't be so gentle next time."

Suddenly, Ethan stood in a room filled with TV monitors. A man watched half of these monitors in which tiny versions of Ethan were lying in a hospital bed. A woman watched the other half of the monitors on which various graphics wiggled and blinked. Two other men sat at a console with a microphone.

The multi-faceted view of all those monitors made Ethan think he was standing in the head of a fly, looking out at the world through a thousand lenses. He turned and peered through a glass wall to where he saw himself strapped to a bed.

"Heart rate is getting up there," one of them said.

23

"He's strong. Let me know if it hits 200."

None of the people in the room seemed to notice Ethan standing next to them. But then he realized he didn't have a body. He was conscious. He was aware. He just wasn't there.

Ethan blinked in his head and he suddenly hovered in bright sunlight on a mountain top. Jagged spires of granite rose around him, thrust up through a world of snow. Wind whipped a curtain of ice crystals into the air and the sun transformed them into a billion glinting prisms.

Ethan blinked again and suddenly floated on a street in a large city. The street teemed with fast-walking pedestrians and bumper-to-bumper cars, but the cars didn't look right. Tall buildings cast stark shadows on their neighbors from a red sun low in the sky.

Ethan rotated his vision, looking down the wide avenue. His mind rebelled. In the distance he saw the twin towers of the World Trade Center. Ethan saw a newsstand further up the block. With no lapse of time, he hovered in front of it. He read a headline on the *New York Times* above which he saw the date. May 14, 1975.

Ethan felt like a frog in a blender. His mind went blank and then he stood in a doctor's office. All around him nurses and clerks talked on phones and filed papers and ushered patients. Ethan peeked over the shoulder of a woman as she opened a file labeled Gunderson.

Ethan read a test report as the woman dialed her phone. "May I speak with Doctor Gunderson?" she said. Ethan noticed her wristwatch said three thirty-seven. The nametag on her lapel said Vanessa Ercig, MD. The desk calendar showed today's date.

Ethan blinked and suddenly he lay in the hospital bed, the attendant just releasing his grip on him. Detached, confused, disoriented, he glanced at the wall clock. 1:32. Here no time had passed, but he had explored somewhere else for an hour.

This made no sense. Gunderson was still attaching leads to his body, yet Ethan had been watching his data already registering on the screens in the control room. And what about that newspaper? What had just happened?

CHAPTER 9

Churchill's eyes locked on the tight-focus television monitor even though he could see Ethan easily through the one-way mirror wall. The attendant strapped him to the bed one limb at a time. To one of the control room technicians Churchill said, "Can you run back the last ten seconds from this camera in slow motion?" He had noticed something, a tiny anomaly. This time, with the video slowed to half speed, he saw it clearly. Ethan's struggles momentarily ceased and his body went limp. An instant later, he animated again and struggled to sit up. Churchill dialed up the sound from the monitor that showed the live feed from the test room.

"Gunderson, get your lab animal off me. I'll give you something," Ethan said.

Doctor Gunderson patted the technician's biceps. "Thank you, Ted. That will be all for now." Without a backward glance, the big man left. "So, what's in the photograph, Mr. West?"

"I have no idea. This is better." Ethan taunted.

"Let me be the judge."

"Okay. You had some tests done recently."

Gunderson cocked his head and said softly, "What?"

Ethan saw the fear. "A biopsy. Your testicles. You'll get the test results this afternoon. A phone call from your oncologist at three thirty-seven. Doctor named Ercig. Vanessa Ercig."

Gunderson gripped the metal rails of Ethan's bed and leaned forward. "How do you know her name? What do you see?"

"Snip, snip, Doctor." A cruel smile turned Ethan's mouth to a gash. "Divine justice, eh? Payback for keeping me here, although I can't see how you'd notice any difference. You're *already* a eunuch."

"I'm afraid you're mistaken, West."

"The first half of that statement is true. You *are* afraid. The second half is wishful thinking. I'm not mistaken." Ethan closed his eyes and settled into the pillow, exhausted. *Am I bluffing? Or is it true? I'll know at three thirty-seven.*

Gunderson tried to maintain his composure, but the thin bead of sweat across his upper lip betrayed him.

* * *

Churchill slapped his left hand against the monitor screen and turned to Dolci. "Ted scared him and he went wherever he needed to go and came back in the blink of an eye."

Dolci stroked his chin, his stubble feeling like a wire brush. "Very interesting. We'll have to wait two hours to see if he was making it up."

"Making it up? How would he make up something as outlandish as testicular cancer? And how would he know Gunderson's doctor's name?"

"Maybe he heard someone talking about it."

"In a locked room? Have you heard anyone talking about Gunderson?"

"Well, no."

"Fact is, it's true. Gunderson did have a biopsy. He hasn't breathed a word of this to anyone, not even his wife. He's scared to death. He confided in me only yesterday."

Dolci's dark eyebrows rose.

Churchill said, "West's been sandbagging, Cliff. He's remarkable. He can pick up information over a distance." Churchill frowned as his brain connected several rapidly moving thoughts. "Oh, my God, I missed the obvious."

"What?"

"This isn't Distance Vision. He doesn't just see across space, he sees across *time*. If Gunderson gets that phone call, do you realize what this means?"

Cliff Dolci slapped his hand against the arm of his chair. "Yes, it means that to know it wasn't a lucky fluke, it has to be repeatable. We'll have to induce fear again. He'll get jaded, so we'll have to up the ante, be more threatening. Andrew, are you prepared for where this is leading?"

Churchill's lips curled into a sneer. "It's leading us out of a very deep hole."

"Or into one," Dolci's eyes glared.

Churchill leaned forward and threw the switch that activated the thin stalk of microphone in front of him. "Mr. West, how did you get that information on Doctor Gunderson?"

Ethan looked up, his eyelids half closed. "Who are you?"

Churchill found it disconcerting to have West look directly at him through the one-way mirror. "I'm Doctor Gunderson's superior. How did you do that?"

26

"I don't know. Why?"

"We're trying to understand how you get this information."

"Just a knack."

"Somewhat more than that, wouldn't you say?"

"No, I just have hunches."

"Well, your hunches are very good. Can you tell us how they form? How you know that the hunch is a good hunch and not just a fantasy?"

Ethan stared at the ceiling where speakers relayed Churchill's voice. "I never really thought about it."

In the control room, with the microphone off, Churchill squinted at Dolci. "Are you buying this bullshit?"

Dolci held his chin in his right hand. "I'm not sure. It's possible he has only a vague conscious sense of his gift. Not easy to tell."

"Vague conscious sense? C'mon, Cliff. You think that was coincidence? West's in a crisis environment and he finds exactly the tool he needs to clobber Gunderson." Though he was talking low, he realized the technicians at the other end of the room had become unusually quite. Churchill turned toward them and said, "That will be all for now, people. Go take a break. I need to talk to Doctor Dolci in private." After the control room cleared, Churchill leaned forward and, louder now, said, "You need to turn up the heat, Cliff. Gunderson is a weenie. Put Ted back in there."

"Ted? Ted's not a trained researcher."

"Maybe that's why he's effective."

"We're on thin ice here. We go much further, we could wind up in jail."

"We don't go further and we wind up in the poor house. Makes jail look good, no? You get Ted in there and scare West's balls off. We're running out of time."

"What the hell is your hurry? What aren't you telling me?" Dolci's dark eyes stared like gun barrels behind his glasses.

Very calmly, Andrew Churchill flattened his manicured hands against the table and said in a low voice, "Cliff, we've been at this a long time. The seed money we got from the Avalon Group has run out. I've kissed and fawned until I'm blue in the face to scratch a few more bucks out of those tight-fisted bastards. They want to see our DOD contract renewed soon or they pull the plug. Then we go bankrupt and they pick

27

our bones clean. The only thing that's keeping this company going right now is my high-risk commodity trading."

Churchill's right index finger lifted off the table and pointed at the TV screen that held a frozen image of Ethan West. "I made that money because of *him*. And right now he's the only resource we have to make revenue to keep this place going. Now, check your bleeding heart at the door and get in there and figure out what he can do and how he does it."

"Goddammit, you're asking me to commit a crime! That's not a lab animal in there."

Churchill lowered his gaze to his hands which he folded and unfolded. "You can walk out that door anytime you want. Just know you walk out penniless."

A long minute passed. Finally, Churchill said, "You're still here."

"For the moment."

"Well as long as you're still here, send Ted up for a come-to-Jesus meeting. I'll explain the new rules to him. Satisfied?"

Dolci gave a grudging nod.

"And Cliff, no more staff in here during tests. All videos are to be kept under lock and key. Tell your people the government just raised our security classification and anybody who opens their mouths will get fired."

"You're not serious."

Churchill rose and crossed to the door. As he opened it, he stared at Clifford Dolci and in a lifeless voice said, "You're right, Cliff. I must be joking."

CHAPTER 10

Techies unstrapped Ethan from the bed and took him to a small suite consisting of a bedroom, bathroom, and sitting area with a big-screen TV. High up against the ceiling, video cameras watched Ethan's every movement. He scowled at the cameras in the bathroom.

Ethan had two hours of rest before Ted escorted him back to the test lab. Gunderson had gone, replaced by Doctor Stewart, a tall, saturnine figure.

Ethan stared straight at Stewart. "Gunderson got his phone call, I see."

After Doctor Stewart connected the Memnon drip to the IV line in Ethan's forearm and hooked up the monitoring leads, he shot a nervous look at Ted and hustled out of the test room.

"It's you and me, kiddo," Ted said, smiling.

"I'm honored."

From a metal toolbox on the floor, Ted extracted a foot-long metal rod with a black handle from which extended an electric cord. He plugged this into the wall and soon Ethan smelled hot metal. Ted smiled and held the tip of the rod near enough to Ethan's face that he felt the heat. "Okay, West. Your prediction on Doctor Gunderson turned out true. We want another piece of information. Anything, just so it's something you couldn't possibly know and that we can verify."

"What's the soldering iron for?"

"That's not a soldering iron, that's an incentive enhancer. The human body has nine square feet of skin. Plenty of room for incentification."

"You're out of your mind."

"Probably. All the more reason to cooperate, wouldn't you say?"

Ethan glanced at his flimsy hospital gown. Great protection. Before he could think much more about options, his skin tingled. Images burst across his vision and his thoughts lurched.

Ethan found himself in a dim room, curtains drawn in the middle of the day. He heard creaking from the bed as he approached. From a tangle of limbs and blankets he heard a woman's voice. "God, baby, that feels incredible."

Ethan peered down at her face. She had lashes so lush, even a deer would feel envy. On the nightstand a photograph featured that same face in a wedding veil. However, the groom in the photograph did not look like the man on top of the woman. The groom in the photograph was Ted.

The bedside clock said 4:11. Below large digital numbers a date glowed in green. Two days ago. Ethan's mind blinked and he returned to the lab. "Ted, your wife has a unicorn tattoo above the nipple on her left breast?"

Ted's eyes went wide.

"Ted, if I were you, I wouldn't go home in the middle of the day without calling first. It could be embarrassing. Further fuel for your feelings of inadequacy." Ethan enjoyed seeing the twitch that jiggled Ted's beefy face. He picked up something else. "You've suspected, haven't you, Teddy? Just haven't caught her yet."

"You bastard."

Scorched human flesh gives off a pungency not unlike that of burning bacon. Some far-off corner of Ethan West's mind made that analogy even as his consciousness danced like a pinball in his head. He howled and twisted in a vain attempt to evade that hot, angry little stem of metal that seared his left armpit. As pain blossomed and Ethan's nerves shrieked he knew he had no way to reason with Ted. Ted continued like a machine.

Maybe not quite a machine. He did have emotions. Why else would he be smiling as he brought the soldering iron against Ethan's skin a third time?

Pain triggered fear and fear triggered instinct. Inside his mind, Ethan blinked again. In one moment, like an insect tacked to a mounting board, completely at the mercy of a remorseless collector; in the next moment, he flew a billion miles or years or a billion somethings away. Like throwing a light switch.

I was there. Now, I'm here.

Where was here?

Here felt vaguely familiar, the stuff of a million childhood daydreams. How many times had he stared out the window of a classroom to set his mind adrift and feel the presence of an unseen land, a different sky just out of reach of his senses?

Witchery. His mother had warned him. He had tried not to feel it, had tried to ignore the images that spilled into his brain, but on a spring morning when he was seven, when the last grains of the school year slipped through the hourglass of his thoughts, he had felt the first irresistible tug of a faraway place, of a dream world. Young Ethan had dipped into the syrupy river of time and experienced the power and pulse of a current far beyond the abilities of a little boy to comprehend.

But grown-up Ethan knew the place existed, like a beating heart on the other side of a door. Dimly aware that somewhere his body suffered, he did not care. He had unhinged himself from physical reality.

He was not having a vision. He had transported to a real place with vivid sights and sounds. He found himself hovering over a landscape. Emerald-green cornstalks jumped out of soil so rich it looked black.

In the distance stood a farmhouse. By thinking of it, Ethan suddenly hovered next to it. He knew this whitewashed building. His house, but from an earlier time.

Ethan watched a tow-headed child waddle across an overgrown lawn. The child's feet tangled in the jungle of grasses and he stumbled and spun and was suddenly sitting upright and smiling as if he had rehearsed the complex maneuver and fell exactly where he wanted to be.

The toddler's pink fingers reached into the lushness around him. His eyes sparkled and his throat bubbled with sounds of joy as he pulled bright green slivers of grass from the ground. Ethan felt dizzy as he recognized his young self.

From the front porch his mother eyed her child briefly, then returned to her task. Fingers brown from the sun split pea pods and thumbed fat, sweet peas into a cobalt-blue bowl.

Gray eyes glanced up, eagle-like, sharp as a judge's decision, and they stared right at Ethan.

Fear shot through Ethan as his young mother's gaze impaled him. He saw the moment of recognition when they blinked and focused, trying to see something more a function of belief than of light. He saw the mind behind the eyes struggle with the image of what it had uncovered on this bright afternoon when a thousand familiar sounds and scents drifted across the fields and felt so normal. He saw that mind rebel at the unnatural something that had jumped into the foreground and pulled her thoughts to a roiled space she had sworn never to visit.

In that brief instant, he saw that she knew him and he sensed her revulsion. He knew how she avoided the place in

31

her mind that spawned such images. She threw down her bowl and leaped from the porch and seized her child. She scowled at the older Ethan as she clutched his young version and she shouted one word into the still, afternoon air.

"No!"

Ethan's eyes flew open and saw Ted above him. A tendril of smoke rose from the tip of the soldering iron. Ethan West lay exhausted and drenched in a sweat that did nothing to cool him.

* * *

"Jesus Christ, Andrew! Look what he did!"

"Sit down, Cliff." Churchill blocked the door.

Dolci said, "He stuck a soldering iron into the guy's side. He's totally out of control."

"You know the saying about omelets and eggs, don't you, Cliff?"

Dolci pointed at the one-way mirror. "That's not an egg in there. That's a man and before you start scrambling him, you need to throw out that ape you think can do research."

"Give him a minute."

"Why? So he can burn him some more?"

"Cliff, the idea was to scare him, not use the damn thing."

"Was this the result of your come-to-Jesus meeting?" Dolci's face had turned almost purple. "I'd say Ted didn't get the message too well, did he?"

"No, he didn't. West pushed him over the edge."

"Are you saying it's West's fault?" Spittle gathered at the corners of Dolci's mouth.

"Hold on, Cliff. Ted was only supposed to scare him. He went too far, I agree. Let's replace the soldering iron with something that gives an electric shock. Okay? If he uses it, no damage, but it gets West's attention. Would that work?"

"We're supposed to do research, not torture. That's a goddamn felony, Andrew!"

"You're right. We have to keep our eyes on the ball."

Dolci squinted suspiciously. "Why are you coming around on this so easily?"

"I just thought of the other egg analogy. The one about the golden goose."

CHAPTER 11

Ethan fought to control his breathing as Ted released his restraints and a nurse dressed his burns. His seething mind wanted to spew from his mouth in a scream that would break eardrums, burst blood vessels, and cause instant death to all who heard him.

If only he could.

A thought had bounced through his brain, disappeared, and then returned. As the thought blossomed, his heart rate dropped and his body calmed.

His dreams and visions had usually been random events. Now, however, with Memnon and the stimulus of fear applied, Ethan saw a difference in his level of control.

More important, he had felt something of the structure of space. He had sensed time as something other than the linear concept he lived within. And that brought him to Beth. Could he navigate back through time and prevent Beth from running into the lightning bolt?

Ethan had almost no control of his visions on his own, but his captors had the chemical that opened his mind to options previously impossible.

They held a big stick.

Ethan would make them use it.

Often.

CHAPTER 12

Buttery sunlight lit up the spring morning as five-year-old Ethan played in the dirt near the clotheslines while his mother hung the day's first batch of wash.

"That man with the funny hair, Momma. He's standing on a corner watching the men put up a telephone pole. They're telling him to move, Momma, but he don't move. He just stands there. One of the telephone men comes over and takes him by the arm and real gentle-like takes him up on the sidewalk. Then they put that pole in the ground and he just watches."

"What man is this?"

"His hair is white and it sticks up all over. He has a pipe. I seed him before."

"Where is this, honey?" she said absently as she fastened clothes pins to a flapping sheet.

Little Ethan furrowed his brow and concentrated. "Place called Prince...Prince-something. Princetown, I think. Everybody's carrying books."

"That's nice, honey."

Ethan saw symbols in his head. Though he had not yet entered school and could not write, he was able to scrawl in the dirt a rough approximation of what he saw. "Look, Momma."

Absently, his mother glanced in his direction. "What is it, honey?"

"I drawed what the man drawed. Look, Momma."

Lifting her empty wicker basket onto her left hip, Eleanor West detoured near Ethan and examined his stick-scratchings. In the dirt, large block letters described E=MC2. Her boy had never written anything before. Einstein had been dead more than a decade.

Eleanor West's face screwed up in a way Ethan had never seen. Her eyes widened as if she were not seeing Ethan, but rather something far beyond him. Like an angry rattlesnake her leg shot forward and her bare foot obliterated Ethan's scribbles. As the boy looked up, stunned, he saw his mother's hand arc through space, eclipse the sun and sky, and slap full against the side of his head. Through the ringing pain that descended over his little world, he heard her say,

"You will *not* become a witch like your grandmother. I'll not have it. Do you hear me? No more of this. Ever. Promise?"

Feeling dirty at what he had done and wanting back into the world of his mother's love, little Ethan blurted, "I promise, Mommy."

But that night the child dreamed. And he woke early in the morning in terror, soaked. He hadn't wet his bed in over a year. Shame shivered through him as he stripped off his pajamas and bed linens and dragged them downstairs to the washing machine in the basement. Many times he had watched his mother put in the soap and turn the dial. Ethan pulled a step-stool next to the washer, loaded his clothes and a cup of powdered soap, and started the rumbling machine. He heard water running inside the white porcelain cube, so he turned away, hoping he had done it right, hoping he could get his wash clean before his mother discovered what he had done.

When he returned to his room, he found Eleanor sitting on his bed. "What happened?"

Ethan ran to his mother's arms. "Oh, Momma, I had a dream. A bad dream. Please don't be angry."

"I'm not angry, baby. I just thought we were past all this. What was the dream about?"

Ethan buried his face in her chest, not wanting to speak.

"Go on, baby, it's okay."

"You won't get mad?"

"No."

"Promise?"

"I promise."

Ethan raised his pale face to his mother's. "It's bad, Momma."

"How bad?"

"There's a funeral."

Her face looked like a birthday cake that had fallen to the ground. "Who?" Then, in an instant, she said, "No. Don't tell me. I don't want to know."

Eleanor watched Ethan closely for the next few days. She noticed that he followed his father, Justin, wherever he went, like a heartsick puppy. One evening, as she rinsed the supper dishes, she watched Ethan and Justin playing catch in the field behind the house. "Is it today?" she whispered to herself. Then, the strength went out of her. She wiped her

35

hands dry on her apron and shuffled into the living room. She settled into the maple rocker her grandfather had built. She stared at the flowers in the wallpaper and rocked and cried until her chest ached.

In the morning, Justin West's body lay cold next to her in the bed.

CHAPTER 13

"How long has he been like this?" said Churchill.

Dolci stretched back in his chair and gestured at the control room monitors. "Fourteen hours."

"Is he okay?"

"Seems fine."

Doctor Sanders chimed in. "Ran a complete physical on him, blood work, EKG, EEG. Everything looks good."

"You drew blood and it didn't wake him?"

"No. We moved him to the bed and he didn't rouse a bit. I think you could set off a bomb in there and he'd sleep through it."

"I'm curious about that EEG. What's his brain doing?" Churchill said.

"Nothing abnormal, though his activity level is higher than the baseline we took when he first arrived here," Sanders replied. "The only real difference is his REM sleep. It's nonstop."

"Dreaming like crazy, eh? Have we seen that in other patients on Memnon?"

"No."

Churchill rose from his chair. "Keep me posted."

* * *

Breakfast. Sweet odor of waffles. Nine-year-old Ethan couldn't wait. He uncapped the maple syrup bottle in anticipation of the first waffle. He heard a thump and looked up to see his mother roll across the linoleum to come to rest on her side. One soft moan came out of her. Then she lay still.

No, no. He didn't want to see this vision. He didn't want God to punish him. But the image continued. Ethan saw his useless struggles to rouse his mother.

Jump ahead. "She had a stroke, Ethan." Doctor James leaned over him. "She didn't suffer."

"Then why did she moan, Doc James? Why?"

The old doctor didn't have an answer. Young Ethan saw the lie forming in his eyes. Young Ethan opened his eyes and made the dream go away.

Frantic, Ethan dressed and ran down the stairs from his room to the kitchen. As he rounded the corner, he heard loud hissing. He watched steam rise as his mother poured waffle batter onto the waffle iron.

No, he was sure it wouldn't happen today. Some other day, but not today.

He stood in the doorway and watched her close the waffle iron and turn to the sink. He watched her sure fingers pluck strawberries out of a colander, pinch off the stems, then run them through the clear stream of tap water. He watched the pile of fat, red berries rise in the green porcelain bowl next to the sink.

She turned. Suddenly engulfed in her gray stare, Ethan broke out in sweat. His breathing became shallow. He wanted to tell her. He wanted to stop it from happening. But he knew if he said anything she would become angry.

Her hard stare turned to ice. She knows, he thought. She knows it will happen soon. She hates me. No, she fears me.

* * *

Ethan trudged across the sun-drenched landscape of his farm. One moment on rolling hills, knee-deep in rustling grass; the next he hiked up a moss-covered pathway along a rocky ravine. He came to a table of rock next to a narrow pool fed by a trickling waterfall, his favorite place in all his six hundred acres. As his eyes drank in the scene, he knew his body slept in a locked room at Neural Research.

How am I doing this?

Dreams don't feel like this. They don't have this level of detail. The scents and sounds are distinct, the light is exact.

As he peered into the shadowed waters, he saw a pale face like a plaster Mardi Gras mask, rise from the depths. As it broke the surface, the eyes opened and the mouth moved. "Ethan, I'm alive."

Bethany climbed from the water and stretched out on a flat, moss-covered rock. Long, lean, tan, naked. She wrung out her hair and then reclined on her side with her head propped against her arm. A shaft of sunlight stuttered through the tree canopy and converted her eyes to smoky jewels.

Ethan knew she had died and he knew he had to be dreaming. He knew he would awaken and feel her loss all the more poignantly for having conjured her up. But he sat next to her nonetheless.

"Feel me, Ethan. I'm real."

His fingers hovered over her flesh, hesitant, not wanting the illusion to disappear. Then he set his palm on her

38

stomach. Despite being wet, her skin radiated heat. His fingers stroked across skin as soft as the petals of a water lily.

Burnt flesh reeked in his nostrils. His body twitched. "Ted, no." He felt the Memnon and his mind blinked and Ted's face leered above him.

No, not here. Not this time and place. Wake up!

Ethan opened his eyes. He lay in his bed. The luminous numerals of the clock on the opposite wall said 4:00 AM. He had returned to the present.

He lifted his right hand and unconsciously rubbed his fingertips against his thumb. He snapped fully awake at the feel of water on his skin. He held his palm to his nose. That special honeyed scent that he associated with Beth wafted into his nostrils.

What am I doing?

He had no explanation.

He breathed her until his fingers dried, feeling her loss, but also seeing that he had gained something. He knew something new. But how could he use it?

Ethan looked forward to the morning's session.

CHAPTER 14

"Why do you fight? The sooner you're done, the sooner you're out of here," Ted said.

"On this table or in my room, what the hell's the difference? I'm still in lock-up."

"Don't make me do it. Okay?"

"Shove it right up your ass, Ted."

"So you want the incentive enhancer?" Ted pulled an old-fashioned cattle prod out of a cabinet. He plugged in the electric wire and tested the button in the grip. The ozone smell of a thunderstorm filled the little room.

"What, no soldering iron? Losing your nerve, Teddie?"

"We don't want to damage you, buttercup. This just gives you a jolt. Ready to cooperate?"

"Where are you getting these tools from? Sadists-R-Us?" Ethan laughed.

Churchill's voice boomed from the overhead speakers before Ted could answer. "Ethan, can you do what you did before? Go forward in time? Bring us back information?"

Ethan's face stayed passive. "You want me to check on Teddie's wife again? See if she's wearing a teddie...or a non-teddie?"

In the control room, Churchill shot Dolci a worried look. Dolci leaned over and cupped his hand over the microphone. "Don't give that psycho an excuse to use his cattle prod, Andrew. Goddamn it, I mean it. I agreed to let you scare him. You hurt him again and I call the police."

Churchill said into the microphone, "No, Ethan. We're not interested in Ted's wife. Can you bring us factual information? A TV news story or newspaper headline?"

"I fly around like a balloon in a hurricane. I can't control this." The lies came easy to Ethan now, driven by his desire to get larger doses of Memnon.

"You've only started with Memnon. Just try, okay?"

Ted's face loomed into Ethan's vision. The big man whispered, "Listen, you freak. I'm ready to fry you down like the wicked witch of the west. Come back with another bullshit story about my wife and I will ram this thing up your ass and leave the juice on while I go to lunch. You got that?"

With no expression on his face, Ethan said, "Called your

lawyer yet?"

Ted waved the cattle prod under Ethan's nose. "You're not too smart, hotshot."

"I like to descend to the mental level of my audience."

Ted glared at Ethan. "You *want* me to hurt you, don't you?"

"Yeah. It makes leaving your sorry ass behind that much more pleasurable."

"Well, have a good trip you warped piece of shit." Ted thrust the cattle prod toward Ethan's face and whispered, "Please screw up. I want to see you spaz out."

"I'll put you on my dance card."

Scowling, Ted said, "I start counting and when I hit ten, this goes someplace sensitive and I pull the trigger unless you give me information. Okay? Now your drip has been on over five minutes. You've got more than enough juice to get started. So, don't shit around."

Yes, Ted, scare me. Make it easy for me. I have somewhere to go.

Ethan closed his eyes and let his mind wander. He thought of a time, a place. Then he heard Ted count. "One..."

Like a watermelon seed spurting from between tightened fingers, Ethan shot into the void, free of his body and into the clean vastness of space. Though having no physical form, he perceived heat and cold, the intense radiation coming off a nearby star, infrared, ultraviolet, radio waves, X-rays, he felt them all, everything up and down the electromagnetic spectrum. And something more. Other forces wrapped around him and through him. Like a blind man being given a telescope, he didn't know how to understand these forces.

He cleared his thoughts and built a specific image in his mind. The space near him seemed to ripple. A strangeness developed in the clean reality of space. Ethan thought himself closer to it. Like stepping around a corner, in one instant, he was here, in the next ... it felt like being wrenched through the guts of a star with heat and pressure and light assaulting senses he could not possibly have until it reached an unbearable crescendo and ... he was there.

"There" was the New York City Public Library. With the speed of thought, he whisked from room to room until he found someone reading a newspaper. He checked the date at the top of the page. Perfect. Two days in the future.

Newspaper. A thought wisped through Ethan's mind. Its smoky tendril thickened into a shape, then an idea, then an image. Even as a prisoner, he could see a way to gain control of his situation. He would prey on that most basic human emotion. Greed.

Ethan waited as the old woman perused editorials. He flitted to several others who were reading papers, waiting for one of them to reach the financial section. Ah, the man in the suit pored over stock listings.

Ethan checked several volatile issues. Then he waited for the man to turn to the futures markets. A heading announced that the Bank of England planned to sell twenty-five tons of gold. The yellow metal had dropped almost ten percent in response. A sudden cold wave in Brazil had put a scare into the coffee market. Coffee had jumped two dollars a pound.

Ethan winked out of there and briefly reentered his body.

"Three," Ted counted.

Ethan had plenty of time. Having gotten the information that would tempt his masters, Ethan now could try what *he* wanted.

Could he go back to that place in the time stream where his wife had been blasted into nothingness? Could he change the outcome?

Ethan concentrated, felt the texture of space and energy, visualized the time and place he wanted to be. Again, he sensed a distortion, a twisting and he willed himself into it.

Only half believing his idea had worked, he arrived just as the blue lightning bolt
passed through his wife, in time to see the surprise and fear and pain in her eyes. Terrified at the raw power crackling around him, Ethan hesitated. He wanted to help her, but didn't know what to do. Faced with the enormous energies coursing through Beth, Ethan froze. He had time to think, "Don't be afraid, Beth," and the moment passed. He had a feeling like an afterimage. Some remnant of her?

He wanted to go back to the moment, but he lacked the strength. Or the courage?

What do you fear, Ethan?

I fear death.

And nothing else? he chastised himself.

He jumped back into his body as Ted said, "Nine."

42

Ethan's eyes bolted open. "Okay. I have something."

Ted took out a notebook and Ethan rattled off stock symbols and their closing prices along with the closing prices for coffee and gold on the day after tomorrow.

Reluctantly, Ted unplugged the cattle prod. He pulled out Ethan's IV line, disinfected the site, and applied a bandage. He winked maliciously at Ethan as Churchill's voice came over the loudspeakers. "Good day's work, Ethan. Someone will come for you shortly."

Ethan still had a hyper-stimulated cerebral cortex. As soon as Ted left the room, Ethan jumped again into the void. He had to develop control. He had to learn how to use this power before it was too late.

CHAPTER 15

"Those trades were incredible, Mr. Churchill. Didn't miss a one."

"My net, Fanning. How much?"

The broker said, "Seven mil and some change."

Andrew Churchill leaned back in his office chair and stared at the ceiling. Heat ran through his thin body. He loosened his tie. All this had resulted from only one of West's Memnon-induced jumps. What about the next and the next? Churchill had been hanging on by his fingernails, but suddenly, salvation dropped into his arms. More than salvation. He didn't want to think of what could result, lest he jinx the outcome.

"Mr. Churchill? Hello? You still there?"

"Yeah, Fanning, I'm still here. I'm just enjoying the moment."

"What should I do with the proceeds?"

"Just park it. I'll have more orders soon." Churchill hung up his phone and thought he might explode with joy. Then he glanced at his watch. Lunch hour over, all the employees would be back in the building. Oh, hell, he thought as he grabbed his suit jacket off his coat rack and headed to the parking lot. He would make the short drive to that hot little minx's house and pound her the rest of the afternoon. He deserved to celebrate.

* * *

"It's working, but he doesn't have much control." Dolci sipped at his coffee and leaned back on the Berber sofa in Andrew Churchill's office.

"How about increasing the dose?" Churchill mused.

"That's not the problem. No matter how much we push into his bloodstream, only a small portion reaches his brain. The blood/brain barrier is restricting absorption."

"So? Inject directly into his brain. Any problem with that?"

"We could never get FDA permission for that."

"To hell with FDA permission. It's our asses if we fail. Goose the dose with neurotransmitters and administer a brain drip."

"A brain drip is risky."

"How so?"

"We don't have any data on where to start the dose. Start too high, we could fry him."

"So, drop way down and build up slowly. Depending on what West brings back, you'll have some idea how you're progressing."

Dolci shook his head and looked down. "Andrew, Andrew, where are we going?"

"Trust me, Cliff, I have a plan. We'll make West our ally. None of what has happened will matter."

CHAPTER 16

"Dolci, how's he holding up?" Churchill said.

"He's fine. Slept eleven hours after that last session. He's up now and I think he's getting cabin fever."

"I want to talk to him face to face."

"You sure? We've limited his contacts. Do you really want him knowing who you are?"

"Why not? Is he dangerous?"

Dolci adjusted his gold-rimmed glasses. "No, but he's far more intelligent than he lets on. We need to be cautious with him."

"All the more reason I should talk with him now before anything can go wrong. I told you I had a plan. We need his cooperation if we're going to go further. I want a partner, not a witness against me in court."

* * *

Andrew Churchill stalked into the conference room and got right down to business. "Mr. West, I know this past week has been stressful on you. But it's for a good purpose."

Ethan's eyes didn't move, hiding his surprise. During one of his jumps, Ethan had seen this suntanned face, these ice-blue eyes, this perfect coif of black and silver hair neatly combed over the bald spot at the top. *What an interesting coincidence. How can I use it?*

"You're skeptical. I understand."

"I'm not skeptical, Churchill. I'm kidnapped. World of difference."

"You have reason to be upset. But I'm also sure you'd be the first to admit that this experiment would never have worked without a feeling of personal threat. It's what got you to jump that first time. I intend to make that up to you." Churchill kept his voice calm, but Ethan sensed the man's anxiety. "You can go home today, right now. I will give you a check for two million dollars and you never have to see us again. If you want to walk away from what we're doing here, fine. But if you'd like to assist us, we'll pay you ten million dollars a year. You'll never have to pick up a shovel again."

"I like shovels. I like farming."

"So farm. Just help us unlock the incredible gift you have."

46

"Why should I?"

"Mr. West, you have talents which Memnon has amplified. The defense of our nation may one day depend on talents like yours."

A vicious little laugh jumped out of Ethan's mouth. "Yeah, that's why I bring back stock quotes? For national security? How much've you made?"

Churchill folded his hands in his lap and smiled across the conference table at Ethan. "Yes, I've been playing the market, but for a good cause. This company almost went bankrupt. To continue our work we needed capital. So, yes, your first assignments have been to bring us financial information from the future. But in the next week, we'll turn a financial corner. After that, you won't need to do that anymore."

"So, this is all for patriotism?"

"I know how easy it is to be cynical, but, yes, it is, Ethan."

"So, I do a few more jumps for money and then what?"

"We need to understand the neurological processes at work here. What's in you that allows these responses to Memnon that are so far off the map?"

"Ten million, you said."

"Yes."

Ethan let his lips purse and his eyes squint a fraction, just the greed-tinged look he felt certain the executive wanted to see. Let Churchill smell a deal. The silence stretched as Churchill waited for his answer. Finally deciding he had made Churchill work hard enough, Ethan let his face break into a grin. Ethan took a fisherman's satisfaction in having used the proper lure. The stock quotes had done exactly what he'd hoped. He'd set the money hook deeply in Churchill's mouth.

Ethan said, "I'll stay."

The shift in Churchill's body language revealed a great release of tension. Good. Ethan had guaranteed his source of Memnon. His search for Bethany could continue. What the hell did he care if Churchill got rich?

Ethan's mind pondered one nugget of information Churchill had mentioned, savoring the knowledge that Churchill had revealed too much. No, the executive should never have mentioned the potential bankruptcy. Like a key in a lock, something in Ethan's mind clicked. He saw a pathway into the future that had not existed before. Alone, seemingly helpless, in a hospital bed behind locked doors, Ethan suddenly had leverage.

He thinks he's in control. But through his greed, I will own him.

And then there was the other thing. But Ethan would think about how to hammer Churchill with that little tidbit later.

CHAPTER 17

"Can you do it without the incentive enhancer? Is the jump easier now?"

"Yes, Mark. Just give me a few minutes."

"Sure."

Ethan smiled inside at the change in approach. The hulking Ted had been replaced by an affable technician with sandy hair. Ted had ceased to exist. Now a member of the team, Ethan no longer wore restraints. Doors unlocked and incentive enhancers disappeared. He just couldn't leave the facility. Yet.

Ethan squirted out of his body and flew along the timeline to a spot two days in the future. More skilled at pinpointing his target time and place, Ethan jumped to the New York Public Library, the easiest place to get what Churchill wanted. Then he'd do what *he* wanted. Closing stock quotes memorized, Ethan tunneled through time to the one place that held his thoughts captive. A second early, he watched the forces gather and realized he could do nothing to change the discharge of enormous energies.

In that horrible moment when the blue bolt of flame shot through Beth, turning her into a burning rag doll, he saw her. Not her body. He saw *her*. Through the incandescent electric flame, he saw and felt the real Beth in the moment of becoming the same incorporeal something that he himself had become.

As he watched Beth scream, Ethan gathered his own forces and thought himself into the lightning bolt. He entered the blue globe that formed around his beloved. He felt chaos, panic, and pain, but for a flicker of an instant, his energy touched hers.

Though beleaguered and fearful she sensed him and they had a microsecond of infinity to remember everything.

"I'll find you, Beth. Don't be afraid."

The energy was going somewhere and Ethan tried to get sucked into it. Then he hovered alone in the gloomy rain, his spirit exhausted by the effort he had just made. In mental shock, he wondered how close he had come to being shredded apart.

For a moment, he felt sick with defeat. He had been so

close.

But he would not accept defeat. In the afterimage of the lightning Ethan sensed something like an echo of Beth lingering in the air. A trace of her led off into someplace, somewhen. Ethan lacked the understanding to follow that trace, but he knew it existed.

He remembered one of his father's sayings. "You can do anything if you have the desire and the time."

Desire he had. And time? He had a universe full of it.

Now certain that Beth still existed somewhere, Ethan felt the first glimmer of hope since her death.

* * *

"What's the meaning of this wire transfer, Churchill?" Churchill heard the incredulity in the voice of Michael Sturm, the CEO of the Avalon Group.

Churchill turned up the volume on his speaker phone. "The meaning is clear. I'm invoking the buy-back provision in our agreement. That's the first payment as required to forestall the conversion of your Class B stock."

"You can't do this. It's outrageous!"

"Just watch me. I'm getting you off my back. You should have funded us faster and made this thing work. Now you can just take the money and shut up."

"The redemption penalty is one hundred percent. You're going to pay an extra fifty million?"

"Whatever it takes."

"You will hear from our attorneys."

"Oh, I'm sure I will. But a week from now, I'll transfer the balance of money we owe you and that will be the end of it. Your lawyers can eat shit and die for all the good they can do now."

"Where are you getting this money?"

"How do you think anybody gets this much money overnight? I'm printing it." Churchill hung up the phone and felt better than he had ever felt in his life.

Churchill loved owning a golden goose. Could he squeeze money out of it even more quickly?

CHAPTER 18

As the serotonin-dopamine-Memnon cocktail flushed directly into his brain, Ethan experienced a wrenching as if his body was being turned inside out. Galaxies spun in the distance, great gem heaps dumped on the black velvet of space. An energy different from his other trips filled Ethan. This experience had a different texture from previous jumps. Now, Ethan could feel something under space, within it, like the warp and woof of a fabric beneath its pattern and color. The cloth of reality stitched forces together that he had never sensed before.

Somehow, his mind reached out to these forces, felt them, analyzed them. Just as a first-time swimmer learns to tread water in a strange new physical environment, Ethan began to feel how the surrounding forces moved and flowed under and through him and everything else in the universe. He rode the energy currents and paddled into the vastness like a child on an inner tube.

He groped out from his vantage point with one thought hard in his mind. The past. She is in the past. Like a beacon it held him to his course as he sifted through layers and currents and whorls of the stuff that made the universe.

He tried to feel that lingering resonance that Beth had left behind. A certain mote in time caught him, pulled him closer. It felt like a starting point. Ethan re-entered the world of physical law in Washington, DC.

He skipped across the city, seeing boxy cars and trolleys. It looked like the 1930s. *Why did I come here?*

Something had tugged at him, but he had no idea how to proceed. He had only a vague, nagging sense that he was getting warmer in his search. *Am I closer in time or in location?*

Though he could see and feel the place around him, Ethan was not satisfied with the sense that he was watching a movie. He had no physical connection to the places he visited. He became convinced that he needed the direct physical link of existence to better judge where Beth might be.

He had pondered this issue many times. Could he somehow enter or control a body? Ethan thought himself into a trolley car. Of the six occupants, Ethan approached a young woman. He reached out with his energy and tried to touch the

51

being inside the body. He radiated feelings of peace and greeting.

No response. The woman continued to gaze out the trolley window. Try as he might, he could not get her to notice him. He moved on to the other occupants, trying to contact each of them in turn. He could not elicit a response.

But he did learn that there existed a link between body and spirit. He had felt it with his own body and here he experienced it again. He realized he would never be able to insinuate himself into a body already occupied by another being.

Ethan scanned the city and considered another option. He felt the stirring energies of recently conceived babies. These tiny agglomerations of cells had no body link. They lay like fertile fields eager to sprout new life. Ethan recognized a big problem. If he chose to occupy a fetus, he would have to wait decades before he had the mobility and resources to continue his search. And what if he'd landed in the wrong time and place? He could waste a lot of effort. No, he saw one other option he now needed to face.

I must enter an adult body. A recently dead adult body.

Ethan's mind reeled as he admitted to himself what had been only a fleeting thought until now. *I must become a ghoul.*

Girding himself, Ethan swept down into the streets, searching, senses heightened. A swirl of distress drew him to someone radiating unendurable fear. At that moment, he felt the energy of a specter like himself as it pulled away from its body and flung itself in panic out among the stars. Ethan moved in toward a riverfront warehouse, one of several dilapidated buildings along Maine Avenue. He would not know if his theory was feasible unless he tried.

* * *

"Dammit, Crenshaw, leave 'im be. He's out. Grab his bindle and let's get outta here. We gotta get to the freight yard and jump that train." Gilly crouched in the tall weeds and peered out into the darkness.

Reluctantly, the larger man released his grip on the body under him. A dim bulb at the far corner of the warehouse offered enough feeble light to show that the body's eyes were open.

"Did ya kill 'im?"

"Nah, that Hobie's one tough nigger. He's just out cold." Crenshaw searched through his victim's pockets.

Gilly scanned left and right. "C'mon. A watchman could show up any time. Let's hop that freight and get the hell outta this town."

"Ya sound like an old woman, Gilly. Make yourself useful and go through his bindle while I finish here."

Gilly kneeled and pulled apart the rope knot that held the blanket roll together. He tossed through some clothes and checked their pockets.

"Anything?"

"Nah. No money, anyway."

"Booze?"

"Nope. Just this." Gilly held up something hard his hand had brushed against. "Looks like a book."

"Lemme see that. Some stiffs keep foldin' green in books."

As Crenshaw grabbed the book and held it up to see, the gold letters on the cover caught the warehouse light. "Shit, it's a bible." He leafed through the pages. "Ain't no money here." He tossed the bible over his shoulder.

"Will, that guy ain't movin'. I don't think he's breathin'."

"One less nigger ain't gonna bother me none."

Gilly's voice dropped. "I seen a light. Off there along the riverbank. Dammit, Will, we gotta go."

"Yeah, yeah." Will Crenshaw pulled off his victim's shoes. "Let's see if he has anything in the shoe bank."

Like a firefly, the kerosene lamp of the night watchman flickered and arced through the blackness along the Potomac as he made his rounds.

A shuddering hiss cut through the silence as the body in the weeds sucked in a breath. Then it wailed with an agony that slashed the night like a scythe. The light along the river bobbed and weaved more frenetically.

"Crenshaw, you're crazy." Gilly grabbed his own bindle and stood. "I'm catchin' that train." He hunkered into the gloom.

As the watchman's light grew larger, Crenshaw threw down the shoe. He fumbled in the dark for his own bindle and then turned back to the body on the ground. He reached into his trouser pocket and wrapped his fingers around the smooth ivory handle of his switchblade. He tugged it free of his pocket and pressed the release button. A satisfying snick punctuated the silence. He crouched and pressed the blade against Hobie's throat. "Thought you was dead, Hobie. Well, I can fix that.

Bye, bye, blackbird."

A hand like a vise wrapped around Crenshaw's wrist and dragged him down.

Crenshaw rolled forward and stabbed into the darkness. He felt the resistance of cloth against the blade and then the grip around his wrist tightened. A small shriek of panic got past his lips as he punched with his free arm.

Then suddenly, the other flipped them over, still gripping Crenshaw's wrist. With his left hand Crenshaw pounded at the head above him, then felt across the face and gouged his thumb into an eye. A hoarse grunt and the grip on his wrist loosened. Crenshaw shook his arm loose and pushed his knife up into the black man's face. It hit bone and then that enormous paw wrapped around his wrist again. With the strength that panic brings, Crenshaw rammed the knife at the shadow above him, but the pressure of the other man's grip dragged the blade away. A forearm crushed into Crenshaw's throat, drove inexorably downward. With his left hand, he hammered at his opponent's face, but the blows could have been slaps from a child for all the effect they had.

Crenshaw felt hot breath against his face and he saw the glint of the warehouse light in two coal black eyes that came closer and closer until nothing else existed. He heard the crackle as his windpipe collapsed, felt a shriek of fire as his own knife pressed into his chest. Then motes of light began to dance in Crenshaw's vision, expanding and coalescing into a shimmering curtain. A great wind sounded in his ears and he suddenly felt giddy and weightless. The wind blew him like a leaf and he skittered away.

* * *

Ethan felt the man under him go limp. Over his shoulder he heard a shout. "Hey, shitbird. What's goin' on?" Glancing back, Ethan saw a lantern jerking through the darkness and heard the rustling of the guard's footsteps through the tall weeds.

Disoriented, Ethan released the body under him and stumbled away, pure instinct, totally immersed in the panic of this person who was not Ethan, yet was. The damp, hot air of a summer night seemed insufficient for the laboring lungs of this big body whose legs and heart pumped like a runaway steam engine. Animal instinct took over and Ethan ran away from the lights of the city. He found the Potomac far south of the warehouses and headed downstream. A crescent moon

54

offered barely enough illumination to pick his way through the rough terrain.

Crickets burred in the underbrush and bullfrogs honked from the riverbank. Far off, a boat horn boomed its doleful voice. Each sound formed a crisp image, a wave of energy that Ethan perceived in some way in addition to what his ears told him. Sensory impressions inundated him. As if he had never lived before, he cataloged every sensation. The pains in his bare feet from brambles and sharp rocks felt almost pleasurable in their intensity. The scent of honeysuckle, thick along the shoreline, wafted and combined with the damp algae rot of the river. No perfume Ethan had ever smelled seemed more appealing. Every nerve in his body seemed amplified, hammering his brain with an unending crescendo of input. He lived and breathed and, like some primordial beast, he cared only for living and breathing as he reveled in this organism that was a man.

He tramped through the dark until he came to the banks of the Anacostia River where it dumped into the Potomac. He settled on his haunches to rest and felt the black water in his mind as clearly as if he could see it.

The adrenaline wore off and Ethan's brain began to work again. He had done it. He had crossed time and space and had come to rest in a living body. Ethan thought back to that moment when he had sensed the panic energy of the being who had previously inhabited this body. Where had that being gone?

And what of the murderer named Crenshaw? Though fighting for his life, Ethan had wondered if he was damning his own soul as he snuffed out the other's life.

Ethan shook himself. *What's done is done.* Though drained, he tried to reach out into the night, searching for Beth. He felt nothing. He didn't seem to have the faculties he normally had. This new body felt like a suit that didn't fit right.

His feet and hands began to tingle. Ethan snapped out of his reverie. The body felt weak.

Ethan shook himself until the tingling went away. Panic returned. He had to concentrate to keep this body animated. Too much daydreaming and he felt like he would slip away, back into the between-space he had navigated to get here.

Have I done the right thing?

Ethan gazed into the gem shop of the sky and saw it in

a new way. He no longer saw the distance to the stars as vast. Any one of those glittering shards of light could be home. It took only a twist of thought, a shifting of space, and he could be there. Wonder swelled through his big frame.

Is Beth here? How many times must I do this if she's not?

Ethan stared again at the stars. Yes, his search might take huge amounts of time. He would have to gird himself against frustration and take each step without worrying about the next million steps it might take to accomplish his goal. He had to trick his mind into believing that he had not embarked on a monumental task. He had to focus on just one step at a time.

He had so much to learn. And each thing he learned brought him one step closer to finding his love.

In his reverie he missed the sound of feet swishing through tall grass.

The sound he didn't miss was the click of a revolver being cocked.

"Stand up, hobo."

Ethan tried to stand, but he did not have complete control of the big body he inhabited. He stumbled and began falling toward the voice in the dark.

"Stay back!"

Two shots shredded the darkness. Ethan felt fire rip through his chest. He fell back into the underbrush. He heard a dog bark in the distance, heard men shouting.

"I got the murderin' bastard." Other feet crackled in the weeds. Lanterns flashed.

Ethan felt this body's life bleeding into the ground. He closed his eyes.

Focus. Get ready.

He waited for the moment when the heart would stop. Waited for his jumping off point.

Now.

CHAPTER 19

"What happened?" Ethan croaked.

Relief washed across the faces looking down on him. Doctor Stewart said, "You gave us quite a scare. Your heart stopped."

"What?"

"Four times. We defibrillated you and then you were back. We need to run tests."

"My heart stopped?"

"Yes. How do you feel?"

"Just weak. How long was I out?"

"Not even three minutes."

Dolci leaned forward. "Did something happen out there? Something different?"

"You might say that."

* * *

During his debriefing the next day, Ethan explained where he had been and that he had actually inhabited a body. He'd found that lying was easier if he told the truth about everything and then held back certain bits. He withheld the part about the killing. And how long he had been there.

As part of his new freedoms, they had installed a computer in Ethan's room. He had internet access, but special software blocked email and messaging capabilities.

Ethan dug deep into the online archives of *The Washington Post*. Sure that he had seen a 1932 Packard he started his search in that year.

The search engine listed nine articles with the name Crenshaw. In the fourth article Ethan saw the photograph of a disheveled corpse nested under the headline, *Victim of Brutal Beating Found*. A sidebar showed a photograph of the ivory-handled knife found next to the body. Under that he saw a photo of Crenshaw, the black and white image showing the stream of blood across his chest as black.

A sickening heave surged through Ethan's guts. His memory shot to those moments when he could smell the onions on the breath of the man he was choking. When he stopped smelling the onions, he knew he had cut off Crenshaw's air. He remembered specifically the little *tick* of sound as the cartilage in Crenshaw's throat gave way.

Ethan stared at a blank wall of his room. A shiver of fear ran through him. He remembered the feel of the night and the smell of the Potomac. *I killed a man. I changed something.*

Ethan now had hard evidence that he had been in the past.

He had no qualms about the future. It didn't yet exist, so what he might bring back as information to use in the present seemed of no consequence. But the past terrified Ethan. What if he changed something that somehow affected whether Beth was ever born? What if his quest for her resulted in her never existing? What would that do to the world? What would it do to him? And would he even be aware of it if he made a change that drastic?

Ethan knew two different pasts: one in which Crenshaw killed the black man named Hobie and one in which Hobie killed Crenshaw. *How can I do this? How can I straddle two different awarenesses? Only one event exists now.*

The two different versions of reality existed only in Ethan's thoughts. This seemed significant. Did he stand outside reality when he traveled through time? But then what reality did he inhabit now? How many realities existed? Had he come back to the same reality he had left or one slightly different?

He had read that in quantum theory *cause and effect did not exist.* If that were so, then all kinds of paradoxes could occur. How could he unravel how he did what he did? He shook his body like a wet dog and set aside these thoughts for now. He would push on and hope that understanding would come.

One thing had become clear, though. Once he inhabited a dying body and reenergized it, he could not leave it unless the body died.

Ethan clenched his hands into fists. *What is happening to me? Good Lord, what am I becoming?*

Like a storm-tossed survivor of a shipwreck, he felt as if he had been washed up on the shore of an unknown land, naked and alone, with nothing but his will to sustain him.

CHAPTER 20

A two-acre quadrangle of trees and grass occupied the center of the Neural Research facility. Employees ate lunch at picnic tables and smoked cigarettes under the trees. Ethan was now allowed in the quadrangle as long as he didn't talk about the research. Easy enough, since he had no intention of telling anybody anything anyway.

At the opposite end of the park from where the employees gathered, he sat with his back against a maple tree, letting his mind roam up into the azure sky. A shadow fell across his face and he squinted at a figure standing above him. "You're West, aren't you?" the shadow said.

Ethan caught a whiff of familiar perfume. "Who are you?" he asked as the woman in green surgical scrubs settled on the grass. Her dark curls and sharp features looked familiar. So did the rounded bulge that pushed out the front of her scrubs.

"My name is Angie Warner. I was one of the nurses working on you the other day."

Now Ethan knew why he recognized her perfume. "Thanks."

She had eyes so dark they looked like all-pupil as they bored into Ethan. "Do you always stare at people you meet?" he said.

She looked dazed for a second, then her face broke into a smile. "I'm sorry. Are the rumors true?"

"What rumors?"

"You leave your body?"

Now it was Ethan's turn to stare.

"I don't care what the rest of them want from you. I just wanted to ask if you ever met others out there."

"Others?"

"People who have passed. Do you encounter them?"

"Why do you ask?"

"My son." She lowered her eyes. "He was only ten when I lost him. And my husband. I never got to say goodbye."

"What happened?"

"A museum trip. My husband was one of the chaperones. It was a freak thing really. A front tire blew, the driver lost control, and the bus hit a power pole. Brought the

59

line down. Half the kids got electrocuted. Now I'm all alone, except for my little girl, Annie. And these." She held her stomach.

Electrocution. The blue globe of energy leaped into Ethan's mind. Beth screamed in his ears and he felt his skin flayed by a thousand spicules of wood. He grabbed at his temples to stop the throbbing.

"Are you all right?" She settled in the grass facing him.

"Not usually. I'm sorry about your boy."

"His name was Steven. My husband was Keith."

"How long ago?"

"Three months."

"How far gone are you?" Ethan gestured to her stomach.

"Almost seven months."

Ethan frowned. "I'm terribly sorry."

She was laying her grief in the open. It pained Ethan to see her loss. The same agony cut through him every day. He just had more skill in hiding it.

"If I meet anyone with those names, I'll tell them goodbye for you."

"Don't humor me, Mr. West."

Ethan suddenly realized what a hard case he had become. He trusted nobody. Grief had twisted him into something he barely recognized. He suddenly found his mouth moving. "Listen to me. Your son and husband are not gone. People die, but their energy goes on. Somewhere, somehow, they exist."

Now her eyes blazed like furnaces. "Don't lie to me. I can get priests to do that."

"I'm not. I only understand a fraction of it, but believe me, they're out there. Somehow, you'll find them. It may take a thousand lifetimes, but you will."

For a moment, she saw into him. Her eyes softened. "You're looking too."

"Yes." He didn't know why he answered her.

"Your wife." A statement, not a question.

A haunted look came into Ethan's eyes. "It's not a good idea to be seen talking to me. You may be questioned."

"They don't have microphones out here. I'll say we talked about the weather." She gripped his hand for a brief moment, rose, and waddled back into the building.

Ethan didn't look down immediately, in case someone was watching. He pulled his knees up and, behind their shield, he opened his right hand. In it nestled a thumbnail-sized photograph, laminated in plastic. A boy's face smiled at him, hair gold in the sun, his permanent teeth looking too big for his mouth.

CHAPTER 21

Suspicion grew in Ted like an ugly weed. Once Ethan had planted the seeds, they sprouted in the dark recesses of Ted's soul, twining and twirling tendrils up and out until they inhabited every crevice.

Ted had traded on the market tips he had heard during Ethan's debriefings and had made twice his annual salary before Churchill yanked him from the project. If Ethan was right about the stocks, wouldn't he also be right about Ted's wife? Ted Buckner had only fleeting reason to question his wife's loyalty until Ethan's taunts.

Or had the farmer just wanted to bust Ted's balls? He had plenty of reason.

Young wives. He'd been warned.

Cheryl Buckner had a centerfold body and she liked to show it off. Ted thought of how men swarmed around her at the company Christmas party and the softball games. Had he made a mistake? With Cheryl only twenty-four, should he have worried more about their fourteen-year age difference?

Ted had no evidence, but over the past several weeks, he had seen little discrepancies in Cheryl's schedule. She showered more, ostensibly from her more frequent visits to the health club. Wasn't she already fit enough, toned enough?

Ted could think of only one thing to do.

* * *

Even though midnight had long since passed, Ethan did not sleep. In his dark bedroom he felt a shift in air pressure and heard the low vibration of the entry door hinge. Visitors entered at all hours, checking his vital signs, drawing blood. He shut his eyes as a light switched on in the living room.

Minutes went by and nothing happened. Curious, Ethan got out of bed and put on his blue terry cloth robe. As he stepped into the living room, he thought he was dreaming. On the sofa sat Ted.

"The leather bars close down early tonight, Teddy?"

Ignoring the jibe, Ted said, "How badly do you want to get out of here?"

Ethan felt surprise for the second time in the same minute. For Ted *not* to rise to the bait was unusual.

"What could you possibly have to say about me getting

out of here?"

"I want your help. You help me, I help you."

Ethan dropped into a stuffed chair. "How could you help me?"

"This place isn't a maximum security prison. I could get you out."

"And what would you want in return?"

"Were you just busting balls about my wife?"

"If I answer that, I'm giving you something free. I'm not inclined to give you anything free." For emphasis, Ethan scratched the burns under his left armpit.

"All right, I'll give you something first. I can shut off any part of the camera system it might take to get you out of here."

Ethan's mind raced. How could he use Ted? "Just shut off? How much access do you have to the security system?"

"Quite a bit. Like for instance, we're not being recorded right now." Ted pointed to a camera near the ceiling. "All dead. A friend of mine is doing maintenance on the video decks that handle this apartment. They'll be off for an hour. All legit and justifiable and entered in the logs."

Ethan nodded. A plan formed in his head. "What do you want, Ted?"

"Two things. I want something concrete to nail my wife with. She's cheating on me, right?" Ethan nodded. "I want her dead to rights so there's no chance of having to pay alimony. Second, I want more of the stock tips you're giving Churchill."

"In other words, you want to get rich and get single."

"That's kinda the idea, yeah."

Ethan stared into the big man's eyes and made his decision. "All right. I'll need several things in return. This is not negotiable."

"Like what?"

"I want the surveillance video from the lab, the one with the soldering iron."

"Now, wait a minute..."

Ethan cut him off. "You can edit the damn thing any way you want so you can't be identified. I just want something that shows what's happening to me and that puts Churchill in the control room while it's happening. I want Churchill. You win a get-out-of-jail-free-card for giving him to me."

Ted stroked the black stubble of his beard. "You're asking too much. Churchill will point the finger right at me no matter what the videos show."

63

Ethan's brown eyes widened into a relaxed stare. He gazed at Ted with a calmness that disconcerted the other man. "Maybe you need incentification, Ted. Remember the incident with your wife?"

The technician's eyes narrowed.

"I've checked on her more than once. She's not sleeping around. She has frequent, shall we say, appointments with the same man."

Ted's nostrils flared. "Don't shit me."

"Ted, I know who the other man is. Churchill. When I met him face-to-face, I immediately recognized him."

"You're making this up."

"Prove it for yourself. Look under your bed. Churchill dropped a Cross pen last time he was visiting and he didn't notice. It has his initials: AC. Andrew Churchill. He has a matching mechanical pencil on his desk if you need proof."

"Bastard goes to my house?"

"Sometimes. Or they meet in a motel near her health club."

Something broke in Ted. "I make my money first. I want to be clear before the hammer falls."

"You'll be rich enough to run so far, they'll never find you. That's if anyone even believes Churchill's accusations. By then he'll have no credibility."

A far-off look crept across Ted's face. "I like that."

"Can you get a video camera in here?"

"Sure."

"I want to record a statement."

"Why not use the videos off the surveillance system?"

"I want to tell my story." Ethan didn't add that the story would have certain embellishments.

Ted screwed his face up and said, "I want to see some gelt up front, before I do any of this. 'Cause once I'm in, I'm in deep."

"That's fine with me. I have something for you." Ethan stepped to the kitchen counter and picked up a slip of paper and a pencil. "Here's a stock symbol. Tomorrow it closes up twenty points. The smart move would be to buy thirty-day call options."

Ted held the paper like it might evaporate any second. He squinted at Ethan. "How does a farmer know so much?"

"Being a farmer doesn't mean being stupid. I went to college and I actually know how to read." Ethan waved his

64

hand in dismissal. "Tomorrow, we start, Ted. That quote seals the deal. How do I get the video camera?"

Ted pondered for a second. "I can borrow a really small digital recorder. I'll put it in a lunch bag and stick it in the bushes near that tree you always sit under. Record what you want, then leave the bag in the bushes. Be careful, though. You're photographed out there too."

"Okay. Tomorrow."

Ted got up to go and stood awkwardly facing Ethan.

"You don't have to shake hands, Ted. I wouldn't want to."

Ted nodded and looked relieved. He left without another word.

A rare smile crept across Ethan's mouth.

CHAPTER 22

"Is this man's life worth the information you're getting, Andrew?" Dolci paced back and forth across Churchill's office. Churchill had never seen him so exercised.

"It's under control, Cliff. He's fine."

"You call cardiac arrest fine? His body's becoming unstable. The longer he stays out, the worse it gets."

"Ask him yourself. He's willing to continue."

"Then he's crazy or he doesn't understand the risks."

Churchill actually did wonder why West continued. What was so important to him? Was it as simple as the money? "Whatever his reasons are, Cliff, what about the science? Did you ever expect you'd be working on something so revolutionary?"

"The science? Please don't blow smoke up my ass. It's not about science; it's about money. How much is enough, Andrew? When do you stop and claim victory?"

"Just a few more days. There's almost enough to pay off the investors."

"I hope there's enough left over to buy back your soul."

* * *

Two days after Ethan's midnight meeting with Ted he made sure he sat in the quadrangle during lunch hour. It didn't take long for Angie to lumber over and settle into the grass under Ethan's favorite tree.

"Ethan, what's happening to you? I'm hearing all kinds of rumors."

"Less dangerous if you don't know. Eventually Churchill will squeeze you."

"Dangerous?" She looked bewildered.

"Yes. Churchill is a snake. Did you know anything about me before that time you were called in on the code?"

"No."

"You know a guy named Ted Buckner?"

Her face twisted. "That creep?"

"Yeah, well, imagine him with a soldering iron and me having something he wants."

Her eyes flashed. "What did they do to you?"

Ethan pulled up the left side of his sweater to show her the livid scars that puckered across his ribs.

"This is outrageous. I'm calling the police."

"Whoa. I'm cooperating with them now. I know what I'm doing, so don't worry about me. But I do need your help on one thing." Ethan pulled up his pant leg a few inches and extracted a digital chip out of his sock. "I need you to get this out of here. To the FBI. But not until I say so. Will you do that?"

"What's on the chip?"

"I recorded a message on it along with transfers of surveillance videos from the lab. Very incriminating for Churchill."

In her anger at Churchill, she reached for the chip.

"No. No." Too late. Angie already had the chip in her hand. "Set it on the ground." Ethan glanced around casually. "Someone could be watching. You don't want to be seen taking something from me."

"Sorry."

"I'll go. You pick up the chip after I leave. Palm it and get it into your pocket before you stand up. Then put it somewhere safe. Not at home. If Churchill gets suspicious, he might have your place searched."

"What in God's name is going on?"

"I'll tell you later. First get that recording out of here."

CHAPTER 23

Like a bird of prey, Ethan swooped into the time and place he had sensed in his mind, drawn by the emanating force of a panicked entity launching into the void.

For an instant, he thought of his body in the laboratory in Rockville. What if this time they couldn't keep his heart going? What would happen to him here? Did it matter?

Pointless to second-guess now. He thought himself into the poor wretch before him. He felt a great whooshing roar that tore his senses to shreds. An unbearable rush of energy became a nova of light, a star furnace.

Someone was screaming.

The sound rang through Ethan's head like a church bell smacked with a thousand hammers.

And pain. He had never known pain like this. It swept in fiery waves through every cell in his body, pulsing, searing, and forcing him *to scream.*

Suddenly, coolness and quiet flowed through him, but the pain continued. His head shrieked with it. He opened his eyes to a dim image of a face, hairy and desperate looking.

"Thought ya was dead, kid. Spooked the hell out of me, you caterwauling' like that."

Ethan's mouth felt dry as ashes. When he tried to speak, his throat hissed.

"Here, Youngblood. Wet yer whistle." The face moved to the side and Ethan heard metal clinking. A tin canteen loomed into view and, in a second, water dribbled into his mouth. He coughed and then swallowed, the muscles of his throat rebelling at this intrusion. He gagged.

"Here, let's take a good look at ya." Hands lifted Ethan's head. Agony scorched through him. The dim world of trees and rocks spun in his vision and he reached out a hand to steady himself.

The pain focused in the left side of his skull. Ethan reached up with his left hand, but he had terrible control. The hand clunked against his head and a fresh wave of nausea ran through him. Sweat flowed from every pore. He tried again and this time the fingers of his left hand felt a hard crusty mass. What had happened to this poor devil?

The light rose quickly. Ethan heard birds chattering in

68

the underbrush. The damp smell of rotting leaves and his own body odor combined into a sickening miasma. His left eye had swollen almost shut, but through his right eye he observed the short wiry man who squatted in front of him.

"Kid, I swear you stopped breathin' last night. How you feel?"

Eyes as blue as a mountain lake peered out from a filthy face. Wrinkles mapped the tanned, leathery terrain around the eyes and down around the sharp beak of a nose that poked out above more beard than any face should be able to grow. The bushy blackness gave way to patches of gray around the mouth.

"Wheh'm I?" Ethan could barely shape the words.

"Don't remember? Hell, I don't blame ya. After the shit-kickin' we got last night, I wish I could forget it too."

Ethan kept fingering the left side of his head. It felt like a groove ran from front to back. "Here, let's take a look-see." The wiry man hunkered down. "Whooee. How the hell ya still alive, kid? Looks like a plow ran across yer head. Goddamn bluebelly bastards." He touched gingerly at Ethan's wound. "Ain't bleedin' no more. Guess that's good. Quarter inch lower and yer brains would be in the dirt."

In the rising glow of the pink dawn, Ethan examined his companion. Filthy and tattered jacket and pants hung from a gaunt frame. The square-collared jacket stood open, revealing long johns that once had been red, but that now sported a collection of dark stains. One lone brass button clung to the gray jacket near the throat.

"Cole, ya look like shit. Can ya walk? We best skedaddle afore it gets much lighter, get you a doctor."

The wiry man stood and stretched and surveyed the area. They seemed to be alone in the world, except for the chittering of insects and the calls of blue jays. A breeze stirred the leaves of the surrounding maple woods to a rushing sound like stream rapids.

Then a sound not of nature punctuated the morning peace: a loud puff, muffled and indistinct in the distance. Another and another quickly followed it until a constant chuffing filled the air, as from a hundred steam engines. The sudden roar of a single explosion dwarfed that sound. Ethan felt the ground stir. Then more explosions ripped the morning calm.

"Goddamn Yankees don't believe in breakfast." Ethan's

companion unbuttoned the front of his trousers and urinated into a bush. He rebuttoned, then reslung his leather satchel over his left shoulder. From under its flap, the butt ends of two pistols protruded. He picked up a rifle taller than him, extended his left hand to Ethan, and said, "C'mon, Cole, we cain't stay here."

Ethan felt the man's callused paw wrap around his right hand, then a dizzying pull that suddenly left him on his feet. The fresh new green world spun in his vision and Ethan almost fell. "C'mon, lean on me til ya git yer bearin's."

Muscles that had been dead rebelled against the first hellish steps. But slowly, Ethan's new heart pumped and blood flowed and his new body began to respond.

In no time at all, the sun launched into the sky and the humidity under the trees grew stifling. Ethan's shuffling gait slowly improved to actual walking and after half an hour, he no longer needed to lean on his companion. The overarching tree canopy broke and they found themselves at the edge of a muddy track. On the other side of the road a field sported tall emerald shafts of corn.

"C'mon, Cole." They trudged into the field and became invisible among the broad-leafed plants. Ethan watched his companion's nimble fingers shuck an ear of corn to expose big yellow kernels. The end of the ear disappeared into the cloud of beard and the blue eyes flashed. With yellow bits erupting from his mouth, the older man said, "Dive in. May not be so lucky tomorrow."

Ethan yanked an ear off one of the larger plants and struggled to get his fingers to pull back the protective leaves. He had trouble with the dexterity needed to pluck off the fine strands of corn silk. By the time his companion had polished off two ears, Ethan had barely started on his first. As Ethan gazed up into the cloudless sky, his teeth raked into the tight kernels and an explosion of sweet juice erupted in his mouth. Had food ever tasted this good?

Ethan held out his free hand and saw long fingers at the end of a thin hand. His wrist protruded from a green shirt sleeve streaked with long runnels of dried blood, now dark brown in the sunlight. Threadbare denim trousers. Heavy brown boots, scuffed and mud-covered.

When the sugar from the corn hit his bloodstream Ethan felt giddy. All he had were the worn out clothes on his back – well, it wasn't even his back, was it? In horrible pain

70

and half-starved, yet he reveled in being alive. Munching corn under a blistering sun with sweat running down his back, listening to the sounds of battle in the middle distance, he was aware of how precious all of this was.

Somewhere in this place and this time he felt sure Bethany was near. But how to find her?

"What's your name?" His unused voice rasped.

The blue eyes squinted. "Ya joshin' me, kid?"

"I...I can't remember anything."

His hairy compatriot stopped chewing. "Ain't shittin' me?"

"I don't remember anything before this morning."

He spat out his corn and crouched close to Ethan. He peered into Ethan's eyes and then examined the wound on the side of Ethan's head. "Spect you *would* have yer brains addled after gettin' shot like that. My name's Jones. Jasper Jones. Ring any bells?"

Ethan started to shake his head, but the pain stopped him. Instead, he said, "No. Sorry."

"Nothin' to be sorry about. You got that damnesia." Jasper chuckled. "Sometimes I wish I could get it. There's lots I'd like to forget." He settled cross-legged on the grass that grew between the cornrows. "Let's chow up and rest. Then we gotta make a beeline back to Sharpsburg."

"Where are we?" Sharpsburg was only a few miles from Ethan's farm.

"West slope of South Mountain." Pointing to the west, he said, "Back where we come from is Middletown. We been holdin' the road that cuts through this gap in South Mountain till Lee gets set up in Sharpsburg and Stonewall Jackson gets back from Harper's Ferry. Then we'll be ready to take on these bluebelly bastards." He gestured back the way they had come. "But they don't seem to be wantin' to cooperate with our plans. They're boilin' up out the Middletown Valley like red ants. Once they get through the gap, ain't nothin' can stop 'em til they reach Sharpsburg."

"How'd I get shot?"

"We was down in the gap after sunset to see if we could pick off some officers in camp. They always stand around their fires like it's a church social. Had a real good spot on a little outcropping. Could see all the way down into the valley. I picked off three of the bluebellies. You got two. Then some bastards rode up on horses and we skedaddled. We was

71

runnin, they was shootin', and one of 'em got lucky. You went down like a sacka taters. Some of our boys let loose from the trees and the Yanks backed off long enough so's I could drag you out of there."

"We're snipers?"

"Damn good ones, too. Too bad you dropped that sweet Sharps rifle down a ravine."

"How old are you?"

"I'm still a girl, Cole. Jes this side of fifty." The beard parted enough to show yellow, beaver teeth.

"What about me? What do you know about me?"

"Met ya six months ago down the Shenandoah. Some of the lads was havin' a leetle shootin' match and you won. My friends started braggin' on me and when I got back to camp, they drug me over. You don't remember none of this?"

"Nothing."

"Well, we commenced to shootin' and we went at it all afternoon. Them damn camp sitters musta had a thousand dollars bet amongst 'em. Crowd kept gettin' bigger. Finally, General Longstreet hisself come over and watched us."

"Who won?"

"Hell, we both did. Longstreet got so impressed, he told us we was too good to be infantry. He made us snipers right on the spot. Had us report directly to General Bobbie Toombs. Toombs lets us wander all over hell an' back, long as we keep makin' vacancies in the Yankee officer corps. Hell, five boys are thankin' us today for their field promotions last night. And we'll get those five tomorrow."

"But who won the shooting match?"

A corncob went back into Jasper's mouth and he looked off to his right. He chewed as he spoke. "Seems I had some bad powder. Had a weak load and my shot fell short."

"So, I won?"

"You *should* win, Youngblood. Yer half my age. Wait til *you* have'ta squint ta see."

CHAPTER 24

"Halt." Two young troopers appeared from behind the trunk of a huge sycamore.

"Sorry ta wake ya ladies." Jasper kept walking at his steady gait.

"Hey, I said stop." The taller of the two pickets stepped forward and hefted his musket.

"Young'un, don't strain yerself on my account. You might bust a gut liftin' that piece of iron."

"You give me the password, old man, or I'll blow yer damn head off," he said, the musket now at his shoulder.

Jasper stopped and took off his grimy hat. He scratched his scalp through a mat of black, oily hair and then replaced the hat. "Boy, you best be savin' that powder for when the Yanks come over that hill back yonder. You'll get all the shootin' you ever wanted."

The young man's eyes darted back to where Jasper pointed. In that instant, the old warrior took two quick steps forward, grabbed the musket barrel and directed it skyward with his left hand while his right hand pressed his Walker .44 Dragoon into the picket's chest. Ethan blinked and the other picket stood dumbfounded.

"Boy, never let a man get that close to ya when ya got the drop on 'im." Jasper released the musket barrel. In the quiet, hot air, the click of his revolver seemed overly loud as he lowered the hammer. "The password is 'garter' since ya asked."

"Old bastard."

Jasper holstered his Walker and picked up his rifle. "Where ya from, boy? Yer lingo sounds like down Charleston way."

"Savannah."

"Close enough. I studded my way through them parts twenty years ago. So show some respect. You could be the bastard son of a bastard son."

"Yer a crazy old coot."

"Rightly so. All the more reason to show some respect. Never know when I might blow my top." Jasper turned and clapped Ethan on the shoulder. "C'mon, Cole, let's let these fellers get back to their beauty sleep. They need it. 'Specially that one."

Two miles ahead, billows of dust towered like cumulus clouds in the still air. In the distance, horses and men scurried around with no apparent purpose.

"Damn, they're pullin' out. They be General Hill and Longstreet's boys."

Ethan knew this place on the western slope of South Mountain. Without thinking he croaked out a word. "Bolivar."

Jasper's blue eyes squinted at Ethan. "Memory comin' back?"

Ethan had to be careful. "Don't know."

The men and equipment in the distance began moving to the southwest. "Must be fallin' back. We do a lot of that," Jasper said. "You won't be seein' a doctor soon, Cole. Not til we get to Sharpsburg."

Ethan's head had cleared a bit. "Jasper, what's today's date?"

"Hell if I know."

"Do you know the month, the year?"

"September in the Year of Our Lord 1862."

Ethan almost fainted. He had grown up in this valley. He knew the stories handed down by the old-timers. He had read dozens of books on the Civil War. If he and Jasper had engaged Union troops last night, today had to be September 16. Tomorrow, the Battle of Antietam would start, the single bloodiest day of the whole Civil War. Thirty thousand casualties.

"My God, what have I gotten myself into?" He barely muttered it, but Jasper heard.

"Yer in the middle of a great big war, son. American style. Men fightin' for ideas, some fightin' for money, some jes fightin' cause it's better than pushin' a plow. And ever damn man that dies is an American. We gotta be the craziest people on the face of this green earth." Jasper cackled and then spit out the twig he'd been chewing.

It felt as if someone had drilled a hole in Ethan's forehead, then driven in a railroad spike. An unwavering shaft of pain scorched across his skull, front to back. He gritted his teeth until the pain abated a little.

A chestnut mound of hair lay in the sun at the edge of the road. Only as they drew close could Ethan make out the distended shape as that of a horse. A million flying emeralds danced across the carcass, glinting in the sun. As the pair approached, the brocade of flies shifted but they would not rise from their feast. A hum like a dozen beehives filled the air.

As the pair passed downwind of the bloated thing, they stepped into an unbreathable wave of stench. Both men grabbed their noses and quick-stepped for twenty paces until the horrible breath of decay was replaced by the loamy odor of the churned earth kicked up by the footsteps of the thousand men who had tramped this road and the adjoining fields not an hour earlier. They still heard the hum of the feasting flies.

Ethan felt road grit in his mouth. His skin itched from the dirt caked on it and the sweat that poured from his body. The coarse fabric of his pants rasped across the raw insides of his thighs. This body had done a lot of walking.

The light was real. The death was real. Though it pained him to move his head, Ethan peered around himself. He saw details of reality etched into every mote of being, every leaf on every tree, every ragged wisp of cloud. He knew he was not dreaming.

I am in a different place and I still exist.

They trudged down the Hagerstown Road until they came to Boonsboro at the intersection with the Sharpsburg Road, where they stopped and slouched in the cool shade of a silver maple tree. The sun outside their shelter created heat shimmers even though the day had barely started. All around them they saw signs of hasty retreat: shreds of newspapers, burlap sacks, smoking cook fires. "Long walk to Sharpsburg. Let's wait here and see if we cain't secure some transport."

They settled on their haunches with their backs against the cool gray bark of the massive trunk. "Even them stupid federals won't have trouble trackin' this army." Jasper gestured to the trampled land around them. "Flies and horseshit. Just a highway of horseshit to wherever we are."

Booming cannons sounded like thunderstorms in the dense air. Townsfolk passing along the road shot furtive glances in their direction, but said nothing to these bringers of war with the rumbling backdrop that was their calling card. The citizens of Boonsboro, some of them for the rebels and some against, suddenly cared nothing for politics. They just hoped it would all pass them by as it had for a year and a half.

After resting fifteen minutes, the pair began the trek to Sharpsburg, passing along the edge of Ethan's home town. Looking across the farmland, he marveled at how the countryside looked almost exactly the same as in his own time. Different trees, but the land's contours seemed as familiar to him as his own yard. He knew some of the houses, but in this time they were only exposed logs and chinking, not the aluminum and vinyl sided facades that he remembered. The stone houses remained exactly the same, just newer, the mortar bright and clean. He half expected to see someone he knew along the road. He had a wild notion to find his own house.

A dirt track led off to the right. Ethan could not stop his feet from heading down it.

"Hey, Youngblood, the road goes thisaway."

"Jasper, it's a little detour. Stay on the road if you want." But the tough little man followed Ethan.

Ethan recognized his land, saw what would become his house in the distance. The brick addition had not yet been built, but the core of the structure looked so familiar. With a sense of foreboding, he gazed up at the hill behind the house. He heard Beth's laughter as her dragon kite navigated the air currents of that afternoon so long ago. The hill grew hay, just as in his time.

"Jasper. Mind waiting here for me?"

"What?"

"I know this family. I just want to say hello."

"Don't take long." Jasper settled on a stone and tugged an ear of corn out of his satchel.

Without thinking, Ethan's feet wove through rock outcroppings on their way to the barn. The tree. Where was it?

Looking nothing like its bonelike remnant, the oak spread out at the edge of the corral behind the barn. In this time a healthy tree, deep green and fully leafed, it stretched thirty feet high with a trunk two feet across. It would more than triple in size by his time.

With almost fearful slowness, Ethan passed under the shadow of the oak's lower limbs, approached the trunk. He pressed his fingers against the gray bark and willed himself inside the tree, deep into its roots. He wanted to hide there, away from this mad time.

Ethan stood motionless under the shaded umbrella of the oak and peered up. Tiny razors of sunlight sliced through the moving leaf canopy, disappearing and reappearing in a random flicker show.

The coolness of space touched him. Without thinking, Ethan felt outward with his power. He could feel the currents of time buoying him along. He willed himself to stand like the oak, defying time, defying the interwoven forces that held him in their skein. For an instant, the motes of light became motionless, particles of dust and pollen suspended in their individual shafts of illumination. Sounds Dopplered down the spectrum to a low rumble.

Frozen, like an ant in amber, Ethan's body stood as motionless as everything else. He looked around himself using the power, the awareness that had been his since birth. For once it was not random, not an image thrust upon him. He controlled it. He felt the intersection of time and space in this exact instant and he gained a tiny fragment of understanding of how they fit together.

This is the place.

He wanted to stay in this place and wait however long it took for Beth and the lightning to arrive. He wanted to let the world flow around him so he would be here when she needed him. He would think of something to do to change her fate.

I don't know how.

He pulled his fingers away from the tree trunk and felt a vast emptiness rise in his soul. His "now" began to move. He stepped back into the stream of time, allowed himself to be swept along. And he suddenly felt very weak, as if he had run a mile. He leaned his back against the oak and slid down to a sitting position, trying hard not to faint.

"Hey there, what ya doin'?"

Groggy, Ethan looked up. A tall man in bib overalls and not much else hobbled across the dappled grass toward Ethan. Though he wasn't brandishing it, a revolver hung at the end of his right arm.

"You all right, feller?"

As the old man got close, Ethan felt a lurch in his chest. That face. Ethan's eyes went wide in shock.

The face of his father.

"Lord Amighty, what happened to you?" The old man stood close now and his eyes locked on the trench of scab along Ethan's skull.

"I...I...was shot."

"That's an understatement."

Ethan's eyes stared into the old man's face. Even his timbered voice sounded like Ethan's father. "What's your name?" Ethan said.

"Caleb. Caleb West. And what's yours, young fellow?" Though solicitous, the old man exhibited caution.

"Ethan. I...I mean Cole." He caught himself. "Ethan Cole."

"From your clothes I'd guess you were a southerner, Ethan Cole, but you don't have the twang. Where you from?"

Ethan almost laughed. "From very far away, Mr. West."

Caleb West squinted his dark eyes, but let it pass. "You feelin' poorly? Want a sip from the well?"

"That would be very nice." Ethan struggled to his feet and took a few unsteady steps. Then his head cleared and he started to walk. Separated by fifty years of age, the two men's movements looked amazingly similar as they shuffled through the dust and around a corner of the barn. One shuffled from age, the other from injury.

They ambled around the left corner of the house and Ethan saw the pump exactly where he remembered it. Next to it stood a thin wisp of a woman, no more than a girl, struggling to lift a heavy wooden bucket to her hip and turning toward them. Her shiny chestnut hair drifted in soft waves to her waist, in dark contrast to the pale blue shift she wore.

Her green eyes met Ethan's and a small cry erupted from her. The bucket dropped and water splashed across her calves as her two thin hands flew to her mouth. She stood motionless, her eyes lit with fright.

"Girl, don't stand there gawkin' like you saw another one of your ghosts. Help this man get a drink."

In that instant of recognition, Ethan knew what she had seen. He tried to ease through the moment by grabbing the pump handle and levering it several times. As cool water flowed out the spout, he cupped his hands under it and lifted water to his mouth. He repeated the process several times until he slaked his thirst. Then he filled the canteen at his belt. The young woman's eyes never left him.

"I best be on my way. Thank you for your hospitality." Ethan had to get out of there. His head spun from the heat and the realization of who these people were. He had to get away before he did something that would affect their lives. He knew that look. This had to be one of his great-great-grand mothers. She had seen who he really was. She was a witcher too.

Ethan turned and shuffled away at his fastest speed, ignoring the hammer that beat in his head. He wanted to run, but he couldn't. In seconds, his pulse speeded and sweat poured out of him. He could feel the girl's eyes burning into his back.

When he rounded the barn and got out of her sightline he felt relieved, but he did not slacken his pace until he was through a stand of trees and saw Jasper lolling at the edge of the road.

"Look like ya saw a ghost."

Ethan almost said that he was the ghost, but thought better of it.

"They kin to ya?"

Able to manage a faint smile, Ethan said, "Yes. Very distant kin."

Ten minutes later a stout wooden wagon hauled by a skinny brown horse trundled up behind them. Jasper stepped out into the middle of the road and waved his arms. "Hey, there, can we git a ride ta Sharpsburg?"

The beady-eyed farmer swallowed his Adam's apple. He clearly didn't want anything to do with them. He eyed the proliferation of weapons Jasper carried. The tone of his voice belied what he said. "Part way. Hop on."

The empty cart tossed and vibrated from ruts in the road. Dust poured up between the planks of the cargo bed. Jasper hung his legs over the rear and Ethan stretched out on his back. After a few minutes, the jouncing felt so bad Ethan had to sit up. A cloud of flinty-tasting grit clawed into Ethan's throat causing a cough that rang like a canon through his head. Ethan retied the bandana that he'd noticed around his neck so that it covered his mouth and nose. He tried to cope with the daggers that sliced through his skull with every unexpected lurch and prayed he wouldn't cough again.

Why here? Why this place, this time?

He tried to go back to that moment of contact with Bethany and relive that nanosecond of recognition. He had felt her twisting into a place. He had re-approached that moment a hundred times, trying to glean some information on how the movement, the displacement, worked. He had jumped through time enough now that he had a feeling for it more than an understanding. Just as he couldn't explain exactly how he rode a bicycle, he couldn't put exact thoughts to this experience, but somehow, deep inside, he was getting the sense of it. That feeling had brought him here. But what should he do now?

Would he have to live out decades of life in this body trying to find Beth? Or was he in the wrong place altogether?

79

Ethan sensed some different understanding just out of his grasp, like hearing a conversation from down a long hallway, familiar voices and words echoing, but distorted to incomprehensibility. A magic word that hung just out of reach could cut his tethers and fly him to a better understanding. But for now he had to slog minute by minute, hoping.

At the edge of town, Jasper grabbed Ethan's arm and pulled him off the moving wagon. "Over this way." Walking felt much better that riding after the jarring Ethan's head had gotten. Now mid-day, the sun baked the hardscrabble road into a reddish dust that rose with each footfall and clung to their boots and pants. Twenty minutes of trudging along high corn and hay fields brought them to a small valley on the far side of which horses and men scrambled. Here they saw intact uniforms that, in contrast, made Jasper and Ethan look like rag men.

They followed a dirt track through a stand of trees and suddenly stood at the foot of a stone bridge over a wide shallow stream. Above it rose a steep ridge. Men and supplies snaked across the bridge. Soldiers dug gun pits along the ridge top. With all the bustle, nobody took notice of Jasper and Ethan.

It took all of Ethan's strength to climb the hill. His head pounded at each step. At the top, a long line of trenches wrapped around the plateau.

Sweet Jesus, I know this place. I know what happens here. He had hiked the area with Buzz many times. Burnside's Bridge.

Soldiers stacked powder and ball at intervals along the trenches. Ethan recognized Pennsylvania long rifles, Hawkens, Colts, and an ancient Brown Bess that must have been handed down since the Revolution.

They trudged on through the hot sun, until they smelled sooty traces of camp life. As they got closer, wood smoke formed a blue haze and all manner of sounds drifted through the trees: the ring of an anvil, a wave of laughter, the snorting of horses. And coughing. Great staccato bursts of coughing caused by the inevitable colds and fevers that close quarters always caused. It even had a name that Ethan remembered: the army cough.

At the edge of the camp, they passed a Zouaves squad bedecked in loose purple and green uniforms. Dried mud clung to the legs of their wide tarboosh pants. Sweat grimed

80

their red silk shirts. What had been exotic costumes months earlier were becoming colorful rags. They looked more like gypsies than soldiers.

In a low voice, Ethan said, "Why do they dress like that? They think this is a party?"

Jasper snickered as he chewed a black-cherry twig he had torn from a tree. "The federals have units like that too. Some damn French idea that became the rage a couple years back. Units in jest about every state. I cain't figure it. When the shootin' starts, nobody can keep track of their colors, so both sides blast the hell out of 'em." He flipped the stick into the corner of his mouth and said, "Jes shows there's no corner on insanity. They do look good on parade, though. Die pretty too."

"If you reckon all this is crazy, Jasper, why don't you just leave? Go out west, chase some gold?"

"Already done that back in '49." He chewed on the stick for a minute. "Y'know, Cole, I wouldn't miss this for the world."

Ethan cocked an eyebrow at the older man as they pressed on.

"When else in your life will you be able to wander round the countryside, take whatever you want from anybody you want to, and with a pull on yer trigger, kill any bastard gets in yer way? Without a war, we'd be outlaws. Now we're heroes." The stub of black-cherry wood disappeared inside his beard.

The smell of burnt meat and garbage and tobacco assaulted them as they pushed into the encampment. "You figure these boys know the federals are only a few miles away?" The uniforms got cleaner. "Officer country. Youngblood, set yerself down here and get some rest. I'll go see what's what."

Ethan needed no further persuasion as he settled under the thick limbs of a white oak. In minutes he half-dozed in the humid, woozy air, that seemed far too hot for mid-September.

Then suddenly his body froze. Patches of snow littered the hard ground and the sky turned a fierce blue. A volcano erupted in Ethan's chest and he couldn't move his body. Ten feet away, Beth's limp form lay on the ground, bright blood soaking into the front of her coat.

This was real. It was going to happen. What did he have to do or *not* do to prevent it?

CHAPTER 25

"Wake up, Youngblood. I found ya a doctor. Did some dickerin' and got you a new Colt's revolver rifle too. Took off the body of a Billy Yank. Ain't as good as that Sharps you lost, but it shoots five shots without reloadin'. One of 'em oughtta hit what yer aimin' at."

Ethan dredged his thoughts from the syrup of time, wondering at the snowy images he had dreamed.

Jasper set the new .58 caliber rifle across Ethan's lap. Then he dropped next to Ethan a canvas bag of shot and another of black powder. "Should test it out, see how true them sights is."

"Jasper, last thing on earth I need right now is an explosion near my head."

The beard parted in a smile. "'Spect yer right. You ready to walk?"

Ethan nodded.

"We'll get you a doctor, then we report to Reno down at the stone bridge we crossed. Yanks come up that way, it'll be like shootin' fish in a barrel."

Ethan struggled to his feet.

"Dizzy?"

"Yeah.'

"Not far to go."

Ethan kept his head level, breathed steadily, and tried not to think about his wound. It suddenly frightened him that if Bethany were here during the battle, might she be killed again? Might he waste a lifetime looking for her?

Activity swept through the dusty streets of Sharpsburg as residents realized what was about to happen. Union troops had begun lining up across Antietam Creek, massing like hungry crows. Lines of barefoot Confederates streamed east from the Potomac River, filling the town and its surroundings with cannons and horses and men wearing every variety of clothing, but all wearing the same grim face. Residents with bundles tried escaping west toward the Potomac, but like trout migrating upstream, they fought against a raging flood of Confederate troops pouring into town. They could seldom use the road, instead having to struggle through ditches and underbrush at its sides. Others cleared shops of provisions and holed up in their cellars and in the woods.

As he trudged through Sharpsburg, Ethan thought it would take only a second for him to step away from Jasper and be lost in the crowd. Even with the rifle, Ethan's clothes blended in with the townsfolk. But Ethan discarded that thought. Weak and disoriented, if he made the wrong move, he could wind up either as a deserter or a prisoner of war. Better to stick with Jasper and use Ethan's foreknowledge of events to try to keep them both alive.

As unthreatening as Ethan looked, Jasper presented another matter. Nobody could mistake the battle-hardened veteran. The three pistols he normally carried in his leather satchel now stuck out the front of his belt. A fourth rode in the holster slung to his right thigh. Those who passed closely stared for a second at the crust of blood on Ethan's head, but they averted their eyes from Jasper, this heavily armed man with the wild blue eyes.

Ethan thought it ironic that in his own time he had crisscrossed the streets of Sharpsburg and the rolling hills around it, trying to visualize the titanic forces that had washed across this peaceful hamlet. Now, a hundred thousand men lined up to kill each other. Ethan's curiosity would be slaked. He would see the carnage first-hand.

At the southwest end of town, a scream rose from behind a stand of sweet-gum trees, dropped to a moan, and then died off.

Jasper cackled, "Always easy to find the field hospital."

The field hospital sported a few fly tents which would soon become totally inadequate. Wounded soldiers had trickled in from the battles at Crampton's Gap and Turner's Gap and orderlies arrayed them in the tall grass under the trees. Some of them sat on camp chairs, with cotton bandages on heads or limbs. Others lay flat on the ground on blankets. Under the fly tents, a few soldiers secured planks across sawhorses to make more operating tables. Four surgeons in leather butcher aprons hurried through their grisly work. As Ethan and Jasper watched, orderlies lifted one soldier off the planking and hauled him to a place in the grass, another orderly sloshed a bucket of water across the vacated table to clear the blood and bits of flesh, and then more orderlies hoisted the next groaning soldier onto the table. Ethan watched this production line of pain.

Just off from the tents, in a small defile, a buzzing

frenzy rose like the sound of angry hornets. Ethan glanced down the embankment as they walked past. Green shiny poison ivy vines grew thick in the hollow and hid most of its contents, but the stench of rotting meat had enough potency to make Ethan and Jasper gag. A pale hand beckoned from the foliage. A foot with only three toes stuck up in the sun. The leaves, the air, the very ground itself teemed with flies feasting on discarded body parts.

Jasper spat. "Now you know why they call doctors sawbones."

Off to the side of the surgery, they approached a narrow-faced man in a bloody butcher's apron. "Sit down, soldier. Let me look at that."

Jasper said loudly enough for all around to hear, "Watch yer head, Youngblood. He's fixin' ta ampeetate."

The doctor pointed to a bucket. "How 'bout you make yourself useful and go down to that creek yonder and fill that bucket with water. I'll need it for your friend here."

"Yessir, Doc. Jes don't cut nothin' off him afore I git back."

Ethan submitted to an examination, while thinking that the doctor looked much too young. Until he looked into the man's eyes.

"Seen it all, eh, Doc?"

A thick, brown eyebrow canted up over the young man's left eye. "There should be pleasure in saving lives."

"I'll be real pleased if you save mine."

"Why? So you can go right back out there and get another bullet in you? In the past three months, I worked on a damn fool lieutenant three different times. Three different battles, three different bullets."

"What happened to him?"

"Amazing. They all healed."

"So, why so glum?"

"Two days ago, his horse shied away from a squirrel in the road. He fell off the horse and broke his neck."

Jasper returned with a bucket of water and set it at the doctor's feet. Then he settled against the base of a giant oak and tipped his hat over his eyes.

The doctor cleaned around Ethan's wound, but left the main scab alone. "This scab is protecting your wound like a bandage. I don't want to disturb it. You have any whiskey?"

"No."

"How about your friend over there?"

"Don't know. Hey, Jasper, you have any whiskey?"

Jasper pushed up his hat brim with a finger. "I might have a tetch."

"Why am I not surprised? Bring it over," the doctor said. He took the proffered tin flask and poured liquor on Ethan's wound. Then he wrapped a bandage around Ethan's head like a turban. "Leave this bandage on. Keep out the dirt. Twice a day, pour a little whisky on the bandage to fight off infection."

"Doc, that's sippin' liquor. Don't seem right pourin' it on someone's head."

The doctor raked his gaze up and down Jasper. "Anything keeps it out of your stomach has to be a blessing to everyone around you. Think of it as your civic duty to western civilization."

"Hey, Doc, they got a library in this town?"

"Why?"

"I think I jes' been insulted, but I need a dictionary to find out."

"You two get out of here. I have work to do."

Jasper elbowed Ethan. "He's got work to do. Real eager for it, ain't he? They musta got a new shipment of saw blades." Jasper cackled and led Ethan away.

CHAPTER 26

Jasper danced a jig on the berm of the rifle pit. Then he leaned over and slapped his ass in the direction of the Union troops a few hundred yards away. In answer, a flash of light and a puff of smoke appeared at the tree line across Antietam Creek. Jasper dropped to the floor of the trench as the Yankee bullet chuffed into the earth berm, followed by the sound of the shot. "Damn good shot there, boy, but now I seen where ya live."

Jasper hoisted his Hawken, rested the barrel on the edge of the rifle pit. He sighted to the right side of the beech tree where the flash had occurred and calculated the range. He pulled back the rear trigger. "Okay, I got the bead on that Billy Yank bastard. I need your Colt."

Ethan handed Jasper his new rifle as he eyed the Hawken Jasper set against the pit wall. "Two triggers?"

"Rear trigger takes up all the spring tension, makes the front one a hair-trigger. More accurate that way."

Off in the distance a Yankee soldier dropped his drawers and bent over. "He's mooning you, Jasper."

"Not fer long."

At sight of the Colt's flash, the Yankee slipped behind the beech tree before the bullet could traverse the intervening distance. The instant after Jasper fired the Colt, he dropped it and picked up the more accurate Hawken. Only a heartbeat later Jasper fired again, at exactly the same spot.

As soon as Jasper's first bullet hit the beech tree, the Yankee soldier stepped back out into the open, his britches still down to continue his mooning. He had not looked for a second flash. He had no idea a second bullet was hurtling through space faster than the sound that would have warned him. Jasper's second shot plowed into the base of his spine and came out through the top of his head. The soldier died before he hit the ground.

Jasper cackled. "Damn fool thought I was reloadin'. Them bluebellies better be a mile out afore they try such tomfoolery. And even then, I cain't guarantee their safety."

As Jasper reloaded his Hawken, Ethan said, "Jesus, Jasper. That thing's a cannon."

"Used to shoot buffalo with it out on the plains. Four-legged and two-legged as I recollect."

Ethan hefted one of the lead balls from Jasper's shot bag. "Big round."

"Sixty-eight caliber. If it don't kill ya, ya *wish* ya was dead."

"Jesus, Jasper."

"Jest thinnin' the herd, Youngblood, jest thinnin' out the herd."

The low sun behind them penetrated the tree line across the fields on the other side of Burnside's Bridge, sparking gold off Yankee uniform buttons. Ethan and Jasper had taken station at the top of the steep cliff that backed the bridge on the west side of Antietam Creek. Five hundred Confederate soldiers had thinly spread across the cliff top with a commanding view of all approaches to the bridge.

All day they had watched Union troops position themselves in the trees and around the small hill to the east. Jasper said, "They charge the bridge and it'll be like shootin' fish in a barrel." Ethan wondered what he would say if he knew that the assembling forces outnumbered them thirty to one.

The sharp edge of Ethan's pain had dulled to a throbbing ache that could flare into dizzying agony if he moved suddenly. Most of the afternoon he had sat in the shade and watched the men dig the trenches that would cause the northern forces such hell tomorrow.

"What they waitin' fer? They coulda waltzed right in here this afternoon afore we got dug in."

"Jasper, you forget who we're facing. McClellan. If he had all of God's archangels lined up and Christ himself as his general, he'd still ask for reinforcements."

"Gotta hand it to Bobby Lee. If he comes up against you with fifty men, he makes you *think* you need archangels. Gave us time to dig in. How long's McClellan gonna wait?"

Ethan said, "Tomorrow. The seventeenth." It just spilled -out. He cast a sidelong glance at Jasper, but saw no untoward reaction to the conviction in his voice.

I need to be more careful.

CHAPTER 27

As the sun dropped below the horizon, its light flooded the underside of the cloud cover, turning the sky to brushed brass. The eerie light cast no shadows and made the landscape glow ruddy orange. Then sunset quickly fell off to a grudging twilight.

Ethan set down his tin plate and the remains of the cold meal he and Jasper had culled from their meager stores. The Confederates had terrible supplies. At least a third of the men had no shoes. He and Jasper had avoided their assigned mess because they didn't want to reveal that they still had corn they had picked earlier in the day. Most of the soldiers had far less to eat.

Jasper emerged from the woods with a handful of twigs. "Got something fer yer headache. Chew on these willow branches. It's an old Indian remedy."

"It won't work for me, Jasper."

"Why not?"

"I'm not an old Indian."

"That's a good-un," Jasper cackled as he settled against a rock he'd pulled close to their fire. "You must be feelin' better." Jasper struggled to roll a cigarette, dropping more tobacco than he got into the rolling paper. "Damn, I wish I didn't lose my pipe. Hate rollin' these damn things."

Ethan chewed a willow twig, remembering this folk remedy that would lead to the discovery of aspirin. "My head feels like a watermelon on a stick."

"Flop yer melon on that blanket and get some sleep. I'm stayin' up. Got to stand watch at midnight. That will be a nice little piece of hell."

Ethan said, "Jasper, we can't stay at this bridge tomorrow."

"Why not?"

"Because you don't know what hell is until you see tomorrow." Ethan stared across the campfire for several seconds before making up his mind. "You're going to think I'm crazy when I tell you this."

"Well, Cole, it don't come as no surprise. You ain't been in a rightly way."

Ethan paused, hesitant to open Pandora's Box. "Jasper,

I wouldn't have gotten this far without your help. I owe you the chance to save your life. You need to get out of here. Tonight."

"Desert? Hell, I reckon the war won't last much longer. I'll see it through."

"It won't end for two and a half years."

Jasper cackled and spit out the black-cherry twig. "You becomin' a seer now, Cole?" The crooked cigarette it had taken him five minutes to roll went between his lips. Using a burning stick from the fire, Jasper lit the end and inhaled deeply, a look of satisfaction softening his rough features.

Ethan mustered his most serious face. "I'm not Cole. Name's Ethan. Ethan West. I won't be born for a century. I grew up in this area, but off in the future."

Jasper's stare lanced into Ethan. "You're right. You're crazy," he said.

"I'm a farmer. Born in Boonsboro. We walked through there. That little detour I made was to see the house I will grow up in."

"How'd you get here?"

"Long story."

"What's it like in the future?" He said it matter-of-factly as if this sort of thing happened in his life every day.

"Fast. Everything is fast. We don't ride horses anymore."

"Donkeys then?" If there had been more light, Ethan would have seen the twinkle in the older man's eyes.

"No, we ride machines much faster than horses."

"You don't say."

"Jasper, I shouldn't tell you too much. I don't know what your knowing might do to things in the future. But you deserve a chance to live through this."

"Live through what?"

"Tomorrow will be the bloodiest day of this entire war."

Jasper stared into the fire and inhaled from his cigarette. "I ain't desertin'. If what you say is true, I want to see it."

"Now, who's crazy?"

Jasper gut-laughed, took another pull on the tobacco. "Youngblood, I cain't believe yer story just by you sayin' it. Can you tell me somethin' convincin'-like?"

Ethan pondered for a moment. "Okay, two things. We'll hold the bridge until about one o'clock in the afternoon when we get flanked from the south. We'll fall back to town and late in the afternoon we'll get reinforcements when General Hill's troops finally get here from Harper's Ferry. And this should convince you: They'll be wearing Yankee uniforms they took from the Union armory."

"All this tomorrow?"

"Yes. September 17, 1862. It's in the history books. My history books."

"Our boys in Yankee duds, huh?" Jasper puffed on his cigarette and tilted his face to the sky. "Christ it's startin' to drizzle." He scuttled under the canvas tarp they'd set up earlier and sat next to Ethan. Thunder growled in the distance. "See, no matter how bad things might be, they can always get worse. Plan on it."

Lightning silhouetted trees on a distant ridge. Ethan scowled at the bolt.

"Yer quite a storyteller, Youngblood."

"You'll believe me tomorrow."

"How you know I don't believe you already?"

"Because if you did, you'd be crazier than you're thinking I am right now."

Jasper doubled over with laughter and almost choked on the cigarette in his mouth. He spit it into the fire. "Sanest thing you said all night."

CHAPTER 28

Ethan sighted down the blued barrel of the Colt and lined up on an approaching figure. The twitch of a finger and a man would die. Ethan retracted his right index finger to the trigger guard.

It looked like the Union soldiers marched across the corn field on a Sunday stroll, a trick of perspective because they were running straight toward the bridge. A great blue tidal wave, they appeared out of the fog that had hung near the earth all morning, rolled across the lush ribbon of cornfield between the woods and the stream, and crashed upon the stones of the bridge.

There, like storm surf along the Chesapeake, they boiled and frothed and spilled away into the creek, bloody tattered remnants of men. Some clung to the weeds along the bank, unable to pull themselves out of the stream, calling desperately to their comrades for help. Others drifted in the current, their blank eyes staring up into glowing fog.

"That stream's so thick with bodies, them bluebellies could jest step across on the corpses," Jasper shouted. The slow-moving water looked like red wine in the hazy light.

Rifles and muskets exploded around Ethan in a continuous, jarring roar that flamed inside his skull and set his teeth on edge. Clouds of gun smoke rolled down the hill, mixed with the fog, and occasionally blocked sight of the stone bridge. Dead grass along the embankment dried enough by mid-morning to catch fire from the gunplay, further adding to the pall that hung over the carnage.

In the distance above the fog, fat plumes of white smoke rose out of the woods from accidental fires started by cannon blasts. The Union forces began pouring canister over the Confederate lines. Jasper pointed up and shouted. "Never seed that before. Heard of it. Flyin' posts. Look, Cole."

The canisters passed overhead at such speed, they created an elongated blur, like flying posts. They exploded further back from the hill face, wreaking carnage in the supply areas and among the Confederate cannoneers. Some rounds exploded short, raining shrapnel down on men and horses near Ethan and Jasper.

Jasper shouted, "Goin' to the supply wagon for more

powder," as he disappeared into the smoke.

A black draft horse stumbled up to the rifle pit behind Ethan. Half its head had been shot away and the poor animal seemed only semiconscious. For a moment, Ethan forgot his own pain. He drew his revolver and began to take aim at the suffering animal's head, when suddenly, red craters appeared all over the dark coat as over a dozen musket balls hit the horse, almost simultaneously. Half a ton of horse groaned and dropped so fast Ethan heard the snap of one of its legs breaking. Oblivious to the battle, a host of black horseflies descended on the corpse even before it stopped twitching, happy guests at the unending smorgasbord of war.

Ethan turned back to the killing field, that flat open farm that served endless Yankees onto the platter of the bridge where Death feasted.

With all his research into the Civil War, Ethan had never imagined this. One endless noise. The constant low, sonic vibrations through the ground made him want to vomit as Confederate cannons fired outward and answering Yankee lead and iron plowed into the earth all around them. Dozens of muskets fired every second, sounding like an endless ripping of canvas.

Men screamed, some entreating comrades to the attack, others begging for relief. Those flung into the open by explosions or their own foolishness lay helpless and unheeded until the rain of random lead eventually found them, finished them, and then continued to punch and move their bodies long after they had died.

This dance of twitching corpses seemed something that should only exist in a nightmare. Ethan's finger pressed the trigger, then stopped halfway in its arc. He could take this life that sat in his sights. Distance and smoke reduced it to a faceless thing.

But Ethan's finger couldn't finish the arc, instead relaxing and releasing the trigger. He didn't want to kill a man, but even larger issues loomed in his thinking than simple morality.

He occupied a body that should have died. If he killed someone who would otherwise have lived, what would it do to his own future time? What if he killed the grandfather of a person who invented a miracle drug? He envisioned an endless list of catastrophes. Ethan felt locked in his own small conflict as the larger conflict raged around him.

"Waitin' for Christmas, trooper?"

Lost in speculation, Ethan did not hear the question. A sudden sharp pain twisted him around to see a black boot digging into his ribs.

"Huh?"

"Gun shy, Mister? Or maybe you just like Yankees."

Ethan craned his head up from his prone position and squinted at the silhouette hunched behind him. "I...I'm feeling dizzy."

The man drew his revolver. "Been watchin' you. Ain't fired a single round. Now you want to shoot or git shot?" Ethan felt the cold barrel of the revolver pushed into the side of his neck. "Now, you shoot somebody so's I can see him fall." The click of the hammer pulling back seemed disproportionately loud in Ethan's left ear.

Ethan felt hot spray across his neck and the officer toppled over the edge of the trench and tumbled down the steep embankment. Ethan blinked. Why had the man fallen outward?

Three seconds later, he had his answer as Jasper scrambled into the ditch next to Ethan, holstering his Walker as he settled into the earthworks. Over the din, Jasper shouted, "Leave ya alone fer five minutes and yer in deep shit agin." He sighted his rifle, fired, and reloaded from the fresh bag of powder.

Ethan stared at the grizzled warrior. "Did you shoot that officer?"

"Damn right I did. Bastard. Sometimes ya need to thin yer own herd too." Jasper pulled the ramrod out of his rifle, turned, sighted, and fired in one fluid motion, not even taking time to watch his target fall. "Cole, I know yer feelin' poorly and that gun punchin' into yer shoulder cain't feel good, but every so often let loose a round so's I don't have'ta kill the whole damn officer corps."

CHAPTER 29

They held the bridge against what seemed like endless tides of northern troops. The butchery sickened even the most ardent Yankee haters. Hundreds of bodies and pieces of bodies lay on the bridge, in the water, on the banks of the creek, and scattered across the now-leveled cornfield that filled the flat land across the stream. Mixed among the men lay numerous horses, some still twitching and screaming in high-pitched wails. The chorus of the dying horses held more horror than the groans and pleadings of the men. Nobody considered a horse an enemy, but when cavalry hit the bridge approach, the Confederates had no time for the delicate marksmanship necessary to peel the rider from his mount. Far easier to shoot the horse, then pick off the dazed and sometimes injured rider.

The shooting diminished in early afternoon. For long intervals, the Confederates could reload and restock their powder and ball as the northern forces regrouped in the woods. In one of those quiet periods, when only sporadic shots punctuated the activities of marksmen picking off those foolish enough to break cover, Jasper said, "What kinda generals they got over there? They don't care how many die?"

Ethan's mind drifted. Dazed by the shocks to his system, he could not focus on the battle. Exhaustion crept through every cell of his body.

"Cole, in case you didn't notice, them fellers is shootin' at us. Think maybe you could fire back?" Jasper loaded his rifle, aimed, and fired before continuing.

"I can't shoot these people, Jasper."

"You think you really have a choice?"

The pain in Ethan's head rang like a cathedral bell.

Yes, I do have a choice. I can stand up, get shot, and die so I can leave this place and try again.

In his weakened condition, Ethan operated more from instinct than thought, which was fortunate or he might have missed the tugging twitch he felt deep inside. As if a tunnel had opened through the random energies around him, Ethan sensed just a flash of Beth and then it disappeared. He could not be sure if he had felt a piece of the future or the past.

"Youngblood, how 'bout you jest load and I'll shoot? That way you won't have to shake yer head up." Jasper handed Ethan the spent Colt rifle.

Ethan pondered this suggestion. So far, he had seen no changes in the future from his activities in the past. And even if changes happened, what did it matter? If he was trying the impossible, it couldn't happen. But it was happening, so it was possible. Probably what made up his mind was the desire to help Jasper stay alive.

"Yeah. Okay." Ethan pulled a powder bag next to his leg. Crouched in the ditch, he measured black powder into all five chambers of his new rifle, pushed in tiny bits of rag for wadding, then dropped a .44 caliber ball into each. With the ramming tool he seated the lead balls tight against the powder. He slopped lard over the front of the cylinder to prevent chain firing and snapped primer caps onto the ignition nipples at the rear of the cylinder. He handed the rifle to Jasper and took the single-shot rifle in return.

"Damnation."

"What?" Ethan said, looking up from his reloading.

"Blew that feller's arm off at the elbow. Lousy damn shot." Jasper sighted Ethan's rifle again.

Ethan squinted and followed Jasper's aim. The smoke parted and Ethan had a clear view of a man writhing on the ground behind the low fence that bordered the road on the other side of the creek. The man fought his way to a crouch and then hunkered away from the bridge on unsteady legs.

"C'mon out from behind that wagon... There." In a cloud of smoke and fire, the Colt hurled another slug. It spun through the air until it hit Jonas Jeffries above his left ear where the soft lead mushroomed to the size of a plum and drove Jonas's brains out the right side of his skull.

"Now he won't be suffering without that arm."

"Jesus, Jasper."

The old veteran cackled. "Jes keep that shot a-comin'. I like havin' a loader." He turned, aimed, and fired. Another faceless northern son died for his country.

An hour later, Union forces regrouped for another assault. Fifteen minutes of cannon volley against the Confederate high ground put several Confederate cannons out of action and detonated one of the supply wagons like a Fourth of July piece, setting dozens of small fires throughout the Confederate line. Bluish-white smoke rose from the fires and sifted among the trees. A light breeze pushed this acrid curtain down the hill and over the rifle pits.

95

"Damnation!" Jasper wiped his stinging eyes. "Cain't see, cain't shoot." He set down his rifle as ragged coughs racked his wiry frame.

The pungent smoke seared into Ethan's lungs and he too began a series of retching coughs, each one setting off a ringing explosion inside his damaged skull.

Jasper's coughs turned to scratchy laughter as he lay back in their ditch, filtered sunlight dancing off his blue eyes. "Ain't this jest lovely?" He cackled again. Then he squinted downhill and immediately began reloading his rifle. He muttered, "Didn't think them bluebellies was jest gettin' rid of excess ammo. Here they come agin." He pointed to the southeast.

Ethan squinted. Through the pall, sunlight glinted off a thousand bayonets. Within moments, Ethan saw distinct forms, men in blue, row after row of them.

"Youngblood, you load as fast as you can. You hear me?" Humor had left Jasper's voice.

Ethan nodded. He didn't dare speak. His Adam's apple seemed lodged somewhere under his tongue as he watched the Yankee troops resolve out of the smoke. For a moment, Ethan did not feel his pains, did not hear the shrill ringing in his head. This was it. Panic almost engulfed him, but Jasper fired and reached for the loaded Colt rifle as he threw his Hawken at Ethan.

Taking up the five-shot rifle, Jasper aimed and pulled the trigger again and again. Ethan couldn't see where he was aiming or if anyone dropped, so massed were the Union troops. Around them, the tempo of firing increased to a steady roar, like the drawn out rippling thunder of a summer storm.

When the front line of Yankees hit the bridge, the Confederate Parrot guns opened up with chain at point-blank range. The first volley hit the line and at least fifty men went down in pieces. Those behind stumbled over the dismembered corpses, half dazed by the sudden appearance of a butcher shop at their feet. Their hesitation allowed the riflemen to get a bead and more Yankees fell in heaps on the bridge. Burnside's Bridge now looked like a rummage sale of old clothing heaped and thrown by frantic shoppers.

Massed troops scrambled over heaps of bloody meat and hit the path at the foot of the hill. They fell, they screamed, they died, but slowly, inexorably, they pushed up the path and up the hill itself in the face of withering fire. The supply of troops seemed inexhaustible. More pushed across the bridge.

Ethan couldn't believe that men could die so fast and in such numbers. And still they came.

The Parrot guns opened up again and sliced the soldiers ascending the wagon path to howling ribbons. This gave the men in the rifle pits a chance to concentrate their fire on the Yankees who scrambled up the steep face of the hill. Some approached the top.

"Youngblood, make sure yer revolver's loaded. This is gonna get close."

General Robert Toombs rode through his meager forces astride a gray stallion. When he cantered to the edge of the bridge overlook, he almost fainted at the sight of so many Union soldiers crawling up his fortified position. One of his captains shouted up from the ground, "We need more men, General."

"Got no more men. We need 'em on the western line. It's worse'n this over there. Use that hill, Captain. It's all you've got." Toombs turned and rode back toward Sharpsburg, lead whizzing past his retreating form.

A canister shell exploded at ground level at the top of the ridge, splitting open the three sharpshooters to the right of Ethan and Jasper as if they were melons. None of the shrapnel hit Ethan or Jasper, but now they knelt alone in the elongated rifle pit. "Grab their guns, Youngblood. The pistols."

Ethan scrambled to the jellied remnants and tugged three revolvers from the dead men's belts. Just as he returned to Jasper's side, a blue cap emerged over the edge of the rifle pit in front of them. Jasper punched his rifle butt into the bridge of the Yankee's nose and the man fell back and tumbled like a rag doll a hundred feet down to the foot of the embankment. "Not wastin' no powder if I don't hafta."

Two heads popped up and Jasper emptied two chambers of his revolver point blank into their faces. Ethan saw motion to his right and turned to face two more Yankees scrabbling over the edge of the rifle pit. They had been fighting all day at a distance but now the battle loomed so close Ethan could smell the mildew on the Yankee uniforms. Ethan watched in horror as one of the Yankees got his leg over the lip of the pit and raised his musket. Ethan could not move.

Jasper hopped around Ethan just as the first Yankee's musket ranged on the younger man. Jasper drilled the young attacker's forehead, then put his last two shots into the chest of the other climber. Spinning back like a dervish, Jasper tossed the empty revolver to Ethan as he yanked another one from his belt. "Get loadin', Laddie. Got us a job of work to do."

With Ethan loading as fast as he could, Jasper emptied all eight of their revolvers to clear the area around the rifle pit. Then, using the rifles, he worked on the Yankees farther down the slope. When the Parrot guns opened up on the bridge again, the stream of Yankee troops got cut off, leaving those who had made it across on their own. The riflemen focused on these stragglers, downing them at a steady rate until they cleared the hillside approaches of any threat. They then fired at the opposite shore, deep into the ranks of the attackers until, finally, the Yankees lost their stomachs and retreated into the trees, their backs to the golden slanting light of the afternoon sun.

And the history books called these "opening skirmishes," thought Ethan. The main battle is coming up. Hell would cross that bridge soon.

CHAPTER 30

General Robert Toombs had lived a nondescript life. He served in the Confederacy with little distinction until the Battle at Burnside's Bridge. His men held that crossing against a vastly superior force and protected Lee's right flank so Lee could concentrate on the main Union thrust. But a little after midday, Toombs's strategic position became vulnerable when Burnside's scouts found a place to ford Antietam Creek. With his right flank threatened, General Lee ordered Toombs to retreat from the bluff above the bridge. Union forces pushed across the bridge and soon threatened the entire southern approach to Sharpsburg.

Toombs's men retreated and formed skirmish lines to slow the Yankee advance, but inexorably the Yanks drove them back toward the town.

"Jeeeesus Christmas!" Jasper's hat flew off his head. He reached down into the hay stubble and retrieved it. Two neat holes had been drilled in it, front and back. Jasper wiggled his fingers through them and then put the hat back on his head. "Guess only one of us gets to be shot in the head." He cackled and resumed leading Ethan through what little cover the farm terrain offered.

Bullets whizzed through the tall grass like maniac mice. Shots from half a mile away flew unimpeded across the flat landscape, striking men who hadn't even been aimed at. Until they reached the town, no decent cover existed.

Ethan raised his voice. "Jasper, we get over that little rise ahead, we'll be at the edge of town."

"Let's skedaddle then."

Halfway up the rise, a small clump of sycamores offered scant cover. Jasper squinted at Ethan. "When we hit that crest, we'll stick out like sore thumbs." He cast a glance behind. Not far off, he saw blue uniforms against dun-colored fields. "Ethan, hand me yer rifle. Then you go first."

Jasper aimed back the way they had come and loosed his first shot. He glanced over his shoulder. "What the hell you waitin' for? Get over that rise. I'll be along presently." He fired another shot and Ethan headed uphill. He could barely stumble. His vision blurred and he thought he would vomit, but he kept struggling up the hill. Just as he reached the summit and saw salvation in the lee of the hill, Ethan leaned against a black-cherry tree to catch his balance.

His head rang like the crash of a sledgehammer on an anvil. Whirlpools of dizziness engulfed his vision. Suddenly, it felt like something bit him between the legs. He doubled over in pain and tumbled over the crest.

He now had pain between his legs that matched the fiery agony in his head. The .58 caliber ball that hit Ethan came from downhill. It had traveled over five hundred feet and had torn through the lower limb of one of the sycamores further downhill. Slowed by the impact, the heavy ball of lead, now misshapen, still carried a lot of momentum. It ripped across the top of Ethan's inner thigh and tore away a testicle before continuing on.

It seemed like he laid on the hill for hours, but it couldn't have been more than a minute before Jasper grabbed Ethan under the arms and dragged him into the outskirts of Sharpsburg. Ethan passed out for most of the trip and awoke at the base of a stone wall that backed onto the yard of a house.

Federals poured over the crest. Jasper dragged Ethan further along a dirt road until it intersected with the main street. He peeked around the picket fence at the corner and swore. "Goddamn bluebelly bastards is all over this town." A column of blue-clad soldiers double-timed it up the street. "Get, down, act like yer dead. You got enough blood on you."

"What about you?"

"I'm gonna take as many of these Billy Yanks with me as I can." Jasper pulled two pistols out of his belt and huddled against the fence. "Put yer head down. Soon as this squad up ahead gets real close, I'm gonna start blastin'. It was nice knowin' ya, boy."

Ethan heard the clank of canteens around the corner. Bad as he felt, he couldn't let this man who seemed to be saving his life hourly die while he huddled in the dirt like a coward. Ethan struggled to a sitting position and pulled out his revolver.

"You don't show good sense, Youngblood." Jasper cackled. "Guess I cain't keep a good man down." Jasper handed Ethan a second revolver.

Jasper cocked his revolvers. Ethan followed suit and breathed in rapid little breaths, trapped between the north and south poles of his body's agony. They waited the last few

100

seconds before taking on the brunt of the attack.
Jasper said, "Here we go."

CHAPTER 31

Katherine Hawley's skin raised in goose bumps despite the heat of the day. Fear and fascination warred in her as the battle wore on. A sheltered young woman, she perceived war as an abstraction, heard its cacophony almost as something musical, a symphony writ large. The deep booming bass registers of the cannons played under the high counterpoint of the small arms fire that rippled and rushed like the skirling of flutes. She heard an operatic chorus as throngs of men shouted and swore and died. Horrible though she knew it to be, the scene filled her with wonder.

The drama of it so reminded her of the opera house in Baltimore to which her father had taken her only two months ago, on her seventeenth birthday. She hugged her arms around her prim breasts and oscillated back and forth with excitement. Her emerald eyes drank in the spectacle of so many tiny figures streaming across the serried ridges, near and far.

"Katherine, come down from there. This instant." Her mother's strident voice echoed up the stairwell.

Katherine scurried down the kitchen stairs to the basement where her father, mother, and the servant, Emily, sat around a long trestle table in polished oak chairs that looked incongruous on the hard-packed dirt. The only light that trickled into the gloomy cavern came from two tiny windows set at street level in the foundation wall above their heads.

Seeing the scowl on George Hawley's heavy features, Katherine took the initiative. "Now, father, I was quick. I was only gone a minute." Before him she set a pewter tankard of cool water that she had taken from the pump in the kitchen.

"Can you run faster than a bullet?" But his gruff voice grew less severe as he hefted the tankard.

Three times she had contrived to go upstairs. Now she settled into a corner on a wooden box and, listening intently, tried to interpret the sounds that reached them.

"Oh, George, should we have gone to the river with the others?" Katherine's mother pleaded.

George Hawley's thick upper lip twisted. "I'll not sit in those river caves with rats gnawing at our toes." His meaty right hand patted one of the two ivory-handled dueling pistols that gleamed against the dark wood of the table.

The afternoon wore on and even fear abated. George Hawley snored softly from the crook of his arm where his head had dropped an hour earlier. Elizabeth Hawley dragged her chair against a wall and leaned her head against the cool stone to lessen the heat of the day. She drifted off and snored quietly. Only the servant girl, Emily, seemed alert, her wide dark eyes darting back and forth as strange new sounds ricocheted up the street. In the distance, muskets chuffed and cannons roared in the syncopated rhythm of death.

Katherine stood and straightened her skirts and shook her copper curls. "Emily, I'll return presently."

The older woman darted her eyes toward Mr. Hawley. "Missy, please, I'll go," she hissed. "What do you need?"

Katherine pressed her hand to her lips and said, "It is not something you can help me with, Emmy. I need the chamber pot."

Emily blanched as Katherine scurried up the stairs. Katherine cleared the basement, her long legs took the servant stairs at the rear of the kitchen two-by-two. She bypassed the second floor and emerged on the third where she ran to the window of Emily's room. Through the rippled glass, she stared down the hill to where blue and white smoke rose above a field. As this gun-curtain lifted, the late afternoon sun transformed the smoke into a veil of pink lace. Through it Katherine watched bursts of yellow light as thick as fireflies on a summer night.

With a sound oddly reminiscent of the cracking pond ice she had fallen through as a little girl, the window before her broke into three pieces and fell inward. Katherine found herself suddenly sitting on the floor. She blinked her eyes and then looked down where a patch of red stained the yellow of her dress. She watched transfixed as the scarlet and the yellow mixed much like red peppers and scrambled eggs. The yellow and the red swirled in her head and she fell back onto the oak floor.

Her last thought was that the curse had come two weeks early this month.

CHAPTER 32

Ethan's pants glistened with blood. Though the sun burned hot, he felt chilly and lightheaded. Through the fence, he watched Union troops approach at a half trot. He looked back the way he and Jasper had come. Blue-clad soldiers streamed over the crest where Ethan had been shot. He and Jasper huddled between two converging enemy forces. But why were Yankees headed toward each other? Ethan peered between the pickets again.

"Jasper, are my eyes playing tricks? Isn't that a Confederate flag they're carrying?"

"Must be a souvenir."

All doubt vanished five seconds later when the troops approaching from the corner broke into a run straight for Jasper and Ethan and the Union forces coming from the hill to the east. Just as Ethan and Jasper were lining up their first shots, a sound Ethan had never thought he'd hear again ululated through the humid afternoon. Ethan's grandfather had once demonstrated this sound for him. It chilled the heart. It rose from the throats of the hundreds of soldiers who dashed up the street to do battle. They roared the Rebel Yell. Ethan could not doubt whose army these bluebellies belonged to, regardless of their clothing.

Jasper gave Ethan a strange look. "Now I seen everything. It's jest like you said, Ethan."

As the Northern-clad Confederate soldiers streamed to the edge of town past Ethan and Jasper, the roar of gunfire drowned out the yell, and then all turned to bedlam as they reached the true Yankees. The Union soldiers didn't know who to shoot at. In the confusion, the fresh southern troops, clad in their spoils from the Harper's Ferry arsenal, pushed the invaders back across Burnside's Bridge and bought Robert E. Lee a draw as dusk thickened to night.

CHAPTER 33

Bethany West stared at endless repetitions of a leaf pattern set in squares that spread to the edges of her vision. They made no sense. She had been running through the rain, laughing and then she woke up here.

She was lying in a soft bed and staring at a stamped tin ceiling. A face loomed over her. Pleasant enough, with wide-set brown eyes and raven hair pulled back off the high brow, the face was nonetheless that of a stranger.

"Where am I?" Bethany did not recognize her own voice.

"God above, Missy, I thought you had passed."

Bethany tried to sit, but a river of pain flowed up through her body. She gasped.

"Now, don't you move, Missy. You been shot real bad. Your father's out tryin' to find Doctor Robert."

"Ethan?" she mumbled. Where was she? Hadn't she been with someone? Someone named Ethan? She remembered running through the rain, racing to a barn. Had she been dreaming?

"No," Emily said, misunderstanding. "He went for Doctor Robert. You lie still, now."

Beth stared at the pattern in the ceiling, following its repetitions over and over, trying hard not to scream.

* * *

"I ain't puttin' no more of this whiskey on yer bandages, Youngblood. You need it in yer stomach, not on yer head. Here, you drink this." Jasper handed Ethan his flask, then threw more branches on the campfire.

Ethan didn't argue. The liquor lessened the pain. Ethan had more than his fill of hurt. Since entering this body, he had felt nothing but agony. "You used my real name."

"What?"

"In town. You called me Ethan."

The campaign veteran stroked his beard. "Everything happened jest the way you said it would. Cain't deny it." They sat silent in the flickering firelight. Then Jasper said, "If you're Ethan, what happened to Cole?"

"Jasper, your friend died. He's gone on somewhere else. I just slipped into his body because it was available."

"Available? How can a man do such a thing?"

"You a religious man, Jasper?"

"Naw. Though I do use the Lord's name right frequent."

"We do have a spirit that goes on after our bodies die. I think we get born into a new life and we forget the old."

"How come you remember?"

"A fluke. I don't know why. Maybe because I didn't go through the shock of death to get here. I was prepared. I remember everything I did as Ethan."

"You have any of Cole's memories?"

"No."

"So, when you die, how'll you keep lookin' for yer wife?"

"I'll find a way. And I won't die. This body will."

"I must be as tetched as you 'cause I believe you."

"It won't be long, Jasper. I don't think I'll last the night."

"Nonsense. A man don't die from gettin' his nuts tore up."

"I've lost a lot of blood. And I'm not sure I want to go on as Cole. This body is pretty damaged. It may be better to move on."

"Sorry I got you shot. I'll miss havin' Cole around even if it ain't Cole."

"You didn't get me shot. Bullets were flying all over the place. I just got unlucky. Don't feel bad. I'm not really going to die. I'll just move on."

"You didn't make no deal with the Devil, did ya?"

Ethan started to laugh, but the pain stopped him. "No. No deals. Someday you'll understand how this works, Jasper."

From somewhere in the darkness behind them, the plaintive notes of a banjo rose from the murmur of voices and cooking. Unsure at first, the notes ascended slowly, but then the picker caught his rhythm and his fingers began the sweet, emotive melody, *Lorena.*

Ethan did not notice the start of the music, but halfway through the first refrain, he realized he knew this song and its sound struck deep into his heart. The cook fires, the soldiers, the war; it all suddenly felt so familiar. Without thinking, he said, "John Ford really knew what he was doing."

"Heh, Youngblood? What's that?"

Ethan looked up with a start. "Nothing, Jasper, just a movie director."

"A what?"

Dammit, I need to watch what I say.

"Long story." *Distract him.* "Who's playing the banjo?"

Jasper sat silent a few seconds, listening. "Yep, sounds like Jimmer. Told that boy if he wants to be carryin' extra weight, he should strap on another Colt, 'stead of that banjo." He cocked his head and listened. "Sure plays sweet, though."

At the start of the second chorus, several men joined in, raggedly following the banjo with gruff, out-of-tune voices. The picker slowed to let them catch up. Then through the inky depths, Ethan heard other voices raised. From across the Antietam. Yankee voices. He turned his head to be sure his ringing ears weren't playing tricks on him. Sure enough, from across the creek, a growing chorus took up the song. How could voices sound both mournful and joyous at the same time? As faceless soldiers joined the growing tide of sound, Ethan stared into the blackness. Eerie energy quivered through him.

A single alto soprano rose through the chorus, providing a rallying point for the other voices. The banjo thrummed at full volume and soon the night came alive with the dreams of men, far from home and the women they loved, but buoyed for this moment by the soulful romance of a song. Lorena was the wife, the mother, the lover for whom they hoarded scraps of paper and to whom they scrawled notes with pen and ink if they could afford it, with charcoal from the cook fires if they couldn't.

The last strains of music swelled up to the pearly clouds that fought to cover the moon. When the song ended, the night seemed more silent than before as if every man held his breath, hoping the banjo picker would break into the chorus once more.

A gruff voice broke the silence. "Private, you play that damn song one more time, you're on report." Men groaned all through the camp.

Jasper cackled. "Captain Tipton. Gave standin' orders not to play *Lorena*."

"Why not?"

"Last time the kid played it, three hundred men got so homesick they deserted." Jasper picked at his teeth with a stick. "If Tipton had half a brain, he'd send Jimmer down to the edge of the creek and have him play so's more of the Yanks could hear. Might even the odds for tomorrow."

"Jasper, there won't be any tomorrow. This battle is over." The nearby fire crackled as a log settled, sending up a column of exploding sparks. "Do yourself a favor and get out of this army."

"It's all I got, Cole, er, Ethan. I'm gettin' old. Cain't start a career now can I?"

Ethan pondered for a minute. "You said you were a forty-niner?"

"Yeah."

"Find gold?"

"Hell, yeah. Had a damn good claim up near Grass Valley in California."

"So, why aren't you rich?"

"Poker. Young jackass that I was, I bet to an inside straight. Lost the whole she-bang. Other feller lives in a big house in 'Frisco on Nob Hill now."

"Jasper. There's gold *here*."

"Here? What are you talkin' about? Ain't nothin' here 'cept flies and horseshit."

"It's not as thick as in California, but it's here. From this area all the way down to Washington. A few years from now, someone will sink a big shaft just a mile or two north of Georgetown. Couple hundred thousand ounces will come out of that mine."

The older man's eyes glowed like hot coals. "You feverish, Ethan?"

"Don't take my word for it. Find a stream in the morning. Make like you're washing your mess kit. Pan the bottom. You'll see black sand. Go deeper and you'll find flake gold. Real fine, but it's there."

Jasper's brow creased. "Only somebody who found him some gold would know about the black sand."

"Stop fighting and go find the gold, Jasper. Nothing you do will change the outcome of this war."

Firelight danced across the bearded face. Jasper's sharp eyes stared at the coals long after Ethan fell asleep.

The next morning, Jasper tugged Ethan awake in the half-light. "You sweet bastard. You was right!" Jasper held a piece of wet denim. "Lookee here." Against the dark blue background, a dozen fine flakes of gold converted the dawn's cold light to noon.

Ethan could not believe he still survived. Every part of his body ached. As he rolled over to look at Jasper's find, he felt like retching. But he had little in his stomach to lose. Clenching his teeth, he squinted at Jasper's gold and struggled to sit. He said, "You let anybody else see that and the war will end right here. Soldiers from both sides will get gold fever and Lee and McClellan can finish it with a game of chess."

"Not a bad idea."

"Yeah." Ethan leaned forward.

Jasper carefully folded his rag and tucked it into a rear pants pocket. "You feelin' any better this mornin'?"

"No."

"Want breakfast?"

"No!"

"Well, don't start spittin' like a wet cat this early in the day. I jest asked."

"I'm angry because I didn't die."

"Then maybe you're gonna make it. You heal up and you'll have a pretty decent young body. Jest won't be no family man." Jasper cackled for the first time that day.

Ethan looked up. "You're in good spirits."

"Certain metals do that to a body. Yes, they do. This time I won't lose my claim. This time..."

"This time what?"

"I'm gonna have a house. With a bathtub. A big damn bathtub and all the hot water I ever want. I'll take a bath every day and I'll go to the barber shop and sit in a barber chair and I'll get a shave. Every day. And I'll have new clothes. I'm sick of bein' filthy. Tired of lookin' like a beggar."

"That's your dream?"

"Damn sure!"

"It's a good dream."

All around them, men packed their belongings and moved southwest to a rallying point.

"What's happening, Jasper?"

"Lee's movin' us around in case the bluebellies attack, but he's pullin' equipment back toward the Potomac in case we have to get out fast."

"Why aren't you packing?"

"You and me's gonna get lost. You cain't travel in your shape anyway."

"What's your plan?"

"Let's jest say I found a place to hole up and we're takin' yer advice."

CHAPTER 34

The pain was real. The stiffness of the sheets was real. And that stench of rotting meat was more than real. Bethany felt sure she was losing her mind.

In her dream, she ran through rain. A man chased her. She laughed and laughed knowing her destination was a hayloft. Then, she felt the prickling warning of a lightning charge building. The bolt sliced through her, searing and crackling and blue. She couldn't even scream as she twisted out of her body and blinked into nothingness. But at the last instant, she felt the man inside her head. With that same demanding intimacy as lovemaking, somehow she felt him within her and around her. He reassured her and then she twisted again, this time out of the nothingness and suddenly here.

Where was here? Had she really been running through a rainstorm? And why was she dreaming about lightning when she had a hole in her belly?

The door of her room opened and a thin man with long fingers entered. He wore a tan cotton smock with large patch pockets and carried a black leather bag. He looked about forty-five. "Hello, Katherine. How are we feeling today?"

"*We* are not feeling anything. *I* am feeling lousy. Who are you?"

He smiled. "Oh, that game again?"

"What game?"

"Pretending you don't know anybody? Not even your parents? Haven't they been through enough, Katherine?"

She didn't protest this time. Let him call her what he liked. Whatever mystery needed unraveling, she could unravel it later. "Humor me. Could you just say your name?"

He smiled again. His blue eyes crinkled as he pushed his graying blonde forelock out of his face. "My name is Robert. Doctor Robert Forester."

"Thank you." She turned her head toward the open window. "What is that killer stench?"

"Ah, it's the bodies, rotting in the sun."

"What bodies?"

"From the battle. Thousands of them out there. It'll take weeks to bury them. Would you like me to close the window?"

"Yes, please." Bethany could make no sense of his answer.

As Doctor Robert returned from the window, he lifted her covers. "I need to examine you."

"What happened to me?"

"You were shot. Do you remember it?"

"No. I woke up in this bed. How bad is it?"

"Not as bad as I first feared. The bullet must have been spent. It went through the front of your abdomen and lodged, ah, well, inside you."

"Inside where?"

"Well, in the, ah, chamber where babies are made." His pale skin suddenly splotched with pink.

"It's in my uterus?"

"Ah, yes, it was. I removed it while you were unconscious."

"How long was I out?"

"Quite some time. I've been here several times in the past few days, but you may not remember. You were delirious."

"Robert, how long have you known me?"

He chuckled as he removed the dressing on her stomach. "I delivered you."

She sucked in her breath as he probed her abdomen. "I'm sorry," he said. "There's some inflammation around the wound, but that's to be expected. The stitches are holding nicely."

As he began to re-dress the wound, Bethany fell back on the pillow, suddenly very tired.

These people, this place, all so primitive. Was all she knew a delusion? Had she dreamed a world with flying machines, and cappuccino, and electricity? A headache built in the back of her head as she felt increasingly confused.

"So, you've known me all my life. Do I seem different to you?"

"You've had quite a shock."

"But do I seem myself?"

"No."

"Thank you. I was beginning to think I was retarded."

"Retarded?"

"Yes. Underdeveloped mental faculties. You know what I mean?"

"Yes."

111

"Robert, what year is this?"

"My dear..."

"What year is it?"

"1862."

She shook her head and blinked. "My God, Abe Lincoln is President."

"That's very good. Your memory is coming back. It's all a matter of time. What else do you remember?"

She tilted her head up. "I don't remember anything about this place. That's just history."

"History?"

"Oh, Robert, that woman who says she's my mother, she says we're in Sharpsburg, Maryland?"

"Yes."

"I got shot in the battle?"

"Yes."

"This is madness. I don't belong here. This must be a dream."

"I assure you, it's quite real." He finished tying a bandage around her abdomen. Then he placed his hand on her forehead. "Your wound is healing and the fever is gone. You're making progress, young lady."

"This was McClellan and Lee faced off across Antietam Creek?" She said the words, unsure where they came from.

"Yes."

"What's the date?"

"September twentieth."

She grappled with a memory just out of reach. An event. Suddenly she had it. "Has Lincoln issued the Emancipation Proclamation yet?"

"The what?"

"It hasn't happened yet?"

"I don't know what you're talking about."

She nodded and stared straight into Doctor Robert's eyes. "You watch. Within the next couple days, Lincoln will declare the slaves in the Confederacy free. It will be called the Emancipation Proclamation."

"This is absurd."

"Perhaps." She closed her eyes, not knowing quite why she had told Doctor Robert such a tale.

* * *

Three days later, on his daily visit, Doctor Robert had a queer expression on his face as he entered Bethany's room. He did not say hello as was his custom. He set his bag on a chair and stared at her.

Seeing his face, Beth said, "What happened?"

"The slaves were freed. Just like you said."

"And you want to think it's coincidence."

"What other explanation is there?"

Her thoughts swirled. For a moment she had felt triumph, but she didn't know why. All the evidence around her – the texture of the sheets, the pain in her belly, the rippled glass of the windows – was no dream. The undeniably sharp details of reality pricked at her mind. Yet she had visions of another place. Each evening when she closed her eyes, she felt the vertigo of a lurching ship in a stormy sea. Other scents and sights and sounds coalesced into vivid images that she also could not believe were dreams. She lived her sleeping hours in one life, and woke to a face that was not her own.

"Katherine, are you all right?"

She stared vacantly. "I have no idea."

CHAPTER 35

"I think they all got kilt when them damn guns opened up on the house. Ain't nobody been around for days." Jasper pulled the barn door closed.

Ethan said, "Part of the main house is standing. Maybe there's a bed."

"Youngster, eventually someone will come around and we don't want to get caught in the house. Down here, it ain't luxury, but it's safe. Ain't much chance they'll ever find us. Beggars cain't be choosers."

They holed up under the floor of a barn. It had been designed for cattle with gapped floorboards to allow the cow manure to be swept off the main floor and collected in the lower level for use in the fields. No cattle had lived in this barn for years, though the sub-level still held the odor of manure. Ethan and Jasper cleared a corner and filled it with straw to hold their warmth at night. Only four feet high, the crawl space provided better shelter than the damp cave where they had slept the first few nights.

Jasper spread out the results of his "hunting" expedition. "Got them a nice root cellar. Enough to last all winter." He'd brought carrots and apples and a fat slice of cheese. He also set in the corner two pistols, a bag of shot, and two bags of black powder.

"You're building an arsenal, Jasper."

"Cain't have too many weapons. Got 'em scattered around in case of trouble."

Jasper dove into the food, but Ethan munched half-heartedly on a carrot.

"Still feelin' poorly?"

"I have a fever. My wounds are festering. I'm a mess."

"Cain't pull through if you don't eat."

Ethan stared into the gloom under the joists and then settled into the straw. He closed his eyes and thought of the place he had started from – the infinite place through which he had searched to come here. Time melted away and Ethan hovered at the brink of that place. He could see it, sense it, but he could not plunge into it. Without Memnon to free him, he remained stuck in this body. Until it died. But then what? Would he once again be able to hold himself together through

114

the chaos of death? He had been here a long time, longer than his other jumps. Did he still have a body alive back in his own time?

"Doze off?"

"No. I was trying to get out."

"Out?"

"Of this body."

"Why you want to die?

"I don't want to die. I want to move on. I'm not getting any closer to Bethany this way."

"Youngblood, why are you in such a hurry? If you can really do what you say, then you have all the time in the world."

"I'm in horrible pain, Jasper."

"In a couple days, you'll either get better or worse. If you heal, you'll have a much better chance of findin' your wife if you have money. Lots of money. If you know where the gold is, you'll have lots of money. Why don't you jes' hang on and stop lookin' fer the easy way out? You may be closer than you think."

Ethan blinked at the shadowy face hidden in its cloud of beard.

Then he reached for a piece of cheese.

* * *

Ethan slept fitfully through the early night and woke to the steady wheeze of Jasper's breathing. Ethan rolled against the rough planking of the wall and peered through the cracks at a sliver of Milky Way. Pain made it difficult to sleep, but something else nagged at him. Like a voice carried on the wind, a rising, falling, intermittent *something* danced just beyond Ethan's grasp as if he were about to remember a dream.

She's here.

He wanted to reach out his senses, see if he was in the right place, the right time. But without Memnon, he didn't seem able to wander out as far as he had done in the lab.

Ethan dug deeper into the straw. He closed his eyes and visualized Beth's face, concentrated on her unique energy. Again he heard something like a distant voice, some vague message he could not understand. Like a ham radio operator trying to tune in a signal from the other side of the globe, Ethan focused on the signature energy of the woman he loved. She seemed closer than ever before.

* * *

The grass felt cool and soft against her back. The blue sky had a tinge of pink cloud. A face loomed above her and blotted out the sky. Chocolate brown eyes came close and she lifted her head to kiss him. His hand stroked her naked flanks and suddenly she could not get enough air into her lungs. She wrapped her arms around his neck more tightly and pulled him closer. Tiny spears of pleasure shot through her in anticipation as the weight of his body settled onto her. She closed her eyes and reveled in the feel of him, the sweet smell of his skin. She wanted him now and nothing else in the universe mattered. Now.

She awoke with a start and became instantly disoriented, floating in a black place. In panic, she reached out around her. Cloth. She felt cloth, not skin. Through the window a star stood as a single spark against the sooted background of space. Where was she?

Her wake-panic subsided. The pleasant remnants of the dream orgasm still washed through her. That man. She felt a deep connection, a complete familiarity with her dream lover. The touch of his hands left a lingering sensation, one she had felt many times before and wanted to feel again. A shiver ran through her, but not from the chill of the room.

Am I losing my mind?

She watched the single star framed in the window. Was it as lonely as she?

Beth watched it until the gathering light of dawn snuffed it from the heavens.

CHAPTER 36

Two gunshots boomed through the woods, followed by a plaintive screech that, once heard, could never be forgotten: the sound Ethan had found most horrible at the battle at Burnside's Bridge – the sound of wounded horses.

"Christ Incarnate," Jasper muttered and pushed on through the red and gold kaleidoscope of falling leaves. Ethan tried to keep up, but pain kept him to a slow walk. The wounds between his legs had healed over, but the internal damage was still mending. The left side of his skull had a narrow line of scab that ran from front to back. He still got severe headaches, but intermittently. Ethan fell behind as he picked his way carefully around rocks and decayed logs over which Jasper nimbly jumped. Soon he could no longer see his friend in the shifting late-afternoon palette of shadow and light. A steady breeze sailed tiny color-kites across Ethan's path and rustled the treetops in the gentle shurring sound unique to autumn.

Ethan had the sudden urge to lay down in the leaves and look up at the sky the way he had as a child. He didn't want to know what was screaming ahead. He didn't want to see the person who had fired those shots. But he forced himself on in the general direction Jasper had taken.

Four more shots rang through the crisp October air. Ethan's reverie gave way to urgency as he pushed his body to go faster, despite the pain. Ahead, the trees cleared where a dirt road, no more than a cart track, cut through the woods. On the road two saddled horses lay in heaps, one motionless, the other raising its head and screaming in panic and pain as it feebly tried to get to its feet. A third horse stood fifty feet into the trees, its hide twitching. On the muddy track near the horses, two men lay in broken clumps. Amidst the carnage scuttled a tiny rag-covered figure, now hunched over one of the dead men, methodically going through his pockets.

At Jasper's approach, the rag-thing stood to its full height of less than five feet and lifted a revolver at Jasper, cocked the hammer. Though child-sized, the creature had a man's face with patchy black whiskers and sideboards, shadowed under a wide-brimmed brown hat. The paw of a full-grown man held the revolver.

Ethan panicked as Jasper walked right up to the specter. "Ain't had much schoolin', have you, runt? Never learnt to count to six? Yer gun's 'bout as empty as yer head. Cain't say the same fer yer pockets, though, you thieving little shit-for-brains." Jasper drew and cocked his Walker in one motion. Ethan hurried to close the distance.

The runt pulled the trigger of his revolver, producing only a loud click. With amazing speed, he hurled his empty revolver straight at Jasper. Caught off-guard, Jasper got four pounds of metal square in the forehead. He went down instantly.

Ethan approached and the filthy dervish in rags glanced from the gun on the ground next to Jasper back to Ethan. Instead of trying for the weapon, he lunged, catching Ethan by surprise. It looked like a punch, but at the last instant, Ethan saw the glint of metal. He ducked and turned and the runt's fist and the knife it contained swept past Ethan's face with only an inch to spare. Ethan yanked his revolver out of his waistband just in time to use it like a sword to parry his attacker's backhand swing. Then Ethan got a solid grip on his weapon. In a blur, he cocked the hammer and pulled the trigger, barely aiming. The runt's knee exploded in red mist and he toppled to the leafy earth. His hat flew off and the young face turned up in astonishment, as if the last thing the robber could imagine was that one of his victims would fight back.

The bandit clutched his knee and began to cry. Ethan lowered his revolver and glanced toward Jasper who was wobbling to his feet. The veteran bent down for his Walker, then hobbled over to the screaming horse. Jasper aimed and shot the suffering animal through the brain. The horse went still, a tendril of steam rising from its open mouth. Jasper shuffled toward Ethan, as the bandit's crying rose in volume.

"Jeeesus Christmas, listen to that caterwauling'."

"Jasper, you all right?"

With his left hand, Jasper rubbed at a spot on his forehead that was already swelling. "I'll live, but afore long, ever' damn squirrel in these woods will be chasin' me to get the walnut on my head."

Ethan pointed with his revolver. "What should we do with him?"

"Only one thing to do with a mad dog." Jasper hobbled up to the bawling young man, cocked his revolver, and shot

118

him between the eyes. The runt groaned and fell back. His last lungful of air spluttered wetly out of his mouth and he lay still.

Ethan's face twisted. "That was pretty cavalier."

Jasper squinted at Ethan. "If what ye been sayin' is true, then ain't no need for regrets. I jest helped this little bastard move onward. Mebbe a mite sooner than he planned, but he had to go sometime."

Jasper surveyed the scene and shook his head. "Just look at this mess. All because of one greedy little bastard." Jasper knelt beside the highwayman and searched him. "He got two pocket watches, a wedding ring, and a handful of silver coin. For this he killed two men and two horses. Damnation! It's trash like this what cut the throats of wounded men after a battle jest to rob 'em."

Jasper stood and fired a round into the robber's chest.

"He's dead, Jasper."

"I know, but my hate ain't dead. This one I'd gladly kill twice. I look forward to meetin' him in hell." Jasper scrutinized Ethan. "You okay? Did he cut you?"

"No."

"Thank the Lord for small favors."

"What should we do?"

"We take their guns, grab that bastard's horse, and skedaddle."

* * *

A mile down the dirt track, they rounded a turn and saw a knot of people huddled at the side of the road. Upon hearing the horse, a small boy ran into the road, oblivious to the mud, and raised his hands. "Buckra, oh, Buckra, please help Gramoo."

The child grabbed Jasper's arm and pulled him to the site of the commotion. As Jasper approached the group, they stood. If the burlap fabric of their clothes and the way they looked mainly at the ground didn't tell him they had been slaves, the use of the all-purpose "Buckra" in addressing whites certainly did. "What you darkies doin' so far north?"

The taller of the two men, a muscular man in his twenties, with skin like obsidian and teeth as bright as Carrara marble, looked straight into Jasper's eyes and said, "We free."

"I know that. But how did you get so far north?"

The young man glanced suspiciously at the wizened old man who supported himself on a stout club of pine. A

119

thousand tiny fissures cracked the old man's skin. From under bushy white brows, his eyes seemed unfocused as they moved in Jasper's general direction. Jasper stepped closer and saw a bluish cast across their surface. Cataracts. "There are people who help travelers such as ourselves. Help us get North." The old man had a dignified voice, quiet, but firm.

A round moon of a face peeked from behind the younger man. She tugged at the man's arm. "Ask him, go on, ask him."

Jasper's eyes wandered to the prone form behind the little group. "Ask me what?"

Pride wrestled with grief across the young man's face, but finally his mouth moved. A rumble of voice said, "My wife's grandmother. Done keeled over. Y'know how to hep her?"

Ethan gingerly descended from the back of the horse where he'd been riding sidesaddle. "Jasper, let's have a look." Ethan stepped forward and the young man stood aside. Ethan knelt next to a shriveled woman whose body seemed lost in the blankets draped over her. Her tiny face showed pain, eyes screwed shut and mouth clamped in a tight line. Thin wisps of white hair stuck out from under a brown woolen cap scrunched down over the old woman's ears.

Looking up, Ethan said, "What happened?"

The old man replied, "My Janna felt poorly all mornin'. We had to slow down. Then she said her teeth and her arm hurt. We stopped for a while and she laid down. She let out a cry and then passed out."

"How long ago?"

"Half hour."

Ethan lowered his ear to the woman's face and felt a faint puff of heat as she exhaled. "Shallow breathing," Ethan muttered. He pressed an index and middle finger under the old woman's jaw, back near the ear. "Faint pulse." Ethan gently lifted an eyelid, saw a dilated brown pupil.

Ethan looked up over his shoulder at the expectant group that had closed in around him. "Anything like this ever happen before?"

The old man spoke. "Ever now and again she gets faint. Says she cain't catch her breath."

"You her husband?"

"Yes, sir. My name is Ezekiel."

"I'm not a doctor, but I think your wife has had a heart attack. I'm sorry."

"Will she live?"

"I don't know."

Ethan and the family knelt around the old woman. Ethan knew he could walk away, but something drew him toward this woman. He felt the need to help, perhaps to expiate some of the horror he'd contributed to at Burnside's Bridge.

Ethan checked the old woman's pulse. It grew progressively weaker.

Ethan placed his fingertips on the old woman's forehead and closed his eyes, aware that the spirit inside this ancient body clung to its anchor in fear and confusion. As the body failed, its panic increased.

Ethan tried to cut through her scattered thoughts, to let her feel his presence. Her eyes opened and the old woman sucked in a gurgling breath.

The two black men rose and stumbled back a pace, their eyes fearful. The young woman fell back and scrambled to gain her footing as the little boy clung to her skirts, pleading, "Oh, Momma, Momma."

Ethan leaned forward in amazement. The old woman's eyes stopped dancing and stared directly at Ethan. The leather lips moved. No sound came out. They moved again and this time the outflowing breath formed a whisper that said, "Hep me."

Ethan leaned closer, his face only inches from the woman's. Jasper scrambled closer to hear.

Ethan said, "Janna, don't be afraid. There will be no pain and you will be freer than you ever thought possible."

"I hear de wind."

"Let it take you. Think of your family and remember all the things you have done in your life. Concentrate. Try to hold your thoughts together. I promise, you will go on and on. You will not die. You have nothing to fear."

Her wizened hand crawled from under the blankets and tried to grasp Ethan. He wrapped his larger hand around her cold fingers. With all his energy, Ethan projected his mind toward her and tried to show her that inner spirit that illuminated him as it did her. In his mind he said, "You see? I have done this too. I have lived other lives. You can too. Just don't be afraid. Let it happen and you will be able to see your family again."

Though Ethan sensed her bewilderment, her struggles diminished.

121

A faint smile dimpled the wrinkles around the mouth. Then the voice, like the rustle of leaves, said, "I see a faraway place."

The granddaughter and her son cowered against a maple trunk ten feet away. In a hysterical voice the young woman hissed, "The debil ketched her."

Ethan said, "Go there now while you can control your thoughts. If you wait, everything will start moving so fast you'll get confused. You may not be able to remember who you are."

Tears streamed down the old man's face as he approached and knelt over his wife. One tear fell onto the dark cheek of the old woman. In a voice as quavering as if it came up from a well, her husband said, "Oh, Janna, I wanted you to see the North. I wanted you to see a different kind of life."

The woman's head rolled back and forth an inch. "Don't be sorry, Ezekiel. You got me free."

The old man's hands cupped the withered face. "Don't go, Janna. Please."

"I see it. I see it."

She closed her eyes and her weak grip on Ethan's hand relaxed. Ethan leaned over the woman's face again. He felt no breathing. The pain lines smoothed out. Ethan dug his fingers deep into the woman's neck in a vain attempt to find the carotid pulse. In his head, Ethan felt the burst of energy that signaled Janna had made the leap. He pursed his lips and stared at the old man. "She's gone. But she's not dead. You'll see her again."

The hazy eyes closed and the man lowered his chin to his chest.

Ethan pulled a blanket over Janna's face. *What makes me such an expert? I haven't even found my own wife yet.*

The granddaughter ran up and flung herself on the body and cried. Sobs racked her so hard it looked like she would jerk herself apart. Jasper put his arms around her and gently pulled her off the old woman as the dumbstruck family looked on.

She turned and clung to him like a child. Jasper led her to her husband whom she grabbed mindlessly, her face buried in his chest.

Ethan caught Jasper's eye and angled his head back toward the road. Jasper nodded and stepped toward their horse. He grabbed the reins and, to Ethan's surprise, led the animal right up to the old man. "Ain't got no shovel and this ground's too rocky to dig a grave. You take this horse, old timer, so's you can carry your wife 'til you can make a proper burial. He'll hold you and the little boy too."

The old man's fingers closed around the reins. His mouth hung open but he could not speak. Jasper left the group in tableau. "Good luck to you, now," he said as he walked away.

Jasper and Ethan hiked in silence for several minutes before Ethan said, "Why'd you give them the horse?"

"Think about it. How we gonna keep hidin' out with a horse? Unless we want to use it to get away from this place. But I don't think it's safe to travel far by road with all the troop movements, so it's no use to us."

Ethan said, "Thought you were a southerner."

"Yup."

"So why'd you help a slave family?"

Jasper squinted. "Ain't never owned slaves. Wasn't fightin' fer slavery."

"Then for what?"

Jasper cackled and shot a malicious grin at Ethan. "Fer target practice."

CHAPTER 37

"Yer gettin' awful restless lately, Youngblood. Must be on the mend. Fixin' to take a walk?"

"Yeah."

"Don't go far. I'm makin' biscuits."

"You sure it's safe?"

"Ain't sure of nothin', but I ain't seen a soldier in a week and I'm right sick of all this cold food. I'll keep the fire small and use dry wood so's I don't make no smoke."

"How long?"

"You git your tail back in an hour. It'll be dark soon."

Ethan emerged into the golden haze of the lowering sun. Fat red and orange maple leaves lay thick on the ground. A breeze shook loose a cascade of russet from a sweet gum tree. Everywhere, the shower of leaf fall seemed unsustainable in its excess. Yet it went on and on as Ethan gingerly pushed west into the woods.

Jasper was right. Ethan felt restless, but not in any way Jasper might suspect. As he lay suffering for weeks in the gloomy confines of the barn's sub-level, Ethan had tried to ignore Cole's damaged body. Ethan had run through his mind a thousand times the chain of events that had brought him to this time and place. He relived each millisecond he had spent with the fading essence of his wife as she was wrenched away by energies too powerful to comprehend.

At night, when all fell silent except for the faint scurrying of mice, more than once Ethan had sworn he could hear her voice in the distance. He felt her presence in this place.

Ethan walked carefully, legs splayed, amazed at how a vital young body could be reduced to near invalid status in so short a time. His muscles ached from the previous day when he and Jasper had encountered the highwayman. But without exercise he would not grow stronger. He pushed on.

He hiked for half an hour. His gait became smoother, his muscles loosened and didn't rebel as they had at the start. Yes, he thought, this body will do.

He heard the snicker of a horse and instinctively dropped to the ground. A voice cut through the darkening air. "No, no."

Ethan crawled to the edge of a tree-filled bowl where he saw three horses tethered to a fallen birch. At the bottom of the bowl three men lashed a fourth man's arms and legs to saplings leaving him spread-eagle face-up on the forest carpet.

Ethan crawled closer, confident that the breeze rattling the trees would cover his sounds.

"Taney, I hear a horse won't step on a man. You think that's true?" The speaker stood tall and muscular, with the white hair and pink skin of a lab rat.

"Well, *Mister* Hulse, my two dollars says it ain't so." Lean and dark, Taney rested both hands on his saddle pommel. His hair stuck out in oily spikes from under a flattened stovepipe hat.

"Well, let's just see." The albino strode to the edge of the clearing and grabbed the reins of his horse. "Hey, McCoy, you be the judge."

The third man stepped away from the struggling figure on the ground and sat on his haunches as the other two men mounted.

"Please, mister. I'm jes a supply clerk. I ain't done no fightin'" pleaded a young voice.

The albino, Hulse, rode his horse up next to the clerk. "I been listenin' to your sorry tales for twenty minutes, Reb. You're a lyin' sack of shit and the more you keep mouthin' the more I want to do ya."

"Honest, mister. I never done nothin' to hurt you."

"Well, somebody killed my brother over in Manassas and looks like you get to pay." He spat on his captive and rode off across the bowl. "Okay, Taney, I go first, then you go. If he's brained, you win." Hulse kicked his chestnut-red Morgan and the horse shot forward.

Ethan felt like he watched a train wreck. He didn't want to be there, yet he couldn't take his eyes away.

Hulse accelerated across the clearing and rode over the man on the ground. As soon as he passed, McCoy scurried forward. Horse and rider sauntered back to the body.

McCoy took off his hat and looked up at the other man. "Hulse, you crazy sumbitch. Ain't a scratch on him."

"You owe me two bucks, Taney," the white-haired Hulse shouted across the clearing. "Now you go. Maybe you can make it even."

The young man on the ground lay motionless and silent, except for tiny panic-puffs of breath whistling in and out of his nose. His mad eyes stared into the darkening sky. McCoy staggered back, his face wrinkled in disgust. "Oh, Christ, the kid shit his pants."

Hulse grinned and shouted, "C'mon, Taney, before it gets dark."

The thunder of hooves echoed through the clearing as Taney swept forward. As the cloud of dust and leaves boiled over the captive, McCoy jumped forward. Again he saw no evidence of damage. The blue eyes of the supply clerk stared straight up, unblinking. McCoy leaned over into the boy's line of sight. "Get hurt that time?" The boy's eyes focused and his head shook back and forth not more than an inch.

Taney and Hulse rode up to examine their results.

"Hey, ain't that a spot of blood on his leg?" Taney pointed.

McCoy fingered the stain. "Yeah, but it ain't fresh."

"Git out the money, Taney. Four dollars and I want it in silver."

Taney sneered. "Hellfire, that was too easy. This skinny kid ain't even a foot wide. Let's go again, but this time, we run over him lengthwise."

"Okay. Double or nothin'." Hulse leered down at the clerk. "Kid, I'm hopin' I lose this time. I break even and you, well, you just get broke." Hulse belly-laughed as he ran his horse across the clearing to join Taney.

Ethan had crept as close as he dared and huddled behind a thick trunk of white oak, twenty feet from the boy. The one named McCoy kneeled in profile to Ethan. Ethan gauged the distance. His instinct told him to get away, to go back to the barn and forget what he had seen. But another part of him couldn't allow this abomination.

Before he could talk himself out of it, Ethan hobbled forward, drew his pistol and aimed at McCoy. As he heard the clatter of hooves and saw Hulse speeding toward him, Ethan swung his aim toward the oncoming wall of muscle. An explosion went off at Ethan's right and he felt a piece of his coat pull away. Ethan shifted and returned fire at McCoy, but his weak muscles were not up to the task his mind had set. His shot went wide. An instant later, Hulse's horse smashed into Ethan and flung him six feet through the air.

Ethan landed in a painful heap, his vision blurred, his head ringing. He sucked in a breath as a revolver appeared inches from his face. Behind that he saw McCoy. Through the ground, Ethan felt hoof impacts. In a second, Hulse smiled down on him. "What have we here? Another Reb deserter?"

Pink eyes loomed close. In a voice so low, only Ethan could hear it, Hulse whispered, "Did you just drop from heaven? Just for me? Now I know there is a God."

A shiver ran through Ethan. Wind howled in his mind. Those pink eyes offered tunnels straight to hell. "Well, gentlemen, this is our lucky day. Let's line him up next to the little one over there." The albino's mad eyes seemed a discordant contrast to his calm voice.

* * *

Jasper found them the next morning. After hearing gunshots the previous evening, he had fruitlessly scouted until the night got so dark he couldn't see his own feet. Now in the cold light of dawn, he cursed himself for waiting so long to go after Cole.

As he cut away the ropes that held the boy and Cole to the ground, Jasper's bile rose in his throat. "What kind of animal does this?" He seethed at the sight of the broken bodies, the tattered bloody remnants of what had been two human beings.

Many hoofprints criss-crossed the area. Jasper ran his fingers along one particularly deep one. Perfectly preserved in the soft ground he saw an impression of a horseshoe that had a fingernail-sized chunk gouged from the trailing edge. Jasper burned the image of the unique print into his mind.

Jasper glared up into the gray dawn, his body trembling with rage. "Lord, I don't ask for much, but I'm askin' you to put the bastards that did this in my sights afore I die." Jasper had no shovel, so he hauled rocks from a nearby outcropping to cover the bodies. He worked until noon, then trudged back to the barn and sat in the gloom of the sub-basement the rest of the day.

CHAPTER 38

"Jesus, Dolci, do something!" Churchill screamed.

Bewildered, Dolci said, "We're in uncharted territory, Andrew."

Doctor Stewart acted as the calm center of the storm that swirled in the test lab. He applied defibrillator paddles to Ethan's chest, said, "Clear," and pressed the button that gave Ethan three hundred sixty joules of electricity. The heart monitor began beeping again, though not with precise regularity. "We can control this in the short term, but he's never been out this long." Stewart glanced at the wall clock. "Four hours. I'm worried about this erratic heartbeat. We need a different approach if he stays out much longer."

"What do you suggest," said Dolci.

Stewart said, "We should consider a defibrillator implant. He would get smaller, more controlled doses of electricity rather than these huge jolts every time we call a code. Less damage to his nervous system."

"Can you do it?"

"I'm not board-certified in cardiology. I think we should have him transported to Johns Hopkins right away."

Churchill grabbed Stewart's biceps. "Can *you* do it?"

"Technically, yes. Ethically, no."

Churchill pulled Stewart away from Ethan's bed and into the hall. "How much will your ethics cost me?"

"Look, I..."

"Just give me a number."

CHAPTER 39

Leaving Cole's body felt like standing naked in a howling hurricane as the forces of the universe tried to rip him asunder, to spread his energy across the stars, to push him to entropy. It went on and on as Cole's body died.

Then suddenly, Ethan launched into the ether and serenity filled his thoughts. He had all the time he would ever need to do whatever he wanted to do. He stayed in the no-place and assessed himself. His thoughts and memories remained whole, his awareness clear. Somehow, he had done it again.

Ethan sensed the tenuous link to his own body. Like a rubber band stretched to its maximum length, his connection tugged at him to return. Should he succumb to that pull?

How am I doing this? Am I existing in more than one place at the same time?

His mind filled with contradictions.

Do I have to return to my own body? If it dies, what happens to me?

Were cause and effect necessary parts of the equation, or just an illusion?

Ethan again faced the perplexing question of how he could know two different histories: one in which Cole died in September of 1862 and one in which he died over a month later. Couldn't only one event be true? Yet Ethan knew both existed.

Or did they? Was one a real event and the other merely an idea? Or did they exist in different planes of existence, different universes so close in detail they could not be told apart?

Ethan could not see how to prove either theory.

Was he a tiny fish in a big ocean, responding to that which already existed all around him, or was he changing what existed? If he could make small changes in the universe, then could he make big changes?

Ethan realized he had caught himself up in the symbology of thinking, using the limited context of physical existence to interpret his experiences. But he had caught glimmers of something else outside comfortable frames of reference. He tried to relax, to let this new information come to him without pushing it for meaning.

He thought of existence as the part of a magician's act that an audience saw. The audience was unaware of the stage hands and the mechanisms that brought about the illusion. For the first time, Ethan began to see behind the curtains and under the props.

Ethan could now cross vast distances, millions of light years from star cluster to star cluster. It had always seemed so huge. Yet, Ethan saw that it was all connected, part of the same thing. Distance really did not exist. The universe existed as an enormous system, expanding exponentially, yet all the same interacting organism wherever one looked. Stars, planets, matter, and energy were merely the tools, the stage props. Behind and under all that existed the magician's art for making something out of nothing.

He sensed something disturbing. He could not pinpoint it, but somewhere out there was chaos and an indefinable force that terrified Ethan.

Am I touching God?

Suddenly, Ethan had an irresistible urge to make sure of his anchor. He needed to return to his own time, his own body.

He thought of where he had been. Like a gopher sticking his head above ground and getting his bearings after hours in the dark, Ethan found the place he needed to be.

CHAPTER 40

The launch team kept Ethan in bed for three days, subjecting him to dozens of tests as they tried to determine if he had permanent damage. Ethan let them talk and explain, but he didn't care at all what they said. He only wanted his next dose of Memnon. It mattered nothing to him that he now had a defibrillator in his chest.

The first time Ethan had told Angie about traveling in time, she laughed. But when he predicted the correct Baltimore Orioles scores three days in a row, she became a believer.

Ethan had struggled with the decision to expose her to this information, but he needed someone to talk to about what he was experiencing and it couldn't be Churchill's launch team. He needed help in sorting out his thoughts, not having his brain picked over.

Today, after Angie joined him for lunch in the quadrangle, Ethan turned strangely silent.

"What's disturbing you, Ethan?"

He told her about Antietam. "The men I helped to kill. I was terrified that I'd change everything in the future. But I get back here and nothing is different. At least not as far as I can tell. I wonder if I've come back to a parallel universe."

"Or maybe your fears were overblown?"

Ethan shook his head slowly back and forth. "I once read a science fiction story where a time traveler killed a butterfly far in the past. When he returned to his own time, some of the words in his language had changed."

"So you thought you'd thrown off the course of history?"

Ethan nodded. "Yes."

"That's fiction, Ethan. Think about it. That's the theory that everything is so interconnected that the slightest twitch has a consequence. But don't forget about entropy. All energy turns to heat and sifts away to become background static in the universe. I think most events also become background static. Let's say that butterfly was to have been eaten by a bird five seconds later. Its death would have no impact. Or it lived another week and then fell into the underbrush. What would that matter? Only if that butterfly flew in front of Wilbur Wright and gave him the idea to fly would it have been

131

important. Or if it flew *into* his eye and caused him to crash."

"But men aren't butterflies," Ethan said.

"There are several ways to think about this. First, maybe the reason you see no change back in this time is that those men would have died anyway. Maybe at Gettysburg or some other battle. No net effect. Second, let's face reality. Most people's lives are not important. Yes, one of those soldiers you killed might have had children if he hadn't been killed; yes, those children would have had children and so on down to the present. There would now be families that don't exist. But what is the effect of their non-existence? If they became farmers or merchants or whatever, unless they would have done something dramatic, historically, we'd never hear of them.

"And what of the men those soldiers in turn would have killed? You saved their lives. Those who should have been dead now have descendants in this time, but unless one of them has had a society-changing idea, how would it affect us? The fact that there has been no change proves that those descendants have done nothing significant and those who would have been alive also never did anything earth-shaking. Their living or dying hasn't changed our lives. Or, the time frame is too short to see what effect their existence or non-existence will cause. Maybe in a thousand years you would see an effect, but after a century and a half, nothing has changed. Most events are small events. Most people live small lives."

"You sound like an expert."

"I am. I've lived a *very* small life."

"Are you saying that if a man falls in the forest and nobody hears, then it never happened?

Angie chuckled. "In a way, yes. If you'd killed Edison's father, you'd know about it. But most people just settle into the entropy of history. They're just static."

"You're a real humanitarian."

"You'd never believe I started out as a philosophy major in college."

"What happened?"

"I realized it wouldn't pay the rent. I became a pragmatist and went into something tangible: nursing. Most people don't even get fifteen minutes of fame. And those who do make very little use of it."

"You don't think your son was important?"

She sighed. "Yes, he was important to me, but I've seen

the way friends and relatives have forgotten him. For whatever reason, they never mention him. Except in my mind, it's as if he never existed. It's sobering, but it's true."

Ethan said, "I've thought of a more frightening possibility."

"What's that?"

"What if there is no cause and effect? What if it doesn't matter what anyone does?"

"Sounds pretty existential."

"What if what goes around doesn't ever really come around?"

"Then good and evil don't matter? There's no karma?" Angie lifted her thick eyebrows.

They both sat in silence pondering the implications.

CHAPTER 41

"I want to know what you talk about," Churchill said.

"His farm. His wife before she died. Nothing earth-shattering."

"Angie, do you like working here?"

"Yes."

"Would you like to continue working here?"

"Don't threaten me."

"Then, don't bullshit me. What does West want from you?"

Ethan had told her this would happen. He had also told her to tell the truth. It would be easier to handle. "It's more about what I want from *him*." She sketched out the story of her son and husband and her hope that Ethan might be able to contact them.

"Hmm." Churchill leaned back in his chair. "Great story, but what did he give you last week?"

"What?" A chill ran through the young nurse.

Churchill picked up a folder off his desk, opened it, and tossed an eight by ten photo across the polished wood. "What did he give you?"

Angie examined the photo and her heart fluttered. It showed her under the tree with Ethan, her hand extended to him. Damn! She made a lousy spy.

"I'm waiting Mrs. Warner."

She noticed that she was no longer Angie. "He didn't give me anything."

"Have you ever been in a really nasty lawsuit, Mrs. Warner?"

"No."

"Well think about what your life will be like after I fire you and then sue you for trafficking in company secrets. I can pay lawyers to work you over for the next ten years. Imagine spending every penny you can ever earn or borrow to defend yourself against a rabid pack of shysters who just won't go away. Is that what you want?" Churchill's syrupy delivery belied the content of his words.

Angie Warner just stared at her tormentor. She had no idea what to say.

"I want you to tell me what he gave you. And any time

you speak with him I want to know what he says. Do you understand?"

Angie remained motionless.

Churchill opened the top drawer of his desk and extracted a single sheet of paper. "Here's your copy of some paperwork that's sitting in the personnel office. You're due for a nice raise, I believe. This goes into effect today if you decide to be reasonable. Can I depend on you to be reasonable?" His smile was like a fist in a silk glove.

When she did not immediately answer, Churchill added, "Annie is how old now, eleven? College right around the corner. So many expenses. Or maybe she won't be able to go?"

Angie's heart raced. This worm had used her daughter's name. What else did he know about her?

"Or the lawsuit. Think of having to sell your house, move into a little apartment to save money. But I'm sure your daughter will understand. Children can overcome anything if they are with their parents. But then, what if you're sent to jail for theft of company secrets? Who will raise the sweet little Annie? And what about the new arrivals?"

Angie squinted hard. "How do you know it's plural?"

"What kind of employer would I be if I didn't take an interest in my employees? I'm concerned about how you'll be able to afford three children. With twins on the way, I think you can use the extra income. Now, why don't you sign this and be done with it?" Churchill reached inside his jacket for his Cross pen. A momentary frown crossed his face when he didn't find it. He reached into his top desk drawer and pulled out another pen and set it on the sheet of paper that sat alone on his desk.

Angie took a deep breath, nodded, and reached for the paper. She knew when she was beaten. It happened so often, she had no trouble recognizing it.

CHAPTER 42

Churchill held the vial of Memnon and absently gazed across the lab. He didn't like being so dependent on West. One man could make or break him. This hadn't been a problem until West started this business of entering bodies. Was that just a story?

But something had changed. Up until this point, West had jumped through time with no complications. He brought back the information Churchill wanted and he woke up fine. But now? These heart problems seemed directly related to West's new endeavors.

Churchill had reviewed hours of West's tapes. What sounded like gibberish made sense if you gave credence to his claims that he inhabited bodies. And that stupid little nurse, she corroborated what West was doing, fantastic as it sounded.

Making a decision, Churchill reached into a cabinet for a syringe. He tore off the sterile packaging and charged the syringe with 25cc of Memnon. Without pausing to reconsider, he slid the needle into a vein in his forearm and depressed the plunger. Nervously, he waited for some change in his vision or his consciousness. Nothing happened. After five minutes, he left the lab. Maybe he needed a larger dose? He'd try that tomorrow.

CHAPTER 43

"She is with child," said Elizabeth Hawley, averting her eyes from her husband.

"What? Are you insane?" George Hawley thundered and rose from the table.

"It is true."

"That's impossible."

Elizabeth raised her eyes again. "Doctor Robert checked her. She is three months gone."

In a sudden reversal of position, Hawley complained, "That little trollop will ruin my name, ruin my business. Damn, woman, can't you watch your own daughter? Who's the bastard's father?"

"She says there is no father."

"She's protecting him." Hawley paced back and forth across the dining room floor. "Three months, you say?"

"Yes."

"Give or take a few days, 'twould put her sinning right about the time of the battle." He stroked his beard. "Had to be a soldier. She says there's no father because she'll never see him again. That little strumpet."

"George, she was in this house the whole time of the battle. And before. When we heard the Johnny Rebs were in Frederick, we kept her in the house, remember? That was a week before the fighting started. After she got shot she lay in bed a month. No man's been near her."

"I have enough trouble believing there was one Blessed Virgin. Is this supposed to be the *second* coming of Christ? You been yakkin' with those Greeleys, those Pope-followers down the road? Good grief, Elizabeth, a man had to get in her knickers sometime for this to happen."

"George, watch your mouth!" Elizabeth immediately put her hand over her own mouth, shocked at her words.

"It's not my mouth you should be worryin' about. It's those neighbors' mouths and the mouths in town. Their tongues will be a'twitch with this news."

"People have more to worry about, George. We're in a war."

The word "war" triggered a thought in George Hawley's mind. His eyes squinted as his right hand tugged at his chins.

"Only able bodied man young enough to interest Katherine is that Anspach boy. Billy is it? He's eighteen or nineteen. Father paid one of his hired hands to take the boy's place when ol' Abe's recruiters came sniffin' around. Didn't Billy come a'callin' sometime back?"

"When he heard she was shot. He came by a couple of times when she was doing poorly."

"Not been around lately though, right? He knows his handiwork would start to show."

"He's in Baltimore City doing business for his father."

"Damned convenient he's out of town when his crop starts sproutin'. He's the one, dammit, he's the one. I can feel it in my bones." George Hawley stormed across the dining room, down the hall, and up the stairs. He boiled into Katherine's room without knocking.

Bethany sat in a straightback chair near the window, a book in hand. She raised her head and her eyebrows.

"You little bitch. Couldn't wait for a decent man to propose to you in a decent way. Had to sneak off like a damn animal in heat. Well, I know it's that Anspach boy. Don't deny it."

"Who?"

"Don't try that with me. Now I know why you've been acting tetched in the head. You knew this day was coming. Thought you could make like some poor wretch who got taken advantage of? You got shot in the stomach, not the head. I saw through you from the first."

She remained silent, grown used to the tantrums of her stepfather.

"Yer precious Billy don't think enough of you to come forward and do what's right? No, he's off in Baltimore City where the whores is thick as flies. Gettin' his fill, I'll wager."

She fixed her calm, green eyes on George Hawley and with the sweetest of voices said, "How are you so familiar with the ways of the flesh in Baltimore?"

If it was possible for a face to explode, Hawley's would have. It turned hot red and his eyes pushed up out of their little pits of gristle. For two seconds his lips writhed like bloodworms in the sun, but no sound came out. "The nerve of you! Live under my roof and dare talk to me like that while yer whorin' up one end of town and down the other?"

He took a half-step toward her, but she remained in her chair and gazed peacefully at his livid face. "I don't know what

138

you're talking about," she said.

For a moment, Hawley teetered, ready to strike her, but disconcerted by her calmness. He calculated the price such rashness would cost with his wife. "Oh, you will, you little slut, you will." Hawley slammed her door so hard, dust dropped from the ceiling.

CHAPTER 44

Ethan struggled to rise to consciousness. He could barely open the eyes of this new body. He felt so weak that his eyes seemed the only things he could move. The bed under him felt soft and the down comforter over him smelled like it had recently been outdoors. The room, though not large, contained expensive furnishings: an oak chest-of-drawers with ornate brass pulls, a small bedside table with a lace doily and fresh daisies in a cut-glass vase.

"That Hawley girl got herself in a bad way," said the young woman in the maid's uniform.

"I heared she's got a bun in the oven," replied the older one, who had to be a nurse. Who else would wear a starched white hat with corners flaring out like the wings of a dove?

"I heared Mr. Hawley beat her with a strap till she bled, but she wouldn't say who the father was. Prolly some soldier wandered through. She always was headstrong."

If his new face had allowed it, Ethan would have smiled. These biddies were so involved in gossiping, they'd never even noticed this bugger had died.

"Headstrong? To let a soldier use you then be on his way? That's not headstrong. That's sheer crazy, Madge."

"Well. I hear she may be that too. Don't seem to know nobody around her. Says her name ain't Katherine Hawley. Why would she make up such a stupid thing?"

"Tryin' to make people think she's not in her right mind so's the baby ain't her fault."

Madge said, "I heared from their maid that in her sleep she says her name is Bethany."

Though the rest of the body seemed immobilized, Ethan's new ears worked fine. Suddenly, upon hearing Bethany's name, getting this body to move became very important to Ethan. He felt his heart begin to race. He needed to get their attention.

"Poor creature. Such a pretty girl. But she won't be much longer for these parts. This much scandal? If 'tweren't for the war, her father would have made her scarce already."

"Where's he sendin' her?"

Madge said, "Don't know. Prolly out west. Marry her off to some desperate rancher in the middle of hell-and-gone who

140

ain't had a woman in years and who don't care what she done long as she has a heartbeat."

"Would you ever do that? Marry off mail-order like that?" the nurse mused.

"Oh, Helen, why would any woman in her right mind do that?"

"It's somethin' to think about 'cause after this war, men are fixin' to be scarce. Unless you don't mind a few parts missin'."

Her eyes bright and her voice dripping with meaning, Madge, the maid, said, "Only one part really counts."

They both convulsed in laughter that they immediately tried to suppress, casting furtive glances at their master's wrinkled face. This only made them laugh harder. At the sound of their choking, Ethan managed a groan and was able to move his head. Madge caught the motion and elbowed Helen into silence. When they saw his eyes open, their laughter stopped as quickly as if their heads had been twisted off their bodies. He had eyes like a demon, a bloodshot mess, with no whites at all around the pupils.

"Mister Watson." The nurse pulled his hand from under the quilt and felt his pulse.

Jesus, Ethan thought, as he saw the wrinkled skin that barely concealed the blue veins of his hand. "Water," hissed out of his throat.

The nurse picked up a glass tumbler from the bedside table and inserted a glass straw between Ethan's lips. He took a short pull of water and found his voice. "Tell me about this girl" he croaked. The eyes of the two women went wide.

Helen, the nurse, said, "Mr. Watson, you should rest."

"I'll rest when I'm dead. Tell me about this crazy girl."

Helen recounted what she had heard on the streets and from Doctor Robert. When Helen repeated the name Bethany, Ethan became energized.

Ethan said, "I must get up."

Shock crossed Helen's face and she exchanged a glance with Madge. "Sir, Doctor Robert said you need bed rest. Your heart can't take a shock. Maybe next week you can sit up in a chair for a spell."

Ethan struggled to sit up. His heart beat in his chest like the wings of a hummingbird and a wave of dizziness washed over him. He took deep breaths and closed his eyes, tried to clear his mind of thoughts. Slowly his heart rate

141

dropped.

When he opened his eyes, the terror-stricken faces of Madge and Helen loomed only inches away.

To Helen, he said, "You the nurse?"

She nodded.

"If my heart stops, you get up here on the bed and you crouch on my belly and press on my sternum. With all your weight. Understand? You do it ten times and then check my pulse. If you don't feel it, press on my chest again. You do this for at least twenty minutes, until I either come back or you can't feel my pulse, you understand?"

"Sir, I ..."

"I know you think I'm crazy, but you can save my life if you do this. It squeezes my heart and makes it pump. I've seen it done. Now, will you do it?"

With eyes so widely open she had white all around the pupils, she said, "Yes, sir."

"So, get up here and show me how you'll do this."

Helen looked at Madge with such pleading in her eyes, the younger girl said, "I'm sure she understands, sir."

The bloodshot orbs fixed their energy on Madge. "You're doing it too." He redirected his baleful gaze at Helen. "Now pull back this quilt and haul yourself up here, nurse."

Gingerly the thin nurse pulled back the covers. She looked so confused, Ethan finally said, "Hike up your skirts and straddle me like you wanted to give me what-for."

"Mr. Watson, I..."

"Just do it."

Both women blushed deep red. Ethan walked them both through CPR until he was sure they could do chest compressions.

Bethany is here. These two women know her location. I just have to keep this old coot going.

CHAPTER 45

Billy Anspach had returned to his father's general store with a wagonload of supplies from the port of Baltimore and spent the afternoon unloading and inventorying the myriad products that could not be produced locally. When he finished, he settled behind the main counter and waited on customers. Seeing that all the new supplies had been stowed, Billy's father, Calvin, hugged the gallon jug of Irish whisky Billy had brought from Baltimore and shuffled the two blocks to their home. With Billy returned, Calvin Anspach could indulge his favorite pastime: rocking on the back porch and getting quietly drunk.

Sunlight slanting in low through the front display window told Billy closing time had arrived. He counted up the numerous coppers and the few silver coins, locked the back door, and put on his hat, thankful for the short distance home. Wind had blown up, the sky had cleared, and the temperature was dropping. With only a few days until Christmas, the weather had been unseasonably warm, but it now looked like the season would catch up to itself.

The bell above the front door jangled. George Hawley's bulk loomed through the entry. Hawley stamped his feet and the pine planking threw up small clouds of dust. "Goddamn cold out there. Like a witch's tit." His deep-set eyes focused on Billy. "Ye know a little about tits now, don't ya, boy? Git your share of tits in Baltimore City? Come home with a good case of the clap, did ya?"

"Sir?"

"Ye know what I mean. Feels like fire when yer pissin'? Man plants his root in ever damn furrow he sees, well, he pays a price someday."

"Mr. Hawley, I piss just fine."

"I jes bet you do, but the piper's fee's come due on yer dance. Yer eighteen ain't you, boy?"

"Nineteen."

"Old enough to be off warrin' instead of whorin'. 'Cept yer old man paid some dumb bastard to go in yer place, didn't he? How much blood money did it cost him, boy? I heard five hunnerd dollars. You think yer life is worth five hunnerd dollars?"

"Sir, I don't know how much my father paid, but it was all legal."

"Yer father bought you out of one mess. Now, tell me, have you thought about how much it's gonna cost to get out of yer mess with my daughter?"

"Sir?"

"Had so much skirt lately, you don't even remember, eh?"

"What *are* you talking about?"

"Either the next words out of yer mouth are to ask me for my Katherine's hand in marriage, or I will make you one sorry son of a bitch." Hawley glared. His protruding jaw ground back and forth.

Billy wanted to run out the back door and down the street and across the bare fields and to just keep running until there was no more light by which to see. "Mr. Hawley, Katherine and I are friends, but marriage is not something we've ever discussed."

"No discussion needed. You either do what's right or..."

"You're out of your mind. You think you can push me around the way you do everybody else? Get out of my store."

Hawley's eyes sank deeper into their sockets. "Then, I'm gonna plug ya, boy, the way you plugged my daughter, 'cept I'm gonna use lead. Yer bastard is gonna grow up without a pappy." Open-handed, Hawley slapped the young man's face. "I'll meet you in the meadow below Burnside's Bridge. Day after tomorrow at dawn. You be there, boy, or I'll hunt you down like the ruttin' dog you are and shoot you in the street."

A gust of cold air blew across the room, the door closed, and Billy Anspach found himself standing alone, the side of his face stinging far more than seemed proper.

CHAPTER 46

Frustrated that he occupied such a frail husk, Ethan spent most of his concentration to keep old man Watson going. Leaving the house to find Beth was about as likely as a trip to the moon.

Hearing the swish of cloth, he opened his eyes to see Helen, the nurse, enter the bedroom. Maybe twenty-five, older than the other one, Helen seemed to have more sense. Ethan made a decision. He couldn't leave the house, but Beth could come to him.

"Helen."

"I thought you were asleep, Mr. Watson."

"No, just thinking. Helen, bring me some paper and a pen."

She set down a stack of sheets and approached the bedside. Her cool hand rested momentarily on Ethan's brow. Her long fingers gently pressed against his neck. "Your pulse seems steadier. How do you feel?"

Ethan chuckled and Helen looked at him with alarm. "Helen, look at this old geezer. How do you think he feels? He's got one foot in the grave and the other one on ice. Other than that, he feels fine."

The nurse's hand went to her mouth and her hazel eyes opened wide.

"It's okay, Helen. You can laugh. Just get me something to write with."

She dropped her hand and Ethan saw her full lips parted in a big smile.

"You should do that more often. You have a pretty face. Don't be so somber all the time."

In complete consternation, the nurse left the room. Two minutes later she returned with a portfolio, a bottle of ink, and a quill pen. She helped her patient sit up in bed and placed two more pillows behind him. "How's that?"

"I promise not to croak in the next ten minutes."

That got another smile.

"Okay, Helen, I'll need some help with this." She opened the portfolio, revealing several pieces of heavy vellum. By folding the portfolio back, she made a writing surface that she set on Ethan's lap. She opened the ink bottle and dipped the quill pen into it.

Ethan watched in fascination as the antique process unfurled. Helen placed the quill in Ethan's hand and he made his first effort to write. The quill scratched and caught on the paper and his first word looked like Greek.

"Helen, stop letting chickens run through here. Look what they did." She flashed him a tentative smile and when he didn't bite her head off, she beamed.

"Are you okay, Mr. Watson?"

"I guess I'm not really myself today, Helen. Enjoy it while you can."

She reloaded the pen and wrote the name "Watson" across the page. "See? Don't press so hard, Mr. Watson. Let it glide across the page."

"Wish I had a ball-point about now."

"What?"

"Never mind." Ethan took up the quill and tried again. This time, the word that came out looked reasonably like the word he had intended.

"That's better."

"Give me a fresh sheet."

Ethan started over. It took almost half an hour for his weak hand to scratch out a message to his satisfaction. "Helen, please seal this in an envelope."

She folded the message and inserted it into one of the yellowed envelopes. Then she lit a candle and poured hot wax on the flap. She reached across the bed and took Ethan's left hand.

"Huh?"

"Your ring."

Ethan suddenly understood. He pressed his signet ring into the soft wax, leaving an impression that looked like a chess piece. The knight.

"Helen, I need for you to take this to Katherine Hawley. But you must give it only to her. You understand?"

At the mention of Hawley the nurse's sunny face eclipsed. "You mean go to the house?"

"Yes."

"I don't like that place, sir."

"Helen, go now before dark."

"I can't. Who will watch you?"

"Go get Madge. I'm feeling fine. You won't be gone that long. I promise to let only you save me next time my heart

146

stops. Okay?"

She pressed her lips together. She glanced out the window. With the sun almost down, fear of being at the Hawley house after dark goaded her to action.

After she left the room, Ethan could barely contain his anticipation. Would Beth come to him this evening? He was almost giddy from the thought.

He shook his head. Giddy? No, actually light-headed. The room tilted and splotches of darkness spread across his vision.

No, not now. Not when I'm this close to her.

With as much breath as he could muster, Ethan called, "Madge!"

Then he blacked out.

CHAPTER 47

The darkness had fallen quickly, as it did this time of year. Wind lanced under Helen's petticoats, raising goose bumps on her thighs. She increased her already brisk pace until she almost trotted, an uncomfortable feat in her high shoes. If not for the cold, she would have gone barefoot.

As she passed the damaged church at the edge of town, she felt marginally safer. She saw a few other pedestrians on the street and she slacked her pace so that she would not draw attention. After all, nothing was actually wrong. But her cheeks flamed red not merely from the cold. She cast a quick glance behind to make sure nobody followed.

What kind of animals did those Hawleys employ? It was one thing to flirt, but the way the hired hands had leered made her feel like a side of beef. Oh, they were thoroughly disgusting! She did not care how her patient might rant, she swore she would deliver no more messages to the Hawley farm.

Helen entered the Watson house through the rear door and stood near the wood stove to thaw. Several seconds passed before she heard thumping through the ceiling. She flew to the stairs and launched herself up them two by two. When she raced through the doorway into Mr. Watson's bedroom, she was not ready for the sight before her.

Madge perched on Watson's chest, dropping her weight onto him and letting out a terrified little sigh between compressions. She turned her panicked face to the doorway, and almost laughed with relief at seeing Helen. "Oh, please, Helen. I'm so scared."

"Keep doing what you're doing." Helen stepped up to the edge of the bed and leaned over. She pulled Watson's head back and elevated his mouth. "Okay, stop." Then she clamped his nostrils shut and covered his mouth with her own. Just as Watson had instructed, she blew into the old man. Again. Then without looking up, she said to Madge, "Now you go."

When Madge had finished, Helen again blew hard into the old man's lungs. They went on like this for several minutes until Helen said, "Stop." She placed her ear against her patient's chest. What was that? She held her breath to hear. Yes. She heard something.

She knelt at the side of the bed and examined Watson's

face. She licked one of her fingers and placed it under his nose. Yes, he was breathing. By himself.

"When did this happen, Madge?"

"Right after you left. He called. I been doing this ever since."

Helen had never seen the younger woman's face so pale. "You did well. You saved his life."

Madge got off the bed and threw herself into the nurse's arms, burying her face in the taller woman's coat. "I was so scared, Helen. I don't ever want to do that again."

"It's okay, Madgie. You go make us some tea and I'll watch him. You did real fine."

After the maid left, Helen removed her coat and draped it across the chair under the window. Then she sat on the edge of the bed and picked up Watson's hand to monitor his pulse. His flesh felt as cold as her own.

CHAPTER 48

Dearest Bethany,

I am near. Do not leave Sharpsburg or it may take years to find you. I know this may all seem confusing to you, but trust me. The lightning was not the end, merely a beginning.

Love, Ethan

P.S. It really is me. If you doubt it, I'll take the Buzz test.

By the single candle in her bedroom, she read it over and over again. How was this possible? The Buzz test?

Some part of her knew what that meant, but like a dream image, she couldn't pull it into full consciousness. And this name, Ethan. It sent a thrill through her, but she did not know who he was.

She examined every scrawling curlicue of each word in the note. This handwriting looked familiar, though shakier than she had ever seen it, but still with the distinctive curls and verticals that she dredged from memory. But again, though she had a piece of memory, she seemed unable to connect that piece with another to build a picture that made sense.

She heard footsteps on the stairs. Panicked, she blew out her candle and hopped back into bed. Her bedroom door opened and George Hawley entered, carrying an oil lamp. He stood next to the canopied bed, staring down.

"I know you're awake. I smell the candle smoke."

Forsaking subterfuge, Bethany sat up and stared at the bulky figure before her.

"Soon as I can make the arrangements, I'm sendin' you west to Nevada. Miners out there pay a pretty penny for mail-order brides. They don't really care if they're sluts. You'll start a new life there. You and yer bastard." He turned to leave.

"How can you do this to your daughter?"

He turned back. "You know you are not my daughter."

Bethany's face twisted in confusion.

"Don't play the idiot with me. Your act does not deceive me."

"How can you be so cruel to your own family?"

"Don't anger me, girl." He turned to the door, his outline silhouetted by the lamp. He muttered, "Whatever possessed me to marry that damn woman?" The door closed and

Bethany's room plunged into darkness.

She groped under her pillow and found the note she had received from a man named Ethan who was also a man named Charles Watson. She clutched the note to her bosom, thoroughly confused.

CHAPTER 49

Why am I early? This is insane, he thought.

The damp morning cold could not compare to the ice that sat in his stomach. Billy Anspach absently watched wisps of fog hover above the wet grass. The field shimmered with tiny gems that held the first sunbeams lancing through the bare trees and patchy mists.

Through the ground Billy felt the approach of horses before he heard them. Four Morgans of the distinctively chestnut-red Hawley line emerged from the trees and wound around the curving track that followed Antietam Creek. The commanding figure of George Hawley led three men whom Billy knew only by sight.

A hundred paces from Billy, George Hawley swept off his horse before it came to a full stop, moving with agility not usually seen in one so large. The three others also dismounted and one of them walked briskly toward Billy. When ten feet away, he said, "Mr. Anspach, I am Jason Weaver, Mr. Hawley's second. Where is your second?"

"What's a second?"

"I see." Weaver turned on his heel and returned to Hawley, who still had not looked at Billy. Billy heard Hawley's voice rise and watched him pound a fist into his other hand. Weaver returned. "Mr. Anspach, Mr. Hawley offers Cornelius Ethridge as your second. Mr. Ethridge has acted as second on quite a number of duels. Will this be satisfactory?"

"Uh, yes."

"Excellent."

In a blur, Billy chose his weapon from a carved cherrywood box that held two ivory-handled dueling pieces. Before Billy knew what had happened, Mr. Ethridge divorced himself from the Hawley entourage, set up a small folding table, and began loading Billy's pistol. Billy watched Ethridge measure black powder and pour it down the barrel, watched him push a piece of wadding down with the ramrod. Then Billy's eyes focused on the gray sphere Ethridge took from a metal canister. Ethridge set this pill of lead on the barrel's mouth, then covered it with another piece of wadding and pushed everything home with the ramrod. Ethridge then pulled back the hammer and set a primer cap on the nipple and handed the pistol to Billy. The metal now hung heavy from the end of Billy's arm.

Across the clearing, George Hawley threw off his riding cape. Billy blinked as he tried to focus on the big man. Hawley wore a gray tunic and pants barely distinguishable from the gray bark of the bare trees and the fog. Billy examined his own brown pants and dark blue jacket that sharply contrasted with the background. He cursed himself for not thinking of such things.

Cornelius Ethridge stepped close. "Have you ever dueled, Mr. Anspach?"

"No."

"That tall gentleman over there, Hamish Wallace, will act as referee. When he calls, both you and Mr. Hawley will assemble in front of him. He will place you back-to-back. Then he will instruct you to take twenty paces away from each other. He will then tell you to turn and fire. Aim and fire as quickly or as slowly as you choose. The duel is not finished until you both fire your pistols or one of you cannot continue. If neither of you is hit, and Mr. Hawley, as the aggrieved party, wants to continue, we reload and have another exchange. Any questions?"

"Which is better? Fast or slow?"

"It depends on your shooting, Mr. Anspach. Some take their time and aim carefully; some let fly quickly to keep from being hit first."

"And Hawley? What does he do?"

"It would not be seemly for me to say."

Wallace moved to the center of the clearing and stood alone. "Gentlemen," he called. In the still morning, his voice seemed unusually loud. Billy found his feet walking of their own volition until he stared up into the dark, haunted eyes of Hamish Wallace.

Wallace nodded to each man in turn and said, "Are we ready to start, gentlemen?"

"Of course, we're ready. Let's get things moving here, Wallace." For the first time, George Hawley looked at his opponent.

Hawley's eyes gleamed like an enraged feral hog, lacking any of God's higher attributes. Billy suddenly felt very small and very weak. He did not understand how he had come to be in this place.

The two men faced each other as Hamish Wallace's

voice droned through preliminaries. In those few seconds, Billy's toe touched something hard in the soft ground. Absently, Billy pushed his toe into the obstruction and uncovered a brass belt buckle. Throughout the area people had been finding strange tokens of the battle that had taken place three months earlier. Here lay a relic of some man's life, now completely forgotten. How much blood had seeped into this soil? Billy wanted to throw up, but he had nothing in his stomach.

Pointing at the belt buckle, Hawley said, "That'll be you soon enough, boy."

One second Billy was looking into the tunnels of hate that held Hawley's eyes, the next he was counting off his steps as Wallace's voice cut through the stillness. Somehow, when he heard twenty, he remembered to stop. Then time stretched and Billy became aware of everything around him.

The pungency of damp oak leaves rose from underfoot. Upstream, a heron's sharp kraaanking call reverberated. Antietam Creek, low now, burbled over smooth stones rimmed with ice. Red-winged blackbirds in low thickets along the shore rang their first metallic notes of the day.

The world was awakening. Living creatures, fat from a summerful of life, poked their heads into the day and chittered and squawked, and scratched, and buzzed. Billy Anspach wondered why he was holding four pounds of metal that could send a heavy pill of lead through space and cleave a man's head in two.

At Hamish Wallace's command, Billy turned, aimed, and fired. At the same instant, a mushroom of blue smoke belched out of the gray fog and a star-hot pellet of metal buried itself in the meat of Billy's chest and cut a tunnel of pain through rib and flesh and shattered his left shoulder blade before it reentered the air, flying on to burrow an inch deep in the soft trunk of a poplar tree.

The bullet had hit no vital organs, but the pressure wave of the bullet's impact stunned Billy's heart. Blood stopped flowing through his veins and his body began to die.

Cornelius Ethridge bent over Billy's blood-soaked body. From across the clearing, Hawley growled, "Ethridge bring me my damned pistol." Ethridge trotted across the wet grass to the cherrywood box and laid the pistol into its velvet-cushioned bed, next to its mate. He closed the lid and turned the key in the brass lock. Straightening up and digging in his jacket pocket, Ethridge then extended his right hand to Hawley, palm up. Beside the brass key a gray sphere of lead sat in sharp contrast to soft pink flesh. They exchanged a silent nod.

Hawley likewise dug in his pocket and extracted a Mormon twenty-dollar gold piece that caught the winter light and turned it to summer in Hawley's meaty paw. "Metal for metal," he said as he dropped the heavy coin onto Ethridge's palm and then scooped up the round shot and the key. He tossed the shot in his hand a couple of times. "You got fast hands there, Ethridge. Remind me never to play poker with you."

Hawley secured the pistol box behind his saddle and swung up onto his horse. "Throw that trash in the creek. Let's fatten up them catfish for spring fishin'." He dug his heels into his mount and galloped away followed by his two other associates, leaving Ethridge behind.

CHAPTER 50

Pain crushed Ethan into the bed while it also felt like it tried to explode from within. Two irresistible forces opposed each other with Watson's meager body in the middle.

Each breath lit a fiery torch in his chest. He had to breathe, but he didn't want to. Ethan fought as best he could, but this old man's body was failing. He was amazed it had survived this long.

He tried to leave the prison of this body, but it was too early, too far from death.

Helen loomed above him. "I'll save you, Mr. Watson."

He felt her hands on his chest. In a torn voice he croaked, "No, Helen, no. Let me go." Ethan knew he could not come back from this one. He hated that he had been so close to Beth and would now have to find another entry point.

Watson's body thrashed without Ethan's control, lurching with more strength than it had shown in years, fighting to save itself.

Now great explosions of light blotted out Helen's face. Suddenly remembering something, Ethan fought back the void and clutched at the breast pocket of his smoking jacket. He dragged a folded sheet of velum from the pocket and held it out. He had written another note.

"Give this to her, Helen," he gasped, battling each word. "The Hawley girl." First he had to suck a searing breath into the furnace of his chest, then he had to master his tongue and his throat while the rest of his body vibrated out of control. "Promise you'll give this to her. My dying wish." Helen touched the paper, terrified, and pulled it out of his clutching fist. "Swear to me, or I'll hunt you down, drag you to hell," Watson's voice croaked.

Just the day before, Helen had sworn she would never go back to the Hawley House. But she could not deny the old man his last wish. Though she had no idea what was in these notes or how Mr. Watson even knew Katherine Hawley, she said, "I swear, I swear."

"Ahhh, God, help me. Help me." Misunderstanding, Helen scrambled onto the bed and crouched over Watson. She set her hands as she had been shown and let her body weight press down on her patient's sternum. He moaned and thrashed as the excruciating pain built to a crescendo. He felt a white-hot pillar rising through his chest. When it reached his head, his vision turned black and Ethan let go.

With a whoosh of energy, the pain vanished. Ethan rushed through star clusters like a freight train passing trees, hurling himself out into the cosmos in an eruption of joy.

Then he thought himself into the place he had been before, that special little nexus of time where Bethany had winked into the other place. He found the eddy and plunged into it. It felt more familiar to him. He knew where to find her. He just had to get back there.

CHAPTER 51

Billy Anspach's body gasped as blood once again lurched through his veins. Nerves fired and his heart chugged as if to make up for lost time. Then Billy's mouth opened and emitted one long horrible wail.

Cornelius Ethridge's heart almost stopped at the sound. He whirled away from his horse, his eyes frantically searching for the source of that horrid noise. Billy Anspach's head rose from the edge of Antietam Creek and his bloodshot eyes drilled into Ethridge.

"Sweet mother of God," seeped from Ethridge's lips. The corpse raised its right arm and beckoned toward him, fingers outstretched and wriggling like worms. Ethridge approached the body cautiously as it quivered and thrashed in the mud and ice at the edge of the stream. Ethridge felt true terror. He had placed his hand on Billy's chest before returning Hawley's pistol; he had felt nothing. No breathing, no heart beat. The skin on Billy's face had been pale and lifeless as wax when Ethridge dragged his body into the stream. But here before him squirmed a living thing. He wasn't sure if it was a man. None of the horrible sounds it was making even resembled words.

Ethridge drew his revolver and for a second considered putting a bullet in Billy's skull. Then he slipped the Colt back into its holster. If Billy's body was found, one bullet hole could suggest he was robbed or in a duel. Even if the duel was ever tied back to George Hawley, there would be no repercussions on a matter of honor. But two bullet holes would mean murder and there'd be hell to pay.

Gritting his teeth, Ethridge grabbed Billy's soggy boots and hauled his writhing body back into the water. Ethridge stepped onto a partially submerged rock and manhandled Billy toward the center of the stream. He set his foot on Billy's back and pushed him under the ice. The dark, slow-moving water carried the body away. By spring, nothing would remain to identify. And if the body was found before then, it would be miles away.

Ethridge's horse had wandered across the meadow. Pacing through the frosty grass, Ethridge scanned around for anyone who might have heard the shots and decided to investigate. Nothing else moved in the mists. He might have been alone in the world. He mounted his horse and kicked it into a trot along the dirt track that would take him back into town. Billy's honorable second didn't even glance toward the stream as he abandoned him once again.

* * *

Horror.

Pain.

Uncontrollable seizures slammed through Ethan's new body. Then the cold hit him. For several seconds he enjoyed the icy contrast to the fire that ripped through his chest. His head cleared and he realized he was under water. Some instinct moved his legs and he bobbed toward the surface. He hit the ice. Ethan rolled face up and couldn't understand why he was looking through a window.

The icy water numbed his wound, focused his mind. He almost laughed as he realized he was trapped under ice. What else could go wrong? With his good arm he pushed against it and his body dropped through the water in response. His left foot hit the bottom. Realizing the shallowness of the stream, Ethan rolled his feet under him and pushed on the muddy streambed. His head broke through the thin ice and he gasped in air for what seemed like the first time in hours. The effort exhausted him. He pushed feebly against the bottom and bobbed his right shoulder up and down to crack a path through the thin sheet ice as he struggled to shore.

Infinities seemed to pass before he floated close enough to reach up and grab the low hanging branch of an elderberry bush. His first feeble tug brought him up to the bank, but as he pulled himself out of the buoyancy of the water, Ethan felt as if he weighed a thousand pounds. He got his head and shoulders onto the shore and then rested.

He felt vibrations through the ground, heard the thud of hooves. Struggling to hold himself in place, he lifted his head and tried to shout. A shadow passed over him before he could make a sound. Ethan looked up and through the thin brush saw a man in profile riding past. Ethan watched the retreating back of the man and the rear of the horse. From the horse's rump down to the right thigh, a white crescent stood out starkly against a chestnut background.

Molten lava poured through his veins. Ethan felt like his head would burst as he tugged on the elderberry bush, grabbed its base and hauled himself further out of the water.

Then he lay exhausted, barely conscious.

Slowly, the pain resolved itself into a hot, throbbing oven in his upper chest and left shoulder. Ethan's right hand gingerly probed and found the entry wound a hand's width above his left nipple. His blood seeped out steadily, though he knew it would have been much worse if he had not been thrown into the icy water.

With an effort that left him dizzy, he rolled onto his right side. By kicking his legs and pulling at clumps of grass with his right arm, Ethan was able to inch his way up the gentle slope of the embankment onto the slick field grass at the side of the dirt track. He lay gasping like a landed fish. *This is madness. I've made a mistake.* He composed himself and tried to escape the damaged remains of Billy Anspach. He battered against the walls of his human prison, but no amount of effort could free him. He could not leave. Yet.

Chilled and shivering, Ethan lay on his back and absently gazed into the azure sky. From pain to pain. Why did he enter only the bodies of those already close to death? But he knew the answer. He could not eject or cohabit with the spirit of one who was living. Only when that energizing essence had abandoned its body could Ethan move in and try to reanimate the empty flesh before it decomposed.

This method sorely disadvantaged him in his search for Bethany.

CHAPTER 52

Calvin Anspach heard loud clumping noises across his front porch. Had some damn fool ridden a horse onto the planking? He stormed through the parlor, filled with righteous wrath. Just as he reached for the knob, the front door flew open and three burly figures stamped into the house, hunched over, carrying something. Then Calvin saw the blood.

A fourth man entered. His long black coat and wide-brimmed hat in silhouette against the brightness outside sent a chill through Calvin. But when the apparition spoke, Calvin recognized the voice of Doctor Robert. "Your boy's been shot, Cal. These men found him alongside the road near Burnside's Bridge. Took him for dead and threw him in their wagon. Brought him to Deagan, the undertaker, but Billy started breathing, so they brought him to me. He's not dead, but close though. Where's your bedroom?"

Calvin pointed and the three men lugged their cargo down the hall. Calvin and Doctor Robert followed like the tail of a comet.

Calvin Anspach had once been a religious man. He wondered if a vengeful God was now repaying him for his many sins. Wasn't that the way of God, to smite down the things one cared about?

The trio laid Billy into Calvin's bed. Doctor Robert took off his coat and dropped it on the floor. He set his hat on the pile and then pulled a short four-legged stool next to the bed. From his black leather satchel, he extracted scissors with which he cut away Billy's shirt.

"Pistol ball. Small hole, but it sure made a mess of him."

"Who did it?"

"No idea."

"He gonna make it, Doc?"

"Can't rightly say."

As Doctor Robert probed the hole for fragments, the three bearded men backed toward the door. One of them said, "Hope he pulls through. We'll leave you to your business." In an instant, they disappeared.

"Cal, help me roll him. Hold him for me." They pulled Billy halfway over, revealing his left shoulder and a ragged exit wound. Doctor Robert felt into it with his fingers. "Shoulder

161

blade is broken. This is a mess. The only good thing is it looks like the bullet went all the way through him. I have to close him up whether there's a piece of bullet in him or not. He's lost too much blood."

For the next half hour, Doctor Robert sewed shut Billy's wounds and applied thick layers of bandage both front and back to stanch Billy's bleeding. "Normally, I'd splint up that shoulder, but we need to change his bandages twice a day. It's going to hurt him like hell, but we have to leave that shoulder free."

As Doctor Robert wrapped his bloody utensils in a cloth and set them inside his satchel, Calvin said, "Doc, how bad is it?"

Donning his coat and hat, Doctor Robert replied, "Bad, but not as bad as it could have been. There's no blood in his mouth or nose and he's breathing regular, so I don't think his lung was punctured and that's a blessing. But his shoulder is smashed and he's lost a lot of blood. That's the biggest danger. He might lose use of that arm, but only if he survives the blood loss."

"What should I do?"

"If he wakes up, give him plenty of water. Other than that, keep him still and send for me if those bandages soak through. Otherwise, I'll stop by this evening and bring some laudanum. He's going to need it."

Sheepishly, Calvin Anspach said, "How much I owe you, Doc?"

"What's my bill at the store come to?"

"'Bout three dollars and maybe six bits."

"How about we just call it even?"

"Done."

CHAPTER 53

"He insisted, Ma'am. It was his dying wish."

Elizabeth Hawley's face glowed red with suppressed anger. "No. After you were here the last time, Katherine became very agitated. I'll not have you upsetting her again. Get home with you." The green door closed in Helen's face.

Dejected, Charles Watson's former nurse retreated down the stairs and hiked up the lane. She turned and squinted back at the green stone house with the white mortar. A movement of the curtains at a second floor window caught her eye. She saw a pale face behind the glare of the glass. On impulse, she pulled the crumpled note from her dress pocket and held it out in front of her like an offering. The face in the window disappeared. Helen turned and trudged home, worried that with Mr. Watson dead she would have to find another situation quickly.

* * *

In her dream, Helen ran through an ice storm. Fists of hail hammered down from the heavens. She ran across an endless field, tripping in the deepening ice, but struggling onward. She had to get somewhere, but she could not remember where. She saw a shed up ahead and almost swam through the waist-deep ice to reach it. She threw her body through the shed door and lay exhausted on the musty straw of its floor. Above her the tin roof rattled with a constant metallic echo as hail rained down on it.

She awoke with a gasp and heard the same gravelly rattle. Fear speared through her bosom and she pulled her blanket tight under her neck. The gravel sound came again and she turned her head to the window. She was not dreaming. She leaped from bed, the night air suddenly cold against her skin. She prickled with more than the temperature as she approached her lone window.

A half moon bathed the side yard in crisp light. She saw an apparition with a bright circle of face looking up. Helen raised the window sash and leaned out as her visitor drew back the shawl that had covered her head. Long ringlets cascaded to her shoulders.

"Where is it?"

Fear left Helen as she recognized Katherine Hawley.

Helen held up a finger and hurried to her bureau. From the top drawer she extracted the note Mr. Watson had given her, returned to the window. Leaning far out, she dropped the note.

Katherine looked like a child chasing snowflakes as she scurried back and forth to match the uneven descent of the paper. A breeze wafted the note away from the house. Just as it seemed to be headed for the meadow, Katherine jumped and captured the fluttering thing. She pushed the note into the top of her dress, readjusted her shawl, and waved. In an instant she disappeared into the shadows.

* * *

Bethany breathed hard after her mad dash up the stairs from the kitchen. Her foray into town had gone undiscovered, but the night chill gnawed deep into her flesh. Her left hand clutched to her chest a brick heated on the stove and wrapped in rags, while her right hand threw back the thick quilted featherbed. She lit a candle, stripped off her outer clothes, pulled on a night dress, and jumped under the heavy bed cover and hunkered down, hoping her shivers would stop soon. With a second goose down featherbed under her, she felt like a mouse in a hayloft, buried deep to fight the cold. She held the swaddled brick against her chest for a few minutes and then transferred it down to the foot of the bed where her feet had become tiny icebergs despite wool socks.

As the heat from the brick thawed her toes and her body heat began to collect in the fabric around her, she bravely poked her head out from under the covers. In the candle illumination, Bethany saw her breath. Despite the sharp cold in the room, Bethany extended her right hand out into the golden light. It held the second yellowed piece of parchment she had gotten from the Watson nurse. She read the scrawled handwriting again and again.

My Darling,

This old body will not last. By the time you get this note, Charles Watson will probably be dead. But Charles Watson is not me. I will go on. I don't know who or how, but someday soon, I will contact you again. I may be young; I may be old. But I will certainly be your husband, Ethan West. Wait for me.

I know this sounds like the ravings of a madman. But have faith. I have found a way to get to you from where we started.

Since I got no answer to my first note, I fear you may have no memories of who we were. But you may remember the lightning. You were struck right after we flew your Tibetan kite. Try to remember. You are Bethany West and you once lived in New York. You taught history. And you hate to be tickled.

Even if this makes no sense, don't leave Sharpsburg until I can reach you. I promise it will all become clear.

With all my love,

Ethan

Three words kept ringing in her mind: *Don't leave Sharpsburg.* He had said the same thing in his first note. Yet, her step-father planned to send her to some godforsaken place very soon.

As she lay back on her pillow and watched steamy tendrils of her breath disappear toward the ceiling, she thought, this is a real place. I can feel the cold, I can see the candle. I am not dreaming. And don't I have some deep feeling for the name Bethany West?

Her thoughts shifted. Was this an elaborate joke? Was George Hawley tormenting her with hope just after he had announced her sale to the highest bidder in some mining camp?

No, this couldn't be a joke. Suddenly, an image – brown eyes and perpetual five o'clock shadow – floated in front of her. This memory seemed clearer than the rest. As if a floodgate had been released, Bethany remembered places and times she had spent with this man. Had she loved him, married him? With a frightening tremble that pulsed through her whole body, she remembered making love with him. Despite the cold, her skin released fear sweat. Her night dress clung to her and she wanted to strip naked and fling it away.

What is wrong with me?

Was this sudden cascade of memories about a husband the product of insanity? How could a dream be so real?

No matter how closely she examined these new memories, she could find no flaw in them. Unlike dreams, they had the smooth and extended details of truth. Then how was she here in a place whose details so thoroughly clashed with memory?

She examined the pink, freckled skin on the long fingers of her hand, the hand of a stranger, yet she could move it, flex it, make it obey her commands. She lived in this body with its copper hair, green eyes, and wide forehead, but she did not feel at home in it. She felt disconnected from everything going on around her. For weeks she had felt hopeless and trapped, but she could not think of a way out of her dilemma.

Then the first note had come and her stoic endurance of something she could not understand began to crumble under hammer blows of memory. Or was it fantasy? She clung to the hope that this man, Ethan, could not be a dream if she held the physical evidence of his existence in her hand. Yet, she wondered if her delusions had become so real that she was hallucinating, creating a reality that nobody else could ever understand or penetrate. She knew such things were possible.

Rather than comfort her, this latest note merely agitated the fears that blossomed like weeds in her head.

How was she in this world when her mind was filled with the images of subways and skyscrapers, of stereos and sports cars, of skim milk and microwaves and central heating? How was she in a world of horses and soldiers and war where a woman's voice was no more than a breath of wind to the forces that swirled around her? She remembered a life of independence and personal accomplishment. So, how was she suddenly transformed into chattel to be sold to a man a continent away? Was it her destiny to be shipped like baggage to another place she didn't know to be used like a tool until her sharp edge would be dulled and she would accept her bondage and sink uncaring into the world around her?

She leaned over and puffed at the candle. The room became an inky pit and Beth curled far down under the featherbed and wrapped her arms around her knees.

A horrible loneliness settled on her and made the room feel even more frigid than it was.

* * *

"Emily, please, you must."

"Your father said I was not to carry messages for you, Katherine. If he finds out, I'll be in a heap of trouble."

"Emily, you don't have to carry a note. Just go to the Watson house. Ask to see him. Talk to him."

"About what? He's an old man and mean as a snake from what they say. Why would he talk to me?"

"Because he sent me another note. Tell him my name and tell him I got his note. Then tell him that Bethany is fine."

The maid's dark eyes shifted back and forth as if she expected George Hawley to materialize out of the walls. "Oh, Missy, please. This scares me somethin' fierce."

"Emily, when you go to town, make a detour. It won't take you ten minutes to go there and talk to him. Then do

166

your shopping. Nobody will ever know."

"I can't do that. Already been to town. And anyways, I won't remember everything you said."

"I'll write a note." Emily clutched her hands in front of her. Before she could speak, Beth pressed the advantage. "You'll do it?"

Emily's lips formed a grim line as she nodded her head. "Only if I can go at night. I don't want your father seein' me."

The fear Beth saw in Emily's eyes made her feel terrible, but not bad enough to relent. This trembling girl could provide a thin conduit to sanity.

Or to confirmation that she had gone truly mad.

CHAPTER 54

The first day boiled in madness. Pain beyond anything Ethan had ever experienced drilled through him in shrieking flashes. He could not hold to a thought for more than a moment before the demands of his shattered body distracted and overwhelmed him. Like an ant on an anvil, he felt trapped in a vast place where any second a hammer blow would loom and crush. And after a blow, he struggled to reorient himself, only to be hammered again.

Then he experienced a sudden respite as if the blacksmith had gone to lunch. The pain rolled back to tolerable levels and, through a soupy sluggishness, Ethan was able to survey the messy room in which he found himself. Weighed down under a huge featherbed of blue muslin, he felt clammy sweat all over his body.

A wide, grizzled face with a flat, florid nose suddenly appeared and hung over him like a furry moon. Droopy brown eyes peered out from under gray eyebrows so large that, up close, they looked like the wings of mourning doves. "Here, Billy, take more of this. Doc Robert said it would help." A huge pewter cooking spoon thrust into Ethan's mouth. Like a baby bird, some reflex opened his mouth and he swallowed a thick substance that was both bitter and sweet. Exhausted from the effort of lifting his head, Ethan fell back into the damp pillow and tried to remember who this old buzzard was. But his mind blanked except for a few nightmare images of lying in a cold field and then being bounced in the back of a wagon until he lost consciousness.

"How does it feel, Son?"

"Terrible."

"How'd this happen? Who shot you?"

"Don't know."

"You was shot in the front. You didn't see who did it?"

"I can't remember."

"Some damn deserter most likely."

The pain trickled away. Ethan asked, "What is that stuff?"

"Laudanum. Doc Robert says it's the only thing can help you. Need more?"

"I will."

"Doc says give you what you need 'till you do some healin'."

"Yeah."

Laudanum. Ethan knew the opiate would be addictive. He had never used drugs and he felt instinctively uncomfortable with taking this medication. However, an hour later the anvil began ringing again, first faintly in the distance, then closer until the vibrations made his teeth ache. As his body began to vibrate, Ethan said, "I need more."

Calvin Anspach eagerly obliged. Anything to stop the screams.

CHAPTER 55

"He's dead, Miss Kate." Emily looked at her feet, not happy to deliver bad news.

Horror washed across Bethany's face. "What?"

"His heart gave out yesterday. His nurse said she crushed on his chest somethin' awful, but she couldn't get his ticker started again."

"She did what to him?" Something about this sounded familiar.

"Says he showed her how to get his heart workin' again. CP somethin'. She did it three other times and got him goin', but this time even breathin' in his mouth didn't work. Sounds like witchcraft if you ask me. Who ever heard of such a thing? Breathin' into a corpse." Emily shivered and scrunched up her face as if she'd swallowed something bitter, then settled in the chair at the foot of the bed while Bethany plopped heavily onto her mattress.

With an expression of hopelessness, Bethany said, "Did the nurse give you a note for me?"

"No, Miss." The servant girl returned the note Beth had sent her to deliver.

* * *

The modest prosperity that the general store offered to the Anspachs made it possible for Calvin to buy his son a steady supply of laudanum. At first, Ethan had tried to space out his doses, but after the first few days of struggle, he gave up. He no longer allowed Calvin to dose him by the spoonful. Ethan now held the brown glass bottle under the covers in his good hand. Almost hourly, he used his teeth to pull the cork stopper out of the bottle and then swigged its contents until the familiar syrupy slowness enveloped him and his pain retreated.

The first half-pint bottle had lasted two days. The one Ethan now held had been opened that morning and would be gone by sunset. Ethan saw the trap he had entered. The shortness of the relief made the drug irresistible. As he swallowed increasing amounts of it, now seeking more than just respite from pain, Ethan wasn't sure which he feared more: the pain or the drug.

Halfway into his second week, Ethan nestled in his

170

stupor. He roused only when some external force intruded on him: Doctor Robert's examinations, Calvin's insistence that he eat.

Ethan reached under the covers and retrieved the bottle. He yanked out the cork and cocked the familiar shape up to start the flow into his mouth. Nothing came out. Ethan sucked on the neck of the bottle like an infant. A minute passed before he realized he held an empty bottle. He hurled the bottle against the far wall where it chipped the green paint and formed a crater in the plaster. Other fresh white craters dotted the wall.

"Calvin!"

The elder Anspach shuffled into the bedroom. "Yeah?"

"More laudanum."

"Billy, you finish that bottle already? That was fresh this mornin'."

"I need more."

"Billy, maybe you best slow down. Doc Robert says you're takin' too much of that stuff."

The pain flowed back like an unstoppable tide. Soon his body would shriek with the knowledge that relief was being denied. It would howl in Ethan's brain. Now that Ethan was able to think again, his thoughts stayed fixated on only this one goal.

Tiny claws of pain snickered along his ribs and up his collar bone. They joined in his left shoulder blade and bit into the marrow. Hot mandibles of a thousand microscopic demons ripped at his nerves, gnawed through muscle. The insistent attack grew and grew. Ethan felt them in there, those hideous little monsters that reveled in bringing him agony. When their assault grew to the point that Ethan could hear their teeth and their claws rattling against his skeleton, he screamed in a rising ululation of horror.

In the kitchen, Ethan's howl sent a spear though Calvin. He rocked forward out of the chair that he had settled into to bask in the heat of the pot-bellied stove. From a shelf next to the window, he pulled down a squat red pottery jug and yanked out the cork. After a long pull of Pennsylvania sippin' liquor, Calvin threw on his coat and stepped out into the cold for the short walk to the apothecary's.

The next week became a tug of war. At Doctor Robert's insistence, Calvin tried to restrict Ethan's laudanum intake. But Ethan would wheedle, plead, cry, or intimidate to get what he craved. His wounds were healing, but from the racket coming from Calvin's bedroom, it sounded as if the patient was getting worse.

Ethan wanted the boy to die so he could move on. He wanted the agony to end. He now rattled around inside Billy, looking for some way out. But he found none. Billy's vigorous teenage body wanted to heal. Ethan began to think of how he might crawl out of bed and find a gun in the house and end this miserable life. But when he tried, the hot magma of pain that erupted in his body slammed him back to the mattress like a beetle crushed under a wagon wheel.

CHAPTER 56

"George, she's just a girl. You can't send her off in the cold. It's the middle of January." Elizabeth Hawley sat on the edge of their bed as George Hawley hauled on his suspenders and threaded a wide leather belt through the belt loops of his clean pants.

"I want her out of town before she starts to show. She's growing a belly."

"It's your imagination. Under a dress it can't be seen. She's only four months gone. She has two months before the baby will become noticeable."

"The baby? You mean the bastard."

"It's our grandchild no matter where it came from. How can you be so cold about this?"

"How can you be so ignorant? People will talk. Then they'll laugh. I'll not be laughed at, Elizabeth. If people don't respect a man, they don't do business with him. And if I lose this army contract, everything I've worked for will go bust." He buttoned up the red flannel shirt that Emily had washed the previous day.

"You think people aren't already gossiping about this, George? You think you can keep this a secret when you shout about it at the top of your lungs?"

"What people think and what they know are two different things. With that wench gone, talk will die out, but if she's here and has that bastard, she rubs their faces in it. Rumor I can deal with; fact I can't."

"Let the weather warm, George. It thaws in March and she'll only be six months along. People will still be wearing coats and nobody will notice a thing. Don't make her go now. I'll never forgive you if you do." The force in Elizabeth Hawley's voice surprised even her.

"Don't you feel shame at this?"

"Yes. I feel shame. But even more I feel disgust at what you are about to do."

Elizabeth felt giddy from the confrontation. She never argued with her husband. She stayed in her place, minded her own business, let him rut against her when it became unavoidable. But her maternal instincts had risen at the threat to her daughter, putting her in a state of mind she had never imagined possible.

"Watch your tongue, woman." He stalked across the rag carpet toward the bed, using his bulk to intimidate his much smaller wife.

Elizabeth stood up from her perch on the bed. She drew her right index finger like a sword and leveled it at her husband's chest. "George, your almighty business is built on my inheritance. This land and this house were my father's and are in my name. The cash he left when he died is what you used to buy your first breeding horses. If I were you, I'd be thinking that the risk to my business came more from my wife than my daughter."

"Step-daughter."

"You never fail to make that point. But hear me, George. You wait until spring thaw or I swear I'll wreck your business worse than any town gossip." Her finger jabbed into his belly for emphasis.

Hawley's eyes bored into his wife. "What could you do? You're just an addle-headed woman."

"Not so addled I don't see what's going on around here. Not so addled I don't notice how your hands round up stray army horses after a battle, change the brand markings, and re-sell them to the army. The right word down in Washington could raise hob with your contract. I have my own money, George, and by God, I'll run your business into the ground if you force me to." Elizabeth Hawley's long face flushed and her fists clenched in front of her. Her husband had never seen her like this.

Confronted with something far outside his experience, Hawley controlled his temper for one of the few times in his life. His pig eyes squinted, trying to gauge how far he could push before his wife made good her threats.

Feeling on thin ice, alone in a place she had never been, Elizabeth retreated slightly. "I feel shame at her pregnancy too. I agree she should leave town. I hope in a few years she can come home, bring her husband. If she's married, the past will never come up. But I don't want her in danger. Wait until after the thaw."

Hawley's right hand pulled at his jowls. "All right. I'll live with it."

CHAPTER 57

In the second month after Billy's duel, after a fitful night's sleep, a horizontal shaft of sunlight cut through the grimy window opposite Ethan's bed and bathed him in blood-red light. As the fat disk of sun hauled itself above the horizon, Ethan remembered being suspended in the black velvet of the cosmos, willing himself toward a star. He remembered how the atomic furnace grew into a huge disk and how the surface roiled as great plumes of scintillant matter flared out against immense gravity and spewed into space. In the pale heat from the rising sun, Ethan felt a faint echo of that ravaging radiation he had marveled at.

He remembered all the places he had been, the vastness of space, and the growing sense he had of the forces at play beneath the surface of what had always seemed real. In contrast, he thought of the pathetic thing he had become and how far he was off the path that led to Beth.

Billy's body was healing well. With the vigor of youth, it had closed the rips in its flesh, was mending its bones, and preparing to move about. Ethan realized how he was hindering that process and turning Billy into a husk. He felt like a ghoul. Where would this lead?

He suddenly saw the predatory creature he could become, a kind of vampire, moving from body to body, always searching for brute pleasures until he would degenerate into nothing more than a parasite, moving through time and space, insatiable and demanding.

Is this what I will do with all the lives that lie before me?

It was his first moment of true clarity since inhabiting this body.

Ethan shouted. Within seconds, Calvin staggered into the room, his eyes wild and fearful, his soiled nightshirt crumpled up short like a skirt around his knees. "Billy, you need more laudanum?"

"Yes, but don't give it to me. Throw it away. Never give it to me again. Do you hear?" Toward the end, Ethan's voice rose to a shout.

The old man nodded and quickly left the room to get the laudanum. But first he stopped off in the kitchen and took a long pull from his jug to start this day.

CHAPTER 58

Ethan leaned heavily on the cane clutched in his right hand, trying to keep his body steady as he shuffled up Main Street. Any misstep lanced pain from his chest to his left shoulder. Maybe he should have worn the shoulder sling, but he was trying to accelerate his healing, pushing the limits of this new body. The March sky, more gray than blue, seemed to suck the heat out of the earth and all that walked upon it. Ethan looked forward to stoking a big fire in the pot-bellied stove in the kitchen and basking in its radiation like a spoiled housecat. But for now, he plodded on, determined to go a little farther away from the house each day.

Through the ground he felt the heavy vibration of horses approaching so he stepped as far to the side of the dirt track as possible. In seconds, two horsemen galloped around the corner and almost ran him down.

Some afterimage came into Ethan's thoughts as the horses passed. He knew one of the horses. Yes, the one on the right had a white crescent across its rump. And the way the rider sat the horse. He knew that too.

Remembered pain washed over him. He stumbled. He caught himself and then planted his feet as if withstanding an earthquake until the spasm passed. Yes, in the moments of his coming into Billy Anspach's body, he remembered that horse and that rider.

Ethan gathered his wits and hurried as fast as his weak, stiff body could carry him. Straining muscles unprepared for exertion, he followed the cloud of dust the riders kicked up.

It took Ethan ten minutes to traverse the town and discover the two horses tied in front of the Brandywine Tavern. He stepped up onto the boardwalk in front of the saloon and reached for the brass door handle. His hand shook. Was he insane? If found the man who shot Billy Anspach inside, what could Ethan possibly do?

He left me, he thought. He left me to die. He dumped me like garbage in the creek.

What had led up to that moment? What grudge or feud or moment of passion had brought Billy out at dawn to a patch of field to take a bullet in the chest?

176

Ethan shuffled away from the Brandywine and retreated to a stout sycamore tree for cover. A thin wind cut down under his collar. He shuddered.

Why am I doing this? What does Billy Anspach's feud have to do with me?

But he knew. Anyone who would leave a boy to die would not leave his handiwork on display. Billy's shooting and recovery were the talk of the town. Surely his assailant had heard. Surely he would want to finish his job of work before Billy was healthy enough for revenge, never knowing that his victim had no idea who had tried to murder him.

A half-hour dragged by before a pair of men exited the Brandywine and mounted the chestnut-red Morgans. They whirled and retraced the route by which they had arrived. As they approached, Ethan slowly circumnavigated the sycamore's trunk, keeping the mottled bark between him and the pair. As they passed, Ethan peeked around the tree and recognized the profile of the man on the left.

I'll send you to hell, he thought. It's what Jasper would say. Now he understood how the old trooper came to such conclusions.

Ethan hobbled through the rising wind toward the Brandywine, a low, log structure with small lead-glass windows. When he stepped inside, a rank cloud of tobacco smoke burned into his lungs. He waited for his eyes to adjust to the gloom and then stepped to the bar, at the end of which two hulking figures in bearskin coats huddled over beers.

Ethan approached the bartender, a squat man with arms like piano legs. The bald top of his head seemed compensated by a dark handlebar mustache so large that Ethan wondered how the man could eat.

"Those two who were in here? Who are they?"

"What two would they be?" The bartender growled. In the dim light his eyes glinted as black as the coal stacked in the bin next to the stove behind him.

"They rode Morgans. They just left."

"Morgans?"

"Yeah, big red horses."

"Seems a man's business is a man's business." The bartender continued trimming the wicks of a half dozen oil lamps lined up on the cherrywood bar.

Ethan stood silent. Why had he assumed he could ask for help? He kept thinking of the past as a time when people showed more civility, but time and again he saw evidence that their cruelty and venality equaled that of his own time. He had to abandon his quaint notions of the "past."

The bartender looked up. "You still here? Why don't you gimp on out before you get into trouble?"

The two men in bearskins turned and eyed Ethan. "Hey, Gimp, how 'bout you buy us a round?"

The meek shall inherit the earth, Ethan thought. Yeah, but not until the strong had made them pay for it. He realized his mistake. This damaged body could barely walk, let alone pursue an impulsive quest. He turned for the door, the sting of their words like a lash in his mind. He transferred his cane to his weak left hand and used his right hand to pull open the thick wooden slab. Heavy boots thumped on the plank floor behind Ethan. He stepped through the door, pulled it shut, and hurried off the boardwalk and into the street, switching his cane to his stronger hand to make better speed.

The Brandywine's door creaked open. "Hey, Gimp, where ya goin'? Ain't nice to turn yer back on a man's talkin' to ya." Clumping footsteps approached Ethan from behind. Ethan's heart hammered and the ever-present throbbing in his shoulder and chest ratcheted up a few notches to searing pain. He increased his pace, each impact of his feet now sending a shudder of agony through him. He breathed shallow breaths and sweat appeared all over his body, despite the cold.

"C'mere, snotnose. You need a lesson in manners," one bear-man growled.

Ethan felt a hand grip his left shoulder, yank at his coat. Pain screamed through his shoulder and by reflex Ethan dropped into a crouch. At the same time, he shortened his grip on the cane in his right hand so that he was holding it midway down the shaft. With as much strength as he could muster, Ethan spun to his left and, almost blindly, stabbed the metal tip of the cane up at the bear man's face. The tip bounced off the man's left cheekbone and juddered up into his eye. Ethan pushed and the bear-man screamed with the voice of a child. Bright blood gushed from the eye socket and the man fell back hard, writhing in the dust of the road. Ethan yanked his cane away from the big man's clutches.

Faint from his effort and from the panic that flooded through him, he shuffle-skipped as fast as he could, wanting to get as far as possible from the Brandywine. He got fifty yards up the street when he heard a shout from behind, but he didn't turn. He just kept his head down and his legs moving as he tried to control the searing white heat that reached up through his chest.

A shot rang out and Ethan heard the whirring buzz of a bullet pass his right ear. He cut right into a side street to put a house between him and his pursuers and to head for the center of town. Ethan did the grim arithmetic in his head. He had a lead, but he couldn't make good time. The bear man would catch up.

Ethan turned left at the next street to break up the line of sight. His breath now wheezed in and out of him in a painful rhythm. Atrophied muscles in his legs burned from effort they could not much longer sustain. And the half-knitted mess of his left shoulder felt as if someone scraped a screwdriver against the bone.

Ethan ducked into an alley between two rows of houses. As he neared its end, he recognized Doctor Robert's house diagonally across the street. The red board-and-batten structure with the gray slate roof had been a frequent destination in his recovery. Now it offered another kind of salvation.

Ethan hastened around to the rear and, without knocking, pushed open the door at the top of a short flight of stairs. The noise of his breathing echoed off the white plaster walls of the narrow hallway and his feet hammered against the pine planking. Surely his pursuers could hear him, like a mouse running inside a kettledrum. Ethan yanked open the first door on his right, spun through the doorway, and slammed the door shut. He slid to the floor with his legs splayed in front of him and tried hopelessly to catch his breath.

"I told you to exercise, Billy, but this is a little bit much, wouldn't you say?"

Ethan looked up and Doctor Robert loomed in the doorway to the adjoining examination room.

Gasping, Ethan managed to spit out, "Hide me."

"What?"

"Men. After me."

Robert hurried to the front of his office and peered out the single window. "I don't see anyone."

"Good."

Robert knelt next to Ethan and helped take off his coat. "Lean forward. Let me examine your shoulder."

As Ethan slowly regained control of his breathing, Robert pulled off Ethan's shirt and probed gingerly around Ethan's bruised flesh. "Your wound hasn't opened. But there's more swelling around this shoulder. Have you kept it in the sling?"

Ethan said, "Mostly, but I'm trying to do without it today."

"So, who's chasing you, Billy?"

Ethan spun the doctor a story of his adventure at the Brandywine, omitting the part about recognizing the man who had left Billy to die.

"Billy, you shouldn't be drinking in your condition. You stay away from the Brandywine."

"No problem there."

Three loud thumps came from the front hall. Robert frowned at Ethan. "You stay here." Robert left through the examining room door which he closed and locked. Thumping and curses. Deep voices. Ethan's heart rate shot up again. *How did they find me?* Any second, he expected the door to the examining room to crash into splinters as the bear-men came at him.

But as minutes ticked by, the sounds diminished to silence that was only occasionally punctuated by a low groan. Ethan crawled across the floor to the adjoining door and squinted through the keyhole. One bear-man sat on a stool at the far end of the room. The other was lying on a table with Doctor Robert hunched over, wrapping bandages around the bear-man's head.

Ethan sat back on his haunches. They hadn't found him. The bear men had merely sought help from the nearest doctor. Relief surged through Ethan.

He suppressed the urge to hustle out the back door. The bear men couldn't see through walls and they would have no reason to enter Doctor Robert's back room. Better to rest a while before the long walk home.

He just hoped he could get home without making any more enemies.

CHAPTER 59

"Pap, who owns that Circle H brand?"

"Where'd you see it?"

"On some Morgans."

"Morgans?"

Ethan quickly realized that in this time the breed hadn't been named yet. He said, "You know, those big red horses."

Billy's father scowled, then spit at the spittoon, but missed. The evidence of numerous other misses had darkened a wide swath of the store's pine floorboards. "George Hawley. You stay away from him."

"Why?"

"I don't like 'im. Hires riffraff. And a crookeder bastard you'll never see." Billy's father turned his head away and glared into the gloom at the back of the store.

Ethan pushed. "Never see his men in the store."

"Hawley don't buy supplies from me and I don't buy horses from him. Works out jes fine."

"What's the grudge?"

"Why you askin' me, boy? You know what happened." Calvin Anspach turned away and began stacking blankets.

Ethan stepped out the front door and shuffled up the street to the millinery shop. He had met the owner, the smiling Mrs. Nichols, several times. She had an arrangement with Billy's father to get her supplies when the General Store made a pick-up from Baltimore. As Ethan entered, a tiny bell above the door pealed. Mrs. Nichols looked up from the counter where she was serving a customer.

"Hello, Billy. Do you have something for me? Just a minute."

Ethan approached the counter. "No, Mrs. Nichols. I just wanted to ask you where George Hawley lives."

Her thin face jerked down and her brown eyes peered over the tops of the rectangular spectacles that perched on her long nose. "What you want with that man?"

"Just curious, is all."

Mrs. Nichols squinted. "You know his daughter. You *know* where they live. What's wrong with you, Billy? Stop sportin' with me. I'm sure your dad has something for you to do 'cept pesterin' me." She turned back to her customer.

Ethan made a hasty retreat.

The day turned warmer than it had been for months. Without his usual two coats on, Ethan felt almost light-footed. His pains had marginally reduced and he had become adamant about exercising his body every day. He made slow progress down Main Street as his mind wandered. Hawley had a daughter? Something sounded familiar about that, but how was that possible? Were some of Billy's memories somehow sifting into him? He mulled this information, but he couldn't quite connect to the memory that hovered at the edges of his consciousness. His months under the influence of laudanum had pushed so many memories out of reach.

Though the town appeared remarkably similar to his own time, he saw many unfamiliar shanties whose poor construction would not carry them much further into the future. Today he headed east, a direction he had studiously avoided. He had not felt up to seeing the battlefields or the place where he, as Cole, had been shot.

He passed the church where the tide of battle had turned. Cannonballs had imbedded in its walls and shattered the steeple. Some debris had been cleared, but no concerted effort had yet been made to repair the damage. Ethan remembered a wedding he and Beth had attended there in his own time. The memory sent a searing flash through him. For a few seconds he stared at the church and imagined it was that spring day so long ago in the future.

When Ethan began walking again, some vague sense pulled him. Too many times in his life, Ethan had suppressed these feelings, but not now. He tried not to think as some inner compass led him.

He limped for ten minutes until he came to a street at the edge of town. Not many houses existed here and long stretches of brush filled unused fields. As Ethan followed the dirt track and rounded a bend, he saw a sprawling white house on a rise with horse fencing surrounding it. As he approached the front of the property, Ethan saw a name emblazoned across the sign that hung above the gate leading to the corrals: HAWLEY.

Mesmerized at sight of the house Ethan realized how much damage the cloud of laudanum had done, how much he had forgotten. Yes, during the battle Ethan remembered being shot as Cole nearby, but a memory from the old man, Charles Watson, came to the fore of his thoughts. He remembered the bedside conversation of the old man's nurse and maid. "The Hawley girl's in a bad way," one of them had said. He groped in his memory. Katherine was her first name. Ethan thought his mind would melt as he remembered sending Katherine Hawley a note. Now he knew why Mrs. Nichols's comments about Hawley had seemed familiar. Beth had to be close.

But he thought of a serious problem. He was sure the man he had seen at the Brandywine had gunned down Billy. He rode a Hawley Morgan. If that man worked for Elizabeth Hawley's father, approaching her directly presented all sorts of dangers.

At first, he thought the wind was keening, but the sound he heard emanated from inside his head, a thin reedy squeal that grew in volume until it consumed him.

Suddenly, he didn't see the house. He saw the cosmos as it had been when he was on a Memnon-induced exploration. He felt the undercurrents of space and time and he rode them back to that moment that he knew better than all others. He saw Beth bathed in blue flame, saw her flicker in and out of existence for a microsecond. He felt himself moving toward her, taking the brunt of the force. He touched her and she knew him. And he thought of something, someplace. Not knowing what he was capable of at the time, he had blinked in his mind. And something changed. Beth disappeared, but something had changed. Ethan did not see it then, but he saw it now.

The energy. He had used it. He had deflected its purpose.

Ethan realized he was standing in the pale sun of a winter afternoon in 1863 and that a quarter mile away his wife lived in the Hawley house. She was exactly where his mind had put her, waiting for this moment. How? He could not fathom.

His feet moved toward the house. He forced them to stop. He couldn't walk up to the front door, not in this shape with the likelihood that someone on this spread wanted Billy dead.

Ethan heard hoofbeats and instinctively he scrambled into the brush to hide behind a stand of pine trees. Three riders approached from town on red Morgans. One of them caught Ethan's attention. White hair, pink skin. The albino cowboy. Hulse, the man who had killed Cole. The scowl on the man's face made Ethan pull farther out of sight. The last time

Ethan had seen the albino, his face was laughing.

After the riders passed, Ethan sat on the pine needles and stared at the house in the distance. He saw it as the intersection of two powerful forces: one that could save him and one that could destroy him.

CHAPTER 60

Ethan had harbored hope of finding the man who had shot Billy for no other reason than self-preservation. He had no memory of what led to Billy's shooting, but if he was to make contact with Katherine Hawley, he wanted to know who to watch out for. Now he knew that the albino had a connection to the Hawleys. And for that man – Hulse – Ethan felt nothing but hatred. Ethan remembered the coldness of the ground against his back as it shook from the approaching horses. He remembered those pink eyes staring down at him as Cole's body died.

And something else had lurked in those bunny eyes. Why had Hulse been so happy to murder a stranger? He had said that Ethan had been dropped on him from heaven. Ethan wanted to bring him a message from hell.

Animal urges rose in Ethan. He wanted revenge on Hulse for killing Cole and on the other nameless Hawley employee for trying to kill Billy. What had more priority? Killing Hawley's minions or getting away with Beth? The answer came easy: Beth. But how to reach her? He couldn't go anywhere near the Hawley house with a nameless psychopath there.

Ethan cursed his crippled body. He cursed the fates that had taken his wife. The frustration of his quest, the pains he had suffered – still suffered – welled up in a thick bile of anger. To have to skulk around the place he knew Beth to be was a lash across his soul, but skulking was all he could do at the moment.

Ethan remembered the Watson nurse, Helen, who had delivered his note. Could he approach her again? What could he say to her that wouldn't make her think him insane?

An idea began to form. Hobbling back to the general store, Ethan got paper and an envelope. First, he would write a message and then figure out how to get it delivered.

Ethan racked his brain for a way to communicate with Beth that would be indecipherable by anyone else. Then he wrote.

Your thirty-fourth birthday. Same date, same time, add five months and look under the trees at the side of your house. Obviously, very different year. Ethan.

185

Today was March fifth. Beth's birthday was October fifteenth. He prayed she would understand his coded message about that magical night and meet him in ten days at midnight.

Then he remembered that her birthday was also the day of the lightning.

* * *

It took several inquiries, but Ethan eventually found the Watson house, a modest brick structure in the center of Sharpsburg. Furls of black crepe fluttered between the columns of the front porch.

Ethan knocked on the formidable front door, his mouth dry, his right hand clutching a sealed envelope. Just as Ethan had decided this a bad idea and was turning to leave, he heard the rattle of the brass doorknob. The heavy oak swung back and he saw a face he recognized. He had last seen it hovering over him in his last moments as Charles Watson.

"Yes, may I help you?" The nurse looked him up and down.

"Helen?"

Her young face squinted into a preview of what she would look like in twenty years. "I don't know you. What's your business here? We're in mourning or can't you see too well?"

"Helen, I know you're a kind person. You took very good care of Mr. Watson. I'm sorry to bother you now, but I've come to ask you for a favor."

She tilted her head, suspicious.

First, Ethan showed her the two-bit silver piece he had taken from the store's till. Her eyes widened at the sight of hard currency. "Helen, how did you get the notes to Katherine Hawley?"

The nurse's eyebrows came down and she stepped back a pace. Ethan sensed she was about to slam the door in his face. "It's okay, Helen. I just want some information. I need to get a message to Katherine."

"Jes walk up to the house, then." The door started to close. Ethan did something he never thought he would do. He darted his left foot between the door and the jamb. This sudden move shrieked pain up his back and through his shoulder, but he stood his ground.

The door opened wide enough for Helen's panicked face to protrude. "I can't take messages there no more. Mrs. Hawley chased me off. Go away."

186

Ethan held up the silver and said, "Just tell me her maid's name. I know you know her."

"It's Emily." A hand snaked out and made the silver vanish. Ethan felt a painful impact on his left toes as Helen stomped his foot. Reflexively, he pulled back and the door slammed shut.

* * *

Mrs. Nichols rummaged through bolts of cloth at the rear of her store, humming to herself, lost in thought.

"Mrs. Nichols?"

She whirled and clutched at her chest. "My word, Billy Anspach, don't sneak up on a person like that."

"Sorry, ma'am. I just wanted to ask you something. Do you know the Hawley maid, Emily?"

Mrs. Nichols's look of consternation quickly remolded into a sly, knowing grin. She saw a possibly juicy piece to add to the cauldron of gossip that stewed in her shop. "Ah, now I see why you were acting so skittish about the Hawley house. Emily is an attractive young woman, no doubt."

"No, no, Mrs. Nichols. I wondered if you had seen Emily lately? How often does she come in here?"

"Oh, once or twice a week. Do you want to meet her?"

Ethan stared at his feet, stuttered, "Well, yeah."

Mrs. Nichols had heard some whispers about Katherine Hawley. Had there been some sparking between her and Billy? But looking at the gawky young man before her, Mrs. Nichols couldn't see how the refined Hawley beauty could ever be interested in this specimen. No, the rumors were close, but wrong. The maid was the more likely match for Billy. But why did he act as if they had never met? Rumor had it that *someone* in the Hawley house was pregnant. Only momentarily slowed as her mind sifted this new information into her never-ending skein of personal intrigues, Mrs. Nichols smiled.

"Billy, I'm sure she'll pop in any day now. I'll see to it you two talk." Mrs. Nichols gave Ethan a knowing nod and shooed him to the door. "Now, off with you. I have work to do."

Gossip was fun, but actually becoming a matchmaker? Mrs. Nichols floated through her chores in heavenly bliss for the rest of the day.

187

CHAPTER 61

Ethan's body healed enough over the next week to allow him to mind Calvin Anspach's store as long as he didn't have to lift anything. Townsfolk obliged. They rooted through supplies and did their own carrying. They only expected Billy to handle money.

One afternoon, in a swirl of pale skirt, the Hawley maid, Emily Blanchard, entered the general store. Her dark eyes glistened from the cold wind and a wind-flush lit up her olive skin. She threw off the hood of her green woolen coat to reveal coils of raven hair wrapped around her head and held by tortoise-shell combs. She had a prim mouth pursed in a tiny smile.

"Hello, Billy. Mrs. Nichols sent me over for a pair of shears. Seems hers are missing."

Reflexively, Ethan reached under the counter, found scissors, and handed them toward the young lady. As she approached, he saw a look of recognition in her eyes. Oh, no, another one. Ethan had the constant problem of encountering people who knew Billy. He endlessly fumbled to squeeze information from people he was supposed to know.

The dark-eyed young woman lowered her head and looked at Ethan from under her brows. "She said you wanted to talk to me?"

Suddenly, it struck Ethan who this was. God knew what fictions Mrs. Nichols had poured into this poor creature.

"Yes, Emily." Ethan's mind raced. If this young woman had romantic notions, the last thing she would do is help Ethan contact Katherine.

That is, if she kept her romantic notions. Ethan hated himself as he opened his mouth. "Can you keep a secret?"

Flames leaped in the young girl's eyes. "I 'spect I can." Her voice told Ethan far more than he wanted to know.

"Good. When you head home, I want you to take something to Katherine Hawley. But you mustn't tell anyone about it. Not a soul. Especially not Mrs. Nichols or the whole town will know by sundown."

For five seconds, Emily's eyes burned into Ethan with an intensity that almost made him shiver. He held up a fifty-cent piece. "It's very important I get a message to her right away." He extended the silver toward the girl.

Her focus shifted momentarily to the money, then back to Ethan's eyes. He watched her hopes crumble. Eyes that had been so vivid and bright now clouded over. Taking the only path open to her, Emily's small fingers reached out for the coin. Her voice had been husky earlier, but now Ethan could barely hear her as she replied. "What's the message?"

Ethan felt cheap as he handed her the envelope he had sealed with wax to thwart prying eyes. All he could think to say was, "Thank you."

Her eyes lingered on him for another second. She turned and put her shoulder to the heavy front door, at the same time flipping her hood over her head. Through the plate glass windows, Ethan watched her hunch against the wind and head back toward Mrs. Nichols's shop.

He noticed that the scissors still sat on the counter. He replaced them in the drawer.

CHAPTER 62

Bethany felt like a teenager as she crept from her bedroom and down the hall. What an idiot, she thought. I *am* a teenager. At moments like this when the thirty-four year old woman clamored inside her head, she wanted to scream. But she threw those frustrations aside, walled them in, and continued her careful navigation of the dark house. She focused on the singular fact that Ethan waited outside in the night.

Her heart thumped at the prospect of seeing him. But was it really him or another delusion? Was she allowing her imagination to overcompensate for her profound sense of loss? Since she had awakened in a stranger's body with bandages wrapping her belly, everything had seemed like a dream. She didn't care. She had to cling to this dream or go mad.

* * *

Ethan shivered in the damp cold. A pale half-moon punched halfheartedly through the high cloud cover, briefly illuminating the Hawley house in sharp lines of black and gray. Ethan turned to the east. A rounded hump of hill rose like an etched and frosted Christmas ball, the illumination of the moon catching in a billion ice crystals that seemed painted onto every surface. The hill. Ethan turned and assessed this house that stood on the eastern edge of Sharpsburg.

He had been here as Cole. On that hill he had been shot. As he had toppled into the hay stubble, he had seen this house. Time telescoped and Ethan suddenly felt the nauseating agony that had seared through his body.

This would take some getting used to. Memories of a different life? Ethan, Cole, the ailing Charles Watson, and now Billy Anspach. The different experiences he had in each body were blending together.

A shadow of black mutated to a shadow of gray. It shifted across the bright backdrop of snow and fluttered in Ethan's general direction. The clouds thickened and contrasts disappeared. The landscape became a soupy gloom. As she approached, Ethan heard rather than saw her. Footsteps crunched through the brittle surface of the snow.

"Over here."

The crunching got louder and a swirl of shadow

emerged from the greater dark. Her loose cloaks like black wings around her, Bethany hurled herself against Ethan. "Tell me you're real," she said.

Arms held him and a warm face pressed against his. Hungry lips searched and found his mouth and suddenly Bethany's presence engulfed Ethan. He did not need to test her with questions for which only she would know the answers. Some ineffable energy radiated from her. He had known its flickering existence as he had searched for her, but now, like a beacon in the cold depths of space, she blazed before him with the heat of a star furnace.

They fell to the snow in a tangle, kissing by touch and by memory.

Gasping, Bethany finally pulled her head back long enough to say, "It really *is* you. I'm *not* crazy. I didn't know what to believe. How did we get here? Ethan, what has happened?" Suddenly, her dreams seemed real and the world around her seemed imaginary as the dam of memory broke loose and flooded her with emotions.

"Later. Right now, come with me. We'll freeze out here." Ethan stood and pulled Bethany to her feet. They brushed the snow off each other and hiked away from the Hawley house, their crunching footsteps constant evidence of the dropping temperature. Ethan navigated to the edge of town, then down an alley to the Anspach General Store. Nobody else walked the streets, the town's residents either asleep or huddled near stoves and fireplaces to fight off the cold. If not for the ghostly columns of smoke belching out of hundreds of chimneys, the place could have been uninhabited.

Using his key at the rear entrance of Calvin Anspach's store, Ethan led Bethany into the storeroom where he had earlier stoked a fire in the small cast iron stove. Ethan relocked the heavy plank door and led Bethany to a corner of the storeroom where he had stacked blankets into a bed. He lit a fat candle, transforming the bare wood walls, the barrels, and the crates into a softly glowing nook. A hundred scents floated through the air: leather goods treated with neatsfoot oil, pepper, the damp odor of wool, wood smoke, tobacco.

They stood for a minute surveying each other's faces in the shifting light. Bethany stroked her hand across the young face with its soft stubble that glowed like gold flecks. "You look like a surfer, Ethan." She took his hand and pulled him down to the makeshift bed. "Would you consider this a barn?"

191

Ethan's face twisted in bewilderment.

"We had an appointment in a barn," she said. "Glad you finally kept it."

A laugh snorted out of Ethan before he could even think. "I see there's only one way to keep you quiet." Ethan kissed her.

* * *

Ethan ran his hand over the naked roundness of Beth's belly. "How long?"

"Doctor Robert says about six months."

"Who's the father?"

"I don't know." Beth shifted her gaze to the yellow candle flame. "But I must say I'm looking forward to having this baby. I like being fertile."

The glow in her eyes could have melted the coldest heart. Disappointment had crushed them when they had found that Beth was not able to conceive. Ethan gently touched the puckered scar below the mound that held the baby. "What's this?"

"During the battle. It's the shot that killed her. Then I woke up inside her. Since then, very little has made sense. I mean, how could I wake up in the body of someone who has died?"

"How'd she get shot?"

"The maid says she found me, her, in a pool of blood in front of an upstairs window."

"Poor girl."

"It's worse than that. The father's a monster. George Hawley. And he blames Billy for this," Beth pointed to her stomach. She outlined all that had transpired during her recuperation.

"That explains why he glares at me on the street." Ethan wondered again how Billy had gotten shot. All clues led to Hawley.

"It gets worse. Daddy Dearest is sending me away. He can't bear the blow to his reputation to have his daughter living here with a bastard child."

"When?"

"I would have been gone already if not for the mother. She wants better weather for the journey."

"To where?"

"You won't believe this. He's sending me by canal up into Ohio far enough north to get around any Confederate

192

actions. Then by train I'll go to Kansas, then on to Nevada by stagecoach."

"He really wants you out of the neighborhood."

She punched his shoulder. When Ethan winced, her playfulness turned to concern. She touched him gently. "What is it, honey?"

Ethan rolled into the candlelight. When Beth saw the ragged crater in the upper left quadrant of Ethan's chest, she gasped. Her fingers flew to the wound and gently traced its outline. "Oh, my poor darling. You had to come back from this?"

Ethan nodded. He told her about the previous bodies he had also inhabited.

"Ethan, how do you do it?"

He stared into the candle flame. "I can't explain it. Do you remember the moment of the lightning bolt?"

Fear twisted her face. She nodded, but said nothing.

"Remember me there in it with you?"

"Yes. I thought I felt you and then nothing."

"We made contact and I think that's why you didn't lose your memory. You're still Beth."

"How?"

"I don't know. It has to do with me. I've been through it four times now and I'm still me. I have a talent."

"But why the dying bodies?"

"The only way to find you. I could enter a fetus; I can feel them out there before I choose a body. But I needed to be grown up to have mobility. I didn't want to wait twenty years to chase after you."

"How could I end up in this girl's body?"

Ethan shook his head. "I'm not sure what I believe."

"But, Ethan, how were you in the lightning bolt with me without being killed?"

"This is difficult to explain. Once I started timejumping, I went back along my own timeline to that moment. I reached out to you and connected with you. Since I wasn't in a physical form, I was able to withstand the energy."

"But that was later, right?"

"Yeah."

"But, it seemed like the same moment. It all happened at once. Then I woke up here."

"That's the most perplexing part of this. I *know* that I visited that moment many times, but for you it happened just once. Another paradox."

"It's more than that. If you somehow changed what happened after the fact to send me here, think of what that means. You rearranged events. How can that be possible?"

Ethan stared into Beth's eyes. "We have this notion that the universe is governed by physical laws. That's a very human assumption. But you remember I read those articles on quantum physics last summer?"

"Yes."

"Scientists find paradoxes all over the place. The physical world seems to be anything *but* lawful. I'm finding the same thing. When I've gone back to our original time, I keep expecting things I've done in the past to have some effect. But nothing has changed. I keep trying to shake off my assumptions about how things are supposed to work."

When he said nothing more, Beth responded, "So, these bodies are ours now? We can stay like this?"

"Yes. Billy is nineteen. How old are you?"

"Seventeen."

"So, we have a long life ahead."

"Then what?"

"We'll cross that bridge when we get to it."

"What about now? Do you want me married off to some miner? Because that's where I'm headed."

Ethan pulled her close to him. "That is not going to happen. We have to get away from here."

"How?"

"Look around you. Billy's father owns the general store. We can take the supplies we need and disappear."

"Hawley sells horses and mules to the army. He won't miss two horses right away."

"Okay, Ma Barker." They laughed and then looked deeply into each other's eyes.

Ethan said, "When is Hawley shipping you off?"

"He won't say when, but he's making preparations."

"Then let's not mess around. Tomorrow's Tuesday. I'll use tomorrow and Wednesday to pull together money and supplies. Wednesday night we'll go. After midnight when everybody's settled down. We'll have all night and the next day to get a head start. They'll never find us."

"The next day?"

"Yeah. Billy or his father always takes the wagon to Frederick on Thursday to pick up freight. If Billy's not around,

194

people will think he left early."

"Where will we go?"

"I think north. Out of the war zone."

"Can we go back to the future, to our old home?"

"I can go back, but I don't know how to get you back. I have my body back there, but yours was vaporized." Ethan sketched out the details of his travails with Neural Research.

"Just when I'm beginning to have some context of where I am, you're blowing it all to shreds. Ethan, are we trapped here? Forever?"

Ethan gazed into the candle flame, admiring the sharp singularity of its form against the darkness. "Honey, this is nothing like forever. The time we spend in these bodies will seem like the blink of an eye. Forever is out there." He looked into the darker reaches of the storeroom. "Even the stars are like toys. Beth, it's far different than we ever imagined. Time and space are like the surface of a lake. We float on it and think we understand. But down in the depths of the lake, all sorts of things are going on."

"What do you mean?"

He shifted his eyes back to her. The faraway look vanished, replaced by vivid intensity. "Beth, a minute ago you said that I must have rearranged events. I changed what happened to you. That sounds insane, but assume that it's true or we wouldn't be here. If it's true, then the universe is not an inert thing in which we happen to live. Instead, what if it's all a manifestation driven by thought? That would explain the paradoxes. Thought doesn't have to be logical to exist. You can think *anything*. Thought has no rules. So if thought makes the universe create and destroy, to mutate and to expand, then there are no real rules in the universe. Anything that we think, actually happens somewhere in it. The trick is in navigating through its vastness to the place you want to be, to the place where your thoughts are real. In saving you from the lightning, I or we have somehow done that."

Beth reached out with her right hand to stroke Ethan's cheek. "Then have we lived before?"

"Probably. We live and die and move through it all, experiencing different realities. But we forget. Each life is new, different. The shock of death and birth wipes the slate clean, except for little snatches of memory just out of reach. Dreams, deja-vu. They're echoes of where we've been."

"Then why didn't you forget?"

"I always had psychic ability. The experiments at Neural Research enhanced those powers. Somehow I transcended the usual cycle."

Beth's green eyes locked to Ethan's. "In other words, you were always a little weird?"

Ethan scowled. "I can never be serious with you."

"Darling, you're usually too serious. If I didn't tease you, you wouldn't love me so much."

"If you don't stop, I won't love you at all."

"Fat chance." She wrapped her arms around Ethan's neck and pulled him close. "Okay, I'll be serious. If you're the one with the power and you made all this happen, then why are we here? If we could be anywhere at all, why did your thoughts bring us to this time and place?"

"I don't know. Maybe because this time always fascinated me. Something in my subconscious served up the information, maybe. Although, I didn't get here my first try."

Beth stared into the shadows, her face becoming wistful. "Oh, darling, I don't want to explore the universe. Can we go back to our home, to Mister Buzz? Can we have things as they were?"

"Maybe, if you really want to. But remember, to do that, both of these bodies have to die. I'd like to put off that little experiment for a while."

"Why?"

"We might be separated. I'm a novice at this. That's why I'd like to live this life with you now. There's no urgency to move on."

Silent for a few moments, she said, "Why didn't you see the lightning bolt before it happened? We could have avoided this."

"I saw the storm inside my head, but I didn't see how close it was. Until I started using Memnon, I didn't have much control. Sometimes I saw visions clearly, sometimes fuzzy. Funny, but when I was a kid, I found it easier to see things."

Ethan's head snapped toward a gloomy corner of the storeroom.

"What?" Beth said, instinctively pulling a blanket over her breasts.

"Nothing. Just a mouse. But we need to get you back soon so this doesn't blow up in our faces. I think we'd have some problem convincing them we're married."

"How long until dawn?"

196

"Maybe four hours, but you need to be back before that. People are up and about by dawn."

"So, we have at least an hour, right?"

"Yes? So?"

Beth kicked off the blanket. "With all the young men off to war and eligible young females crawling all over this town, I want to make sure my husband is too pooped to do anything but look. Come here, you, whatever your name is." Her arms wrapped around his neck and pulled him down.

"Okay, Little Miss Jailbait."

CHAPTER 63

"You're going Thursday mornin', you little baggage. There's nothing you can do about it." Beth's eyes froze in shock.

Elizabeth Hawley stared, aghast. "George, she's almost six months gone. She'll never make it the whole way before the baby comes."

Hawley sneered. "No thanks to you. Delay, delay. Well she's goin' now. She only needs to make it to Chicago. She can have the baby there and wait for her new husband to come for her. I telegraphed him. He's on his way. There's wagon trains headin' west all summer to take the newlyweds back to Nevada."

"But you promised she didn't have to go until the weather broke."

"The weather's fine. It's time."

Beth had to get word of this disaster to Ethan. She would cajole, threaten, even beat Emily, the servant girl, to get her to take a message tonight.

"Start packing your things, girl. You leave at first light Thursday. Ethridge will take you to the C&O canal. Most of the ice is gone and barge traffic is movin' again."

Beth wanted to argue, but she had long since realized the futility of it. Resistance to her step-father only produced rage. She had to make her own plans.

Hawley called after her. "I'm locking you in your room tonight. Don't want no sleepwalkin'."

* * *

It was after eleven when Emily, the servant, found the courage to creep down the back stairs to the kitchen. She had pulled on two coats against the freezing chill of night. In the pocket of the outer one, the blanket coat, she held Miss Katherine's letter tightly in her right hand.

Earlier in the day, she had slathered lard on the back door hinges to keep them from creaking. The rear door opened without a sound. She stepped onto the back porch and tiptoed toward the stairs. The clouds had diminished and the moon provided sufficient illumination to navigate the streets with ease. She had just reached the top step when a familiar voice rasped from the dark.

"Bit late for a stroll, Emily." The floorboards of the porch creaked as George Hawley loomed out of the shadows. His big hand looked like a bunch of pale sausages as it reached out to her. "Give it to me."

"Sir, I..."

"Don't even waste yer breath. Just give me the note." With a hand whose shaking had nothing to do with the cold, Emily handed Hawley the folded paper.

"Who's it for?"

Emily's small voice replied, "Billy Anspach."

"Now go back to bed and don't breathe a word of this to Katherine. If she asks you, the note was delivered. Understand?"

Emily nodded and flew through the door before Hawley could think of a punishment.

A Lucifer match flared in the gloom and Hawley lit the oil lamp that sat on a crude table at the end of the porch.

Dearest Ethan, my so-called father has done the unthinkable. We cannot leave tomorrow night. He is sending me away Thursday morning and I will be locked in my room until then. Do not come here. I'm afraid he suspects something. You must try to intercept me on the C&O Canal. Somehow, we'll slip the hounds and raise our baby away from all this madness.

All my love,
Bethany.

Hawley's eyes gleamed in the lamplight. He *had* been right. "*Our* baby." The little trollop had given herself to Billy Anspach. Here held proof of their sins. And this game of calling themselves Ethan and Bethany. It must be code in case their letters got intercepted.

Hawley's thick lips worked into a sneer as he set paper to flame. In the sudden light, the sweat on Hawley's face sparkled like frost. The paper burned out and Hawley dropped the ash to the planking where tiny sparks winked across its surface for several seconds. Hawley squeezed out the lamp wick between thumb and forefinger.

Darkness reigned.

CHAPTER 64

A cloud of dust roiled up Main Street, kicked into the air by a dozen riders and a freight wagon pulled by two draft horses. The clatter of so many hooves and the whooping of the riders caused heads to pop out of windows and doorways all along the street. Ethan stepped out of Calvin Anspach's store. George Hawley drove the wagon while a second man held a scattergun on someone in the rear. The ground trembled as the wagon passed. Ethan's eyebrows rose in disbelief at the sight of the man trussed up in the wagon.

Jasper.

Ethan scurried as fast as he could in the wake of the commotion. Townspeople gathered, eager to hear the news. Hawley's group stopped at the unofficial center of town, in front of the telegraph office and the tiny cubby from which Newton Chiles produced the weekly newspaper.

Breathless, Ethan joined the circle of onlookers, all now engaged in heated discussion. Ethan turned to one of the shawled women to his right. "Mrs. Kelly, what happened?"

"They caught that Reb under the McAlister barn. Had guns and powder and a whole cache of food. Seems he's been stealing the countryside blind."

"Let's hang 'im. Murderin' reb bastard." Lucas Brady's fist punched the air. Several in the crowd supported his call for immediate justice.

George Hawley raised his arm and then his voice. "Remember that traveler we found shot on the road a couple months ago? And two of our local boys was dead next to him? Maybe this reb shot all three?"

"I say we hang 'im," Burt Scoggins chimed in.

Hawley had to play this right. He wanted the town worked up, but he wanted them moving toward the solution that he had been going over in his head since his men had found the reb that morning. "Let's bring our prisoner up here and see what he has to say." Three of Hawley's hired hands muscled Jasper to the boardwalk in front of the telegraph office. "What's yer name?"

Jasper stared into the crowd.

Hawley punched him in the ear. "I said, what's yer name."

200

"Ya fixin' to carve it on my tombstone, are ya? Right generous of ya." Jasper said.

Hawley wound up and punched at him again, but Jasper ducked and the force of Hawley's follow-through almost caused him to fall off the boardwalk. Several people snickered as Hawley's face reddened. His eyes sunk into their pits of gristle. "You won't even get a grave, reb. First they starve you in prison, then they feed you to the pigs."

"Reckon you know a lot about the habits of pigs, you tub o'guts."

Someone in the crowd yelled, "Prison? Hell, we should hang 'im."

Hawley recovered himself. He held up his hand again, signaling for silence. "Nothin' I'd rather do than hang this murderin' thief. But we don't want trouble with the army. They want all stragglers and deserters delivered to them. I do a lot of business with Uncle Sam and I don't need no trouble. This bag of bones should go to Fredericktowne to the county sheriff. They can turn him over to the army."

"It's damn cold, George. Who's gonna take 'im all that way? Easier to hang 'im." Several in the crowd examined the gray sky and nodded.

"I'll take him." Hawley scanned the crowd. "You there, Billy Anspach. Don't you go into Fredericktowne for supplies on Thursdays? How about I go with you tomorrow? While you drive, I can keep an eye on the prisoner. That'll be a lot safer than puttin' him on a horse."

Several men made sounds of support. One dissenter said, "I still think we should hang him."

"Chester, this is an army matter. They'll send him to a prison that will be worse than hangin'. We hang him, he dies once. In prison, he dies every day." Looking around the crowd, George Hawley raised his voice. "Are we in agreement on this?"

Scanning the crowd, Ethan didn't see that many people nodding.

Hawley said, "Okay, then. We're in agreement." He called out, "Billy, when you leavin' tomorrow?"

Ethan didn't respond, seemingly frozen in place.

"Billy, I said, when you leavin'?"

Not wanting to let the moment pass, Hawley announced, "Alright, that's settled. We leave tomorrow morning. Early." Hawley smiled and shouted to his men. "Okay. Let's haul this trash to the livery stable overnight. You men take shifts watchin' him."

As the crown dispersed, Ethan stood trancelike looking at the spot on the boardwalk where Jasper had been.

CHAPTER 65

Ethan waited outside the Hawley house until well after midnight, shivering badly until he could take no more and finally trudged back to the general store. He left the back door unlocked and buried himself in blankets, hoping that Beth might show up in the wee hours.

Just after dawn on Thursday, roosters awakened Ethan. He forced himself to get up and shuffled into the barn behind the store. He hitched two horses to the supply wagon and drove to the front of the telegraph office where George Hawley and three of his men stood stamping their feet against the cold. Jasper's head lolled against his chest, as if he was still asleep. Hawley's men manhandled Jasper into the Anspach wagon. For George Hawley's benefit, Ethan made a great show of roughness in tying a heavy leather thong around Jasper's wrists. But he didn't cut off Jasper's circulation. The old trooper wouldn't be comfortable, but he wouldn't be in pain. With a stout yard of rope, Ethan fastened Jasper's wrists to an iron ring in the side of the wagon.

Hawley inspected Ethan's handiwork, grunted, and heaved himself into the wagon's front seat. "Let's go, boy."

Something about Hawley caused Ethan's hair to prickle. He was used to Hawley treating Billy like a field hand, contempt just under the surface for the young man that Hawley blamed for his step-daughter's pregnancy. But something else hovered there this morning. Smugness, even a touch of concealed joy. Why? What did he know? Had he been aware of Beth's planned escape? Ethan fought hard to keep his face normal.

Just as Ethan was reaching to unhitch the wheel brake, the wiry figure of Newton Chiles hustled out of the telegraph office. Only in shirtsleeves, he hunched his shoulders as if that would keep him warm against the morning chill. "Billy, could you take this to the post office in Fredericktowne?" Chiles offered a flat, paper-wrapped bundle tied with rough string.

Because Sharpsburg had no official post office, Billy often took letters and packages back and forth on his trips to Fredericktowne. As he reached for the package, Chiles grabbed Ethan's arm and pulled him lower. Not much above a whisper, he said, "Careful with this, Billy. It's important."

203

Ethan glanced at the black, spidery writing in the center of the parcel addressed to the Department of War. "What is it, Mr. Chiles?"

"My two boys found it. It's a dispatch case, from the battle. Has papers for General McClellan."

"Where'd they find it?"

Chiles looked down for an instant. "They didn't just find it yesterday." He gave Ethan a knowing nod. "Don't want no trouble here, Billy. Just want to get this back in the right hands." Chiles slapped Ethan's shoulder and ran back to the warmth of his office.

Ethan tucked the package under his seat.

The day started clear and, though still chilly, markedly warmer than the previous week. As they bounced out of Sharpsburg, Ethan noticed that icicles along the fronts of houses had begun melting. Patches of earth showed through the snow. He'd had enough cold wind to last a lifetime.

Over his shoulder, Ethan said, "So, tell me, soldier, where you from? Got the sound of Charleston in your voice."

Ethan glanced back and got a weird look from Jasper. So much for coded messages.

Hawley half turned on the seat and glanced at Jasper. "Tryin' to make a friend, Billy? It's like you that the only friend you can make is a worthless reb soldier."

The first hour, they remained silent. Then, as they ascended the heavily rutted trail into Turner's Gap, Jasper called from the rear of the wagon. "Hey, I need ta shit. Think we can stop for a minute?"

Hawley laughed and said, "Shit in yer pants for all I care."

Ethan said, "If he does, he'll stink to high heaven the rest of the trip. Why don't you hold a gun on him and I'll untie his wrists?"

"Untie his wrists? No. Those wrists stay tied 'til we get him to Fredericktowne."

"You want to pull my drawers down, wipe my ass for me? That's fine by me," drawled Jasper.

Hawley growled, "Hold it 'til we get up the hill. At the top we need to rest the horses anyway."

They rode in silence for ten minutes. Hawley barked, "Stop the wagon. Pull into this clearing on the right." Hawley drew his Colt as Ethan released Jasper's hands from the iron ring. "Let's go down in this brush over here." As they walked,

Ethan noticed that the snow and dead leaf cover had been churned up recently by a horse's passage. At the end of the hoof prints, human footprints had packed down the snow. Who had ridden a horse this far off the road? And why?

A large copse of mountain laurel stood out in lush green against leafless trees. Behind them, the land dropped off, revealing the Middletown Valley stretched in patches of brown and white and tan. Jasper said, "I'll jes' go behind there. Won't take a minute."

Hawley growled, "No. Keep walking."

Thirty feet farther, they came upon a gorge in the earth. The underlying rock had parted into a deep chasm only three feet across. Jasper squinted and looked back and forth at Hawley and Billy. "Jes' give me two heavy tree limbs to stretch across there and that'll be the finest latrine I ever used," Jasper cackled.

"Reb, thirty seconds from now, the last thing on yer mind will be the latrine. Now, you want I should shoot you first, or you just want to jump down in there?"

"Hawley!"

"You shut up, Billy." Hawley waved the revolver in Ethan's direction for a second.

Jasper craned his head over the edge of the gorge. "Looks like a hundred feet down. Man could get pretty busted up fallin' in there. I think you better shoot me first. Or mebbe you ain't got the stomach for shootin' a man? Rather I just make it easy fer ya and jump?"

"You Reb bastard. I don't care how we do it."

Ethan's face twisted in shock. "Why are you doing this?"

A grin sliced open the red jowls of George Hawley. "Getting' even, Billy. Nothing in the whole world feels better."

Jasper's calm voice carried through the clean air. "I'll turn around. If I was runnin' away, you'd have to shoot me in the back."

Hawley spun his weapon back toward Jasper. "You die no matter what, you scum, so shut up."

"Getting even for what?" Ethan said. "He never did anything to you."

Hawley's eyes glinted. "This reb is just a tool, Billy. I'm gettin' even with *you*." He leveled his Colt at Ethan. "This piece of scum tried to escape, grabbed my gun and managed to shoot you, Billy, before I could overpower him. In the fight, I got hold of my gun and pushed him into the pit. Good story, huh? The town will eat it up. All my problems go away."

"How am I your problem?" Ethan said.

Hawley's eyes got their most piggish. "They say you lost your memory, Billy. Don't remember who shot you. You don't remember the duel?"

Ethan frowned. "What duel?"

"To make you pay for gettin' Katherine pregnant, for not marryin' her. How you think you wound up in the creek? We had a duel. You lost."

Ethan shook his head. "No, it was that Ethridge. He's the one I saw riding away."

"He was your second. I was the one who shot you. Though I do owe some of my success to Ethridge." Hawley swelled like a balloon. Now that he had started, the boasting felt too good to stop. "Ethridge made sure you didn't get lucky. When he loaded your pistol, he palmed the ball. You only fired powder and wadding at me. So now I have the pleasure of shooting you again. Only this time, you stay dead."

As Hawley lifted his pistol to sight at Ethan's chest, Jasper jumped into the gorge. Hawley instinctively turned his aim toward the movement, fearing an attack. In that moment of confusion, Ethan drew a Colt .44 from inside his coat. Time slowed. Ethan smelled wet earth wafting up from breaks in the snow. He heard a woodpecker hammering against a tree trunk. The sun that filtered through the bare branches warmed his face. Where the sun struck the barrel of his revolver, it formed a bar of light that pointed directly at George Hawley. Beyond the muzzle, Ethan watched Hawley turn away from the gorge, his arm swinging toward Ethan again. With no haste, Ethan thumbed back the hammer, sighted along the bar of light, and pulled the trigger.

A ball of fire and smoke roiled out of the big Colt and wrapped around Hawley's chest. George Hawley's eyes opened wide and a great groan rumbled out of him. With a mind of its own, Hawley's big fist arced up again toward Ethan, but before his revolver could fire, another ball of flame hurled into George Hawley and he toppled backward. Ethan walked the few steps needed to stand over the heaving body. Hawley's legs thrashed as he sucked great lungsful of air into his damaged chest.

Ethan thought of Jasper's body now crumpled and broken at the bottom of the gorge and he fired again, taking pleasure at how the jellied mass quivered from the impact. Still that great body battled death, but blood began to flow out the sides of Hawley's mouth, bright blood, like barn paint in the sunshine, thick and shiny.

Ethan had always thought of himself as a peaceful man, but something in him snapped. He emptied the Colt into that black heap of cloth that just wouldn't stop moving. Finally, George Hawley looked like a beached whale left behind by an ebbing tide.

Ethan stood with the Colt hanging in his fist. Life after life he just saw pain and more pain and greed and the wreck of human lusts run wild. He had leaped through the cosmos, had seen stars born, yet here he stood with a smoking gun and another dead body. He now knew why someone had left a boy to die on cold ground. Knowing the answer gave him no pleasure. He looked down on the corpse with scorn.

"'Nothing in the whole world feels better?' You stupid bastard." Ethan looked up into the sky. "God help me."

"Maybe God could help me too, feller, 'cause it don't seem nobody else is fixin' to."

Ethan thought he had lost his mind. He hurried to the edge of the gorge. Six feet below the edge, standing on a boulder wedged into the cut, Jasper squinted up, his beaver teeth yellow in the sun. "Sure could use a hand."

"Jasper, you old bastard."

Jasper blinked. "How you know my name? I never told my real name."

Ethan smiled. "It's me, Ethan. Or Cole, whichever you choose. Can you get your hands in front of you?"

"Yeah, hold on."

Jasper crouched and worked his bound hands under his bottom and then under his legs. He muttered, "Don't rightly care what yer name is long as you get me on outta here." He stood.

"Hold your hands up." Ethan reached down with his jackknife and cut the leather. "Okay, here goes." With Jasper bracing his legs in crevices in the rock wall, Ethan hauled him up over the edge where they both collapsed. Ethan felt Jasper whirl and then he felt a tug at his coat. As Ethan sat up, he faced the business end of his own Colt as Jasper scrambled to his feet.

"Jasper, my gun's empty. You must be tired. I thought you could count better than that runt of a highwayman." Ethan sat back on the rock and folded his legs, waiting.

"How you know about that?" Jasper craned his head

207

back and forth to examine Ethan's face. He quickly checked the Colt.

"Jasper, go over there and get Hawley's sidearm if it makes you feel better. I know having less than a half dozen guns makes you nervous."

The old campaigner's eyes shifted toward the corpse and back to Ethan. Those blue orbs scrutinized every detail of Ethan's face.

"Jasper, it won't do any good. I won't look like Cole. This is a completely different body."

"I don't know how I can believe this."

"I'll prove it to you." Ethan pointed north. "Up there is where we started, above Turner's Gap. We ate green corn that morning. Then we walked down through Bolivar and Boonsboro and caught a ride on a cart to Sharpsburg. You drew your Walker on a sentry from Savannah. I got my nuts shot off in the battle and I showed you these streams contain gold. We holed up under a barn. You shot that highwayman who killed two men and two horses. The third horse you gave to a slave family. Isn't that enough? Who else could know these things?"

Jasper shook his head as he brushed himself off. "You know, Youngblood, a few months back when you spun this yarn, I thought you was like half the men in this war. Tetched. Ain't nothin' wrong with that. But I must be tetched too, 'cause even though I'm lookin' at a different face, I do believe it's you." He shrugged and shook his head and let out one of his cackling laughs. "What shall we do with this tub of guts?" Jasper handed back Ethan's revolver. He leaned over and picked up Hawley's Colt and let down the hammer. He tucked the revolver into his belt and picked through the dead man's pockets. "I vote we throw him in this gorge since he liked it so much."

Jasper took something from Hawley's vest and rolled it in his hand for a few seconds before looking up at Ethan. "Here, Youngblood, I think this was for you."

Ethan extended his hand and felt something heavy drop into it. The gray lead glowed dull in the morning sun. Ethan rolled the pistol ball between thumb and forefinger, examining it. Scratched into its surface he saw a date: 11-7-62. Calculating back, Ethan said, "Bastard scratched the date of the duel on this damn thing." He pursed his lips and dropped the bullet into his pants pocket.

"Whoowee." Jasper stood up and held out his hand to Ethan. "Lookee here." Seven disks of fire nestled in Jasper's palm. "Double eagles. Mormon twenty-dollar gold pieces. Ain't seen one of these since I was out west. This day is lookin' up. We can go a fer piece on this kinda money."

"I won't be going with you, Jasper. I'm going back."

"What? They'll hang *you* instead of me."

"No. I'll tell them we got ambushed by deserters. They grabbed Hawley and the wagon, but in the commotion I jumped off and ran into the woods. They shot at me, but I wasn't hit. Last thing I know, they were headed up the road to Myersville. That way if anyone ever finds Hawley's body, it won't get put on your shoulders."

"That's a real fine story, Youngblood. But why go back and have to tell it?"

"I found her, Jasper. Bethany, my wife. She's back there in Sharpsburg. She's young, I'm young. We can live a life together."

Jasper cackled and danced a little jig. "Good fer you, Youngblood. Good fer you."

Together, they struggled to push and drag Hawley's big carcass to the hole in the earth. When they got him to the edge, Jasper said, "Mind if I do the honors?" He stood straight, saluted, then kicked the corpse hard. "See ya in hell, ya bastard."

Two seconds later, a loud thump echoed out of the pit.

Ethan commented, "So, another fellow for you to meet in hell."

"Yeah, my dance card's gonna be pretty full."

"Jasper, why didn't you get out of here? I thought you would be gone months ago."

"Once winter came on, I didn't care much for tromping across the countryside to head south. Had plenty of food and that barn was kinda comfortable."

Ethan lifted an eyebrow and teased, "Had nothing to do with leaving the gold behind, did it?"

The old scout snickered and tugged at his beard. "Well, maybe a leetle bit."

Ethan stepped closer to Jasper and held out his revolver. "Here, it's not a Walker, but you may need this. Give me Hawley's." Jasper swapped guns and smiled so wide his beaver teeth showed. Ethan threw Hawley's gun over the edge of the cliff.

"Hey, that was a damn nice gun."

"Yeah, Jasper, with Hawley's initials engraved on the barrel, what do you think would happen if you got caught with it?" Ethan shrugged out of his greatcoat and handed it to Jasper. "Here, take this too. Your uniform is beat up but it still sticks out like a sore thumb." Jasper donned the big garment. Then Ethan said, "Take the horses and the wagon. I have to walk back to town for my story to work."

Jasper leaped up onto the wagon's plank seat and reached down his right hand. "Good luck to ya, Ethan. Thanks fer gettin' me out of this jam."

They shook hands. Ethan said, "I thought you needed a latrine?"

Jasper's blue eyes twinkled. "Nah. Was jest lookin' to get somebody to make a mistake so's I could cut loose."

"You fox. Hole up in some place like Baltimore until the war is over. Lots of southern sympathizers in Baltimore. Then I expect you'll be a rich gold miner a couple years later."

"You get half my share. I'll deliver it personal."

Ethan laughed. "You do that."

"What name you got now so's I can find you?"

"Billy Anspach. The father is Calvin Anspach. He owns the general store in Sharpsburg. But if things work out, Jasper, you won't find me there. Beth and I will be long gone." Remembering something, Ethan said, "Almost forgot. Hand me that package under the seat."

Jasper fumbled around and then caught hold of the package twine. "What ye got there?"

"I don't know. Now, you get out of here, Old Timer."

"Don't you 'Old Timer' me, you little pup." In answer, Ethan slapped the nearer gelding's rump and the wagon lurched ahead. He watched until Jasper disappeared among the naked trees. Then he turned and followed his shadow down the hill. Ethan faced a long walk, but he needed time to go over the story he would need to tell.

After an hour, Ethan stepped off the muddy road and settled on the thick trunk of a fallen oak to rest his feet. The sun warmed his face as he cut the string from around the parcel. As he pulled off the paper wrapping, the sun caught the scarred surface of a leather dispatch case. Ethan unfastened dull brass buckles and opened the flat case. Inside he found several folded papers and one large envelope. He unfolded the papers and saw manifests, listing supplies and

210

provisions in neat columns. Ethan set those back inside the case and pulled open the stiff, brown envelope.

Ethan had always been a student of history, had spent long hours in the library during his youth. In later years he had hiked all over Maryland and Virginia, exploring the sites of great and small Civil War battles. But that had all been abstraction compared to this moment. Ethan realized he *was in* history. A glow ran through him as he fingered through the documents.

He read battle orders from General McClellan to his subordinates with scribbled replies from each. He perused hand-drawn maps of Sharpsburg and the surrounding countryside. Amazed, he handled orders from Robert E. Lee. Someone must have intercepted a Confederate messenger.

He had seen such documents in museums, but they had been yellowed and tattered with the ink faded by sunlight and blurred by water. These documents had clean surfaces, the writing crisp. Ethan riffled through the packet, reading letters and notes until he came to one document that took his breath away.

His attention telescoped into single-point focus as Ethan read these words: "Dear General McClellan, though I have pushed and prodded you to engage the enemy over these past months, my heart quells at the sight of the product of these exhortations. I stand here now in the church at Middletown, some miles in the rear of your position. My aides will not let me proceed further than this toward the front. Hundreds of young men lie here in this makeshift hospital, under the eyes of their God as they expire in silence and with a courage that humbles and rebukes me. Though my sense of duty urges me to see the fighting first hand, to know the consequences of my decisions, some part of me finds relief in knowing I will not be allowed to view the Horseman of Death as he scythes through the fields of Sharpsburg. Know that my good wishes and prayers ride with you and your men in this hour of calamity. Yours, in God, Abraham Lincoln."

As Ethan's gaze wandered up to the china-blue sky, his vision blurred. As vast as he knew the universe to be, he marveled at how the actions of one being on one small planet in one average solar system could ring through eternity with such compassion and humanity.

Ethan carefully folded the letter and placed it back into the larger envelope with the Lee and McClellan papers. This he

211

tucked into a pocket in the inner lining of his coat. The remaining papers Ethan tossed to the wind. As he stood, he flung the dispatch case spinning into the trees. Then he continued his trek back to Sharpsburg.

CHAPTER 66

Halfway down South Mountain, in a sharp left turn, Jasper felt the wagon's traction give way. The iron-rimmed wheels slid on snow and ice and the wagon began to drift sideways toward the edge of the cliff. Jasper risked a quick look and snapped his eyes back to the road in horror. He damned himself for driving too fast in his haste to get away from Hawley's body. Had he traded a slow, almost certain death in prison for a swift demise not a mile from his liberation?

Jasper yelled, "Yah" and the horses jumped in surprise. He pulled on the wheel brake as he loosened the reins to make the wagon drag against the increased pull of the horses. The wheel moaned as Jasper put all of his weight against the braking lever. Smoke rose from the brake. Just another few seconds.

Jasper steered the horses to the side of the road as they raced onward. The rear wheels spun dangerously close to the edge, spewing up a white curtain as the outside wheels plowed through a foot of virgin snow that no other traveler would have been foolhardy enough to drive through. The added drag of the deeper snow began to work. The wagon stabilized. The horses pulled the wagon out of its skid.

As the road straightened, Jasper reined in the horses and pulled hard on the wheel brake. He sat puffing in the still air and watched steam rise in lazy tendrils off the backs of the geldings. "Damn, Jasper, this is no way to end it," he mumbled to himself.

The bright day had gotten warmer. No longer in a hurry, Jasper pulled down the collar of the greatcoat Ethan had given him, clucked at the horses, and released the brake.

Once off the hill, he covered the remaining four miles to Middletown in short order. He did not stop. Someone might recognize the Anspach's wagon and horses. Jasper pushed on to the much larger settlement of Fredericktowne where he could lose himself in the crowds.

It was not even noon when Jasper trotted the horses through the center of Fredericktowne. To be safe, he continued to the eastern edge of the city, believing that the Anspachs probably did their business on the western side that was

213

closest to Sharpsburg. Jasper found a livery stable and commenced to a leisurely haggle that resulted in him riding away on a serviceable used saddle strapped to one of the geldings.

Jasper stopped at a general store and half an hour later tied several brown-paper bundles behind his saddle. They contained wool pants, shirts, and socks and a new pair of black boots. He'd bought a gunbelt which now held a heavily used Walker .44 for which Jasper had gladly parted with one of the Mormon gold pieces. The Colt Ethan had given him now nestled in his saddlebag.

As Jasper finished securing his parcels, a gruff voice addressed him from behind. "Hey, theah, mistuh." Jasper turned. Before him shuffled an old man whose pale, pious face sported a ridiculously bulbous nose that glowed cherry red in the cold. The red of his nose matched the bloodshot eyes that peered out from under a crumpled gray stovepipe hat. This walking scarecrow wore a gray suit so wrinkled that the sleeves and legs rode up several inches from the man's paper-white wrists and ankles. The man's left hand held a bottle in which a few inches of amber fluid sloshed as he gestured with both skinny arms.

Jasper cackled at the sight. "Hey, old-timer, looks like somebody sat on you."

"You a liah, a cheatahr 'n you doan kno God."

Jasper laughed and replied, "Guess I'm in the right town." Before he could get sucked into a conversation, Jasper swung up onto his horse and trotted it away, leaving the gesticulating drunk standing in the middle of the muddy street.

He stopped at a tonsorial parlor. After taking two bits in silver from Jasper, an old Chinese woman with skin like wrinkled parchment led him into a low shed of wood slats at the back of the property. Jasper stooped to enter a small room dominated by a huge iron pot that sat in the center of the dirt floor. Two feet away stood a blazing wood stove. On top of the stove sat a massive copper kettle with a spigot attached to a length of iron pipe that extended into the cauldron. The old woman turned the spigot and a stream of boiling water flowed into the big pot. She hobbled out the door and screeched a string of incomprehensible gibberish. Two boys scrambled in toting buckets of water almost as big as they were. They couldn't have been more than six or seven, but they hustled in and out and, with the help of a stepladder, dumped their loads into the makeshift bathtub until they had it half filled with water.

When they finished, the old woman returned and felt the water. She turned off the spigot and flicked her thin hands at Jasper. "You bath now." She handed Jasper a small tin pot that contained something that looked like curdled milk.

"What's this?"

"Soapee-soap. Me makee."

Jasper dubiously set the pot on a wall shelf and dropped a parcel of new clothes onto a little bench next to the bath. He began unbuttoning his clothes as the old woman closed the door. When his battle grays lay in a heap on the floor, Jasper stared at them for a long moment. Was he really doing this? Was he out of the war? Just like that? All he had to do was shed his skin like a snake and the past fell behind him?

Using his shirt like a pot-holder, Jasper yanked open the stove's heavy iron door. A blast of reddish light bathed his naked skin with heat. He threw his pants and shirt and longjohns into the gaping stove mouth and watched them turn black, then burst into dancing yellow flames. The stove devoured his past as Jasper fingered the last brass button on his uniform jacket, now tarnished to a dull brown. He yanked it free of the fabric, then threw the jacket into the fire and kicked the door shut. He set the button on the bench that held his clothes bundle.

The water felt hot, but not too hot as Jasper lowered his thin body into the bath pot. He couldn't stretch out, but the cauldron was deep enough that he could float with only his face above the surface. He could not remember feeling anything so luxurious for a long time. The heat leeched the stiffness from his bones and for a little while Jasper didn't think about anything.

An hour later, Jasper emerged from the bath shack in his new clothes and boots. In the white-tiled shop that faced the street, Jasper reclined in a barber's chair as the old Chinese woman first cut Jasper's hair to a respectable length, then attacked his jumble of beard. His face had not known a straight-razor for a long time. When he peeked into the wall mirror, he almost fainted. He had not just shed his skin, he had been reborn. He winked at the stranger whose face now looked ten years younger.

215

While in the bath, Jasper had thought long and hard about his next course of action. The prospect of holing up in Baltimore City had seemed less appealing. From the talk he heard in the general store, Jasper learned that federal troops permanently bivouacked in the city to quell the riots and general orneriness of the population there. Though Jasper looked prosperous now and nothing like his former self, he faced prison if he got caught. Going to Baltimore would simply be hiding. Jasper didn't like the idea of hiding. He had spent too much time hiding under that barn and had almost gotten his neck stretched for it.

With an hour of daylight left, Jasper rode west out of Fredericktowne and in Middletown checked into a small inn. Early Friday morning, he would set off for Sharpsburg. He had made a decision.

CHAPTER 67

By the time Ethan hiked back to Sharpsburg, he looked sufficiently bedraggled to sell his version of recent events. Townsfolk gathered around to hear of Billy's most recent tragedy. Several Hawley riders set off to look for their boss. Ethan shuffled home, begging off further discussion. After feasting on roasted potatoes and mutton he found bubbling on the back of the stove, Ethan hobbled to the store.

"Back awful fast." Calvin had not yet heard the news.

Ethan sketched out how his day had gone, undersensationalizing as much as possible.

"Son, you need to start carryin' a sidearm. How many times you need to get waylaid? First you get shot, now you get robbed. That was a damn good wagon."

"I need a flat piece of wood and some screws."

"Ain't you listening to me?"

"I hear you fine, but I can't change what happened." Calvin Anspach looked puzzled at his son's lack of concern, but he pointed to a back corner of the store. "Got a couple pieces of pine over there from a crate that busted. How many screws you want?"

"Four should do it. An inch long."

Ethan found a screwdriver behind the counter and dropped it and the screws into his pants pocket. The short plank he stuffed into the front of his pants. Off one of the wall racks, he pulled a dark blue coat and wriggled his arms into the wide sleeves.

"Now, what about a hogleg? What do we have in stock?" They walked over to the weapons counter. Though McClellan's quartermaster corps had scoured the major battlefields, local residents still found guns in the most unlikely places where they had been flung by dying men or hurled through the air as the result of a cannon blast. Many were damaged. During his recuperation, Ethan had spent long hours mixing and matching salvageable parts into serviceable weapons to sell.

Ethan reached for a Colt's .44. In excellent condition, it had probably been the service gun of a Union officer. He worked the action and spun the cylinder. He unhitched the cylinder, pulled it off the frame, and held a piece of newspaper at the base of the barrel. When he peered down the barrel from

217

the other end, the reflected light off the paper showed the interior of the barrel clean and unpitted.

"Someone took care of this gun."

"Where'd you learn to handle a gun like that, Billy? I never taught you nothin' like that."

"There's a war on, Dad. Makes sense to know," Ethan answered evasively. In his own time he had been an avid target shooter. He pulled boxes of powder and ball off a shelf and loaded the six big chambers of the Colt. Then he selected a second Colt, not in quite the same condition, but serviceable, and loaded it as well.

He slung a leather gunbelt around his waist and dropped the better revolver into its holster. The second Colt went into one of the coat's capacious pockets.

"Fixin' to fight your own war, Billy?"

"It's dangerous country out there," Billy said in a voice much older than his nineteen years.

* * *

Ethan waited until the funeral procession marched far down the main street before he entered the Presbyterian Church. He slipped into the darkened interior and waited for his eyes to adjust to the gloom. As he hoped, the place had emptied, all religious individuals drawn into the comet's tail of the afternoon funeral ceremony. Ethan stepped to the left, his eyes surveying the interior architecture. Except for electric lights that would be installed sixty years in the future, the church appeared just as Ethan always remembered it. No renovations other than paint would occur in the future.

Ethan checked the pewter name plaque at the end of the last pew and committed the family name to memory. Bauer. Ethan stretched out on the maple planking and squirmed under the bench. From under his belt, Ethan extracted the square, flat piece of pine crating that closely matched the dark-stained oak of the pew. From his coat he pulled a flat packet of paper he had sealed with wax. Using the screwdriver and screws, Ethan attached his plank of wood to the underside of the pew, with the packet sandwiched tightly between the two surfaces.

He stood, dropped the screwdriver into his coat pocket, brushed himself off, and stepped out into the slanting sunshine of late afternoon.

* * *

As Ethan approached the rambling white house, he

again had a feeling of familiarity with it. He climbed the broad, wide steps of the front porch and hammered the brass door knocker twice.

"Mrs. Hawley."

"Hello, Billy. Won't you come in?"

She led him through a beveled glass doorway into a parlor furnished by overstuffed chairs and sofas of crushed burgundy silk, over the arms of which hung ornate lace doilies. She closed the door to insure their privacy and indicated a chair for him as she settled onto a wide divan.

"Is there any word of George?" she said in a conversational tone.

Knowing the fate of her husband made Ethan nervous. More lies. "Afraid not. I'm sorry, Mrs. Hawley. Has his crew gotten back from South Mountain?"

"No." The older woman's face appeared calm, not with the resignation of loss, but with a contentedness absent when he noticed her in town. Ethan saw the similarities between mother and daughter. But where, in Katherine, the ineffable mix of factors that comprise beauty had joined in perfect harmony, in the mother, they had not quite coalesced. Her bronze hair, wide-set green eyes, and straight nose, though pleasant, did not appear singular. Her full lips, however, perfectly matched her daughter's.

"How can I help you, Billy?"

"I'd like to see Katherine."

The calm features twisted. "I'm afraid that's not possible."

"Why?'

"She's gone."

"What? When? Where did she go?"

"*She* didn't actually go; she was sent."

Though Ethan wanted to pull the answers from her mouth, he controlled himself. "Please explain, Mrs. Hawley."

"My husband has sent her away." Her gaze settled in her lap as if something of great importance happened there.

This couldn't be. Ethan tried to remain calm, but his pulse thrummed in his temples. "Mrs. Hawley, where was she *sent?*"

Elizabeth raised her eyes from her lap. "Are you the father?"

Ethan knew nothing of what went on between these two young people prior to Beth and Ethan's arrival. He stammered

219

an answer. "Her, ah, her condition was as much a surprise to me as to you."

"I'm sure you were surprised, but that doesn't answer my question. Are you the father?"

A faraway look crept into Ethan's eyes. "I wish I were."

Elizabeth's features softened. "You want to know where she is?"

"Yes."

"They left early this morning. Headed for the C&O Canal. They'll be going to Ohio and then to Chicago. George has picked her a husband."

"So I heard."

They stared at each other. She seemed to be waiting for him to say something. Finally, Ethan rose to leave. He hesitated and suddenly asked, "Could I see her room?" Something nagged at the edges of his awareness. As much as he wanted to hit the road, he couldn't resist this urge.

Elizabeth Hawley tilted her head, her eyes quizzical. "Yes. Follow me." She led him through several rooms to a stairway. On the second floor, she turned right down a hall and opened a door.

As soon as Ethan entered, he felt Beth's presence. Some faint scent of her occupancy still hung in the air. Instinctively, Ethan went to the window. "Is this where it happened? Where she was shot?"

"No. That happened upstairs in the maid's room while she watched the battle. Do you want to see?"

"Yes."

Elizabeth led him to Emily's room. Ethan stepped over to the window. At his feet a dark, irregular stain marred the pine planking. He pointed. "Here?"

"Yes."

"And the bullet came through this window?" Ethan noticed the bead of new trim around the perimeter of the glass, lighter than the original wood of the window.

"Yes."

Ethan peered through the rippled glass. He felt the rumble in the earth beneath his feet as artillery crushed iron into it. He heard the random firecracker sound of hundreds of rifle and pistol shots that went on and on like a Chinese New Year gone mad. He smelled the sharp bite of burnt gunpowder that hovered over the ground like a curtain of fog.

He had been out there. Now he stood here in a different

body.

"Are you alright?" Elizabeth Hawley said.

Ethan realized he had collapsed into the straight-back oak chair beside the window.

"Billy, you look like you've seen a ghost. Are you sure you're alright?'

"Oh, yes, yes, I'm fine." He wobbled to his feet. "I'll be on my way."

She led him through the house to the front door. As he passed her on his way out, she laid her hand on his shoulder in a moment of maternal care. "Be careful, Billy. She's traveling with Ethridge and Hulse. Watch out for that Hulse."

"Yes, Ma'am, I'll be real careful." *Right up to the moment I blow those bastards away.*

The thought of Beth with a weasel like Ethridge and a psychopath like Hulse lit a fuse inside Ethan. His search had ended. His confusion had ended. He now had a clear understanding of what he needed to do and what forces had arrayed to stop him. He hurried from the house, the fog of the last few minutes lifting as rage built inside him.

Three men in leather chaps gathered at the end of the dirt track that led through the Hawley's main gate to the road. Three tethered circle-H horses munched at tufts of grass under the fence rails beside the gate.

"Hey, there, Billy. Mr. Hawley said you might come sniffin' around one of these days." The tallest of the three, a lanky, swarthy man with a scar down his left cheek, spoke in an outwardly friendly tone, but his voice held an undertone of sarcasm. Maybe twenty-five or thirty. A wide-brimmed brown hat rendered his eyes invisible in its shadow. He leaned against the left gate post. He looked familiar.

The second horseman, a wide-eyed boy no older than Billy, pulled off his work gloves and rested his thumbs on his gun belt. A heavyset giant of red hair and florid skin finished off the trio. Ethan ignored them and kept on for the gate.

"See here, fellers, this is a boy don't have the manners to speak when spoken to," the tall one said.

"Teach 'im, Taney," urged the red man.

Ethan reached for the gate latch and the lanky one slid across the intervening yard quick and silent as a shadow. Suddenly a blade pricked the underside of Ethan's chin. "Got your attention now, do I, boy?" This close, Ethan could see under the hat brim. The eyelids looked like mere slits over black marbles. Yes, Ethan knew this face. It had been one of the last things poor Cole had seen. This man, Taney, and the albino, Hulse, betting on whether a running horse would step on a man.

"Not thinkin' of goin' after the girl, now are you? That wouldn't be smart and you look like you might have a little bit of smarts in that pinhead of yours." The grin that slashed across the stubbled face held no good humor.

Ethan said, "Look down, Taney." Taney's grin got wider.

The click of a hammer being cocked sounded as menacing as a diamondback's rattle. Taney stepped back half a pace, keeping the tip of his skinning knife under Ethan's chin. His false grin disappeared as Taney saw the dull gleam of Ethan's revolver between them. Taney's companions stepped away from the fence, no longer lounging.

"Now lose that knife and step back." Ethan's finger so wanted to pull the trigger. His mind filled with the memory of Taney and Hulse staring down on Cole, taunting him before they mutilated him with a ton of horse, but his need to get to Beth won over his temptation. Shooting Taney would cause complications and delay.

The blade dropped to the ground and the lanky horseman retreated. The grin reappeared. "Lots can happen on the road, Billy. Stragglers, deserters, they make travelin' real unhealthy. You be careful, now, y'hear?"

Ethan surveyed all three, checked their hands, watched their posture as he kept the revolver trained on Taney's chest. No, they wouldn't do anything now, not in daylight, not with him just a finger twitch away from blowing a hole in Taney. Ethan threw back the gate latch and stepped through. He didn't re-latch the gate as he backed off. All three men stayed motionless. He held the Colt on them until he had gone a hundred feet.

Turning, Ethan walked briskly toward the center of town. Now too far for a pistol shot, Ethan's back still itched in anticipation of a rifle bullet. No, it would be too difficult for Taney to explain how Ethan presented such a threat that Taney needed to shoot him in the back from a hundred yards. Several minutes passed before Ethan realized he still had the revolver in his hand. He lowered the hammer and dropped the revolver into his holster as he double-timed to the livery stable.

His lingering pains seemed minor compared to the acid fear in his gut.

CHAPTER 68

Beth felt Hulse's eyes burning into her back. With Ethridge riding in front of her and Hulse behind, she had little hope of cutting free. The canal path stretched like a railroad line; one could go only forward or back. Along most of it, steep embankments rose on the land side. Between the road and the embankments a deep ditch had been formed when the builders hauled dirt and stone up onto the roadway. Over an embankment on the other side rushed the torrent of the Potomac River.

Beth acted passive, but stayed alert for an opportunity to bolt.

Hulse rode up next to her. She felt his Easter Bunny eyes rake across her breasts. He made no attempt to hide his interest. "Tired?"

Without turning her head, she said, "No, Mr. Hulse, I can sit a horse as long as any man."

His pink lips leered under his white mustache. "Good rider, eh? That could be handy tonight."

* * *

The C&O Canal stretched from Washington, D.C. to the Ohio River. George Washington had been one of the original visionaries who developed and funded the canal to allow for commerce from what was then the frontier to the settled areas along the coast. The dirt and gravel canal track used by the barge mules also provided a smooth, level road for travelers on foot and horseback.

When Ethan reached the canal late in the day, he didn't see much traffic. He rode northwest until he encountered a lock. He dismounted and banged on the lock master's door until a grizzled old man came to the entrance. Pulling on his red braces, he bellowed, "Lock's closed. Cain't you see?"

Ignoring the outburst, Ethan said, "Did two men and a young woman ride past here this morning?"

"Lotsa people rode past this mornin'. You think I keep track of 'em? I keep track of barges and there ain't no barges this afternoon."

"She was young, very pretty. Long red hair. When did they go by?"

His stubble of white whiskers stood out in starker

223

contrast as the old man's skin changed from pink to red. He stopped fussing with his suspenders and glared into Ethan's eyes. "I smell trouble in you, young man."

"What time did they pass?"

The lock master gave in. "'Bout eight. Now off with you."

Ethan remounted and kicked the horse to a trot. At eight o'clock, he and Jasper had been riding up the hill to Turner's Gap. Ethan's emotions warred. If he hadn't helped Jasper, he and Beth might be far away by now. Together.

And he would have spent the rest of his days in guilt for condemning Jasper to rot in a military prison.

Ethan rode until he could barely see the tow track. When the horse stumbled and almost fell into the canal, Ethan knew he had to stop for the night. A cautious mile later, he saw a dim light ahead. As he pushed on, the light differentiated into individual candle flames dancing behind window panes. Seconds after Ethan rode up to the front of the whitewashed stone structure, the front door opened and an ancient black man shuffled out carrying a glass and metal lantern that held a fat candle. "Stayin' the night, sir?" The old man reached for the horse's bridle.

"Where am I?"

"Big Spring, sir."

"Enough room?"

"Yessir, couple nice rooms left. Oats for the horse and a soft bed for you."

The odors of cooking meat and wood smoke wafted through the air. Ethan suddenly felt famished. "How much for dinner too?"

"Two bits for the horse, dollar for dinner and the room, sir."

"Done." Then a trick of the lantern revealed the old man's face and clouded eyes. Ethan caught his breath. "How's your family doing, Ezekiel," Ethan blurted out before he could catch himself.

The lantern came up between them and the old man squinted his cloudy eyes to examine Ethan's face. "Do I know you, sir?"

Ethan shook his head. "No, no."

Ethan dismounted and handed the reins to the puzzled old man.

As Ethan pulled open the heavy front door, he felt transported from the world of ice to the world of fire. The great room glowed with dancing flames from the wide fireplace along the far wall. Huge logs shimmered red and gold on the thick andirons whose metal glowed like the setting sun. Thick odors suffused the air: the sweet smell of burnt fat, the comforting alcoholic tang of mead, the subtle undercurrents of cooked parsley and squash.

Ethan catalogued the room's inhabitants, though he knew Beth would have passed here much earlier in the day. Two men huddled in a back corner. A man, a woman, and two girls picked slowly through the remains of their meal, large wooden trenchers between them filled with chicken bones and the skins of yellow squash. A lone man huddled near the fire, wrinkled hands wrapped around a pewter flagon.

Ethan settled at the end of one of three long tables that filled the room, close enough to the strong radiation from the fireplace to thaw out but far enough to not overheat before he finished his meal.

It seemed a week since he'd said good-bye to Jasper, but it had only been this morning. His thighs had chafed from the day's ride and every joint in his body ached from the long walk down from the place he'd killed George Hawley.

As he stared into the fireplace, Ethan heard his own voice.

You killed a man today, Ethan.

Yes.

How does it feel?

It feels good.

His meal arrived and Ethan ate like a starved wolverine.

CHAPTER 69

The sun had set and only its rapidly diminishing afterglow remained pink in the sky as the trio pulled up in front of a road house in Indian Springs. Hulse said, "Made good time today. Didn't think we'd get this far."

Hulse dismounted. "Ethridge, you think you can keep an eye on missy here while I get us a couple rooms?"

"How many rooms?"

"Two should be just about right." Hulse leered at Beth. "Ethridge, you don't mind sleeping alone, do you?"

Ethridge didn't answer as Hulse strode up the steps of the front porch.

Beth spat out, "He's a royal bastard."

"You should know."

"What's that mean?"

"You grew up with one."

Beth felt no fealty to George Hawley, but she resented Ethridge's presumption. "So, you work *for* a royal bastard and *with* a royal bastard. What's that say about you, Mr. Ethridge?"

"And who was the royal bastard you spread your legs for, little girl?"

"You hypocrite. You want a woman to spread her legs, then you condemn her for doing it." Beth dismounted and began walking to the left of the inn.

"Where you think you're going?"

"I'm going over into those bushes to pee, if it's any of your concern. Do you want to watch? Would that make you happy, Mr. Ethridge, to watch a woman relieve herself?"

"Just so I can see the top of your head."

Beth squatted in the mountain laurel, her mind bouncing in her head like a hornet in a jar. She had to do something. Now. She had no illusions about what would happen tonight. Sometime before dawn, those big pink fingers would smother her mouth, those pink eyes would loom close, and Hulse's pale slug of a body would rape her. Once he crossed that threshold, she could expect the same every night. How many weeks was this journey? She shivered and drove the repellent image from her mind.

She had succeeded in tricking Ethridge about relieving

herself and needed to use this time to best advantage. Kneeling, she ran her fingers down through the tall grass. She found a stone protruding above the soil. Too small. She felt around some more. Ah. She tugged a fist-sized rock out of the ground. As she ambled back toward the horses, she concealed the stone in her right hand which she kept buried in the right-hand pocket of her blanket coat.

Beth's horse stood on the other side of Ethridge's, so she walked around the rear of Ethridge's horse. He had no reason to fear a seventeen-year-old girl. He remained facing toward the inn, lolling in a fog of fatigue, as Beth passed behind him.

She glanced fearfully at the front door of the inn. If Hulse came out, her plan would fail. Tiny breaths puffed in and out of her mouth. She felt giddy with fear. If she failed...

I will not fail.

She stood directly behind Ethridge.

With her heart beating like a racehorse, Beth set her feet, reared back, and hurled the stone with all her strength. The two-pound missile crossed eight feet of space and hit the back of Ethridge's skull with a loud thunk. Ethridge cartwheeled out of the saddle and landed on his left shoulder. He didn't move.

Petrified, Beth approached his limp form and stood over him for a second. What if he was faking and was waiting for her to get close enough to grab her? Panicked, she glanced at the front door of the road house, expecting Hulse to come crashing down the stairs.

Beth stopped breathing as she lunged for Ethridge's pistol and yanked it from its holster. Ethridge didn't budge. She tucked the gun into one of her big coat pockets and glanced again at the door of the inn.

Feeling as if every eye on earth was watching her, Beth untied the reins of Hulse's horse and tried to tug him next to Ethridge's. Hulse's horse reared and whinnied at the strange touch. Beth's heart pounded so loud, she could hear it in her ears. She ran her free hand along the base of the horse's neck. "It's okay, baby, it's okay." Hulse's horse still fidgeted and muscles along his flanks twitched in nervousness, but he stopped crow-hopping and allowed Beth to tug him closer to Ethridge's horse. She grabbed the second set of reins and then untied her own mount from the hitching post.

She felt like she was moving in slow motion and naked

227

for the world to see as she climbed onto her mare. She tried not to look at the door of the inn, tried to focus on balancing into the saddle, getting her feet properly set in the stirrups. God, she wished this wasn't a real horse, but rather her old V-8 Mustang.

She wanted to ride like the wind, but she was afraid the sudden clatter of hooves would bring Hulse outside. Though Beth was an accomplished rider, dragging the reins of two tired horses proved difficult. Half turned in her saddle, she had to yank the reins hard to get the two horses moving. They knew it was the end of the day and they expected to be fed, not start a new trek.

No more than fifty feet down the path she heard a shout behind her. "Goddamn you little witch!"

Beth kicked her horse's flanks and held onto the saddle horn with her left hand while her right pulled at the other two mounts. In that moment between when her horse accelerated and the other two horses began to respond, Beth was pulled off the back of her saddle. Bouncing on the rump of her horse, only her legs clamped to its sides kept her from tumbling to the ground. She hung suspended between two opposing forces as Hulse raced after her.

Looking back, Beth gasped at how quickly Hulse closed the gap. For an instant, she thought of letting the other two mounts go, but thought better of it. Once Hulse had a horse under him, Beth knew she would be recaptured. She suddenly had a gutful of ice at the thought of what his anger would make him do to her.

All three horses accelerated now, with Beth in the middle, Hulse only five feet behind the last horse.

Beth jerked hard on the reins of the two following horses to get their attention, then hauled the reins toward her, literally dragging them across the gap. She had no choice. If they didn't speed up, Hulse would capture one.

Beth groaned relief as the gap closed. As the tension on her arms lessened, she hunched forward and managed to get back into the saddle. She took one last look over her shoulder and shuddered. Hulse's churning legs had gotten him near the rump of one of the horses. He stretched out his left arm.

Beth saw Hulse grab a handful of the streaming tail. She screamed and kicked her heels into her horse again. Bathed in fear-sweat, her hand almost lost the reins. In panic, she screamed at the horses, "Run, Godammit!" Her right hand looped the reins around her saddle horn as she frantically kicked her horse's flanks. All three animals smelled her fear and accelerated, the thrill of the chase getting into their blood.

Beth's last view of Hulse was of him still running in the middle of the road, a fistful of black horse tail in his left hand, as a dust cloud enveloped him. As the tree canopy above her thickened, she lost sight of him in the gloom.

The faint ribbon of roadway stretched in front of her as she headed back the way they had come. The light got bad now and she feared a misstep, but she dared not stop. Somehow, she had to push on through the night, retrace her route, and hope that Ethan had figured out what had happened and was trailing her.

She had no plan other than to keep moving. Though she was expanding the distance between her and Hulse, she would not feel safe until she saw Ethan.

Clouds hid the moon and Beth slowed. She hoped the horses could follow the canal track.

When she was about three miles from the inn, her horse stumbled, almost throwing Beth from the saddle. She lost the reins of the two other horses as she scrambled to stay in control of her mount. The chestnut mare regained its footing, but Beth realized that she was pushing her luck. Her horse might go lame.

Beth tried to remember how far the next town was. Should she keep on or stop?

It depended on what Hulse's and Ethridge's horses did.

As soon as Beth continued east on the canal track, the other two horses stepped down the embankment to munch the grass that grew in the ditch.

Would Ethridge and Hulse be on foot tonight or wait until morning? Either way, if they headed back this way, they'd find their horses.

Beth thought she could reach Big Spring before midnight, but then she realized she had no money for food or shelter. If she stopped at a public place, she would be easy prey for her followers if they pursued tonight. The safest thing was to get off the road.

Beth dismounted and felt her way off the land side of the path. She led the horse through the gully and allowed it to drink from the trickle of water at the bottom of the depression. Then she dragged the rebelling animal up the embankment. At one point, it reared and she was terrified it would topple back

229

into the ditch, but it righted itself and followed as she yanked on the reins. They reached the tree line and the earth leveled. Beth could see nothing but inky darkness. By feel, she worked her way through a stand of small trees. When she felt dry leaves underfoot, she stopped.

Feeling her way around the horse, she pulled a coarse blanket from one of the saddlebags, then tied the horse's reins to a sapling. She gathered a large pile of fallen leaves around her and spread the blanket over them to hold them together. She burrowed down into the crackling leaves. When she had settled, she pushed her hands into the opposite sleeves of her coat, like a nun. A horrible way to spend the night, but she could think of nothing else. She hoped she could sleep, but feared being unable to wake up due to hypothermia.

After midnight, when the temperature dropped well below freezing, the horse settled onto the forest carpet to keep its legs warm. Half asleep, Beth wriggled up against the broad, warm side of the animal. It snorted once and she fell back asleep.

* * *

At dawn, the horse stood, jostling Beth awake. She felt a hundred years old as she tried to stand. At first, she couldn't feel her feet. Then came pins and needles so excruciating that a small cry of pain seeped out between her lips. She stamped until the pain diminished, then led the horse back to the canal.

Looking down the embankment, she could not believe she had scaled it in the dark. She feared descending with the horse behind her. If the horse lost its footing, it would crush her. She scanned to the east and decided to ride the horse along the top of the canal embankment until she found a better place to descend.

Beth looked over her shoulder every few minutes.

Hulse followed somewhere back there.

She kicked the horse into a gallop.

CHAPTER 70

With five Mormon gold coins and various silvers still in his pockets and a full breakfast under his belt, Jasper felt right with the world as he rode into Sharpsburg with the rising sun over his left shoulder. Residents glanced at him, but after more than a year of war, they had gotten used to strangers passing through and paid no particular notice to the man they had almost hanged.

Not far into town, Jasper found the sign heralding Anspach's general store. He hitched his horse and entered the large, barn-like establishment. Jasper acted like any other customer. He selected a wide range of items he would need on the trail: dried beef, a mess kit, a cook pot, a coffee pot, flour, beans, lard, and blankets. He treated himself to two pounds of real coffee, a supreme luxury. Jasper had drunk enough chicory to last the rest of his life.

As he settled his bill, Jasper examined the man behind the counter. From the man's hands, Jasper judged him to be roughly his own age, but the man's face seemed much older. The burst blood vessels on the man's nose and the watery eyes signaled the ravages of drink.

A matronly woman bundled up like a pigeon waddled into the store. "Mornin' Calvin."

"Mornin', Mrs. Pushcar."

Calvin, Billy's father, just the man Jasper wanted to see. As he waited for his change, Jasper said, "So, how's that boy of yours doin'?"

Calvin squinted at his customer. "You know Billy?"

"Met him once or twice."

"Boy ran off. He's actin' crazy lately."

Jasper watched Calvin's hands shake as he counted out change, noted the alcohol smell coming off the man. "Have a bender last night?"

"Hate getting' up this early. Billy usually opens the store."

"Young'uns is like that. Gonna take the strap to him when you find 'im?"

Calvin chuckled. "Kinda big for that. He might jes' take the strap to me."

Jasper laughed too. "Couple times I been in here, he always seemed like a good worker. When you 'spect him back?"

"Not sure."

"Where ya think he run off to?"

Calvin's wrinkles shifted into a sour expression. "Heared he chased after a girl. Never knew the boy was even interested. He just up and takes off after her."

Jasper shook his head. "Makes ya wish ya was young, don't it?"

"No. Didn't have shit when I was young."

"Which way'd he go? I might run into him."

"Unless you take the canal, not much chance of that. I heared that's where the girl went. You want some help gettin' this stuff outside?"

"Much obliged."

With Calvin bringing out armfuls of supplies, Jasper had time to properly pack his saddlebags and distribute the weight evenly.

"That's the last of it. Where you off to with all that?"

"Driftin' north and west."

"Well, good luck to you." Calvin slapped his hands against his arms and ran back into the warmth of the store like a man on a mission.

Jasper leaped into his saddle and tapped the horse's flanks with his heels. Ethan was chasing after some girl? It could only mean he had found his wife. For an instant he thought how crazy that sounded. Before yesterday's ride he could never have had such notions. But he had seen Ethan as Cole and as Billy and he knew both times he saw the same man. So why couldn't the same be true for Ethan's wife?

We're all crazy, he thought as he began whistling *Lorena.*

CHAPTER 71

Long before dawn, Ethan ate a hurried breakfast of fresh bread and apple cider and persuaded the innkeeper to hard-boil a dozen eggs while Ethan saddled up his horse. Ethan wrapped the eggs in two handkerchiefs and placed them in the large side pockets of his coat. He paid the innkeeper and hurried out into the cold pre-dawn.

Before the sun even peeked above the horizon, Ethan had traveled several miles on the canal track heading west. He wanted to kick the horse into a gallop, tear a hole in the wind, but he knew to do so would be to tire his mount before noon. He had to maintain a steady, mile-eating pace to ride all day.

As he rode, Ethan peeled one of the warm eggs and popped it whole into his mouth, wishing he had a salt shaker. His eyes surveyed the path ahead for the next lock master's shack. No one else ventured on the path at this early hour.

* * *

"He's a mile ahead." The young man breathed hard from the fast gallop back to Taney.

"Good goin' Conrad. We'll take our time. Don't want to ride up on him until past Indian Springs. Nice and quiet along that stretch."

They rode in silence for several minutes. Then Taney said, "Hey, Conrad, how's about you roll us a couple cigarettes?"

The young man, eager to please, pulled out his fixings.

Taney eyed the towpath ahead and smiled.

Mentoring. Tough work.

* * *

Movement far ahead on the towpath caught Ethan's eye. When he identified it as a single rider coming toward him, he dismissed it. Ethan wanted three riders, moving away. He concentrated on peeling another egg.

At the clatter of hoof impacts, Ethan looked up. For a second, he thought he saw a hallucination. Copper hair streaming behind her like a kite tail, Beth leaned forward in the saddle as if by will alone she could propel her mount faster. Her face squinted into a mask against the cold air.

As she closed the distance, she sat up straight. Ethan heard a small shriek from her as she recognized him. He

233

reined in as Bethany brought her mount to a halt in front of him. The rising sun splashed full in her face, transforming her skin to gold and her hair to fiery metal.

Holding onto the reins, she dropped from the saddle a second before Ethan dismounted. As he hit the ground, she threw herself into his arms. Their mouths locked and the steam of their breath billowed above them.

Finally pulling her face back, Beth blurted out, "Oh, my darling. We have to get away. Hulse and Ethridge are back there somewhere." Her excitement was part love, part fear.

Ethan peered along her back trail, but saw nothing. "How far?"

Breathless, she said, "I got away last night. I don't know how close they are by now." She smiled up into Ethan's face for an instant, then looked in panic over her shoulder.

"It's alright, honey. Let's get moving."

Ethan reversed course and they trotted their horses east.

Ethan said, "We have to get off this canal. We're too easy to spot. Back a bit, we'll hit a cutoff road that goes up to Huyett and then on past Hagerstown."

"How far?"

"At Williamsport, maybe six or seven miles."

"Piece of cake." She flashed him a smile. Her panic subsided in Ethan's presence.

"Want an egg?"

"Thank, you, kind sir, but I'm already carrying the biggest egg I can handle." She patted her stomach.

Ethan laughed. "No, I'm serious." He pulled one of the hardboiled eggs out of his pocket and held it out.

"Good Lord, I'm famished." She grabbed the egg and immediately began peeling it.

"I'll peel you a couple."

It took five eggs to sate her.

They approached the tiny settlement of Pinesburgh. "We better stop to feed and water your horse. She looks a little worse for wear."

"Oh, please, not for long."

"Not for long."

* * *

As Ethan and Bethany rode past the place where Taney and his companion had left the road, Ethan pointed to the torn up earth. Beth said, "That's what I did last night to get off

234

the road."

Caution instantly spiked through Ethan. "Just happened. The hooves broke through the frozen crust. Two riders." He peered up into the trees, but saw nothing. As they rode, Ethan said, "Now why would someone do that?"

"Detour?"

"Or they didn't want us to see them."

Five minutes later, they approached the outskirts of Williamsport. Ethan reined in his horse. "Beth, I don't want to go through there. Too many places for ambush."

"Were you followed?"

"Knowing Hawley's bunch, let's assume yes." He glanced over his shoulder and then up into the trees. The embankment here formed only a low berm, easily crossed. "Let's cut up through here and avoid the intersection down at Williamsport. It's just a short ride and we'll hit the Hagerstown road running north. I want to get into some cover and see who's behind us."

"Sounds like a plan."

They rode up the berm into the trees, paralleling the road for a few hundred yards. Then Ethan dismounted and rummaged through his saddlebags. "Here we go." He pulled out a collapsible telescope. Leaning against a tree, Ethan scanned the canal road.

"Ethan, I'm getting nervous. Let's get out of here."

"Easy, honey. Better to know what we're up against."

Five minutes later, Ethan spied two men on horseback along the edge of the forest at the top of the towpath embankment. He adjusted the focus. "This damn thing is really primitive. What I wouldn't give for a pair of 7x50 Bausch and Lombs right now."

A minute later, Ethan identified the riders. "Jesus Christ."

"He's behind us?"

"No, it's that weasel Taney with some kid. They followed me from Sharpsburg, cut up into the trees when they saw us coming back, and now they're behind us."

"Oh, Ethan. Let's go."

Ethan handed Beth the telescope. "First, take a look. I want you to be able to recognize these bozos on your own."

Beth hastily focused the telescope, peered at their pursuers, and said, "Oh, God, through this they look way too close. Okay, now please can we go?"

"Yeah." He hopped onto his horse and set off into the woods. "Let's get to that Hagerstown road. We'll make better time than through the woods."

* * *

Taney saw fresh tracks climbing the berm and kicked his horse's flanks. "Dammit, they spotted us. Now it gets hard."

Taney's sharp eyes picked up the trail of disturbed leaves and moss. Part of him wanted to rush the pair, but a little voice in his head kept asking what happened to Hulse and Ethridge? Taney remembered how Billy had poked a pistol into his guts. The kid had more skill than expected. Maybe he should wait until dark, catch them tired or sleeping. A gunfight could get messy and if the girl got hurt, Jesus, Hawley would personally skin him.

Yes, maybe better to hang back.

* * *

"I don't like this. Let's just keep moving." Bethany darted glances at their back trail.

"Beth, these people won't go away. We have to stop them."

She squinted and stared into Ethan's eyes. "You don't have to kill them, Ethan."

"What do you suggest?"

"Keep riding."

"Listen, this is going to get out of hand sooner or later. If they don't know yet, they'll find out soon enough that George Hawley is dead. He's got enough psychopaths on his crew that they might just hunt us for sport. I'd rather pick the time and place than have them do it."

"What?"

"He's dead. I shot him."

Bethany's hands flew to her mouth. "Why?"

"He tried to kill me and Jasper." Ethan sketched in the story of his short trip with Hawley.

She sat stunned. Then shaking herself, she said, "What do you want me to do?"

Ethan pointed. "Take my horse and ride up there, across that clearing, to the edge of the woods. Tether my horse further on, out of sight. Then come back to the edge of the clearing, get off your horse and make like you're inspecting your saddle. When you see Taney, ride east away from here. Leave my horse. Wait at the road. I'll catch up."

She edged her horse up against Ethan's, leaned over and kissed him. "You'd better."

Ethan dropped from the saddle and handed Bethany the reins. "Get moving." He settled behind a rock outcropping ten feet from the trail their horses had made through the brush. He unholstered his Colt and waited.

It seemed like hours before Ethan heard the muffled impacts of horse hooves. When the sounds got close, Ethan looked back and saw Beth ride off, just the right bait to distract Taney. As the hoofbeats got closer, Ethan rose just far enough to sight around the rock without making a target of himself.

When Taney got fifty feet away, Ethan fired. Too soon. Too ambitious, particularly since Ethan was trying not to hit the horse. Taney dropped from the far side of his horse and rolled into a thicket.

Ethan had to move quickly before the second rider reached the scene. He peeked around the rock and a belch of fire and smoke boiled toward him. He screamed and flopped over in the dirt, coming to rest on his stomach with his right arm outstretched and his pistol a foot from his hand. He moaned feebly.

Ethan heard footsteps and turned his head to see where his gun had dropped. He extended his right arm as far as he could, but he couldn't reach the weapon. Suddenly, a boot ground his wrist into the dirt as a shadow appeared over him. "I'll take that you little snot-nose." Taney picked up the revolver and stood over Ethan, a gun in each hand. "Tell me where the girl went and I'll let you live. On second thought, I take that back. I can track the girl, but I want your little ass dead. I'm gonna put one right in the middle of your sorry face, Billy."

Taney aimed at Ethan's head. Taney's toe fished in Ethan's armpit and then pushed to flip Ethan onto his back. As Ethan rolled, an explosion ripped the air between them.

CHAPTER 72

On the eastern side of Hagerstown Road, Beth fidgeted, looking first along the path she'd made out of the woods, then south on the road. The mare sensed Beth's nervousness and snorted. Little ripples jerked the skin along the horse's neck. The mare lifted one foot, then another, eager to be moving again.

Beth saw a rider make the turn off the canal road and head toward her. He rode the distinctive red of a Hawley Morgan. She recognized the hat of the younger of the two followers she and Ethan had watched through the telescope just minutes ago. Beth's heart accelerated and she backed her horse into the scrub along the road.

"Please, Ethan, hurry," she whispered to herself.

The rider kicked his horse into a trot. In a minute he would come upon her. What to do? Ride into the woods or back to Ethan?

She heard a shot. Then another. Dear God, no. Ethan.

The rider picked up his pace. Beth frantically backed her horse even further into the scrub along the road, but knew he would see her soon.

Another shot boomed out of the woods. And another. Every nerve in her body spasmed.

Something had definitely gone wrong.

CHAPTER 73

Taney spat, "I'm gonna put one right in the middle of your sorry face, Billy."

As Taney rolled Ethan onto his back, Ethan's left hand appeared from under him and pointed up toward Taney. His hand held his second revolver. Before Taney could pull his own triggers, a blinding tongue of flame licked out from Ethan's hand and slapped Taney in the chest. Taney didn't even hear the explosion as his heart flayed to ribbons.

Taney's eyes looked down in shock as he began toppling backward from the impact. "Not today, Taney." The gun in Ethan's left hand fired again and Taney spun and hit the earth face-first. His legs twitched for a few seconds and then he lay motionless.

Ethan stuffed the Colt back into his coat, then picked up the other one and pushed it into his holster.

Ethan stared down on Taney's unmoving body, watched the blood spread on the cloth of Taney's coat where the big .44s had exited his back. Taney looked small now, huddled face down against the cold earth. Ethan's breath hissed loud in the still air. His initial horror passed and he felt a cold satisfaction. All his life, he had been crammed into a little world inside himself, his desires thwarted, but, first with Hawley, and now with Taney, these explosions of emotion felt liberating.

Ethan sensed the departure of Taney's spirit, the silence in the clearing now complete.

Ethan ran across the clearing, leaped onto his horse, and kicked it to a flat-out gallop. It worried him that the kid with Taney had not shown up.

In no time he came to the Hagerstown road. As Ethan cleared the trees, he spotted Beth waiting in the scrub across the road, wearing a mask of fear. The look of relief that washed across her face told the story of what she had thought after hearing shots in the woods. As Ethan rode up to her she pointed toward the canal track. "Ethan!"

Ethan spun in time to see the kid kicking his horse to a gallop. "He didn't follow Taney. He checked the canal road." Ethan jumped from his horse and handed Beth the reins. "Go on into the trees. Wait for me."

"Ethan..."

"Do it! We don't have time."

Ethan ran straight toward Conrad. As the boy drew his gun, Ethan dropped to one knee and sighted carefully. Firing from the back of a bouncing horse, Conrad missed Ethan with his first two shots. Ethan didn't make the mistake he'd made with Taney. Hating himself, he shot the horse three times. The animal screamed and reared and Ethan fired again. Fifteen hundred pounds of horse fell over backwards and rolled onto its side, crushing its rider under it.

Ethan didn't approach to investigate. Instead, he ran into the woods, mounted his horse, and raced through the trees with Beth close behind.

* * *

Jasper reached Williamsport late in the morning and looked up the turnoff that cut north to Hagerstown. A knot of people gathered in the road north of the intersection. A hubbub of voices carried through the cold air. Jasper instinctively wanted to avoid them and continue west on the canal road.

Bright metal flashed in the sun. Jasper became wary when a tall man in the group waved his arm, beckoning Jasper to approach. Jasper thought of riding up into the woods and making himself scarce, but that would arouse suspicion. He gritted his teeth and rode north, abandoning the canal path. As he approached, he focused on the man who had signaled him. The man wore brown pants, a green flannel shirt and a long black coat. His brown hat had a tiny brim that looked foolish on a man of such size. Most important, a brass star flashed on the chest of the man's coat.

"Hey, there, hold on fella." The voice held the twang of New England.

Jasper's stomach dropped as the lawman called to him. The last thing he wanted was to talk to the laws, but running away now would just compound his problems.

"Yeah, what you want, young feller?" Jasper rode closer, reined in his horse, and sported his best shit-eating grin.

The man with the badge huddled with a stocky man and woman who kept glancing at Jasper as they spoke. Jasper couldn't hear their words, just the subdued stridency of their responses. After they shook their heads, the tall man with the star strode purposefully toward Jasper. "I'm deputy sheriff for this county. Seen anybody hightailin' it back along the canal?"

His dark eyes examined Jasper with the keenness of a hawk.

"Ain't seen nobody since early this mornin'."

"Ye sure? Didn't see a man and a woman riding two big reds?"

Jasper's mind raced back and forth over his time in Sharpsburg up to this moment. Roughly a day. What had happened on the road ahead of him during that day? Had Ethan and Beth found each other? "Didn't see nobody like that. What happened here?"

"Boy dead up ahead. Couple townsfolk saw the fella what killed 'im." The lawman gestured at the couple. A half dozen other gawkers stood at the edge of the road about ten yards away, chattering among themselves. In the ditch at the edge of the roadway, a chestnut-red horse carcass lay with its legs sticking toward the sky. An arm stuck out from under it.

Jasper's heart chilled. Had Hawley's men caught up to Ethan and Beth? Was he too late? Trying to appear casual, Jasper said, "Hey, there, sheriff, mind if I take a look?"

"What for?"

"Never know who I might know."

Now that Jasper seemed to have no useful information, the sheriff lost interest. "Help yeself," he said.

Jasper rode up to the fallen horse and dismounted. He yanked at the dead animal's bridle until the horse's head flopped over, revealing the face of the rider pinned underneath. Jasper recognized one of the young piss-ants that had captured him and dragged him into Sharpsburg only days earlier. A crusted line of red flowed out of his nose and meandered across the smooth alabaster flesh of his face. More blood lay in an enormous pool around the bodies. Thick red runnels had flowed into the ditch and twenty feet down the grade.

His tracker's eyes noticed that the blood in the shadow of a boulder at the side of the road had a light coating of frost. It happened near dawn, he thought. In his mind he saw the horse rear on its hind legs as lead punched into it, saw it fall over on its back, crushing the rider.

Jasper casually looked around and saw signs of flight into the woods at the eastern edge of the road: broken branch tips, torn leaves where horse hooves had churned up the forest floor. Appearing to stretch, Jasper wandered over to the opposite side of the road. Someone had ridden out of the woods here. Had it been Ethan?

241

Jasper approached the nearest man and in a conversational tone said, "You see what happened?"

The stranger tore his eyes away from the saddle and rubbed a forefinger across his red nose. "Not much. I was in them woods over there." He nodded to the east. The liquor on his breath made Jasper take a step back. "Heard some shootin' but thought somebody was huntin' like me. Then I seed two horses runnin' through the trees, a flash of skirt on one of 'em. Then they was gone." The man's eyes went back to the saddle on the dead horse.

"Much obliged." Jasper mounted his horse and rode into the trees at the west side of the road, backtracking along the clear trail of horse sign for a quarter mile. His horse snorted and got an answer from off in the trees.

Jasper dropped to the ground and, like magic, his Walker filled his hand. He tethered his mount and cut perpendicular to the course he had been on. Using a holly bush as cover, he hunkered down and became motionless for several minutes. Up ahead he heard a twig break. Jasper surveyed the ground around him. To his right, a flat outcropping of rock stretched about fifty feet. He hopped onto the stone, thankful to avoid the rustling leaf-fall that spread almost everywhere through the trees. At the end of the outcropping, Jasper dropped into a hollow where moss and snow cushioned his footfalls. He peeked above the underbrush and saw movement. He froze.

Through the gray curtain of bare branches, Jasper watched a riderless horse raise its head and shake its mane. The animal's nostrils flared. Jasper took note of the slight breeze that pushed through the maze of trees and hit the left side of his face. Downwind from the horse, it could not smell him, would not signal his presence to its owner.

The horse's head dipped and came up again, the grinding of its teeth sounding clear through the air. It appeared calm, eating something. Where was its rider?

Far off, Jasper heard a shout. "Hey, feller, where are ye? What're ye doin' back in here?"

That damn deputy.

Jasper sifted through the heavy woods, stepping on the outstretched roots of maples and beeches where he could, on clumps and patches of snow when he had to. He had spent a lifetime tracking both four- and two-legged prey and he knew that to hurry was a sure way to get yourself killed, but with that jackanapes sheriff on his heels, he needed to take a chance.

Jasper listened for a few seconds and still heard nothing but the horse ahead grinding up forage. Jasper plotted his course through the trees, imagining each footfall before he moved. Then, with a fluidity that belied his years, he accelerated through the woods with almost no sound except for the harsh click as he pulled back the hammer of his revolver.

At the feet of the horse lay a man face down in the leaves. He had Billy's dark hair. The black fabric of the man's coat shredded around a hole as big as Jasper's fist. The surrounding fabric had been soaked with blood that was now congealed like a reddish-brown pudding slopped from its bowl. As Jasper approached the body, the horse whinnied and shied away.

Half in panic, Jasper poked the toe of his left boot into the corpse's right armpit and rolled the body. Then he stopped to catch his breath. A grin broke across the frown that Jasper had been wearing as he saw the black marbles of Taney's eyes looking no more animated in death than they had in life. The chilled skin of Taney's scar stood out from his whiskered face like a chalk stroke across a blackboard. Jasper kneeled next to the body and touched the corpse's throat. The body felt cold, though not frozen hard. Jasper looked up at the sun. He calculated that Ethan and Bethany had half a day's head start. But in what direction?

"Hey there, what the hell ye doin'?" The sheriff made a racket plowing through the underbrush.

"See for yerself."

The tall man puffed steam as he approached Jasper. His brown eyes fixed on the body for a few seconds, then cut to Jasper. "How'd ye know this was here?" He squinted at the revolver in Jasper's hand.

"Jes followed the trail." Jasper let down the hammer and holstered his Walker.

"What trail?"

"Broken twigs, strands of horse hair caught in tree bark, crushed moss. You know."

"Ye some kinda tracker?"

"Used to be."

The sheriff knelt next to the body. "Ye know this feller?"

"No," Jasper lied.

243

"Why ye be interested in what happened here?"

"I lead a boring life."

The sheriff glared at Jasper as he went through the corpse's pockets. "Make yeself useful and go get that horse."

The horse munched the underbrush twenty feet away. When Jasper retrieved it, the sheriff said, "Nother one of them circle H brands. Same as on t'other horse. Somebody don't like George Hawley, I reckon."

Not wanting to let on he knew anything about the situation now that Jasper suspected what had happened, he said, "Who's George Hawley?"

"Big shot horse trader. Evahbody this side of the mountain knows Hawley. Ye're not from 'round heah are ye?"

"No."

"That accent. Where that be from?" The eyes raked across Jasper again.

"Grew up in the Nevada territory."

"What brings ye here?"

"Got kin up in Pennsylvania."

"Where?"

Jasper hid his nervousness and with his peripheral vision checked if anyone else approached. He might have to shoot this curious son-of-a-bitch. He said the first thing that popped into his head, something Ethan had mentioned. "Gettysburg."

"I got kin up that way. What's ye name?"

Jasper saw no reason to lie more than he had already. "Jasper Jones."

"Don't know no Joneses in Gettysburg. Ye wouldn't be one of them southern infiltrators, now, would ye?"

"If I was, why would I spend time lookin' at dead bodies and chawin' the fat with a sheriff? Wouldn't be too smart."

The hawk eyes danced for a second. "So, mebbe ye ain't so smart."

"I'm beginning to think so."

"So, why ye be chawin' the fat with me?"

"Like I said, I lead a boring life."

The sheriff squinted and examined the details of Jasper's face as if perusing a treasure map. Jasper didn't blink as he stared back. He'd already noted that the sheriff had his six-gun holstered on his right side inside the flap of his long coat. He'd need a half-second to clear the coat before he could draw. The sheriff clearly wasn't a gunfighter or he'd have

244

hitched that coat flap behind his holster. Jasper gauged the distance to his horse.

The sheriff's eyes changed. He'd made a decision.

Here it comes, thought Jasper. He spread the fingers of his right hand in preparation for drawing the Walker.

"Ye want to make a few dollars?"

Jasper couldn't keep the surprise off his face. "How?" He relaxed his fingers.

"Ye seem to know how to track. Ye follow that trail through the woods and let me know what ye find? There's three dollars in it fer ye."

"How long?"

"Three dollars, one day. Ye said ye was bored."

"So I did. You got a deal, Sheriff."

The sheriff mounted Taney's horse and together he and Jasper rode back to the road. Several more travelers had gathered around the corpses. Jasper grinned as he noticed that both the red-nosed onlooker and the boy's saddle had vanished.

Playing his role, Jasper said, "Where do I find you?"

The sheriff pointed down the road toward the river. "Got an office in Williamsport. I'll be back there gettin' together some deputies to go after whoever did this. But don't worry 'bout comin' back. Ye stay on the trail. See if ye can find out where they headed. We'll catch up."

"Got a name, Sheriff?"

"Dunsfield. Think ye can score off some tree bark here and there, so we can follow? We'll be along late in the day."

Jasper tipped his hat and lightly tapped his horse's flanks, heading east into the trees. Within minutes, his experienced eyes spotted a long hair wafting like a flag from an overhanging tree branch. He reached up and pulled it loose, then drew it between his fingers. It stretched two feet long and held the color of burnished copper. No doubt a woman's hair. Jasper now felt sure of his quarry.

He rode for the rest of that day, not once marking a tree trunk.

* * *

Late in the day, Jasper dismounted to check a collection of hoofprints in the muddy bank of a small stream. Earlier it had been warm enough to thaw the mud, but the dropping temperature of late afternoon had gelled the soil, perfectly preserving four sets of tracks.

The first pair showed that one horse carried a much lighter load than the other. Ethan and Beth? When his eyes gauged the tracks that overlaid the first pair, Jasper's heart rate increased. One of the followers' horseshoes had a fingernail-sized gouge torn out of the left trailing edge. Jasper had encountered this track at the site of Cole's death. The old trooper ground his teeth together, then whispered, "Thank you, Jesus."

As he remounted and cantered off along the trail, Jasper worried that two other riders tracked this same trail. Ethan led Beth along untouched ground, away from roads or trails, clearly trying to avoid being seen. The two followers never wavered in their duplication of the couple's path. Who were they? Surely not part of the sheriff's people, not with Cole's killer on the scent. More of Hawley's men?

"Things can always get worse." Jasper resolved to be careful about riding right up behind them. Well, maybe not too careful.

CHAPTER 74

"Killed that boy Conrad." Ethridge reined in his horse to stay even with Hulse.

"That kid wasn't gonna amount to nothin' nohow," Hulse sneered.

"Yeah, well, Taney was no kid."

"Taney was an old woman to let somebody like Billy Anspach get the drop on 'im. Christ Jesus, Billy's a damn storekeeper's son."

"And your father would be the King of England?"

Hulse glared at Ethridge, but Ethridge's response was to kick his horse in the flanks and pull ahead. Over his shoulder he said, "Hulse, maybe we could go stumble around and try to find this store clerk before he finds us?"

They rode another ten minutes. Through a break in the trees, they saw the main road to Hagerstown again. The trail of their quarry ended there.

"Damn, they're back on the road," Ethridge complained. "This will slow us up. We'll have to check every town, every cut-off, every rat hole."

"If it was easy, we wouldn't be the ones doin' it," replied Hulse.

* * *

The last remnants of the day glowed in pink and red ribbons that stretched across the western horizon. Ethridge and Hulse slowed as they approached a small inn at the edge of Maugansville, a few miles north of Hagerstown.

"Let's check the stable," said Hulse.

"I tell you, they're back in Hagerstown holed up somewhere." Ethridge said the words, but he lacked conviction.

"No, it's too close to home. They couldn't risk running into someone they know. I'm sure they're headed north and this is the best road. The kid will want things easy for his girlie. Let's check the stable."

It took no more than three minutes to find the pair of circle H Morgans, munching happily on alfalfa hay in adjoining pens. Hulse leered at Ethridge. "They're holed up in Hagerstown, are they?"

"So, you're a genius. What do you want to do?"

"Wouldn't be smart to barge into this place. Let's camp near the road north of here and set up an ambush tomorrow. We'll pick a nice quiet stretch."

"We have to sleep outside all damn night?"

"What's wrong, Ethridge? Need yer mommy to tuck ya in and tell ya a story?" Hulse laughed wickedly.

"What's the point, Hulse? What about this?" Ethridge pulled a crumpled scrap of paper from his pocket. "Ever since we telegraphed Sharpsburg, none of this has purpose anymore."

"So Hawley's dead. That don't change nothin'."

"As of this afternoon, we no longer work for him. His wife can't stand us. No way she'll keep us on. Doesn't that mean anything to you?"

"It means something that they found Hawley up near Turner's Gap. That damn Billy probably killed him when they rode up there."

"Let the sheriff deal with it."

"If we're out of jobs because of that little bastard, then I want him to pay. I want him to pay for takin' the girl."

"It doesn't matter anymore."

"It matters to me."

Ethridge studied the pale pink eyes peering from under the white hair that flopped across Hulse's forehead. "So noble all of a sudden? I don't believe you. What's the real reason?"

A sly grin rearranged Hulse's pink lips. "I want that little heller. She made us look like fools. You ain't never felt a stitch in yer guts when that uppity green-eyed witch walks by? Hawley's dead. We can dance and there ain't no piper to pay."

It sounded good, but Ethridge sensed there had to be more. Much more.

* * *

Ethan twined his fingers with Beth's on the pine tabletop. Their eyes glinted like prisms in the ever-shifting light from the fireplace that dominated one wall of the common room.

"Isn't this romantic? Fireplace. Wine. It's like a storybook dinner."

Ethan chuckled. "Honey, in this time, this is all they have. They look at a fireplace as a thing to feed and stoke and clean. I'm not sure there's much romance in it."

Her nails dug into his palm for an instant. "Spoilsport. People pay big bucks to get away to places like this."

"Well, then we're hands-down winners because this is the farthest anyone has ever gone to 'get away'."

Beth shook her hair out of her face and beamed Ethan a smile. "And this whole evening cost us about two dollars and that includes putting up the horses. We'll have to mention this to *Zagat's*."

Ethan marveled at how he recognized his wife even though she looked nothing like herself. "You know, when you shook your head, it was pure you. I don't think that's something Katherine Hawley did."

"Yes, I notice it too. Even though I'm looking at a different face, I still see all your expressions."

The innkeeper, a portly man with a bald head and snow-white muttonchops, approached the end of the trestle table where Ethan and Beth sat. He cleared his throat and said, "Sir, is your wife ready to turn in? I'll have my boy run the blanket warmer under the covers for you." His eyes twinkled.

Ethan said, "Yes, that would be fine. Thank you."

Beth smirked. "I'm definitely not used to this lack of central heating."

"I think I can keep you warm." Ethan winked.

"You'd better."

CHAPTER 75

In the dream, Ethan heard wind blowing through tree branches and felt its cold fingers touch his neck. On his back and staring up into an eggshell blue sky, he watched bare branches sway in spidery lines above him. Something felt wrong with his legs. Then a pair of Easter Bunny eyes filled his vision and Ethan awoke with a start.

Ethan's movement woke Beth. In the crepuscular light, she rolled over and held him. "Honey, how did we get here?"

"What do you mean?" Had the dream been only a dream, or something real?

"This particular time and place. Why here?"

Ethan turned on his side and put an arm over Beth's waist. He'd think of the dream later. "I've given it a lot of thought."

"And?"

"This is a little difficult to explain. We think of time as linear, so it isn't easy to grasp this. It's taken me months to figure it out and I'm still not sure I'm right." He raised his head onto his right hand and looked directly into the dimly lit eyes of his wife. "Think of the moment in the thunderbolt when I was there with you. That didn't happen at the same time as the lightning."

"What do you mean?"

"You got hit by lightning, but I didn't find that moment in time until later. But once I found it, I could revisit it over and over, almost like playing a video in a loop. You sensed me then, after the fact, but for you it felt like it was happening in the same moment didn't it?"

"Yes."

"What for you was one event, was many events for me."

"How can that be?"

"I don't know. But time doesn't work the way we think it does. And I'm becoming convinced that I somehow changed what happened."

"You made us come here?"

"Yes."

"But why?"

"That I don't know. Maybe because this is a time that always fascinated me. I know I wasn't thinking about it

250

consciously, but somehow in that fleeting moment, my mind dredged up a vision and I think you were put into it."

"What did you mean, you 'changed what happened'?"

"You were already gone, but after I found you in the thunderbolt, I think I manipulated the event. I changed the timeline. I tucked you here until I could find a way to get here myself."

"How can you change what already is?"

A long sigh came out of Ethan. "Are you ready for this?"

"Why so dramatic?"

"Because this will change the way you see everything."

"I'm a big girl, Ethan."

He ran his hand over her belly. "And getting bigger."

"You..." She tickled him mercilessly for half a minute. They lay panting in a tangle of bed clothes. "Now spill it. What's the big secret of the universe?"

"The secret is it's not what it appears to be."

"Oh, that's really helpful."

"Think of a piece of yarn. It has many fibers that compose it. Think of our timeline as being one of those fibers. Now think of the other fibers in that same piece. They're also timelines that extend from the past to the future. Now imagine stepping from one fiber to another. The strands rest together in the same piece of yarn, so they are similar, but in each one, the strands contain different lives, different rules."

"Alternate universes?"

"Yes, if you think about it in the most basic way. But our view of alternate universes is kind of rigid. We think of each one as a closed system. Here's the tough part. I don't think they're closed. What looks like the beginning or the end of a strand of yarn is just the limitations of the image, the metaphor we use to explain it. In reality, there's no beginning, no end, no middle. You can cut a piece of yarn into a thousand pieces and reconstruct them in a totally different sequence. You can loop the yarn back on itself. You can weave it with other strands and make a fabric that blends together many different strands. You can manipulate it in any way you can imagine."

"And get what?"

"Whatever you want. Something new."

"You're losing me."

"Beth, the universe, all the timelines are constantly changing, recreating themselves. And I think the force behind

251

all that change is thought. When I went into the lightning bolt, I changed the outcome for us. My need to rescue you became reality. You moved into this place."

"It didn't exist before?"

"I think it did, as a possibility. As a set of choices somewhere along one of those strands."

"This isn't the real Civil War?"

"Oh, it's real and it seems accurate to the original, but it may be a different one of those strands. It's laying right next to the other strand, the one we were born into, almost identical to it except for the fact that we are in this one. Or maybe the two strands have blended together. And there are other strands, other versions where the lightning never happened and where we never met and so on."

"You're saying thought does this? Moves us in and out of different universes?"

"Yes, or changes the one we're in."

"So, think us out of here."

"I have no idea how to do it. I'm still groping through this, taking baby steps."

Beth's eyes lost focus as she tried to assimilate what Ethan was saying. "So, which is it? Did we move from one strand to another or did you change the strand we were in?"

"That I can't figure. Maybe both. I don't know. But when I went back to my old life, even though I had been in the past and had changed things, I saw no effects in what used to be our present. Maybe I stepped between two alternate universes so that what I did in one didn't affect what happened in the other."

"So, this is all a theory? You're not really sure how it works?"

"I don't know anything for sure. I learn a little bit each time I make a jump. I can send my mind along a timeline, but each variable shifts what I see. It's confusing."

"And you controlled where you wound up each time?"

"Not at first. After I developed a little more understanding I was better able to focus on this time and place. Each choice I make, each variable in everything around me, changes where I go. I kept sifting through the reality in which you existed and kept looking for an entry point. Each time I got closer and it got easier."

"Can I do this?"

"Probably, but I don't know how to give you practice."

"Let me get this right. Your bodies died, you got loose, then you found another body to inhabit."

"Yes, but I picked bodies that had just died, empty. They were my entry points to your time and place. But there's another issue. My body back in our original time still exists. I go there each time the body I'm in here dies. Your body back there is gone."

"What does it matter?"

"My body is linked to me. To stay with you, I may have to go back there and die."

"You're saying I'm stuck here, but you have options?"

"No. I think the safest thing for us to do when the time comes is for me to die first so I can wait for you, maybe guide you."

"And you don't think I can do that alone?"

"I didn't say that. The problem is dying, Beth. It's a shocking experience. If you don't focus and keep yourself together, you get reshuffled and pop out in some reality God-knows-where. I can barely do it and I had lots of practice before my first try. You experience pain and confusion and all sorts of distracting forces, but you have to focus to stay the same person."

"But the lightning thing showed that we might be able to do it together."

"Yes, but I no longer have the Memnon to release me from my body. I have to die at the same time you do."

"Oh, Ethan, this is creeping me out. You mean if one of us is going to die, the other has to commit suicide?"

"Until you get the hang of it, I think, yes."

"It seems wrong."

"Right and wrong take on new meaning."

The light had risen slightly and Beth could now clearly see Ethan's eyes. Her mood shifted. "Ethan, you killed two men yesterday. You can't live like that."

His jaw tightened. "Yes, I can."

"Is it right or wrong? Do such concepts exist in your new existence?"

"They would have killed us. I sent them onward. They still exist, but somewhere else, working out their own versions of being."

"Nice justification, but I saw your face afterwards. You liked it."

Ethan said nothing.

253

"Do you get to play God now, Ethan? Send people onward whenever you like? Kill yourself whenever you get tired of the body you're in, the place you're living? It sounds like a video game where you get to reset and you never have to put in more money. And you want me to do this too?"

"I want us to be together."

"But at what price?"

"We don't have to decide this now. These are young bodies. Let's live these lives and prepare for what will come next."

"And if you get run over by a horse, what am I supposed to do? Commit ritual suicide on the spot, wait a week, live the rest of my life alone, what?

"I don't know."

"Ethan, I don't want to be a ghoul. I had a horrible experience waking up in a stranger's body. I thought I had gone insane."

Ethan's eyes lost their focus as he looked inward. He *had* enjoyed killing Taney. And Hawley. After Hawley it had been easy because he didn't really think he was killing. He was just keeping them from killing him. But Beth made him feel ashamed. It triggered a fear he had had earlier. Could he become a body-jumper, just living easy and not caring about consequences?

He refocused and saw the green eyes of Katherine Hawley staring into his. "Ethan, the quality of a life counts for something. Even if you get an infinite string of lives, each one has meaning."

Ethan said, "We'd better get up and on the road."

"Why should we?"

Halfway out of bed, Ethan turned, puzzled. "What?"

"Why should we run? Let's just stay here and let Hawley's men find us and kill us. Why drag it out? Let's just get to the next life and see if we like it better than this one. If we don't, we can off ourselves and move on to the one after that."

At that moment, Ethan saw nothing of Katherine Hawley in the woman confronting him across the bed. Beth and Beth alone radiated out of the young face, her fierce determination a palpable force. Ethan pointed at Beth's bulging belly. "What about the baby?"

"What about it? He or she can just go on and live another life somewhere else." Her voice cracked like a whip.

254

Ethan settled back onto the bed.

"Ethan, when we get to the next life, what will be different? What will our purpose be?"

"Beth, you haven't been out there. You don't understand."

"I don't *want* to understand what you're telling me. It's wrong. Can't you see that?"

For a few moments, they stared into each other's eyes. In a calmer voice, Beth said, "Yes, you have much more experience at this than I have. You've been rolling around the universe while I've been right here in this one body. This young woman 'went onward' as you put it. But I'm her now. And I don't want to go somewhere else. I want to live out her life and deliver her baby."

"Then we may have to kill others so you can do that. We're in the middle of this now. People are after us. You can't have it both ways."

"You're saying conflict is inevitable? Someone wins and someone loses?"

Ethan shrugged.

"If this corner of the universe reflects your thoughts, Ethan, if you did make it happen the way you believe, then maybe the conflict we're in merely reflects your view of existence. Could you turn another corner and be in a place where we don't have to make these choices? Where we don't have to push others onward to survive?"

"Maybe you should design our next universe."

"I'm serious. If you have tapped into the secret of the universe and can choose where and who you want to be, then aren't you limited by your own experiences, your own beliefs? Think about it. Why here? Why now? We are in the middle of the Civil War. You didn't will us to a peaceful fishing village in Tahiti or a prosperous farm in the south of France. No, you willed us to one of the bloodiest chapters in history. Why, Ethan?"

"I don't know."

"Ethan, don't morality and decency count anymore? Is this what life is supposed to be, what we see around us? Lies and murder and rape? Isn't there something wrong with us when we have to call those few who don't live like everyone else *saints*? Those few holy people are the exceptions? Why is it like this, Ethan? Isn't God supposed to be merciful? Why then do we suffer so much?"

255

"I don't know."

She slid across the bed and pressed her naked body against him, curled her arms around his neck. "Babe, couldn't we live on a beach where we make love all day, where we don't have to run and hide? Isn't that paradise? Couldn't we be in paradise instead of here? Or back home? On our farm, with our dog? That would make me so happy."

Ethan's mind staggered. For months his life had been dominated by the recurring agony of trying to survive in the damaged bodies he had found. His sole objective had been to find Beth, all else be damned. He had her now and he realized he hadn't thought much beyond this goal, since accomplishing it had seemed so difficult and improbable.

Ethan gazed out the window at the rising light as his fingers sifted through the copper curls of his wife's head. Suddenly, he felt deflated, questioning everything he had done. The manic energy that had kept him going against all odds, never questioning his goal, turned off like the twist of a spigot. "You're right. Maybe I'm exactly where I wanted to be. No more, no less." He turned back and searched the emerald eyes that stared at him from only inches away. "Yes, I have a gift and I continue to let it make me suffer as it has my entire life. I thought I was freed, but I'm still a prisoner of my own past."

The look on his face was unlike anything Beth had ever seen in her husband. The melancholy she felt pouring out of him shocked and scared her. "Oh, Ethan." Beth cupped her hands around his cheeks. "Tell me."

The words started as a trickle and built to a flood stream. He told her of his childhood, the visions and the punishments. He told her of his mother's rabid need to stamp the witchery out of her son. He told her how he had feared his gift, but had used it occasionally for his own enrichment. In a halting voice he recounted the tortures he endured at Neural Research to amplify his abilities once he realized it might be possible to find her.

When he was done, tears streamed down Beth's cheeks. Her red eyes darted back and forth across her beloved's face, mapping the pain there. "My darling, I had no idea. No idea."

She pulled him down next to her and cradled his head in her arms, peered into his eyes from a distance of only inches. "Darling, listen to me. If you were drawn to this time and place, think of why. You've been fighting all your life. With your mother, with your gift, with yourself. But remember what you told me about fighting and martial arts?"

"Fighting is the last resort."

"Yes. The best solution is to avoid the fight before it happens."

"Beth, we're past that point."

"But what about next time?"

Ethan gave her a grudging smile. "Easier said than done."

"If it was easy, everyone would be doing it."

Ethan's smile widened.

"Ethan, you were right. I don't understand all of this. Maybe I never will. But I want to be with you. Here and now. Can we stay here? I want this baby. You and I were never able to have one. Can't we make this one ours? Raise it? Then we'll figure out the next steps. Okay?"

He kissed her. "You win."

CHAPTER 76

"This is a good spot, Ethridge. You hide in the trees along the road. I'll hide round that bend up ahead. When I see 'em, I'll head back this way like I was comin' from north of here. You just be ready when I make my move."

"We shootin' the kid?"

"You're not shootin' nothin', ya hear? Any shootin' needs doin', I'll do it. You just be here in case all hell breaks loose."

"Lotta trouble for a lousy storekeeper's son." From the sneer that crossed Hulse's face, Ethridge knew he had scored.

* * *

Hulse slouched in his saddle like a man who had been journeying for days. His head lolled forward and shielded his face behind the wide brim of the black hat he had pulled from his saddlebag. As he approached Ethan and Bethany coming in the opposite direction, he kept his head down. Instinctively, Ethan edged Beth toward the right side of the road so that he was between Beth and the stranger.

Ethan examined the oncoming horse and rider. Mud caked the horse's legs and flanks like it had been running, but the rider wore a clean oilskin slicker, like he had just put it on. Not a drop of mud marred it. His hat, a crumpled, wide-brimmed affair had seen a lot of wear. His slicker hid the man's hands and body. His horse shuffled almost abreast of Ethan. Ethan kept his own hat brim low while his eyes examined the man. Something about this rider caught Ethan's interest. Ethan's right hand dropped from his reins and brushed against his thigh, coming to rest near the Colt.

The rider passed on Ethan's left and didn't change position or even turn his head. He looked asleep in the saddle. Judging by appearance, the man presented no threat, yet Ethan's fingers wrapped around the revolver grips. He sensed something here. Something evil. Ethan heard wind in the trees though no wind was blowing.

Seeing his hand move to the gun, Beth said in a disapproving whisper, "Ethan, no."

By reflex, Ethan's head swiveled toward his wife, but he quickly turned back to rake his eyes across the horse and man. At a distance of only fifteen feet, Ethan saw strands of white hair peeking out from under the side of the rider's hat. The man had passed slightly behind Ethan and Ethan's eyes jumped to the circled H on the rump of the man's horse. Ethan drew his pistol too late. The fraction of a second he had taken to turn toward Beth gave Hulse the advantage. Hulse had his sidearm already in his hand under his slicker and in the instant before Ethan drew, Hulse snaked out his left arm and fired a round into the base of Ethan's back.

Ethan tumbled from the saddle as his horse reared. Beth screamed. Hulse leaped off his horse before Ethan hit the ground. He stomped on Ethan's right wrist and yanked Ethan's weapon out of numbed fingers. He smashed the gun into Ethan's temple, knocking him unconscious.

Ethridge rode out of the trees as Hulse fought with Beth's horse. She dug her heels into the animal's sides, trying desperately to get free, but once Hulse had a grip on the bridle, he was able to control the panicked mount.

"Ethridge, grab her, dammit." Ethridge hauled Beth, kicking madly, out of the saddle. Hulse whistled and his own horse sauntered up close. He pulled a rope out of a saddlebag and looped one end over Ethan's right ankle. The other end he tied to the saddle horn. Then with Hulse leading all four horses by their bridles and with Ethridge manhandling Beth, the group left the roadway and pushed deep into a thick stand of hemlocks.

When they passed far out of sight from the road, Hulse tethered the horses to a tree and hauled Ethan to the edge of a clearing at the base of an ancient beech tree with a trunk four feet across. As Hulse coiled his rope he delivered a fierce kick to Ethan's ribs. Ethan's eyes flickered. Hulse swung the coarse rope and raked the coils hard across Ethan's face, leaving thin streaks of blood. Ethan returned to consciousness and lifted his head.

Ethan didn't understand why his legs didn't work. As he came out of his daze, he remembered where he was. He recognized Ethridge twenty feet away with Beth in a hold from which she could not escape. He vividly remembered Hawley's words about how Ethridge had set up Billy to be cut down in the duel with Hawley. Red rage rose in Ethan at the memory of Hawley's laughing confession. And now this animal was handling his wife. Ethan wanted Ethridge dead. Now.

Then a face suddenly loomed over him. White, wispy locks peeked out from under a hat brim over eyes the pale

259

pink of an Easter rabbit. The dream. He saw the face from the dream he had awakened to this morning. And something else floated in those eyes. But before Ethan could understand what it was, the face turned away.

Ethan managed to raise his upper torso onto his elbows. Ethan wanted another close look at this man. Hulse spoke. "Hawley didn't like you. I don't like you." Hulse waved his pistol at Ethan. "How's that bullet feel? Bet it hurts like the devil."

Ethan didn't try to answer. A sharp sword of agony sawed at the base of his spine, but below that, Ethan felt nothing, his legs lifeless.

"Did that once to a feller out toward Winchester after he tried to cheat me on a horse. Heard it took three days for the bastard to die. Near the end he was beggin' for somebody to put a bullet in his head. You want, I can finish you off right now."

Ethan wasn't giving this bastard any satisfaction. He said nothing as his mind vomited up the image of this same leering face standing over Cole. Involuntarily, Ethan felt the crush of horse hooves as this one – Hulse – rode over Cole months earlier. Ethan wanted to exterminate both these vermin.

Ethan's vision blurred and from the growing roar in his ears, it seemed a freight train was passing nearby.

"Well, then, have it yer way. But I'm gonna have *my* way with yer woman. Now you jest lay there and watch me do what you cain't do no more."

Ethan sunk into the awareness that he had suppressed for so much of his life. Billy's body could not last. In a very short time, Ethan would be loosed once again into the raw, elemental stuff of existence and would need to find a point of entry back into this particular plane in order to stay with Bethany. He needed to prepare.

Ethan concentrated. He needed to drift out as he had during the Neural Research testing. He needed to be a wraith. He called on everything he had learned during his previous deaths. He pushed outward with his awareness. He tried to remember the texture of the experience, the feel of space-time. Then as if he had merely blinked, he was there. He could feel the unique quality of his present plane of existence, but he also saw the alternative pathways that led off in an infinite jumble from this moment. This huge set of options had always confused him.

He focused. He only needed to stay with one path at a time, leading outward, into the future. He saw something he did not want to see. Ethan thought his way back and forth along many possible futures. Yes, in every one he faced a nightmare scenario. He saw Beth and blood and then he saw nothing. His own fate was certain. In not one of the scenarios did he see Billy's survival.

Ethan's mind writhed in panic. After all he had been through, all the energy he had expended to finally be with his beloved, it was now falling apart. Billy would not survive and Ethan would have to find another way to Beth. If Hulse raped and killed her, Beth would be gone. She was here only because of Ethan's intervention. But if she died in panic, died without being able to focus herself or to have Ethan's help, her consciousness would disappear, possibly forever.

Ethan's mind bounced like a pinball as he considered the factors, the chances, the odds. A whole new set of futures opened up. The further out Ethan tried to project, the more complex and difficult it became to make the right choice. More nightmare scenarios. But in one, there seemed to be a way. It all depended on choosing the next three minutes. He saw a way out, but to take it he had to trust. And to do something terrible. Would Beth understand? Would she ever forgive him for breaking his promise?

Ethan focused his thoughts, made his choices, and threw his energies into believing in one particular version of events. Then inside his mind he blinked and he could feel the tumblers of fate realigning and moving like some great machine.

Ethan frantically scratched himself back toward consciousness. He had no time. The factors started shifting, reality began rearranging itself with each new possibility. Ethan had to move quickly, play his role at the right second or it would be too late. A lifetime too late.

Ethan swiveled his head toward Beth. He felt his abdomen filling with blood, becoming distended as if he'd eaten a feast. Shards of lightning went off at the edges of his vision and began closing in toward the center. He knew he had to take this chance. His window of opportunity had almost shut. Billy had to die now to release Ethan so he'd be ready when Beth's spirit broke free.

261

When he inhaled, his guts felt on fire. In his mind, Ethan said, "Honey, forgive me. Stay alive. I'll be with you soon."

At the sound of Beth's scream, Ethan's numb fingers began their difficult journey under his coat for the revolver in his belt. It seemed that it would take forever to get this damaged flesh to obey his commands. But slowly, the Colt came free and Ethan dragged it up and up until it pointed at his own head.

Then something he hadn't foreseen stopped him from pulling the trigger. All hell broke loose around him.

CHAPTER 77

A single pistol report ripped through the cold stillness of the morning. Three crows cawed their annoyance at the disturbance and burst out of the stark trees ahead of Jasper. Squinting, the seasoned campaigner tried to penetrate the distance. He saw nothing but the net of gray branches that choked off his view at less than a hundred yards. Off to the right, open field stretched along the road. Jasper kneed his horse into a trot and took to the softer ground where the sound of hooves would be muffled.

Jasper had spent most of his life outdoors. He had the indefinable senses of a woodsman. Without thinking, his brain calculated the distance of the gunshot and, knowing that whoever had fired it might be wary of travelers coming from the road, Jasper looped around to approach from a different direction. When his senses told him he was close, Jasper tethered his horse to a sapling and continued through the woods on foot.

Jasper crossed a well-worn game trail, saw horse tracks leading off into the woods on the other side. The disturbed leaf cover told him something heavy was dragged. He spied a clear horseshoe print in the frozen mud. It had a fingernail-sized gouge along one edge. Jasper gritted his teeth. He avoided the leafy piles of detritus and placed his feet on the remaining patches of snow whenever he could to dampen the sound of his approach. He melted through the interlacing branches and trunks that seemed like an impassable screen from a distance.

Jasper heard a man's guttural voice, then the cry of a woman. He drew his Walker, accelerated deeper into the stand of hemlocks. He heard sobbing, then the sharp tone of a man saying, "Dammit, Ethridge, hold her still."

Jasper gauged the distance to the commotion and, with a slight adjustment of course, put a huge beech tree between him and its source. He cautiously stepped along small hillocks of moss until he was among the fat gray roots than spidered out from the forest giant.

Jasper peeked around the right side of the smooth silver-gray trunk. He saw three horses tethered to a fallen tree at the edge of the clearing and a fourth that had wandered off and was munching at the underbrush. On the ground not ten

263

feet from Jasper a body lay in the leaves, its young face gazing into the sun. He recognized Billy, but the name that jumped into Jasper's mind was Ethan. Grief ripped through Jasper. Thirty feet away, two men struggled on the ground with a copper-haired young woman.

A ragged female voice rasped, "Don't do this."

"Well, Missy, ya cain't get pregnant twice, so stop makin' such a fuss. Ethridge, cain't you hold her still? The way she's flailin', I'll have to cut these damn knickers off."

Jasper watched the one called Ethridge grip the girl's arms more tightly while a white-haired giant pulled out a huge knife, cut away her clothing, then unhitched his pants.

"Okay, girly-girl, time to take you down a peg."

The young woman sunk her teeth into Ethridge's hand and he released her momentarily. "Hulse, get off me, you animal," she screamed.

"Don't be so uppity. I know ya done this before. How else did ya get that belly?" He chuckled and speared a look at Ethridge. "When I'm done with 'er, you can show us what kinda man you are, Ethridge." He laughed again and spat to the side. "Okay, feller, you hold her arms while I work on the business end of this little hellcat."

"Hulse, she'll scream like a banshee."

"Aw, let her. Who the hell can hear her?"

Jasper saw his opportunity. With all the commotion, nobody would hear his footfalls. He erupted from behind the beech tree at a run. As Jasper covered the distance to the group, Ethridge, seeing motion, looked up, drew his pistol.

Jasper didn't want to risk a shot while he was running for fear of hitting the girl, but when he saw the glint of metal in the young man's hand, he had no choice. He squeezed the Walker's trigger just as Ethridge's own gun went off.

As Beth felt the heat of Hulse's skin against her naked thighs, she writhed in panic as the double gunshots tore through the air. Suddenly, she could free her arms. She reached for Hulse's face and plunged her thumbs into his eyes. Then she heard more explosions and she screamed.

Ethridge's first shot whizzed past Jasper's head so close he heard its whine louder than the girl's scream. But his own shot caught Ethridge in the shoulder and punched the young man away from Beth. Ethridge's second shot went wide before Jasper's Walker belched flame and smoke twice more and Ethridge fell to the forest carpet with runnels of red pulsing out of his chest.

When Hulse's vision exploded into multi-colored pain from Beth's thumbs poking into his eyes, his first instinct had been to pull back, but when he was deafened by shots, he grabbed for Beth. He rolled and got her on top of him as a shield while he groped for his holster. Blinking, with no sense of a target, Hulse extended his right arm and fired just to give his attacker something to think about.

Beth felt the explosion of hot gases against her face and, for an instant, she thought she would die. She almost welcomed the belief that her life was now finished, that she would be released, and that somehow she would be united with Ethan in the vast universe he had described to her. She felt sick at the loss of the baby she would never know.

But she felt no pain. Just an incessant ringing in her ears. And she still felt Hulse's arm like a band of steel across her chest. The sky hovered bright and blue and she suddenly realized she had not died.

A long-barreled Colt arced across her field of vision, the heat-mottled blue barrel so in contrast to the lighter blue of sky. She watched the shiny hammer slowly move backwards under a thick pink thumb. Then, still an observer, she watched her own hands reach out, saw them wrap around the hand, saw the hand come close. Then her teeth sank into the pink skin and another explosion erupted all around her and then everything went dark.

With the girl flailing, Jasper couldn't get a clean shot at the man who held her. He watched the other man's gun appear, saw it level toward him. Jasper dove, but in the last instant, the struggling girl deflected the man's shot. Jasper landed on the pair and with his left hand grabbed for the hand that held the gun. He got a grip on the barrel and pushed it away just as another shot rang out. Jasper thought his hand had been dropped in scalding water, but he held on as he struggled to get his own pistol under the girl.

Again, the stranger fired and now Jasper's left hand went numb from the vibration. He barely felt his grip on the other's barrel as he heaved forward with his legs, rolling the trio. Working by feel, Jasper thrust his right arm down, under the limp bulk of the girl, and pulled the Walker's trigger. The other man screamed as the heavy lead ball tunneled through his arm.

Battle instinct told Jasper he had two shots left. Taking

a chance, he released Hulse's gun barrel from his left hand and, using his arm like a shovel, he scraped the girl toward him and off the stranger. Jasper scrambled to his knees as the prone figure of Hulse swung his revolver toward Jasper. Just then, Beth rose back to consciousness. She lurched and threw off Jasper's aim as he fired. The bullet slapped into the dirt. Too late, Jasper realized that the girl was now like a shield in front of him. Jasper flung Beth to the side as Hulse fired again.

Jasper felt fierce heat rip through him. A kettledrum banged in his head and he collapsed onto the frozen ground. It hurt to breathe, but he struggled to breathe anyway. Jasper's view of the blue sky narrowed as sharp explosions of light erupted around the periphery of his vision. He saw a swirl of skirts through the explosions and then a burring rasp grew in volume inside his head.

For a moment, Jasper didn't care about Hulse or the girl or gold or the taste of fresh coffee. His vision narrowed further as something inside him began to expand. When his eyes could no longer see, some other sense took over and he began to sense things he had never thought possible. It seemed that eons passed before his eyes, yet only a second had transpired.

Hulse rested against the hard ground and let its cold seep into his fevered body. He filled with the elation of victory over this formidable old man whose last shot had gone wide. He touched his injured arm. Not life-threatening. He holstered his gun and struggled to his knees as every muscle screamed.

He saw movement and turned in time to see the girl rushing toward him, wielding a rock the size of her head. As her arms arced down, Hulse fell back and kicked out with his booted feet. Beth's legs twisted and she went down in a heap. Hulse jumped on her in a flash.

"Now girly-girl, you gotta pay for all this." From the top of his right boot, Hulse yanked a pearl-handled straight razor. He flicked his wrist and the blade hinged out of the handle.

Beth screamed as Hulse's fist smacked into the side of her head.

266

CHAPTER 78

One of Hulse's stray shots sliced into Ethan's throat. Fighting off the darkness, he struggled to collect his thoughts. He knew he had only seconds.

Don't panic. Ignore the pain. Stay focused.

Ethan heard the roaring of space and suddenly he left Billy's mangled body.

Clean and free.

Ethan felt a disorienting ripple of energy, like a dark wave, run through his being. His grip on the fabric of time began to slip. He was here, yet he wasn't. Part of his mind began to see other images. This had never happened before.

God, no. His body link. That thin tendril of energy that somehow tethered him to his body back at Neural Research tugged at him. He had no idea what would happen if that body died. It had been his anchor. If it pulled loose, what chaotic sea of energy might he be cast into?

No, Godammit, no.

Ethan wanted to go back to the clearing. He felt Ethridge's life slipping away, knew he could inhabit Ethridge's body. Not to heal and live, but to squeeze out the few moments he needed to save Beth. By using Ethridge, Ethan could go back to almost the same moment he had left. He had to do it. But he felt himself slipping away, losing control. All he had to do was relax his thoughts and he knew he would be back at Neural Research. But he fought it.

Then he felt Beth. He felt her fear. And he knew she was going to die within moments back in the clearing. He heard her cry in the void. "Ethan."

Ethan's mind screamed. He was being torn in half, wanting to stay, yet being pulled back to his body. His energy writhed. He fought with every scrap of will at his command.

He was yanked away. All the anger and frustration he had ever felt turned to scorching rage. Like a game fish being pulled out of the ocean, Ethan was being yanked out of time.

He needed a nanosecond to connect with Beth, but it was denied him. Could he find her on his next jump?

He had to go back. He had no choice.

So, he made a quick detour. It only took a second.

God help you, Churchill, here I come.

267

Ethan yanked off the oxygen mask and lurched to a sitting position on the examining table, his head a roiling nightmare. Part of his consciousness lived in the clearing in the Maryland woods, part of him struggled to see the events that splintered off from that moment. Only a small fraction of him seemed back in Neural Research.

"Ethan, lay back down. We need another EKG. You had a bad one this time."

"No, I have to get out of here." Hands pulled his weak body back onto the table.

Ethan struggled. "Are you insane? I need to jump again. Now! I need Memnon."

"You're not going anywhere. You almost died. Now lay back down," Dr. Stewart barked.

Ethan fought against hands that clamped down on his arms, secured them with restraints. The cold jab of a needle pierced his left forearm. "That should calm him down."

"No, damn you."

Ethan's thoughts swirled. He had to stay in the time stream. He had to stay aware. But his body went limp.

His howling rage subsided into a corner of his brain and growled. They would pay for this.

* * *

"Tomorrow, after its FOMC meeting, the Federal Reserve will surprise the market with an interest rate hike. Not a small one. Three quarters of a percent. The Dow will nose-dive a thousand points. NASDAQ will tank." Ethan scribbled a series of stock symbols on a notepad. "These are the biggest losers. You short these and make a ton." He handed the paper to Churchill.

"Does the market turn around?"

"Not until the next day. So, tomorrow, you sell short like crazy and then hold on. During the day, you'll see all kinds of whipsawing. Don't worry about price fluctuations. Just know that at the close tomorrow, those will be the final prices." He pointed to the piece of paper in Churchill's hand. "The next morning, the rally begins. That would be the time to cover the short sales and get back in."

"Excellent." Churchill's eyes beamed as he folded the sheet of paper and slipped it into the breast pocket of his suit. He could taste victory.

Ethan returned to his room. He turned off all the lights and sat on his sofa, unseen by cameras, grinning in the dark.

* * *

Churchill said, "When can he launch again, Cliff?"

"*When?* Don't you mean *if?*"

"What the hell are you talking about?"

"Andrew, are you oblivious to what just happened? We almost lost him. He was out for three days. We implanted a defibrillator, for Christ's sake. One more jump and he may not come back at all."

Churchill's brain raced through a stream of numbers. With what West had told him yesterday, he would have the big score he needed to break free of their investors. If West didn't come back from his next jump, well, it might make things difficult, but he would find another time jumper. "Cliff, he says he wants to jump again."

"He's become crazier than you."

"Does he have any permanent damage?"

"We put a machine in his chest, Andrew! That's no laughing matter."

"You're being an old woman, Cliff. His heart is fine. Millions of people have defibrillators."

Dolci's eyes flashed behind his glasses. With clipped words he said, "We're going to run tests and we're going to make sure West is okay before we make any decisions."

Churchill wanted to slap his research director, but instead, his mind churned through West's Federal Reserve revelations. If he could get that broker, Fanning, to really press, really leverage his position, it was possible to squeeze enough out of West's latest data not only to pay off the Avalon Group but to have a few million left over for himself. Let Dolci run his tests. Whether it took a week or a month to greenlight West's next jump, Churchill could afford to wait. Tomorrow he would have the money he needed. "All right, Cliff. I leave the decision in your hands."

Dolci rose. However, he cast a suspicious glance at Churchill. Dolci sat down again.

"You agreed too easily. What are you up to, Andrew?"

Churchill's smile revealed too many teeth. "You're becoming cynical, Cliff."

Dolci, examined his boss's face. "You're not worried about what happens to West because you think you can find another timejumper?"

"I'm sure there are others with his talents."

"But you'd run into the same problems of control. If the

269

subject doesn't want to cooperate it's a mess."

"West's on board. What's the problem, Cliff?"

"But wouldn't it be better not to deal with an outsider?" Dolci's hands snaked across the conference table and pulled up the left sleeve of Churchill's lab jacket. In the instant before Churchill pulled away, Cliff Dolci saw the telltale bruises. Dolci's eyes squinted. "No, Andrew. Are you insane? How long has this been going on?"

Churchill's face turned surly.

"How long, Godammit!"

"Couple weeks," Churchill grudgingly mumbled.

"How much have you been taking?"

"Seventy-five millileters."

"Jesus, that's twice the arterial dose West was taking and he was off the charts."

"But it has no effect."

"That you know of. Andrew, you're playing with fire. Look what's happened to West. His heart's unstable. We don't know where this is headed."

"I don't want to be dependent on West. I want to know what he's experiencing. Now stop mothering me, Cliff."

Clifford Dolci rose from the table and tugged at the stubble on his chin. "I'll be watching you. Anything weird happens, I will have you strapped into an ambulance to Johns Hopkins and this project comes to a screeching halt. You understand?"

"Oh, yes." Their history together was not enough to stop Churchill's thoughts from taking a wicked turn.

As soon as the door closed behind Dolci, Churchill grabbed his phone and dialed Clark Fanning's private line. "Fanning, how's the market?"

"Dropping like a stone after the Fed's announcement. Just like you said."

"Good. Can I leverage any more? I want to be in with every nickel I have. Leverage my ass to the sky."

The broker began explaining the intricacies of short selling. "The exposure on this kind of trading is enormous."

"Fanning, when you know the outcome of an event, you have no exposure."

CHAPTER 79

Ethan hung out in the cafeteria all through lunch hour, waiting for Angie. She didn't appear. He drank coffee until he thought he would burst, read old newspapers. He didn't want to search the halls or somebody might get suspicious. He tried not to look at the wall clock though he knew his timetable was being shot to hell.

Just after two o'clock he saw her get into the cafeteria serving line. Even though not many people inhabited the cafeteria at this hour, Ethan would not talk to her. Passing behind her, he dropped a small, folded square of paper onto her plastic tray and hurried to the exit. When he glanced back and saw the expression on her face, he began to worry.

Angie waited until she sat at a table in the corner of the cafeteria before unfolding the tiny square of paper. Her heart raced as she read, "Call the FBI now. Tell them to arrive just at 4:00 PM. Not before. And I need 100 ml of Memnon and a syringe sometime before the feds arrive. Thanks. I'll be in the quad all afternoon."

Angie stared at her shadow on the plastic surface of the table. She wondered how she had enough substance to even cast a shadow.

* * *

She sat for ten minutes, not touching her food. Finally, she dropped the contents of her tray into the trash can near the door and shuffled out of the cafeteria. She returned to her office, gathered a handful of folders and stalked into the halls, looking busy. She headed for the lab complex, swiped her ID card through the slot next to the door, punched her PIN into the keypad, and entered the main testing rooms. Two technicians concentrated so hard on their work, they didn't look up. Angie crossed through two rooms to a refrigerated storage area. Stainless steel doors hung from all four walls. She opened one near the corner and a wave of fog dropped out of it. Inside racks of glass vials sat in neat rows, all numbered and sealed. Memnon. She reached into the cold recess.

"Excuse me."

Angie almost fainted at the sound. She whirled around.

"What are you doing in here?" The uniformed guard scowled.

"I, I'm getting something for Dr. Stewart."

"Security codes are being changed. You're no longer allowed in here, Mrs. Warner. You'll have to follow me." He held the door open for her.

The guard took her to the security office, where she sat alone for a long time. Finally, one of the security managers came out into the waiting room and handed her a new ID card. "I'll take your old card." He held out his hand.

Sweating, Angie extracted her old card from the plastic holder that hung from her neck. When the manager had the old card in his hand, he smiled. "Your security status has been downgraded. You won't be able to enter the lab unless accompanied by someone with a higher clearance."

Angie sat wide-eyed in shock.

"Is there anything else," the manager said.

"Uh, no." She rose and hurried out of the security office. She headed straight for the quadrangle. Her swollen ankles hurt. She wondered how bad it would get by the ninth month, carrying two.

She found Ethan under his favorite tree and settled next to him. Ethan held Angie's hands cupped in his own. "Thank you for helping me."

Tears welled in her eyes. "I did nothing."

Ethan stared into her eyes and said, "Angie, I want you to do three things. First, go straight to personnel and resign. Don't listen to arguments, just fill out the papers and get out of here as fast as you can. Second, go to Sharpsburg. Take a claw hammer and a screwdriver with you. Drive down the main street until you see the white steepled church on the left. Go inside and sit in the last pew in the back on the left. It belonged to the Bauer family. The medallion with their name may or may not still be on the pew. Kneel down and look under the seat in front of you. There should be a piece of wood about eight inches square, half an inch thick, screwed into the bottom of the seat. Pry it loose. Between it and the seat you'll find a packet sealed in wax."

"What is it?"

"Something I found. A letter written and signed by Abraham Lincoln among other things. Collectors will pay a fortune for those documents. You'll be set for life. You can be home with your babies and never work again."

Awe pulled Angie's eyes wide open. "You found? How could you find something like that?"

272

"My last jump. I got my hands on a dispatch case. I sealed the document in a wax packet so it'd survive until now."

Her face twisted into what Ethan thought was surprise. "You're serious? You did this for me?"

"Just go to the church. Then you'll see how serious I am. It's my way to pay you for getting that video out to the FBI. Now, for the third thing I want you to do."

"What?" Angie looked near panic. Her response was not what Ethan expected.

Ethan pulled an envelope out of his pocket. "Here's my address. It's a farmhouse not far outside Sharpsburg, near Boonsboro. You'll find a big foxhound running the property. Name's Buzz. He's friendly." He handed her a shirt that had been on the ground next to him. "Take this. He'll smell me on it and he'll be easy to catch."

"Catch?"

"I'd appreciate it if you would take care of him."

Tears welled up and slid down her cheeks. "Why? What about you?"

"This phone number on the envelope is for an attorney Beth used. You give him this envelope. I guess that's actually a fourth thing to do."

"What's in it?"

"A codicil to my will."

"Your will? What are you doing?"

"I'm making an unscheduled jump."

Angie's face went from consternation to curiosity to fear. "Ethan, did you ever feel my little boy or my husband out there?"

"I tried to feel them, but, no, I haven't encountered them."

"But you looked?"

Ethan felt like the world's biggest charlatan as he said, "Yes." He had fed her hopes because he couldn't trust Ted beyond getting the video and witnessing the codicil. He'd needed this woman to link him to the outside world.

"You're sure they're out there?"

She seemed so forlorn. Ethan felt guilty for how he had used her. What choice did he have? Did he really think his gift to her would expiate his guilt?

Ethan held her shoulders and said, "Angie, they exist. Where, is anyone's guess. But somehow in the eternal vastness I know is out there, they will learn to do what I have

273

done. You may meet someone someday who seems to know you, someone you feel immediate attachment to. It could be Steven, or Keith. And if they were able to hold their memories together, they will tell you who they are. Anything's possible."

Her green eyes glittered from her tears. "You give me hope."

"I also gave you things to do. Now, get moving. You don't want to be here when those feds arrive."

Her face showed panic. To hide it, she buried it in his chest and sobbed. Ethan held her in bewilderment for a few seconds feeling the wetness of her tears against his shirt. Then he gripped her upper arms and held her away from him. Splotches covered her face and she avoided his eyes.

"What's wrong?"

"Oh, Ethan, I'm a terrible person. I've done a terrible thing."

Ethan cocked his head to the side. His stomach sank.

"The FBI won't be coming. Churchill threatened me." She looked at the floor. "He said he'd fire me and bleed me dry in court if I didn't tell him what we talked about."

Ethan's grip tightened. "What did you tell him?"

"As little as possible. But I told him about you and Bethany and how you were trying to find her."

"What did he say?"

"He laughed and said he didn't care what you did as long as you gave him what he wanted."

Ethan started sweating as he asked, "That was the terrible thing?"

She looked down and in a feeble voice said, "No. I gave him the video."

The sinking in Ethan's gut turned to nausea. All he could think of to ask was, "Why?"

"He had a surveillance photo of me reaching for it that day in the courtyard. He knew it existed. He wore me down." Her blotchy face twisted into a pained mask. "Oh, God, I hate myself for being so weak."

"And the Memnon I asked for?"

She looked at her feet. "I can't get near the lab. They downgraded my security status."

Ethan closed his eyes and bowed his head. He heard Beth's words on the last morning they had spent together, remembered the promise he had made. When he looked up, Angie saw a strange expression on his face. "I'm a terrible person too. I've stepped over the line and I know the feel of evil. I don't like how it feels. You can do good or you can do bad. And if you do bad, you should pay. I wanted Churchill to pay, but maybe I need to pay too. The price for me to move on is to forget about revenge on Churchill. So he gets away with his crimes. In the vast scheme of things, he doesn't really matter. I should just leave him and all his bullshit behind."

"You're not angry with me?"

Ethan managed a faint smile. He imagined his face probably had the same weary expression that Jasper's sometimes had. "You're human, Angie, and Churchill isn't. How could you possibly hold out against him?"

Her tears resumed. "I was such an idiot. I'm *so* sorry."

"Forget it. You tried to help me and for that I'm grateful. I should never have put you at risk. Get the documents from the church. And when you contact the attorney, don't say no."

"No to what?"

"You'll see."

Her eyes snapped wide and she grabbed at her belly. "Oh, God."

"Are you okay?"

"They're really kicking." She grabbed Ethan's right hand and placed it against her bulging stomach. "Feel?"

"Yes."

"When they both get kicking, I feel like a bowl of jelly."

"I'm happy for you." Ethan withdrew his hand.

Tentatively, she said, "What are you going to do?"

Ethan chuckled. "I'm leaving." He pointed straight up at the sky. "For good."

Her eyes opened so wide, the whites showed all around the pupils. Her right hand came to her mouth as she realized what he was saying. "Oh, my."

"Angie, I know what I'm doing. I found Beth and I'm going back for her. Don't worry about me, okay?"

She nodded then turned quickly away. Right before she entered the building, she gave him a last frightened glance.

Ethan let out his breath in relief. He hadn't been aware he was holding it. He checked his wristwatch. If the feds weren't coming, his timetable was shot. He decided to go to the lab, steal the Memnon, and make his final jump. If he couldn't send Churchill to jail, he had no reason to hang around.

CHAPTER 80

"It will turn around, Fanning. He said it would drop. We have to wait. At the close those stocks would be way down, he said. Then tomorrow we cover the short positions and buy long. The market rallies like crazy."

"What, like it's Easter? Our portfolios will rise from the dead? C'mon, Churchill, the market's only open another ten minutes and it's still rising like a kite. If I don't liquidate these short positions now, we will be deep, deep under water."

"Tomorrow. Let the market close. He said get out in the morning. In the next ten minutes the market will dive again." Churchill's voice sounded desperate.

"Maybe he made a mistake. I told you we should have gotten out earlier today. After the drop at noon, you would have made fifty million. All that's gone now. If the market keeps rising, our losses can be astronomical. How do you intend to cover these short positions?"

Sweat broke out on Churchill's forehead and palms. Everything had been going so well.

"Churchill, you get this West on the phone. I want to talk to him. I need a very big reason not to pull the plug."

Churchill barely heard Clark Fanning's voice as his mind churned over his plans. He intended to pay off the Avalon Group tomorrow. He had to hold on. This *had* to work or everything would fall apart.

The broker interrupted Churchill's reverie. "Andrew, I'm watching real-time quotes. Right at this moment, if we bail, I will have wiped out my entire retirement, a lifetime of savings. You won't even be able to make payroll next week. We are seriously, deeply in shit. The market's open for eight more minutes. If we wait..." He didn't want to say it.

Andrew Churchill ran through recent events. The wolves had been at the door, but he had fought them back. He had made the breakthrough that would make him a billionaire and a power broker unlike anything the world had ever seen. Then in the bat of an eye it all washed away? He thought of Ethan. Reality triumphed over hope. His thoughts imploded and he saw how he had been manipulated for the fall.

"That goddamn royal bastard farmer screwed us, Fanning. He set this up. I'll rip his liver out."

276

"Six minutes left. I just pushed a button on my computer, Andrew. I'm out. I've lost everything, but I won't go in the red. What do you want to do? I've already set up the trades. I just have to push a button."

"Oh, God."

"You've lost ten million dollars since we started talking."

Andrew Churchill knew when he was beaten. He wouldn't be able to pay off the Avalon Group. He would lose everything and be so deeply in debt he would never get out. And for what? Some dumb-ass shit-kicking farmer. "Godammit all to hell! Just do it, Fanning. Get me out."

"Done."

"How bad? How much do I owe on margin?"

"You don't want to know, but thank Roosevelt for Social Security."

Churchill hit a button on his intercom. "Mary, get me the sky taxi from BWI. I need it on the roof helipad ten minutes ago. And have Dolci meet me in the lab." He hung up and dug in his bottom desk drawer. He pulled out a Taurus .38 revolver and made sure it was loaded. The intercom buzzed.

"Sir, Doctor Dolci is headed for the lab and the sky taxi just made a drop-off across town. They'll be here in ten minutes."

"Christ, at least something is working out." He headed for the lab.

* * *

Without even thinking, Ethan punched in the security override code for the test lab's door. Inside he rummaged through the refrigerators until he found a vial of Memnon. He grabbed a hypodermic from a drawer and sat on the bed from which he had launched himself so many times.

To hell with Churchill and all the rest. I have to go back and get Beth.

The past two days did not matter now. He would go back to that clearing and enter Ethridge's dying body like he had never left.

Ethan did not hear the door open, but he felt a presence. When he turned, he stared down the barrel of Churchill's revolver. "West, you must be incredibly proud of yourself."

Ethan glanced at the wall clock. "Market just closed, I see. Have a tough day?"

277

"Not half as tough as the day you're going to have."

Ethan continued to prepare his syringe, ignoring Churchill.

"You're not jumping out of here, West. Not yet."

Ethan smiled. "Getting a little melodramatic there, Churchill." Ethan lifted the syringe to the top of his head and began lining it up with the tiny plug in his skull.

"Stop that."

"You're beginning to bore me, hotshot. Be glad you're not behind bars."

Churchill lifted the revolver and aimed from only four feet away. He pulled the trigger and the lab rang with a deafening explosion. The plastic syringe disintegrated and part of the heel of Ethan's right hand went with it.

"Jesus H." Ethan yanked his arm down and gawked at the blood oozing out of his hand.

"I'll kill you if I have to West, but I'd prefer you going along with my plan."

"I'm sick of your plans."

"Yes, well, you just ruined *all* of my plans. So, I'm taking you somewhere and I'm not letting you up for air until I've recouped my fortune."

"And how do you propose to do that?" Ethan wrapped a towel around his hand and scowled at Churchill.

"No more Memnon to the brain for you. We go back to the weak dosages. Just enough to get you a day in the future. You give me winners every goddamn day until I say stop. Then I let your sorry ass go." Churchill's nostrils flared and he breathed as if he'd been running.

Ethan said nothing. He saw the signs of panic in Churchill. The sudden shift in his finances had pushed him to the brink of madness. Ethan couldn't afford to provoke Churchill too badly or he'd lose his source of Memnon. He needed it one more time. The bastard had him over a barrel.

The lab door arced open and Dolci strolled in only to come up short at the sight of Churchill with a gun on Ethan. "Andrew?"

"Glad you could make it, Cliff. Over here please." Churchill unlocked the door to a storage closet.

"What's going on?"

"Just stand here, Cliff." Churchill waved the gun at Dolci. With his other hand he pulled a loaded syringe from his pocket and flicked off the plastic needle protector with his thumb. Before Dolci could react, Churchill rammed the syringe into Dolci's neck and emptied it. Dolci spun around, his eyes wild. He lost his balance and Churchill heaved him into the closet where Dolci clattered to the floor.

Churchill spun around and pointed the .38 at Ethan. "Over here, West. In the closet." Ethan stepped near. "Inside you'll find scissors. Cut Dolci's shirt up the middle." Ethan, now curious, did as he was told.

"Now open that nylon satchel on the floor." Ethan found the parcel and zipped it open. "Take it out. Now unravel those wires and get the red electrode. Yes. Take off the plastic protector and press it to Dolci's chest above the sternum. Yes. Now the other one. Put it on his left side on the lower ribs. Good. Now press the power button." Lights danced across the small console at the other end of the electrode wires.

Dolci's panicked eyes looked up at Ethan, pleading. His limbs no longer moved. He could barely open his mouth to say, "It hurts, Andrew. Oh, God, it hurts."

"Be over in a minute, Dolci."

"Why, Andrew, why?"

"You shouldn't have threatened me with an ambulance ride earlier, Cliff. That was the mistake that got you here."

"But why, Andrew? Why are you doing this to me? What can it give you?"

"Dolci, you're an insurance policy, just in case.

"For what?"

"You don't need to know."

A sickly moan came from deep inside Dolci. His voice hissed out, barely a whisper now. "Jesus Christ, Andrew, this is killing me."

"I know. That's the idea."

Dolci's eyelids fluttered and closed. The breath he had been holding sighed out of his mouth.

"West, lean down and put your ear to his chest."

Ethan kneeled over Dolci's motionless body. "Nothing."

"The wonders of pharmaceuticals. Now press the big red button on that device." Lights danced across the machine. It beeped and Dolci's body jerked. Churchill pulled a second hypo out of his pocket and flicked off the plastic needle protector. "Now place this in Dolci's hand. Put his thumb on the plunger. That's right. Now hold the end of the needle against your neck."

"What?"

"Don't break the skin. Just hold it there. A little more forward. Good. Now set his hand down, pull those electrodes off his chest, and close the door."

Churchill motioned to the exit. "Up to the roof. We're going for a little trip."

Ethan paced into the hall and up the stairs. He needed a minute to clear his head and try to figure out what the hell just happened.

They reached the helipad and waited. In the distance, a tiny dot grew larger. Soon they heard a thwocking roar and a six-seat Bell commuter vectored in for a perfect landing. Churchill kept the revolver in his jacket pocket as they boarded. Once seated and airborne, Churchill asked the pilot to close the connecting door to the flight deck for privacy.

Ethan's mind raced. He had missed something.

Churchill pulled a clear glass bottle out of his jacket. "This will last about a week. That should be long enough to get rich again. Then you go free."

"Why didn't we just stay at the lab?"

"That little video. I still don't know how you made it. Somebody else must have helped you. You have the means to bribe anybody at NR. One fat stock tip and they're rich. That place isn't safe. The cops could show up any time if your little nurse friend gets a conscience. And I don't need that place anymore." Churchill's gaze wandered off Ethan to the chopper's ceiling as he visualized his redemption. "Make me a billionaire and I think I'll be happy without my company."

Ethan spat, "You'll *never* be happy."

"Oh, you're a farmer *and* a psychologist, I see. Happiness for me right now would be to shoot bullets into your body, West. The only thing that's stopping me is that if I kill the golden goose, I don't get the golden eggs. And I really want the golden eggs."

Ethan calmed himself, thought of the big picture. Churchill seemed as insignificant as an insect. "I don't need special powers to see into the future, Churchill. You're a bully. You like to win. Why would a megalomaniac like you be willing to let me have what I want after you get what *you* want?"

"I'm not a greedy man," Churchill leered.

"People like you get what they think they want, then they find what they really want is *more*."

"A philosopher." Churchill grinned.

"No, a realist. Without my death you'll always have jail

time hanging over you."

"A cynical philosopher."

Then it hit Ethan. Why did he need Memnon at all? He had body-jumped without returning to the lab for Memnon. He had no Memnon when he jumped from old man Watson to Billy. Why did he think he needed it now? He saw the flaw in his assumptions. His real body remained alive. To leave it he needed Memnon. But if his real body died?

If I'm wrong, I'll be dead and Beth will pay the price. But Churchill will kill me anyway. Same result.

Ethan closed his eyes and went through the sequence of thoughts he used before a jump. He got to the point where the only thing linking him to the here and now was the link between his spirit and his body. He attenuated that link until he barely felt it. Outside his body, held to it by a thread of energy. Memnon had been the tool that made it easy to get to this point. Now, what if he went further on his own?

For a moment he felt panic so encompassing that he froze. Like leaning out over Niagara Falls, he felt all that energy that could so quickly gobble one up, knowing that the slightest misstep would spell annihilation. In desperation, Ethan reentered his body. He willed his heart to beat, his lungs to gasp. He fought the inertia of all that blood, all that fluid that had come to rest in his veins. Feeling like he had been drugged, he opened his eyes, lifted his hand off his knee. It looked as it always had, but it felt heavy. His body weighed a ton.

Churchill looked at him strangely.

Ethan's systems began to function again. He began to feel normal. He had learned something significant. He believed he could step off without Memnon.

What if I'm wrong?

Then you'll never see Bethany again.

He had only one way to find out. Only one way to truly free himself from this time and the anchor of his own body.

Ethan jumped to the helicopter's exit, threw the latch, and swung open the door. Immediately, a siren blared, warning the pilot. Wind howled through the passenger compartment.

"What the hell do you think you're doing?" Churchill screamed.

"I'm leaving now, Churchill. I don't need you or your drug."

"Are you insane?"

"No. I just want to have no way to return to this body. I don't want to be tempted to come back." Ethan put one foot on the threshold and lanced a malicious grin back at Churchill. "Thank your stars I don't have time to really deal with you."

"I'll shoot you!"

"Be my guest." Ethan began to step through the hatch.

Churchill screamed, "I'll kill that nurse! Her daughter and her babies!"

Ethan hesitated.

"I'll kill them slow, West, and it will be your fault." Churchill's eyes danced like pinballs as his thin lips smeared back in a grimace.

Ethan had thought he could walk away from Churchill and all of it. A vision of Jasper executing the highwayman came into Ethan's mind. "Only one thing to do with a mad dog," Jasper had said. Ethan turned, shaking his head. "Everywhere I go, I meet vermin like you. Where do you people come from?" Ethan stalked straight for Churchill. Fire belched from Churchill's revolver, then again. Ethan grabbed the gun and yanked Churchill out of his seat, ignoring the pain that screamed through his guts. This pain held no comparison to what he'd experienced as Billy. He grabbed the executive in a bear hug and grappled him toward the hatch. "You just couldn't leave it alone, could you, Churchill?"

Churchill fought back and howled like a banshee when he realized what Ethan intended. Twenty years younger than Churchill and working a farm, Ethan's muscles knew how to work. And work they did, dragging Churchill to the hatch and beyond.

As they fell through the sky, Ethan gripped Churchill. He stared into those ice-blue eyes that flashed so madly with panic that Ethan wasn't sure the executive would even understand as he yelled, "Looks like no more plans for you, Churchill. See you around. Then again, maybe not." He released Churchill and watched him pinwheel through the air.

CHAPTER 81

The humming in Ethan's ears blared so loud he could barely think. As he opened his eyes, he saw Hulse striding across the clearing, a straight razor in one hand, Billy's head in the other. He blinked and thought himself insane. He'd jumped so fast, he completely disoriented himself. Then he heard Beth scream.

"We'll be takin' along this little souvenir of your boyfriend, okay?"

"You monster!"

"Don't want it? Okay." Hulse laughed like a hyena as he tossed Billy's head into the dirt.

"No!" exploded from Beth's lips. Sobs flooded from her as she tried to crawl on her hands and knees toward Billy's head. But before she could go three feet, Hulse strode up next to her and crushed her to the ground with his left boot in the center of her back. "Where ya think yer goin'? Save some of that spunk fer me." He wiped his razor on her dress, closed the blade, and pushed it into his boot.

Ethan heard Beth's panting sobs, a blow, then silence. A minute went by as he tried to focus his thoughts. The pain in Ethridge's chest felt like molten lava. Pink eyes suddenly stared into his face.

"Ethridge, you let that old geezer get the drop on you?"

Ethan didn't try to speak.

"You're a mess. Nothin' I can do for ya. Want me to put a bullet through your head? 'Cause you ain't I' better."

Ethan stared into the bunny eyes.

And he saw something that shook him to his core. Just seconds before, as Billy, he had sensed something familiar about Hulse, but Hulse had backed away, as if wanting to hide himself from further scrutiny. Ethan's witchery could not be fooled. Now Ethan saw Hulse in his mind, not just his eyes.

"Churchill?" Ethan croaked.

The pink eyes opened like saucers. Hulse sat back on his haunches and shook his head. "Well, I'll be damned. Is that you, Ethan? I'm certainly glad you jumped into Ethridge's corpse. Billy died too damn fast for me to give you the send-off I wanted. Thought I'd have to track you halfway across the universe again."

The affected accent of Hulse disappeared. Ethan had no doubt he faced Churchill.

"How?"

"Do you think I just arrived here, Ethan? Don't be an idiot. I've lived a dozen lives since you dragged me out of that helicopter. I've developed skills."

"You should have died."

"I'd been taking Memnon for weeks. Nothing happened 'til I was scared shitless falling through the sky. Remember how fear of Ted caused your first time jump? Fear was the key."

"Hulse?"

"Stupid bastard fell off his horse crossing a stream, got knocked unconscious and drowned. I followed your wife to this time and knew you'd eventually show up, so I jumped into Hulse and got a job at Hawley's ranch. Fat bastard had a lot of grudges. He liked my, shall we say, problem management."

"You're insane."

"Who's to say? But sane or not, I'm here to take away the one thing you want."

"How would you know?"

"I listened to your tapes. All those hours in your quarters when you slept after a Memnon jump. You talked. It all sounded like nonsense until I watched you voluntarily haul me out of that chopper. I never thought you were a suicide. The things you told your little friend Angie about dying and leaving your body and looking for your wife had to be true. I held onto that belief until I hit the ground and saw that you were right. Now I may be better at it than you. More practice."

The body of Hulse, animated by the spirit of Churchill, raised his revolver toward Beth. "She doesn't know how to do it, does she, Ethan? You wouldn't have fought so hard to save her if she knew. You'd have just jumped with her and gone somewhere else."

"She got here didn't she?" Ethan bluffed.

"Nice try. You have an innate talent and I think you helped her get here. And anyway, even if she knows how to jump, all I have to do is panic her in her last moments and she won't be able to hold together. Her spirit will scatter across the great beyond and even if it's possible to find her, she won't be the same person." His thumb pulled back the hammer. "Watch how it's done."

"What good can this do you, Churchill?"

284

"I don't like to lose, West. You made me lose everything. So, I thought I'd return the favor."

"If you can jump through time, why do this? You can make all the money and have all the power you want. You don't need to have anything to do with me."

Churchill said, "I have all the time in the world to do that. But first I want to watch you suffer. Nobody does what you did and gets away with it." He pointed his revolver at Beth's unconscious form. "She's never had Memnon. She doesn't know how to jump. Without your help, she's gone."

"I'll find her."

"You think you're skilled enough to do that? Even if you could, you'd still have to deal with me, because I'll keep track of you. Then someday, somewhen, I'd meet you both again and get to kill you all over. I could hound you through eternity, West."

"Don't bet on it."

"You're right. I'd rather have the sure thing. It ends here."

Churchill strode over to where Beth had fallen after he punched her. With his free hand he slapped her face back and forth. Beth moaned. Churchill turned toward Ethan. "See, she's not dead yet. Just out cold." He slapped her again. Bright welts rose on her skin and her eyes fluttered open.

"You're basically a good person, West. Good people are soft. They think things always turn out for the best. But people like me know there's no such thing as happy endings. I've learned to take my pleasure where I can and I must admit that thinking about destroying you and your little honey has given me an enormous amount of pleasure the past two years. You know how many times I've watched her little rump walk by at Hawley's ranch and savored what I would do to her?"

Churchill squatted over Beth and pointed his revolver between her eyes. Beth panicked and squirmed. Churchill's head turned toward Ethan. "See the panic. Say goodbye."

Churchill slapped her again and again until she screamed. Churchill pulled the trigger and Katherine Hawley's body lurched. He fired two more shots into her.

Ethan's mind caught fire.

CHAPTER 82

The clearing turned silent as a crypt.

"There she goes, West. Out, out where you will never find her again."

In Ethan's head, a clock began ticking. The longer he had to wait, the more difficult it would be to find Beth's trail. "Two years here have driven you insane, Churchill."

"Two years here have been more fun than I've ever had. I've killed seven men already. It's the best sport I can think of."

"Well, make it eight. Finish the job."

Churchill hovered over Ethan. "You'd like that wouldn't you? Go chasing after that little bitch?" A malicious grin spread across Churchill's face. "Nah. Just to be sure she's long gone, I'm going to hold off killing you. Just in case."

Ethan focused all his energy, all his will, thinking of Beth. He felt her flying away from him like a comet.

"Oh, no you don't." Churchill slapped the revolver barrel across Ethan's face. He rapped the barrel back and forth until he drew blood.

Ethan's head became a ringing cauldron of pain. He struggled to maintain his mental connection with Beth. He felt her slipping away.

The bunny face loomed close. The hammer of Churchill's revolver pulled back and Churchill fired next to Ethan's right ear. Ethan's mind went blank and he lost the connection to Beth.

Ethan's eyes opened in rage.

"Yes, get angry. That will make you lose focus and when you least expect it, wham, I pull this trigger and you're gone. And you'll scatter too. If you're not centered when it happens, poof. You know that don't you, West?"

Churchill grinned. "But not just yet. I'm enjoying this too much." He pressed the barrel of his Colt into the wound in Ethridge's chest, drove it in and wiggled it around. Ethan gritted his teeth and held his breath. "Broke some ribs, that bullet. The old geezer was a good shot."

"I'll find you too, Churchill."

"No you won't. Once your energy scatters there will be no more *you* to come after me."

Ethan started to laugh. The bunny eyes squinted and

drew close. "You're a fool Churchill. You think you know the rules of the game." As if a switch had been thrown, Ethan's smile disappeared.

The bunny eyes looked perplexed.

"I'm going to teach you the rules, Churchill. The hard way."

Churchill let out the breath he had been holding. "Pretty feeble threat, West. I thought you really had something."

Ethan calmed his thoughts, focused, played his bluff. "I do. You'll find out in a few seconds."

Churchill held his revolver against Ethan's forehead. "You don't have a few seconds." He pulled back the hammer.

Yes, Ethan thought. Do it. I'm ready.

The pink eyes examined Ethan's face closely. "What's going on in that brain of yours?" Churchill pulled the revolver back from Ethan's head. "Almost, Ethan. You almost got me to cut you loose. You're all ready, aren't you? All focused and prepared to jump."

He placed the gun muzzle against Ethan's thigh and pulled the trigger. Ethan's body twitched. "Did you feel that? No? Let's try higher." Churchill pressed the gun barrel against Ethan's right hip and pulled the trigger.

Ethan's face turned almost purple as he writhed from the pain. But he kept his mouth clamped shut, not willing to give Churchill the satisfaction of hearing him scream.

"Oh, hip fractures are nasty, I hear. My grandmother fell down, broke her hip, and bitched about it day and night. How's that feel, Ethan?"

Ethan pulled back from his anger. He had to stay focused. This was Churchill's way of scattering Ethan's thoughts before he fired the fatal shot.

"I wanted to end you here, but I just decided to do something I think I'll like a lot more." Churchill leaned close, so his eyes stared into Ethan's face from inches away. "How about I destroy your timeline?" Churchill fired into Ethan's other thigh. "You stay here and suffer while I use my back door."

Between gritted teeth, Ethan said, "What the hell are you talking about?"

"Remember Dolci? He's laying in a lab closet, heart stopped, just waiting for me to inhabit his body."

Ethan raised his head. "What?"

287

"That chemical I injected into Dolci paralyzed his heart. He died. But the chemical breaks down quickly and there's no real damage to his body. Dolci's body's ripe for reanimation. The machine you hooked to his chest is a defibrillator. It restarted his heart for a second. That's the second I go back to. Remember the hypo against your neck? It's charged with morphine. All I need to do is kill Hulse's body here, enter Dolci, shoot the syringe into your neck and you won't be able to put two thoughts together. A minute later, you'll be dead of the overdose. Then all of this doesn't happen. This timeline gets sheared off and the other one goes on without you in it. Except that in Dolci's body I will know what I know now. Because for me, there is no interruption in my timeline. It's like I looped back from here to there. After that, without you to bother me, there will be no stopping me from doing any damn thing I please. You've caused a little detour, West. Nothing more."

"If Dolci wakes up, don't you think your past self will try to stop him? You'll probably get shot," Ethan said.

"If Dolci suddenly comes to life, my past self knows why. It's the reason I killed Dolci to begin with. He's my safety net."

"Then two of you existing at the same time. How's that going to work out?"

"That will be an interesting experiment to see whether cause and effect rule the universe or whether everything's disconnected. Newtonian physics or quantum mechanics."

Regardless of the physics involved, Ethan knew Churchill had a real potential to cut off Ethan's timeline. He had to cut off Churchill's before the madman's greed and lust wreaked havoc, not only on Bethany and Ethan, but on other innocent lives.

But Churchill held all the cards in this game. Ethan watched the revolver barrel arc toward his face, felt the ringing impact in his skull, tasted the salt of blood in his mouth. Then the barrel came back from the other direction. Ethan began to lose consciousness.

His mind coughed up the bitter thought that Churchill had won and that he and Beth faced destruction.

CHAPTER 83

The bunny eyes loomed close. "I don't intend for you to pass out. I want you to feel every moment, every pain until you disappear. I want you to know without a doubt that you're done, West."

"Then let's jest see if it works like that," Jasper's voice croaked. Churchill spun to see Jasper propped up on one elbow. Jasper had tugged the Colt out of his belt. His shot plowed into Churchill's right shoulder, knocking the revolver out of his fist. Churchill's face became a billboard of amazement rather than pain.

"You're about to have a real bad case of losin' yer focus, Mr. Hulse, or Churchill, or whatever you call yerself." The second shot caught Churchill above the right knee. Red mist puffed up as he toppled to the leafy earth, screaming.

"Havin' trouble concentratin', are ya?"

Churchill struggled to right himself, his left leg churning as he twisted to see Jasper.

"Look like ye might be unfocused, there, Mr. Churchill." Jasper put a shot into Churchill's side. The pink lips squirmed as a howl tore out of Churchill's throat.

Jasper punched two shots into Churchill's stomach. "Gettin' gut-shot will take yer mind off jest about anything, Mr. Churchill. Feelin' a mite panicky, there? Well, then, you're ready to say goodbye."

"Jasper, NO! Don't kill him."

* * *

"Bastard needs to die."

"Jasper, it's me, Ethan. If you kill him he might be able to do what he said. Listen to me."

"How I know it's you?"

"You know. Cole, snipers, gold," Ethan gasped. He needed to rest for a few seconds. He gazed up at spidery tree limbs twitching in the wind against a robin's egg sky. Ethan had seen this image in his dream that morning. He wished he had seen more.

He struggled to turn his head. A few feet away, Jasper examined himself, his hands slowly crawling over his torso like hairy spiders searching for food. With an enormous effort, Ethan inhaled enough air to croak, "Jasper, you bad?"

289

Jasper's hands travelled over his midriff. "Best I can tell, he got me in the side. Cain't tell how bad. I can breathe okay."

Ethan's heart lurched as he watched Jasper crawl across the leaf bed to what looked like a jumble of rags. The old scout put his hat over Beth's ruined face. "That bastard needs to die, Ethan." He crawled over to Churchill who lay on his back two feet from Ethan. "He's still breathin'. Why cain't I finish this piece of shit?"

"You can. Just not yet," Ethan whispered.

The old scout groaned and rolled over to face Ethan, blue eyes blazing.

"Jasper, I need your help."

"Hell if I can even help myself, Youngblood."

"You can do this. Put your revolver to my head and kill me. Then you can kill Churchill." Except for the creaking of branches in the wind, Ethan heard nothing. He forced his eyes open. "Jasper."

"Yeah, yeah, I heard you. Jes' don't see how that helps."

Ethan gathered his shreds of remaining strength. "Can you help her now, Jasper?"

"No."

"Well, I can."

A rattle came out of the old man's throat. "How's that? You're worse off than me."

"Why did you call me Ethan? You know it's me, but how could I be in Ethridge's body unless what I told you was true? And you heard what Churchill and I said. You know the power I have. You know what he intends to do."

Jasper snorted. "After that bullet hit me, I had me some visions. I went someplace and then I came back. Maybe I can see a little bit of what yer talkin' about."

"I can save her, Jasper, but I need to get free first. Help me now."

"It don't seem right."

"Jasper, would I ask you to do this if I didn't know what I was doing?"

"You may know what *you're* doing, but I don't know what *I'm* doing."

"You're just helping me. This body will die soon anyway. I have one chance to change everything that's happened and I have to do it now before Churchill has a chance to go back. Do it!"

290

"I'm out of bullets," Jasper said lamely.

"Use Ethridge's gun. It has to be around me somewhere."

Ethan turned his head to look for Ethridge's revolver. When he looked away from Jasper toward his right, he saw Churchill. He gazed into those pink eyes. -"Hurry, Jasper. I have to die before he does."

Freezing metal lightly touched against Ethan's left temple.

"God help me, Ethan."

"God has nothing to do with this, Jasper. I promise."

"I done a lot of bad things in my life, but this is the worst."

Ethan struggled to extend his left hand out of his field of vision. He felt Jasper's warm, callused paw wrap around it. "You're a good man, Jasper. Far better than you know. Goodbye and good luck with your gold mine."

"If I live."

"If you live."

Suddenly the sky burst into a nova and hard light screamed through Ethan.

CHAPTER 84

Ethan immediately felt the difference. The death of his original body had released him from its anchoring influence. He no longer needed Memnon or anything else from the physical universe.

And with that snapping of his tether, Ethan's abilities took a quantum leap. He no longer felt that he was groping through time and space.

He flashed to the moment in the clearing as Hulse's body tumbled to the forest floor and thrashed in pain. He saw Jasper lining up the shot that would end Churchill.

Plenty of time. I have a promise to keep.

Where would he find the fulcrum point to change everything? Ethan blinked inside his mind and returned to the lightning bolt.

He had been here many times and had been unable to change the outcome. He saw why. He had always believed in the insurmountable power of the lightning, but had fought it anyway. He had focused on the wrong point in time. He needed to go back earlier.

Which point? Could he go back to the kite delivery, confuse the UPS driver and make him unable to find Ethan's address?

No. Ethan could not influence other minds. He had tried. And then in a flash he knew the place that he needed to apply pressure. He saw the moment that could change the course of everything and where he had some chance of success.

But he also saw incompatible consequences.

Ethan thought of another time and blinked in his mind. He saw himself with Beth as they ran down the hill, trying to avoid the rain. He would not waste effort trying to change Beth's actions. The true potential was with himself, his own body. His own spirit animated that body. He couldn't influence other entities, but might he align himself with his own energy? If a chance for success existed, that would be the entry point.

Ethan probed gently at the outer edges of his then-consciousness. The touch felt strange. He did not feel the wall he had encountered in trying to contact others. Ideas and impulses flooded him, the waves of conscious thought that made up his being.

Ethan felt the frenzied excitement of running through the rain with Beth, the joy of their love. He did not experience a flash of memory, but rather the moment as it unfolded again, now intensified by the rush of energy from his physical self, his own senses as they lived the experience.

The torrent of his own emotions caught him up, dragged him along and intoxicated him with sensations. He relived a singular moment in his life which could be a turning point of ultimate importance.

Ethan mentally shook himself for almost allowing opportunity to slip away. In a few seconds the lightning would arrive. He had fought to get here, had worked to insinuate himself into his own mind. Now he must act. He must change what had been. If it worked, he could not turn back. He would have looped back along his own timeline, cutting off everything that had been.

Beyond that image of what Ethan intended, he could see nothing, as if a wall had been erected in time. Would he cease to exist? But Beth might live.

The first fat raindrops began to fall. Ethan willed one command: TRIP HER NOW!

Beth turned to Ethan and ran sideways, looking at her husband with sheer mischief. "Meet you in the barn. Try to find me. I'll be the naked one."

TRIP HER NOW!

Beth turned and lifted her right knee, the first step of her sprint. His past-self did not hear him, did not respond. Or perhaps the stubbornness inside his other self rejected an idea that seemed alien.

Ethan pushed his energy up to the being that had been him. He lost himself in it, tried to blur the edge between them. Frontal assault would not work. He had to make himself think that this was his own thought. Ethan lost himself in the effort.

At exactly the right moment, Ethan's past-self snaked out his left leg and planted it in front of Beth's right foot. As she brought that leg forward, it collided with the solid part of Ethan's calf. She twisted to the left, stumbled, and went down on the slippery grass.

The sky burst as a billion volts of electricity found its grounding. It flashed to the old oak tree, the highest point in the vicinity.

The lightning bolt lasted a nanosecond, but that

amount of time stretched like eternity. Ethan lived inside that tiny blister of time as forces beyond his ken sputtered and pulsed and became incandescent reality around him. He was in it now. For an instant he felt only chaos...and then everything changed.

The oak exploded and Ethan smacked into the mud, face-down. One of the lightning streamers crackled across the ground and brushed past him, feeling like a hot steamroller running over his body. It spat and hissed and slammed across the clearing like a whip in the hands of a madman. It hit Ethan again.

Ethan's heart stopped. His mouth gaped wide, trying to suck in air. But all around the edges of his vision, triangles of iridescence danced, then closed in toward the center, slowly at first, then more rapidly. When they hit the center of his vision, Ethan lost consciousness. His body settled into the mud with his head turned to the right side. Muddy water trickled into his open mouth. Ethan's eyes remained open but unseeing.

A second passed. And then another. A slow procession of seconds marched over and around Ethan's body as the world went on without the Ethan who had been.

As fierce energies continued to writhe through space-time, Ethan's spirit moved above his body. Here is where it ended. Or began.

He had traded Beth's life for his own. Payment lay in the mud.

He had seen nothing beyond this point. He had deleted his own timeline. He waited for his past self to die, waited for the moment he would cease to be. But some deep instinct refused to accept the inevitable. Some part of him wanted to find another way.

Why couldn't he enter his body at exactly the moment when it died? Just as he had with Cole, and Watson, and all the others? Why couldn't he bridge what had been to what could be? He hovered above the body, waiting. He would have a tiny sliver of time in which to act.

He felt the kettledrum of his heart pound its last beat. He hurled his mind at himself and became himself. The past-Ethan died as the present-Ethan energized his body.

And he went on.

As a peel of thunder died away, a new sound cut through the clearing. A grunting cough. Then another.

The taste of dirt and death filled Ethan's mouth. He

294

spat out the mud and sucked in a sweet lungful of air.

I'm here.

His thoughts jerked and fumbled as he reoriented inside his body.

I've done it. I'm back. Before Churchill, before Neural Research, before all the rest of it happened.

The lightning's fierce voltage had paralyzed Ethan's body. He struggled to regain control as the seconds ticked by. First breathe. Then move fingers. Then roll over and push off the ground. Then get onto those screaming knees and numb hands and crawl through the storm. One hand in front of the other. Then a leg. Move!

He would have his answer now. Had he looped back through time to the place his nightmare had started? Would the change he envisioned occur? Or was he alone? What would he find through the curtain of rain? He prayed it wasn't the steaming smear he had found before.

He felt through the gloom until another crash illuminated the mud ahead. He saw a body. He crawled to her, mud sucking at his hands. He pushed her onto her back, and knelt above her to keep the rain out of her face.

"Beth," he said, barely a whisper, lost in the wind.

Ethan knelt down and placed his ear over her mouth. Beth was not breathing. He pressed an ear to her chest. She had no heartbeat for all he could tell with the shriek of the storm around him. The whip-lightning had caught her too.

Without hesitation, he straddled her and set his palms against her sternum, then dropped his weight onto her and began chest compressions. Each time, air rattled out of her throat. Ethan continued like a machine. "Beth, come on. Come on."

He hated the rattling sound. He wanted to press harder, to crush the life back into her, but he was afraid of breaking her ribs, puncturing a lung. He moved faster, desperation now consuming his actions and thoughts.

"Please, Beth. Please."

His tears combined with the rain, one great drenching sorrow. Had all of his efforts been for nothing?

Time stretched out and Beth did not stir. Except for her bubbling exhalations after each compression, she felt like a rubber doll. Ethan worked in a rising panic, his thoughts skittering through his mind like butter on a hotplate. Did he have to find a way back, try another path through time? Could he loop back like this again?

What was the best thing to do?

He saw no solution.

I have failed in the only thing that ever mattered.

I can't even kill myself.

I am trapped in time.

And then some part of him rebelled. It grabbed him like a terrier with a toy and shook him. What was he doing? How could he let panic and failure overwhelm what he had learned?

He stopped the chest compressions, stopped waging war with the physical. Why fight with matter? He had to deal with something far more fundamental.

His being here and now proved that he had reentered his own timeline before the lightning blast vaporized his wife. He had branched the timeline in a new direction. This answered the nagging question of whether he was stepping between alternate universes. He now knew he remained in the same universe he had started from. Only one vast universe existed. But it startled him to know how much it could be changed. His theory that it was like a rope whose fibers could be snipped and rearranged was pretty accurate. The universe did not function as a fixed system like the workings of a clock. Instead it was freewheeling, flexible, nonlinear. Knowing that was the key to his problem.

Ethan concentrated. He pushed his thoughts into that state of transition from which he timejumped. Relax. Think. Just like with Memnon.

He felt the fabric of space-time. He felt the flow of forces. Aligning himself with these forces, his mind flashed images. Like something under a microscope, he saw himself in that tiny moment of time. Then, he saw the scenarios of shifting possibility, the imagined futures. In several of them, Beth died. But in one, she didn't. He needed to bridge the gap, shift his timeline again.

How many times had he felt those subtle shiftings, suspected that he somehow influenced them? Then this jump, where he had excised a major timeline to retrieve this moment, this possibility with Beth. It had been difficult, but what he could do once, could he not do again?

All that lay between what was and what could be was the power of thought. He had the power to do more than merely move through time. He had hints over the past months that he could actually change that which he thought

296

constituted reality. Wasn't his being here proof that he had reorganized energy and matter?

He saw that this timeline did not hold a solution. He had chosen the wrong thread. Once again, he had fixated on the lightning, trying to make small changes in what had happened. He needed a *big* change, a completely different thread in the timeline.

There is no time. There is no distance. There is only what I believe.

Ethan untangled the skein of possibility and visualized his desires. Then he believed. He did not *try* to believe. He *believed*.

And his mind blinked.

And he felt that odd shift again. He felt the bubble of his thoughts rip free from existence for an instant. The threads of existence re-wove into a new fabric.

Yes, there and there, he needed that and then and this. Snip snip and mend and pull the threads together.

Then everything began again.

CHAPTER 85

"Ethan, I still think you're insane. Your family has owned this land for two hundred years."

Ethan tossed the last of their suitcases into the back of his pick-up, squinted against the afternoon sun. "C'mere, Buzz." The dog leaped into the passenger compartment and settled on the bench seat next to Beth. Beth opened the passenger door and started to get out.

"Where are you going?" Ethan said.

"I'm not sure if I locked the back door."

"Beth, no!"

"What the hell is wrong with you?"

"Stay in the truck. We have to get out of here. The real estate agent can check the doors."

"What's your hurry? All week you've been a madman."

"We have to go. Too much damn dawdling."

"Ethan, you're creeping me out."

"I know. Trust me."

Ethan got in and started the ancient heap. Beth pulled the truck door closed, creases distorting her brow.

"Beth, you once told me your dream was to live on a beach and make love all day long."

"I don't remember ever saying that."

"We were in a country inn a long time ago. A very long time ago. It's true, isn't it?"

Beth squinted at her husband. "That time in Vermont?"

"It doesn't matter. It's your dream-life isn't it? Your vision of paradise?"

"Well, yeah."

"That's what we're doing."

"How will we make a living?"

"We don't need to make a living."

"Selling the farm won't last us the rest of our lives."

Ethan grinned. "It doesn't need to."

Beth shook her head and stared out the windshield as the truck bounced down the gravel driveway. She still couldn't believe the For Sale sign next to the mailbox.

Ethan turned left onto the paved road and gunned the engine. "See this car coming toward us?" He pointed at a black Lincoln Continental.

"Yes."

"See the two men in suits?" The car whooshed past.

"Yes, what's going on? Who are they?"

"They're a future we need to avoid. I'm through fighting, Beth. I don't need to fight anymore. Not ever again. I see that now. I was such a fool and you were right."

Beth's mouth hung open and her eyes flashed gold in the sun. "Ethan, you better explain. I mean *really* explain, because I think you've lost your mind."

"I promise I'll explain it all, but right now, trust me."

Ethan drove into Sharpsburg and parked in front of a white-steepled church. Reaching into the glove compartment, he retrieved a screwdriver. As he got out of the truck, he said, "This will take a minute. It's one of the threads I pulled. Make sure Buzz doesn't jump out the window."

Beth stared at Ethan. Threads? Her left hand clutched Buzz's collar. She could think of nothing else to do.

Three minutes passed, actually, before Ethan returned. He dropped a wax-sealed packet on Beth's lap. "There's the future, the beach house, and a comfortable life."

"Ethan!"

"I'll explain it all when we're on that beach." He started the truck and turned onto Main Street, picking up speed slowly. Wind blew through the open windows and ruffled Ethan's hair back and forth.

Bethany pulled open the packet and unfolded the thick wrapping paper, then the yellowed papers it contained. "What is this?" Her eyes scanned several sheets, then stopped. "Oh, my God, Ethan. Is this real? Abraham Lincoln?"

Before Ethan could answer, Buzz stuck his cold nose into Ethan's ear, then gave his pack leader a rare three-lick kiss. The dog turned to Beth and snuffled at her hair. She leaned away and held the papers near the windshield. "No drooling, Buzz. Not on *these*."

Ethan rubbed the dog's ears and smiled a real smile. It felt like the first time he'd smiled in ages.

I kept my promise to you, Beth.

THE END

If you've enjoyed *Time Jumper*, please visit Amazon.com and leave a review.

And visit Matt at matthewbayan.com or on Twitter or Facebook.

65559498R00181

Made in the USA
Lexington, KY
16 July 2017